Nan

A Six Sigma Mystery

Also available from ASQ Quality Press:

Six Sigma for the Office: A Pocket Guide
Roderick Munro

Six Sigma for the Shop Floor: A Pocket Guide
Roderick Munro

Six Sigma Project Management: A Pocket Guide
Jeffrey N. Lowenthal

Customer Centered Six Sigma: Linking Customers, Process Improvement, and Financial Results
Earl Naumann and Steven H. Hoisington

The Six Sigma Journey from Art to Science
Larry Walters

Office Kaizen: Transforming Office Operations into a Strategic Competitive Advantage
William Lareau

Defining and Analyzing a Business Process: A Six Sigma Pocket Guide
Jeffrey N. Lowenthal

Improving Healthcare with Control Charts: Basic and Advanced SPC Methods and Case Studies
Raymond G. Carey

Measuring Quality Improvement in Healthcare: A Guide to Statistical Process Control Applications
Raymond G. Carey, PhD and Robert C. Lloyd, PhD

To request a complimentary catalog of ASQ Quality Press publications, call 800-248-1946, or visit our Web site at http://qualitypress.asq.org.

Nan

A Six Sigma Mystery

Robert Barry

ASQ Quality Press
Milwaukee, Wisconsin

American Society for Quality, Quality Press, Milwaukee 53203
© 2004 by ASQ
All rights reserved. Published 2003
Printed in the United States of America

12 11 10 09 08 07 06 05 04   5 4 3 2

Library of Congress Cataloging-in-Publication Data

Barry, Robert, 1938 Dec. 29–
    Nan : a six sigma mysery / Robert Barry.
        p. cm.
    Includes bibliographical references and index.
    ISBN 0-87389-612-2 (Soft cover, perfect bound : alk. paper)
    1. Six Sigma (Quality control standard)—Fiction. 2. Hospitals—
Administration—Fiction. 3. Quality control—Fiction.
    I. Title.

    PS3602.A7776N36 2003
    813'.6—dc22   2003017581

    ISBN 0-87389-612-2

Publisher: William A. Tony
Acquisitions Editor: Annemieke Hytinen
Project Editor: Paul O'Mara
Production Administrator: Barbara Mitrovic
Special Marketing Representative: David Luth

ASQ Mission: The American Society for Quality advances individual,
organizational, and community excellence worldwide through learning,
quality improvement, and knowledge exchange.

Attention Bookstores, Wholesalers, Schools, and Corporations: ASQ Quality
Press books, videotapes, audiotapes, and software are available at quantity
discounts with bulk purchases for business, educational, or instructional use.
For information, please contact ASQ Quality Press at 800-248-1946, or write to
ASQ Quality Press, P.O. Box 3005, Milwaukee, WI 53201-3005.

To place orders or to request a free copy of the ASQ Quality Press Publications
Catalog, including ASQ membership information, call 800-248-1946. Visit our
Web site at www.asq.org or http://qualitypress.asq.org.

 Printed on acid-free paper

Quality Press
600 N. Plankinton Avenue
Milwaukee, Wisconsin 53203
Call toll free 800-248-1946
Fax 414-272-1734
www.asq.org
http://qualitypress.asq.org
http://standardsgroup.asq.org
E-mail: authors@asq.org

For Vivian, Chuck, Amy, Matt, Jessica, Raj,
Howard, Harvey, and Audrey, all of whom add
special somethings to the story

Table of Contents

1

The Baby Is Dead—So Is the Board Chairman

"Jack, oh Jack. That baby died." Nan put the telephone back on its cradle and closed her eyes to stop the flow of tears, without much effect.

"Is that the Thompson baby you told me about yesterday?" Jack asked, trying to find something to say that would not make Nan feel even worse.

"Yes. The Thompson baby. Not even a year old. Last week he was a healthy baby boy with happy parents. Today he's dead. The parents must be devastated. I can't even imagine how they must feel. How would we feel if it were one of our boys? The Thompsons took the baby to the hospital where he was born because he had a bad bout of diarrhea and had lost a little weight. They figured to take the baby home that same day or maybe a day or two later. They didn't figure on this."

"But Nan, you're taking this baby's death pretty hard, pretty personal. You've seen babies die before, and so far as I know, you've never even set eyes on this one. Aren't you letting this one get to you, maybe more than you should?"

"Oh Jack, I know that birth and life and death are all one package. I was holding that Mrs. Carlson's hand when she died just the week before we came here. But she was old and ill, beyond what medical care can provide. She was calm and at peace. I was sad when she died because she was a nice old lady. The hospital had done everything it could to make her comfortable, so her death didn't make me cry. I haven't cried over a death since I was in training at that pediatric transplant ward. Do you remember that? Those little kids would get transplants. Some would get well immediately and be discharged, healthy for the first time in their lives. Others were about the same as they were before. A few of them died. They would be in the ward for three or four weeks, so we student nurses would naturally get attached to them. Then their little bodies would reject the transplant, and they would die. That was tough duty.

"But most of those kids had been sick all their lives, and they were getting the best treatment the world knew how to give. So it was a personal loss, but not a professional loss, if you know what I mean."

Jack knew. He almost always knew what Nan meant, the same way that Nan almost always knew what he meant, no matter how few words were spoken. It wasn't telepathy, just a closeness that was almost as effective. Nan knew about telepathy, having been raised with an identical twin sister. So did Jack, having been raised with an identical twin brother. Jack and Nan met at a college freshman mixer, where a computer had matched them up as having "common interests." Indeed. They were from high schools of the same size in the same state and they were born in the same month. They were both left-handed. The same computer had matched Nan's sister with Jack's brother because those two were both right-handed. The highlight of the evening was a different match-up the computer had made, matching a freshman with his own twin sister.

Nan and Jack had hit it off from the start, dated, and found that common interests grew into love as well as friendship. They were married the summer before their senior year, moved into a tiny married-student apartment, and produced their own twin sons the week after graduation. The highlight of the graduation ceremony was getting Nan up on the stage and back down again in cap and gown, given her state of glorious pregnancy.

They'd stayed at the university one more year while Jack earned his master's degree on a research fellowship, making ends meet with more than a little help from both sets of grandparents, who themselves knew how hectic and expensive the first year of raising twins could be. Twins having twins led to chaotic naming. Nan's twin sister was baptized Anna Claire. Nan was baptized Mary Claire. Her name, Nan, came from being "Not Ann." Jack was baptized Jacques and his twin brother John. They were called Jack and Jick. Their own twin boys were baptized Jacques and James and practically from birth were called Jake and Bake. What's more, Jake and Bake were both left-handed.

Eventually the twins were in school, and Nan started practicing her nursing profession. She took a graduate course here and there to get her own master's degree in a mere 10 calendar years. She also took a couple of courses toward an eventual doctorate. Jack had earned a good living in software engineering, and five years earlier he had left the big company he worked for to start up his own one-man software consulting business. He had a reputation in software architecture, so his business prospered. He did most of his work from his home office, which had computers and networks and gadgets galore.

Nan had moved up the ladder to supervisory positions and this year had been named to the position of head nurse for her hospital, which came with a fancy title of vice president. Because she was now part of the hospital's executive team, the board decided she first needed some executive management training and had enrolled her in a six-week management course. So, while she had the new title, she had not yet been in her new office. With the twins off to college, Jack decided to enroll in the same program, making it a second honeymoon, particularly since they had skipped the honeymoon the first time around.

Now, with only the graduation ceremony of their management program remaining and a happy second honeymoon behind them, instead of basking in the glow of it all, Nan was in tears.

"Jack, that baby was not like Mrs. Carlson or those transplant kids. That baby was not in jeopardy of life or limb when it went into the hospital. That baby is dead because the hospital killed him. I don't see how it could be any other way. I haven't seen the medical record yet, but I will on Monday. Maybe it will tell the whole story, and maybe it won't. I just have this feeling that while I've been studying up on finance, governance, and operations, my nursing service failed to prevent, or maybe even caused, this baby's death. That hurts, Jack. It really hurts."

Jack had nothing to contribute, so he clenched his jaws, formed a sympathetic half grin, and held Nan's hand for a long time.

The next day, after the graduation ceremonies, the class photo, and the good-byes, Jack and Nan talked during the two-hour drive home. They often talked, finding it more interesting to talk to each other than to anyone else.

"So, Nan, are you thinking about the new job or about the management course we just finished—or are you thinking about me?"

"You. And the new job. And the course."

"Are you glad you decided to take the general management course instead of a hospital management or a nursing management course?"

"Yes. If I had signed up for a hospital management course, you would not have come with me."

"Sure I would have."

"Yeah, for about a week, and then you would have discovered a crisis with some client in Walla Walla."

"Winnebago."

"Wauwatosa."

"Okoboji."

"You lose. That doesn't start with W."

"West Okoboji."

"That doesn't count. You still lose."

"Okay. You win. You think you can apply general management to your head nurse position?"

"I don't know. I've had the job for six weeks already, and I haven't been there to see if I am doing a good job or not. I must not be doing too badly. They didn't call up and fire me—yet."

"They might be saving that for next week. Are you going to do the ritual of handing in an undated letter of resignation like cabinet officers do?"

"I thought about that. It would add a little drama. It depends on how permanent I feel after a few weeks on the job."

"So, don't you think, though, that the big picture issues we have been learning about are the same for a big hospital as they are for a big industrial company?"

"I suppose. Market. Strategy. Finance. Personnel. Operations. The headings are the same. Maybe seeing how others deal with their issues gives us some clues on how to cope with our own set of issues."

"Give me a big issue that impacts your nursing department."

"Really big picture, medical error. You read about it in the papers all the time."

Jack nodded and replied, "When I'm not reading about that, I'm reading about software screwups like virus attacks that get through the computer firewalls. You and I picked the most visible fields in the world for publicity on the errors we make."

"I don't know what to do about medical error. Down the ladder and closer to home, there aren't enough nurses to go around, so we have high turnover. We've been robbing Peter to pay Paul with staffing. I don't know what to do about that either."

Jack said, "Economically speaking, the shortage drives up salaries, which attracts more people into nursing, so the problem solves itself in the long run."

"I suppose. In the short run, every hospital is short of nurses."

"Since nurses have their choice of jobs, what influences their decision?"

"Salary matters. After that, I think nurses are like everybody else; they work where they want to work. That might even be more important than salary. Take yourself, for example. You could make more money if you hired some people and got bigger consulting contracts, couldn't you? I think you have said as much in the past."

"Yes, I probably could. But I like doing it this way, and now that you're going to get a big executive paycheck, I can slack off."

"You don't fool me, Jack. You still make more than I do, and you're doing what you want to do. That's what I was saying about nurses. They'll work where they want to work, all other things being reasonably equivalent."

"Okay, what did you learn in our course that's going to make your department more attractive to nurses who have lots of choices?"

"I've been thinking a lot about that. The stuff the human relations professor talked about probably doesn't help. He seems to be most interested in reducing stress and dealing with people who are under stress. There's stress by the carload every day in any hospital, so I didn't learn anything new from that professor. The operations guy, though. He had something interesting to say about managing personnel, and it gets back to the error topic. He said that you can't yell at people when they do something wrong, which I already knew. He said you can't even criticize them in the mildest terms, which I didn't know. He said that the person didn't mean to do it wrong and therefore should not be criticized. Just retrain them in a nonjudgmental fashion. That seems simplistic, don't you think?"

"You've been doing nursing for 20 years. Have you ever seen a nurse make an error?"

"Nurses, doctors, accountants, orderlies, floor sweepers—I might have even made one or two myself."

"Did you make your one or two errors maliciously, or were they inadvertent?"

"Maliciously? No, of course not. No malice. I just did something that turned out badly. The same is probably true for all the others."

"So maybe the operations professor was right. If there was no malice, then maybe you and the others just needed a retraining jolt about then."

"Maybe. If that would really work, we could have a new slogan: Nurses, work here, we don't yell at you when you drop the ball."

"The marketing professor was the most entertaining, don't you think? He was a regular vaudeville act every class. He still got his point across every day, though. In my one-man business, my marketing is pretty simple. I answer the phone when it rings. I'd think that hospitals wouldn't need much marketing either, since people get sick pretty regularly."

"There is still a lot of hospital competition in most cities. But we don't have to make up reasons for people to need a hospital, so it's not like dreaming up halitosis to sell mouthwash. It's a matter of getting people and their doctors to want to come to our hospital rather than going to the other hospitals."

Jack said, "That operations guy had some good information. I was surprised to find myself paying attention in that class. I thought I already knew all there was to know about operations. Didn't you feel the same way to start out?"

"Yes. I did. Then he started explaining that the way to reduce errors is to change the way the work is done. Don't yell at people to do it right. Instead, make the task easier to do right than wrong. That sounds like something out of a fortune cookie, but I think that might be worth a try, even in nursing."

"All three of his rules—make it easier to do it right than to do it wrong, make errors obvious, and allow the worker to fix the error on the spot—might even work for software. See how much I learned? He says the Japanese learned these rules from Americans, except that Americans seem to have forgotten them."

"His way of looking at problem solving was a little different from the way we do problem solving in hospital cases. We have a set drill we do, sort of a form to fill in, that conforms to the way the Joint Commission on Accreditation wants it done. He didn't exclude that method; he just went a little further and got to something that might be a better management solution. I want to give that some thought. And he had something useful to say about work flow. What he had to say about error detection and change management seemed to be okay, particularly about getting a lot of information out of a little bit of data. So those topics were good, too, although maybe they don't have the same immediacy as problem elimination by proper task design."

"The operations guy probably took the marketing guy's course and figured out that he would get better attendance if he told the students they could earn a Six Sigma Black Belt by completing his extra cases and doing projects. I'm glad we did that. We each got two certificates for the price of one."

They drove on for a while, letting the scenery pass, just enjoying each other's company. Then Jack asked, "So, Nan, you haven't told me yet, what are you going to do first on Monday morning?"

"I guess I ought to try to find out how the place ran so well without me. Then I'm going to try to find out what happened to that baby so that it doesn't happen again."

"Going to find somebody to yell at?"

"That's always tempting, isn't it? Maybe hit somebody with a stick. Maybe write a stiff letter to file. Or, maybe I'll just yell at you and try something a little more modern on the job."

"You can yell at me if you want to. Just don't hit me with that stick anymore. It makes me grumpy."

Traffic was light, so they were making good time. The weather was pleasant, making it a very nice day to be together on the road. As they were getting closer to town, Nan said, "Jack, I talked to Marcy again this morning. She told me that William Schneider died last night, probably from a heart attack suffered while he was lying in bed up in the VIP suites. I don't know if you knew him personally, but he's the Mr. Bill whose face is plastered on billboards all over town urging people to go buy a car from one of his lots. He was chairman of the hospital board, which means he had a lot of money and a lot of community interest. I met him in person when the interviews were going on for the new job. He looked healthy enough to me, although I would have guessed his blood pressure was a little on the high side from his more-than-rosy complexion. You can't always tell from that, though. In any case, I'm not his cardiologist. People die of heart attacks, even in hospitals. My father used to talk about a guy he worked with who had gone to get his annual management physical. While he was getting dressed and tying his tie after the physical, he dropped dead on the spot. So, I don't read anything special into Mr. Bill having gone to meet his maker. Neither did Marcy—it was just a news item because he was so well known around town and was on the hospital board. I guess it would have looked worse if he had gone to some other hospital."

"I've certainly seen his mug on a lot of billboards. Didn't Mr. Bill have his Aunt Agnes on the billboards, too? Was she for real?"

"I don't know Aunt Agnes personally, but now that you mention it, she does show up on those billboards, doesn't she? Buy a car where Aunt Agnes will take care of you, or something like that. Or maybe it's buy a car or Aunt Agnes will get on your case. They used the same tag lines year after year, and they certainly must have sold a lot of cars to make Mr. Bill as rich as he was. Maybe Aunt Agnes has a little put away, too. I don't know if the Aunt Agnes pitch will work as a solo act."

Nan continued. "Marcy told me the unofficial version of what happened to baby Thompson. I'll tell you now before I see the record because this case is likely to wind up in court. I don't want to tell you anything after I see the record because some lawyer with too much imagination might subpoena you. The unofficial version, subject to change later on, is that the parents brought the baby to the emergency room because he had lost some weight after a prolonged siege of diarrhea. Babies get diarrhea pretty easily, and they didn't think too much about it. They just wanted to see about the loss of weight and whether they should change the feeding or give him some medicine or vitamins. The emergency room doctor consulted with their pediatrician, and the pediatrician decided to admit the baby for treatment and observation. That's all pretty normal. The baby was transferred to the pediatric ward, where the pediatrician ordered a drip and a drug. The drug was one that they use routinely in pediatric care and the dosage was normal, so the charge nurse carried out the instruction. By the next day, the baby was in very bad shape. He was transferred to Children's Hospital, and after about a day there, he was dead.

"It looks like the wrong drug was used in the pediatric unit. You might think that it was a blunder by the pediatrician. Maybe it was and maybe it wasn't. You know the pediatrician, Maria Escobar. She's the best pediatrician I know."

"Yes, I think I met her at some hospital event. Was there a language problem or a language translation problem?"

"No, she's a native-born American, so English is her mother tongue. Her ancestors have been here for 400 years. In fact, some Costa Rican trainees who came through here last year were laughing about how funny her accent was when she tried to speak to them in Spanish. Not that mine was any better, but they didn't expect any better from an Anglo like me."

"Well, isn't it what gets written in the doctor's order that counts?"

"Yes and no. What Marcy says is that Dr. Escobar told Mary Cummins, the charge nurse who has been there since the buildings were built and who is a wonderful nurse, to use drug A but wrote down drug B. Mary followed the verbal order, and tragedy resulted. Maybe Dr. Escobar said it wrong, or maybe Mary heard it wrong. In that situation, the charge nurse follows the verbal instruction, as would only be natural. Nobody expects the doctor to misspeak. Especially in a pediatric ward where care is always taken to get the right dose for the weight of the child."

"How are you going to find out which one of them made the goof?"

"I don't know. Maybe we'll never know. Remember that scene in the movie, *Cool Hand Luke,* where Paul Newman is lying in a ditch with the stuffing beat out of him, and the warden with the whiny voice looks down and says, 'What we have here is a failure to communicate.' Well, it looks like we had our own failure to communicate." Nan's attempt at levity fell a little flat.

"Well, if the parents sue everybody in sight, who has to pay the damages, the hospital or the pediatrician?"

"I don't know. I haven't been an 'executive' long enough to know that stuff. Everybody is insured, so one or the other insurance company will pay, or maybe both, and then everybody's insurance rates will be that much higher next year.

"Oh Jack, I sound so cold blooded, don't I? No amount of money is going to bring that baby back for those parents. No amount of financial punishment is going to cause this kind of error to be avoided the next time. It's going to take some way of eliminating that error. If financial punishment worked, we would have solved this problem and all the others a long time ago."

"Enough on that subject, Nan. I don't want to sit here in gloom for the next hour until we get home. Tell me about your new office. Speaking of which, are they really redecorating it for you? Nobody ever did that for me. I don't even do it for myself in the home office."

"Redecorating might be a more generous word than the case warrants. They painted the walls, which needed it, and they selected a brighter color than the bilious green that was there before. It's probably a light bilious green now," said Nan with the beginnings of a smile. "I gathered up some family photos to put on the credenza, and I'll have my diplomas and the two new certificates to hang as soon as I can get frames for them. I like the idea of having a Black Belt certificate up on the wall, just to intimidate people so they won't make any sudden moves for fear of getting a kick in the side of the head or a chop to the knee. I figure it will take six months before some folks understand that the Black Belt is in Six Sigma and not in tae kwon do.

"What are you planning for this next week, Jack?"

"Well, I've got to run the traps to make sure all my clients remember me after six weeks out of the limelight. Then I'm going to fly down to Houston to the closeout meeting on that last project. We did most of the project meetings on the video link, which is certainly handy and good enough for fixed-agenda meetings. I need to press the flesh, though, to make sure the client makes the final payment and to make sure I see all the people who might be planning new projects.

"I'll go see Jick while I'm there. I haven't seen him in a while, and don't tell me to look in the mirror. He might know of something of interest at NASA. NASA likes advanced projects, so they're always interesting to me, professionally speaking. The aggravation is that it takes NASA so many years to put anything into practice that you can hardly live long enough to see whether something works or not. Still, my part is usually at the front end, working on the architecture for the new scheme. To get NASA to think about me when they're thinking about new projects, I have to show my face once in a while. I have often thought about giving Jick a box of my business cards and asking him to fake it. Just like when we were kids. I don't suppose you and Ann ever went on each other's dates, did you?"

"They were all my dates. I just let Ann have a few of the dates I had left over." Nan leaned over against the restraint of her seat belt to put her head on Jack's shoulder and wrap her arm around his. Jack leaned her way a little so that they would be comfortable the rest of the way home.

2

Nan's First Day
on the Job

Nan had a spring in her step as she carried a cardboard box of office bric-a-brac into the hospital. Her heart was filled with joy and anxiety and enthusiasm and trepidation, all appropriate to taking on her new and important job as head of all nursing services for the hospital.

Nan arrived early, hoping to get a jump on setting up her office before the rush of everyday tasks took away her discretionary time. Nan looked forward to meeting Marcy Rosen, her new secretary, in the flesh. Marcy had been on the job only five weeks, having replaced the previous secretary who had earned a promotion into the president's suite. Because of a retirement in the purchasing department, there were two executive secretary positions open at that same time, and the most senior candidate had her choice. She made it, passing over Nan in favor of the other opening. Nan had spoken to that candidate by phone but was never told why she chose the other job. It was nothing Nan had any control over; it was just a matter of curiosity to her.

Marcy was the next most senior candidate. When they spoke on the phone, Marcy said she wished very much to have the opportunity to show that she could do the job to Nan's satisfaction. Nan checked with the head of personnel, who told Nan, "Marcy is not for the faint of heart nor for the insecure." This information was delphic and not very helpful. Having no grounds for rejecting Marcy, Nan welcomed her to the job and explained that she would be away until the management program ended. She told Marcy to use her own judgement and ask around for advice if she got stumped.

Nan had known Marcy by sight but had never had any actual dealings with her.

So far, Marcy had done a good job of forwarding information to Nan by post and by e-mail, with a few phone calls thrown in. No one had called Nan to complain about Marcy, so Nan thought the arrangement was off to a decent start.

Nan had never had a personal secretary before, and she wasn't sure what a secretary actually did in an office anymore. Nan wrote her own letters, which were largely e-mail messages these days, and the filing was mostly electronic. She supposed there were administrative tasks to be done in a department as large as hers, and the secretary's position was a given, so for Nan on the first day in her office, it was one more unknown.

Nan walked into her office at 7:40 AM.

Marcy greeted her at the door, dressed a little more formally than most secretaries, but then Nan was a little overdressed herself, at least for the first day.

"Hello. I know you're Marcy Rosen. Please call me Nan."

Marcy took Nan's extended hand and pressed it warmly, responding with an enthusiastic and sincere smile, "Oh, Mrs. Mills, I hope you will understand that I couldn't possibly address you by your first name. Please let me address you as Mrs. Mills or Ms. Mills if you prefer."

"Well, let's make it Mrs. Mills then, although I'm accustomed to informal relations with my coworkers."

"Mrs. Mills, you're very kind to call me a coworker, but I know that I'm just the secretary here, not one of your group managers. I know my place. I do look forward to working for you, and I hope that my work has been satisfactory to you so far. You told me to use my own judgment in routine matters, and I expect you'll find I dropped the ball on a few things, but I don't yet know which ones. I do feel honored that you trusted me from the very first day, sight unseen. I hope I'll continue to earn your trust."

Having put down her cardboard box, Nan looked around the room. The new paint job had worked a miracle by brightening up the office, and the shade of green was actually quite pleasant. There were accents in two darker shades, and everything was spotless.

Marcy referred to her steno book—Nan hadn't seen one of those in years—and started through the work of the day. "Mr. Crawford wishes to see you immediately, which I interpret to mean as soon as he appears in his office. His secretary is clued in to telephone me the moment he appears. He generally gets in a few minutes after eight.

The teapot is hot, and here's a clean cup and saucer." Nan hadn't seen a saucer in the hospital, ever. Rank may be revealing its privileges. "The staff meeting you asked for is set for 9:30 in your conference room. Dr. Wong from the anesthesiology service confirms that she will attend as your guest, and she asks that she be told whether to bring her hand puppets or a tank of laughing gas." At this point Marcy paused, pencil poised, looking up to Nan for direction.

"Please tell her that I would like her to talk for a few minutes about the work of Professor Gaba at Stanford. If that doesn't ring a bell for her, tell her to bring the laughing gas."

"Right," replied Marcy, who then stepped out to her own desk and came back with a young man in tow. "Mrs. Mills, this is Sanjar Subramaniam from the information technology department. He's here to set your computer access up. This will only take a minute. Sanjar?"

Sanjar extended his hand with a respectful bow and said to Nan, "Mrs. Mills, I am honored to be of service to you. This will only take a few minutes. Please consider me your computer geek and your security officer. I serve at your pleasure, and I will be replaced by my boss at the slightest word from you. I accept that, and please be assured that I do not wish to be replaced. Therefore, I will strive to serve you in every way.

"If you wish to be informal, you may call me Subramaniam. Oh, that is my little joke. Everybody calls me Sanjar, and I will be pleased if you do so, too.

"To start with, place your left index finger on this electronic reader. Thank you. Now, your right thumb. Thank you. To use the PC on your desk, place your left index finger in this depression here on the keyboard, so that the computer can check your fingerprint against this master. Your computer now knows you, Marcy, and me. No one else. If all three of us are absent and the computer needs to be accessed, then there is an additional emergency procedure that requires three signatures and the physical presence of two of my superiors. So, consider that the information on your computer is confidential among the three of us. All files are immediately encrypted on your PC, and the network backup copy of all files stays encrypted. The encryption key is controlled by the same fingerprint. This is actually quite old technology. Biometric computer access has been available for commercial use for a decade if not more. With the recent terrorist concerns, the hospital has elected to apply the available technology in this way. It is actually quite inexpensive, and we have had no difficulties with it at all.

"Here is your digital assistant. It is a cell phone, a two-way text pager, a wireless e-mail terminal, and a general organizer for schedule, telephone numbers, and smaller files. Place your right thumb on the screen for access. This device synchronizes its information with your desktop PC by its wireless infrared link, which is again rather old technology.

"Your computer desk has a pencil drawer and two file drawers. The file drawers are locked and are reasonably secure. They can be opened with a crowbar but not with a nail file. The lock is controlled by the computer. When you tug on the drawer, a window pops up on the PC, and you are asked to provide your index finger for examination. The drawer then opens. The drawer on the left is a standard drawer for hanging files. The drawer on the right, as you will see, has a place for your handbag, a resting place and connections for this medium-quality digital camera, and a connection dock for this laptop computer. Here is the charging point for batteries for your cell phone."

"Sanjar, if all this works off the computer, what happens if the lights go out?"

"Well, Mrs. Mills, we have been pretty careful in that regard. Your PC is on the vital mains, so if the power company's grid trips off, the hospital's diesel generators will start automatically and provide power to your PC and the rest of the vital loads. In addition, there is a battery backup right here under the desk that will carry the office load for perhaps half an hour.

"The reliability of the electric power supply is getting a lot of attention just now. When the contractors started to remodel the north wing, they found that the old engineering drawings had many errors. As you may know, that that is the oldest part of the hospital and has been remodeled many times over the years. Since errors were found, the hospital has hired a consultant to check the rest of the wiring setup both for electricity and for data connections throughout the hospital. The consultant is also measuring the electric load of the important medical equipment and computers so that a better database of design information will be in hand. That study has been going on for a month now, and it continues, so you see that it is not a small matter in a building complex like this one."

"Sanjar, this computer and desk setup is pretty nice, much nicer than I've had before. Is this standard issue to all managers or all employees now?" asked Nan.

"Mrs. Mills, this is the first actual installation of this type, but I expect it to be our new standard computer desk for all employees.

Since this is a beta application, if I may use computer jargon for the first field application, the cost of the desk is charged to our security department's budget and not to your budget.

"You will find the digital camera good enough for informal use, but for posed photos or important subjects, please call the hospital photographer, who will bring professional equipment and proper lighting to handle any need.

"Now, if you will give me your car keys, Mrs. Mills, I will attend to getting the right bar-code sticker on your windshield so that the gate will rise as you approach the executive parking area, which is known as the executive corral. That is where you parked this morning, but you will recall that you had to use the intercom to get the guard to open the gate remotely. This will now be automatic for you. If you have a second car that you drive sometimes, please allow me to repeat the same procedure for that car."

"Very well," Nan replied, digging her car keys out of her purse and handing them over.

"Finally, Mrs. Mills, I believe I am right in saying that your husband is the famous Mr. Jack Mills."

Nan was surprised and, she found, flattered by this remark. "Yes, Sanjar, at least he is famous with me."

"I mean, of course, famous as a computer expert. We will wish to make sure that the computer setup at your home is secure in this same way and that you have ample bandwidth for your home computer network, in case a situation arises in which you find yourself working at home. I do not doubt for a second that Mr. Jack Mills will have a computer setup far in excess of our modest infrastructure, but I wonder if you would permit me to visit with Mr. Mills on this point in the near future?"

Nan, still bemused but finding no reason to object, replied, "I'm sure Jack would be pleased to show you his setup and hear your advice and concerns on network security. That's one of his particular interests."

Marcy's pencil was flying again. "I'll contact Mr. Mills, introduce Sanjar, and work out an appointment time convenient to Mr. Mills."

Sanjar excused himself and left. Nan had never before seen anyone bow and walk backward at the same time, so seeing Sanjar perform this feat of balance was something else for her to remember to write in her daybook for her first day in the office.

Marcy took a phone call. Nan then realized that Marcy had a wireless telephone headset that was so small as to be nearly invisible. The microphone was in the earpiece and the telephone was voice activated. Nan had heard of such gadgets but had never seen one. The call was from Mr. Crawford's office, announcing that Mr. Crawford was awaiting Nan's arrival.

Marcy handed Nan her new digital assistant and relieved Nan of her handbag, saying that she would take care of charging the spare batteries and putting a spare battery pack in the handbag. Nan surrendered her purse and walked briskly to the office of Philip L. Crawford, chief operating officer and immediate superior to Nan on the organization chart. Philip Crawford was a known quantity to Nan. She had been in scores of meetings with him on budgets, projects, and committees. He was always intense, sincere in his manner, and neatly dressed—very much the executive. Nan liked and respected him.

"Nan, it's so good to have you here. You must tell me all about that management course one of these days. I've been trying to get away to one of those for years now. I signed up for one at Harvard twice now, and I've had to cancel both times. I understand Jack was with you as a fellow student, which certainly made you the envy of all the female students and him the envy of all the male students.

"It has been hectic here, and we need you to jump into action on many fronts. First of all, you must have heard about the tragedy of the Thompson baby. So sad. Dr. Anderson, the chief medical officer, is meeting this morning with his counterpart at Children's Hospital to determine whether they will handle the morbidity and mortality review as a joint group or as two separate groups. Needless to say, this is likely to attract lawyers. If we have been culpable, then we'll shell out or get our insurance carrier to do so. If somebody else was culpable, then we'll make sure we don't carry the can. If nobody was culpable, that will be fine, too.

"These things happen, and that's why we are prudent enough to carry insurance. Nobody wants them to happen, they just happen. In the long run, I'm more concerned about the public's perception. I don't want the public to get the idea that we take this sort of thing lightly. With that in mind, we need to tell and show the public that we are taking corrective action. The way things stand right now I think that's going to be on your plate. If I learn otherwise in the next day or so, we can deal with it at that time.

"We'll also need to get organized to handle a Sentinel Event analysis and report and ship it off under seal to the Joint Commission on Accreditation. Our compliance officer will hold the baton on that, but you'll be deeply involved, I'm sure.

"Then there's the matter of the untimely death of Mr. Bill. No one has told me yet how he managed to die, lying in bed in our VIP suite with a nurse not 20 feet away from him standing by to apply the defibrillator if his heart acted up. All that electronic stuff right there, and he dies and nobody notices. So far, this is just in the strange-event category, but I'm not going to let it go until I get a lot better answers than I have gotten so far. Dr. Anderson told me that he is digging into this one. I told him to set aside the fact that Mr. Bill was chairman of our board of directors and to just dig up the medical facts—that's what we all need right now.

"This Mr. Bill event is just too close in timing to the Thompson baby event. I think we're going to have Woodward and Bernstein wannabes all over us on this. They could make us look pretty stupid, particularly when our head nurse was off on a junket when both of these troubling events happened.

"I think you know the drill. All public statements are made by our public affairs officer or our hospital counsel. If anyone reaches you, decline to answer any questions whatsoever. At the appropriate time, we may want you to make a public statement or take a tame interview, but that will be carefully prepped before hand. You have full right of approval on any words put in your mouth by lawyers, and we never ask anyone to take an ethics dive. I won't ask you to, not now and not ever. It's just that this is a new experience for you, and it just happens to involve the most worrying cases I've seen in years and years. Well. I've been doing all the talking. What do you have on for the next few days?"

Nan, pretty well rocked back on her heels at this point, replied, "Well, I have a staff meeting later this morning, and I'm planning get-acquainted meetings with the whole staff over the next few weeks. I want to study the medical records for the Thompson baby and for Mr. Bill, then talk to the people involved before I form any opinion on what happened and what, if anything, went wrong. So, the first week or so will be mainly catching up and learning the ropes. Soon, though, I would like to try out a few of the things I learned in the management program, particularly on how to stop ourselves from making errors. I'll tell you about that later on, when I have a better handle on how to proceed." She smiled politely and waited for further direction from her boss.

"Nan, we're counting on you. You can't imagine how relieved I am that you're back here pulling the wagon along with the rest of us. I know there is a lot to adjust to in a short time, and I know it's rough that these cases have popped up just when you are getting your feet wet. I want you to know that my door is open day and night and that you will get every support possible from all the other department heads. We're in this together, and we need to do this as a team. A good team. A solid team. It's a stronger team, now that you're here playing your position.

"Let's have lunch later in the week and compare notes. I understand Marcy Rosen is your secretary. She might take some getting used to, but I swear you'll never know a more loyal and dedicated worker than Marcy. Figuring out how to manage your immediate team is part of the game, you know. I'm sure you'll do fine. Have Marcy set up a lunch date for us pretty soon. Go get 'em. I'm counting on you." Mr. Crawford gave Nan his most sincere smile.

Just for a moment, Nan considered bowing and walking out the door backward, but then she thought she might need to practice that maneuver before trying it out in public. So, she took Mr. Crawford's proffered hand, shook it once, smiled politely, turned on her heel and marched out of the executive presence.

What an experience that was, Nan thought to herself. So now I'm part of the executive team, yet I feel more alone than I have ever felt in my life. What I have I gotten myself into this time? And it's not even nine AM!

3

How Things Work in the Nursing Service

As Nan walked into her office, she met a young man going out, carrying a stepladder and wearing the coveralls typically worn by the building maintenance personnel. They smiled in passing. Nan entered to find the same bright office, but now her diplomas and certificates were hung, all in a straight line, in matching frames. Her family snapshots were placed on the credenza to good advantage, and the potted plants from her old office were right there, starting to bloom, and looking remarkably clean.

Marcy came into the office two steps behind her, steno pad and teapot in hand.

"Mrs. Mills, since we have some time before the staff meeting, perhaps this would be a good time to go over some routine matters. Is that all right?"

"Yes, Marcy, this is as good a time as any. Where do you want to start?"

"We can start at the beginning. When your appointment was announced, a number of vendors and organizations sent you flowers and notes. I took snapshots of the flowers with the digital camera and saved the photos and notes on your computer for you. I sent thank-you cards in your name. The flowers went to the hospital auxiliary, which always needs flowers for the waiting rooms and hallways.

"Then last week, there was another announcement that you were graduating from the management course, and some of the original flower senders sent more flowers. I again sent thank-you notes, making sure I didn't send the same message to the same people.

"This time, the announcement mentioned your Black Belt, so you got congratulations messages from two Korean and one Japanese martial arts clubs. You've been offered honorary membership in the local chapter of the American Society of Quality Control Engineers, and you're invited to speak at its annual banquet. I sent thank-you notes to the karate clubs, accepted the speaking invitation, and put the date on your calendar.

"Practically all of the other department heads and vice presidents have asked if they could set up get-acquainted sessions with you, so I have booked them for lunch in twos and threes spaced out over the next two weeks. The cafeteria will cater small lunches in your conference room, which can be set up with a table for four. I have the bio sheets for each of them organized for you in a folder for each luncheon. I didn't know which of these people you already know and which ones you don't, so I did them all."

It occurred to Nan that she had not yet tried her tea. She sipped her cup and found it to be her favorite oolong blend. She was starting to feel at home in her bright, new, well-equipped, well-organized office.

"Marcy, this is my favorite tea. Is that a stroke of luck, or did you know?"

"Well, I asked around."

"Marcy, I can't get over how well this office has been painted. Did you have anything to do with that?"

"No, it was painted by Eddy and Joe, the regular painters from the maintenance department. Hospital policy is that all management offices are repainted when there is a new occupant."

"That may well be the policy, Marcy, but I was just in Mr. Crawford's office, and I didn't notice any accent colors there."

"Well, after Eddy and Joe finished their standard painting, I noticed a few dings here and there, so I sent down a touch-up order to the maintenance department. Touch-up work is billed to the same order as the original paint job, which in this case is to the overall maintenance budget, not to yours. As long as they were here, and since you were not needing the office right away, I asked them how they would have done it if they had been given a little more time. You know, they like to do things right just like everybody else, and they rarely get anything but rush jobs to do. I also had them touch up your conference room as long as they were here."

"Marcy, Sanjar says this computer desk is new, but the credenza is built-in, so it must be old. Why does it look new?"

"Eddy and Joe have a helper named Willy, the kid who was just going out with the stepladder when you came in. He works here part-time as a gofer. He's a real nice kid who is going to trade school to learn to refinish furniture, and he wanted a little practice."

"Wanted?"

"Well, it turns out he likes cherry pie, too."

"Eddy and Joe worked here for a week, and Willy refinished the furniture in my office and in my conference room, all for a cherry pie?"

"Eddy and Joe are in my bowling league, and it sort of turned out that they owed me one. Willy just likes to keep busy. You know how it is with young men, with you having twin sons in college. And Willy is a little sweet on my sister's niece."

"Marcy, that leaves one mystery in this office. This chair. I have never had such a wonderful chair in any office, and it looks like it's brand new. What's the story here?"

"Well, it turns out that the accounting department ordered a lot of new furniture when they redecorated that wing a year ago. Then when the department was reorganized, there was one more executive chair than executives. The extra chair went to storage. Sanjar and Willy traded chairs with the storage department and created new capital equipment tags for the inventory records. The capital tags are kosher. It seemed to everybody that it would be better to have the best chairs in use rather than in storage. Besides, when the accounting department staff members buy something for themselves, they go first class."

"What happens if they hire another executive and can't find their chair in storage?"

"They're the records experts, I'm sure they'll find everything recorded the way they say in their instruction manual."

"So I have new and refinished furniture, new paint, a new computer desk, fancy electronic gizmos, and none of it charged to my budget?"

"Yes, ma'am."

"Marcy, I think we are going to make a team.

"How have you handled administrative matters on my behalf for the past five weeks? I ask because I think I'm going to like the answer."

"Well, the organization is so large, with permanent employees, part-time employees, pool employees, casual employees, candy-striper volunteers, and the 200 students in the nursing school who aren't employees but work in the patient care units, that there is a lot of paperwork to cover hires, departures, salary changes, grade changes, departmental transfers, and the like. Anything involving salary or grade requires a vice president's signature, so there is always something to look at and sign. In five weeks, you've had more than 100 personnel actions to take care of. You told me to take care of things, so I took care of them. I signed your name to those actions that were in the annual plan. I sent the actions that looked odd back to the unit manager for justification. There were only two of these, both salary increases for employees who had been given written cautions within the past six months so that a raise now looks a little fishy. Neither of those has come back with justification yet, but they might."

"You forged my signature?"

"Yes, ma'am."

"Marcy, we're going to make a fine team. What else have you been doing?"

"Mostly keeping your schedule up to date with various invitations to meetings so that you don't get yo-yoed around every day. The invitations that look like they can't be refused but don't look like anything to spend an hour of your life on I triple booked so that you can get out of at least two of them. In the afternoon, I hand-carry something or other around to each of the units and drop it off at the administrator's desk. Usually there's an opportunity to chat for a minute about what's going on in that unit. That's how I knew about the Thompson baby and Mr. Bill. I never gossip myself, but I can't avoid hearing what gets said around the building."

"That reminds me, Marcy, I want to see the medical records for the Thompson baby and Mr. Bill. Can you take care of that for me?"

"I thought you might, so I asked the unit and the medical records central storage administrator about those records. The word is that the records are in the care and custody of Alice Newcomb, the chief counsel. Senior managers such as yourself can examine them in Alice's office, but no copies and no notes. Looks like they figure on litigation in both cases."

"Okay, that seems a little on the extreme side, but so long as they let me see the records, it doesn't matter where. Will you set that up for me?"

"I set it up for eight AM tomorrow. Alice Newcomb doesn't get in very early, so you can read the files without having her looking over your shoulder or trying to get you to second-guess one of your nurses. Do you want to meet with Mary Cummins, the nurse in the Thompson baby case?"

"I do, eventually, but I want to keep that within the chain of command so my supervisors and unit managers won't think I'm cutting them out. I need to build their confidence in me and my judgment. Let's let that go for a day or so. "

"Well, then, you have a few minutes to freshen up before the staff meeting. Do you want me to attend and take minutes? I can set the telephones to transfer calls down the hall. We do that all the time to cover for each other."

"Yes, Marcy, I think you need to be in this staff meeting."

4

The Monday Staff Meeting

As they stood up to head into the conference room, Nan wondered if she should have invited Sanjar, since he seems to have placed himself on her personal team. "Marcy, do you suppose we could invite Sanjar to the staff meeting?"

"He's already there. His cover story is that he's observing the videoconferencing system in the redecorated room. Something about light levels."

"Why do you say 'cover story?'"

"If it hadn't been light levels, it would have been something else."

"I like that in a man. Let's go."

As they entered the conference room, it was immediately obvious that everyone had decided to attend this meeting in person, not by video link. Was that driven by curiosity or fear? Sanjar was adjusting one of the three cameras. The cafeteria had sent up a trolley with coffee urns, and the little teapot was next to Nan's spot at the head of the conference table. Nan would have preferred a round table, following the King Arthur symbolism, but the room was long and narrow. So, eight managers, Marcy, Sanjar, and Nan made for a full house. Dr. Wong was also present and gabbing with two of Nan's managers. Nan wondered whether they were talking shop.

At the stroke of 9:30, Nan invited everyone to find a seat, an invitation not requiring any repetition that day. "Good morning. Welcome to our first staff meeting. I look forward to meeting with you all in smaller groups over the next few days. I'm happy that we can all be here in person at least for this first meeting. Video links are fine, but they are not quite the real thing yet.

"Most staff meetings are taken up with administrative matters. I hope to minimize that so that we can spend our meeting time on more strategic matters. Let me say that another way . . . administrative matters provide their own urgency and get attended to because they can't be avoided. Strategic matters, if left to themselves, just don't get done. So we as the senior management of the nursing services have to provide the push to get strategic matters attended to.

"Nothing is more strategic for us than to provide nursing services at the highest standard of care that can be attained. When I went off to this business short course, I expected to be thinking about business, finance, and strategic planning. What I found myself thinking about was how to reduce the incidence of errors in the way we do our work. I don't expect anyone here to be opposed to reducing the error rate. The hospital has had quality programs and continuous improvement programs for as long as I can remember. Frankly, I don't think they have done very much besides pile up paper and generate forms.

"Years ago when I was in college, a line from Emerson stuck in my head. He wrote, 'The greatest courage is the courage of having done the thing before.' What we have done before is pretty good, probably the best in the world. But maybe other hospitals have done their thing better than we do ours, and maybe we can borrow a little courage from them. With that in mind, I have invited Dr. Mei-Ling Wong, head of the anesthesia service, to talk with us. Dr. Wong."

Nan started things off with some mild applause, which was then taken up by the group. Dr. Wong had taken the seat at the foot of the table, so everyone could see her from their own seats.

"Thank you, Nan, for inviting me here this morning. When I have seen most of you before, you were on maternity tables with vacant looks in your eyes. It's nice to see you upright.

"My given name is indeed Mei-Ling, but everybody calls me Suzy. I have a sister, and everybody calls her Suzy, too. We even call each other Suzy. So, call me Suzy.

"Our role in healthcare is to get patients through procedures that would otherwise be too painful to endure. Modern medicine would be impossible but for us. America has led the development of anesthesiology for the past century, and our outcomes have always been as good or better than anybody else's. Better, I'd say.

"Even so, we weren't very good at keeping score. Nobody knows how many patients were going home dead because something went wrong in the anesthesiology, but the number was somewhere between 100 and 500 per million procedures. The United States does about a million procedures a month, so that was 100 to 500 people who didn't make it every month. That's with the best we knew how to do. Every place else was worse.

"Today that number is *five* per million, and we're pretty sure it's five because today we keep score.[1] We think we can do better than five. Nan, you're a Six Sigma Black Belt: congratulations to you. I know your magic number is 3.4 per million. We want to get to that number and then maybe do a little better than that.

"How did we get to five per million? Computers? Robots? New gases? Blind luck? Acupuncture? I'd say we got there by stopping doing things that were not well considered. We do things right by not doing them wrong. We do things right by making it easier to do things right than to do them wrong. When I was in fifth grade, the nun used to spend a lot of time wagging her finger and telling us girls to avoid the near occasion of sin. I don't know if that did much good sin-wise, but it's a good metaphor for better anesthesiology. We try to avoid the near occasion of killing our patients.

"It was not one magic bullet that reduced the number to five per million. It was the result of many things. I'll rattle off a few so that you can get the idea. An important part of keeping the patient alive is to keep the blood oxygen level right. In many cases, that requires feeding an oxygen tube through the nasal passage into the larynx so that the oxygen goes into the lungs. That means getting the tube past the epiglottis. Otherwise, the tube goes into the esophagus and the oxygen into the stomach, which causes heartburn and doesn't get oxygen into the bloodstream. This intubation is done by feel. The margin for error is a fraction of an inch. If it's done wrong, the error has to be found within a couple of minutes, or else.

"Several years ago, practical monitors were invented that read out the oxygen level in the blood. You would think these monitors would have been snapped up by anesthesiologists because they immediately indicate whether the intubation was fouled up. Some did. Some did not. The reasons why some didn't use them might sound familiar to you. 'Not the way I was trained.' 'Expensive equipment, and no added reimbursement.' 'Relying on gadgetry isn't good medicine.' 'More things to go wrong.' 'No one can tell me how to do my profession. I'm the expert here, and I'll decide what equipment to use.'

"It's true that almost nobody can tell a doctor, particularly an anesthesiologist, what to do. The hospital can't or won't. Legislation usually protects old practices rather than encouraging new practices. Well, finally, in this case, the anesthesiology professional organization itself put its foot down and issued a guideline that said the standard of care is to use a blood oxygen monitor. At that point, the financial incentive changed from avoiding equipment costs to avoiding loss of insurance coverage. That's one near occasion of error eliminated.

"At that time, there were two major suppliers of gas control equipment. Believe it or not, with one brand, you turned the knob clockwise to get more gas, while with the other brand, you turned the knob counterclockwise. What could be sillier than that? It's like getting into a rental car on a rainy day and spending 20 minutes trying to figure out how to turn the wipers and headlights on because the car makers can't agree on a standard configuration. Again, it was the professional organization that got the manufacturers together, locked them in a room, and told them they couldn't come out until they agreed on a standard configuration.

"Fatigue was a factor, especially at teaching hospitals that use anesthesiology interns for most procedures. It's part of their training. It's also part of their training to be on call for ridiculously long periods of time, during which they might or might not get enough sleep. If not, then the anesthesiologist is apt to be nodding off just when something happens. So, the professional organization introduced rules about how much downtime an intern has to have between procedures or shifts. In this, we follow airline practice, which requires pilots to spend so many hours on the ground at their hotel between flights, even if that means flights will be late the next morning.

"Another thing we learned from airlines is how to train anesthesiologists to deal with emergencies. Our medical training is the same as everybody else's: study, observe, try it under supervision, and apply it in your practice. Well, something like a heart attack during an appendectomy is pretty rare and therefore hard to observe. You can read about it in a book, but you might be in practice for 10 years and never see a case. Then, all of a sudden, it happens and you need to do the right thing, right now. It's the same with airline pilots, who might fly for 10 years without ever having an engine fire. Then they have one and they have to do the right thing, right now. Airline pilots drill themselves on how to handle emergencies by flying a simulator. Now *we* have simulators for training anesthesiologists, computerized mannequins that give off the same symptoms as a patient having a heart attack, a stroke, an obstruction, or a sudden loss of blood. We can run drills on those procedures without putting patients at risk.

"One lesson we learned about simulator training is that it isn't enough to train for emergencies. We need to provide retraining for the routine tasks, too.

"Here's why. Think about a curve shaped like a bathtub, high at the beginning, then low and flat, and then high again. Now think about making errors.

"First we make mistakes when we're learning something. Next, we do it correctly without any thought, as a matter of habit. Then we start to make mistakes as bad habits creep in. It's human nature. Well, the antidote is to move back to the middle of the curve by repeating the routine procedure under the supervision of the simulator instructor. Pilots do this, too. It's called checkout testing.

"I could go into additional examples, but I think you've grasped the idea. A lot of this work is due to Professor Gaba at Stanford. He has published quite a bit. The professional organization is not resting on its laurels. One matter of current research, and argument, is in the complexity of computer displays. Experienced practitioners, let's call them the experts, generally say they don't need any help, that they do just fine with the present displays, which I admit are pretty complex. Others say we are just trying to keep secrets away from the public to cover up for ourselves. Anyway, that's a current hot topic.

"Other medical specialties have announced that they're going to do the same types of training, including simulator training. That might be even more difficult for them than it was for us because we, in fact, perform a limited range of actions.

"Nan, I'll answer a few questions if you like. I will tell you, though, the question and answer session is between you folks and the cake."

Cake? Nan turned around in her chair to find Willy coming in the door pushing a trolley carrying a large sheet cake decorated to say "Congratulations Nan" in pink frosting. Given the seating arrangement, everyone else had seen it before Nan did. That put an end to the Q&A session before it started. Nan worked her way through the throng to reach Suzy Wong to thank her for coming and for making her case so clearly. Suzy was balancing a coffee mug and a paper plate in one hand and a fork and napkin in the other.

"You should try doing this with chopsticks," Suzy remarked to Nan. "By the way, Nan, have you seen Maria Escobar? She was always so regal and so beautiful with those high cheekbones and that Castilian visage. Well, I have high cheek bones, too, but it works better on her. Now she looks 10 years older. That Thompson baby case has really been eating at her insides. Have you read the record?"

"No, I haven't seen the record yet, so the only thing I know about the case is the general run of gossip. I've only been in the office for a couple of hours since that happened. It is a grabber, that's for sure. Once we figure out what happened, maybe we can make sure it doesn't happen again. Suzy, do you know about Six Sigma?"

"Well, I know the most general stuff about Six Sigma. I know that it was developed as a better way of getting manufacturing to get very high yields, that some service industries have taken it up, and that if you want to be a supervisor in the mail room at GE, you'd better get yourself a Green Belt and maybe a Black Belt. Do you think you can get it to work in a hospital setting?"

"I don't know. The need is so great, and we've tried every other kind of improvement program. Maybe we've made some progress—in fact, I'm sure we have. But we have a long way to go, and maybe we ought to take a few steps down the path to see where the path leads."

"Glory. All paths lead to glory. I think I remember a hymn to that effect. In any case, the cake is good, the audience was kind, the day is short, and I have some people to gas. Congratulations on your new degree and your new position. Anyone who provides me an audience and feeds me cake is a friend for life, so let me know when I can help. In the meantime, I'm going to stop at Dr. Anderson's office and complain that your decorator is better than ours."

"Suzy, I think you're joking. I hope you're joking. I'll loan you this conference room any time you want it, just don't make waves!"

People were drifting back to their seats, so Nan returned to hers. As she was about to call the group to attention, Miriam Caldwell, the most senior of the managers in the department, beat her to the punch. "Nan, before we get back to the meat of the agenda, I want to interject a few words on behalf of the staff assembled here. I believe I speak for all of us, but you know us well enough to know that anybody who doesn't agree with me is going to sound off immediately.

"First, I love the way you have redecorated this conference room. If you never do another thing for the hospital, you will have already made your mark.

"Second, Suzy Wong is a delight. I love getting a message in an entertaining way.

"Third, this is the best prepped staff meeting I can remember. How you did the preparation while you were off at the university, I don't know, but I'm impressed. The Web site links you sent last week gave me, and I think the others, a chance to get acquainted with the Six Sigma notions, although I think I still have a lot to learn.

"Fourth, I don't know how we're going to do this, but I do want you to know that I'm on your side, by your side, and pulling on your rope in the same direction. If I can learn to do things better at my age, then it's going to be duck soup for the rest of you.

"Fifth, how do we get started?"

Wow, thought Nan to herself. It looks like Marcy found Web citations for Six Sigma background material. Why didn't I think of that myself? How am I going to top Miriam's speech? Nan was reminded of a remark made by the big management guru in her program, who said control of an enterprise is an illusion. There are tides and winds and torrents, and the best you can do is to keep your oar in the water and try to steer the best you can. Lots of tides and winds and torrents here, Nan surmised silently, so I'd better get my oar in the water. Meanwhile, I'm in love with this staff.

"Miriam, you're too kind, and I take you at your word. I'm going to talk about Six Sigma for just a few minutes. This is not a factory. Therefore, much of what Six Sigma consultants talk about doesn't apply. Factories today are highly automated. We are not. We do manual work. We use our hands, we touch our patients, and we even hold their hands sometimes. Maybe robots will do that a hundred years in the future, but here and now, we are in manual mode. So, we need to look at some Six Sigma principles and see how they apply to manual operations.

"So, let's start by learning a new word. Like aspirin and shampoo this word has the same meaning in all languages. It's *poka yoke.* That's poka as in Pocahontas, and yoke as in OK with a 'y' in front of it. It means prevention of inadvertent error. That's not only polite, it gets at the main point here. We don't have people trying to do things wrong; we have people trying to do things right and who sometimes make errors inadvertently.

"Poka yoke is not a slogan. It's a set of three very basic guidelines for designing any work task. They are: one, make it easier to do the right thing than the wrong thing; two, make it immediately obvious to the worker when a mistake is made; and three, make it easy to correct the error on the spot."

Nan clicked the mouse on the laptop computer controlling the projector so that a slide appeared on the wall with the three guidelines. This was an act of blind faith that there would be such a slide, since she had never seen the slide before in her life. Did Marcy set this up, or did she call in more favors from the bowling league?

"If we take some of the examples Suzy Wong gave us, we can see how these rules come into play. For the faulty intubation, what rule jumps out?"

Miriam spoke up. "I'd better answer the easy question so I won't have to answer a hard one. The old way, with no blood oxygen meter, ran against rule two, because it was not immediately obvious to the anesthesiologist that the tube was down the wrong passage."

"Do we all agree?" Heads were nodding in the affirmative. "Okay then, how about the gas machines that had knobs that went in opposite directions?"

Claudia Benedict spoke up. "I'm not sure about this, but wasn't the problem that it was just as easy to do it wrong as to do it right? That would be against rule one. Making all the manufacturers use knobs that turn in the same direction would make it better, more likely to do the right thing than the wrong thing, at least after people got used to doing it in the uniform way."

Heads were nodding in the affirmative again, and people were murmuring to their neighbors, which probably meant that they were catching on. So Nan continued. "How about the fatigue factor that Suzy mentioned—that interns working long shifts would maybe not be alert?"

Several people said, "Rule one again."

Miriam added, "Boy I can see where that applies when we require nurses to work a double shift just because we're short on bodies. That's just asking for trouble, and rule one is so obvious, now that I see it there on the wall. Even the suits ought to be able to understand it. I've always known it was a bad practice, and now I have something to point at. I like this kind of sushi better than that raw fish."

More nods, more vigorous nods. More chat with neighbors.

Nan took the floor again. "Okay, it looks like everybody has the idea. Before we attack any barricades, let's try for some context.

"Poka yoke is indeed a word from the Japanese, but it has caught on in all languages. If you look at the Japanese source documents, you'll find the Japanese quoting American authors, so this is a worldwide development. Other concepts that we will look at later on are not Japanese at all. They are pure corn-fed American. Poka yoke is a cute name, and that's fine with me.

"Let's take note of one other thing that Suzy Wong said. She said that the anesthesiologists learned a lot by studying how airlines use simulators to drill pilots on routine tasks and to drill pilots on emergency situations. These doctors were willing to learn from the experience of others. That flies against the established American practice of refusing anything that was not invented here—I think NIH is the buzzword. They were also willing to make changes as a profession and to find ways to force everyone to follow best practices by muscling them if they had to.

"They started out not knowing how many deaths were attributable to anesthesiology. Maybe they didn't want to know. Maybe we can say the same about nurses, surgeons, therapists, or nutritionists today."

"Okay, for homework, please look at the routine tasks we do in each of our units for a week or so, and see whether or not they conform to poka yoke. Don't try to fix things on the fly. Let's just do some observation first. Maybe we can fix some things ourselves, maybe not. And let's be looking for those things that we can get done during our lifetime.

"Poka yoke is not the whole of Six Sigma, but I think it's the part that has the most relevance to our manual work. Eliminating error caused by inadvertent actions. That's us. Now, before we break up, let's take a few minutes to hear from anybody who has something to say."

Vivian Smith, the manager of the pediatrics unit, spoke up. "Have you read the Thompson baby's record yet?"

Nan answered, "No. Not yet. Can you give a quick recap?"

Vivian said, "Yes. The pediatrician gave a verbal order for a drug and wrote down a different drug in the written order. The charge nurse followed the verbal order, as any of us would. Inadvertent error. Now I don't know if the doctor misspoke or if the nurse misunderstood, but I do know that I would trust my life and that of my children and grandchildren to this doctor and this nurse. They are the best I know. So if the best people can have inadvertences, then the system needs some work."

Claudia then spoke. "Let me recap the case of Mr. Bill. He was on an EKG monitor, which was connected to an alarm at the unit station. The alarm went off, and the nurse went immediately to the bed and hit him with the paddles. No response. Why he didn't respond is an open question. The word going around is that Dr. Anderson, our chief medical officer, thinks the nurse waited several minutes doing her nails, watching a soap opera, or talking to her boyfriend, so that by the time she got to the bed, it was too late to do Mr. Bill any good. Dr. Anderson got the family to agree to an autopsy, which is booked for tomorrow. The autopsy will certainly show that he is dead, but whether it will show anything else, I guess we'll have to wait and see. Dr. Anderson is interviewing all parties himself, including everybody on the cardiac emergency team that rushed up to Mr. Bill's room when summoned by the nurse on duty. From what I've been able to learn, the setup and the nurse's action were both by the book. The EKG and the alarm system appear to have been in good working order. The alarm did go off, and the nurse responded.

"Mr. Bill was in to get a pacemaker. That was put off for a few days to clear up an unrelated infection with a course of antibiotics. He was not thought to be a high-risk patient, even with his arrhythmia, at least not up until the time he died."

The room fell silent. Nan concluded the meeting by saying, "I think we'll hear more about both of these cases. I hope we can learn from them. Both are likely to get a lot of attention in the press, so just smile and say, 'No comment' if asked anything by anybody on the outside. A Sentinel Event project has already started for the Thompson baby and might be started for Mr. Bill if the autopsy reveals anything. You know the drill. Everybody cooperates, as we always do. The Sentinel Event reports stay confidential and do not get released to the public press. If litigation arises, then that is all in the public arena.

"I thank you for the cake and for your good wishes. I look forward to talking with each of you in the next few days about your particular operations. And let's remember that as senior managers, we need to keep in mind that we have to do strategic planning and succession planning, because if we don't, nobody will. Thank you for coming. Meeting adjourned."

Nan stood up and exchanged pleasantries with each of them as they filed out. Nobody seemed to be in much of a rush, so the exit process went on for several minutes. Nan took this to be a good sign, but she wasn't sure.

As the last of the managers left, Nan called Marcy and Sanjar to sit down with her. "Marcy, did you do the poka yoke slide yourself?"

"I did the slide, after Sanjar told me what to write. Sanjar hunted down the Web citations that we put in the meeting notice. Sanjar's very good at that Web stuff," said Marcy as she turned with a sort of motherly smile in Sanjar's direction.

Sanjar did one of his patented bows and replied, "I am pleased to be of service. I am particularly pleased to be attached to this department, which has such keen interests in the betterment of the hospital's services."

Nan went on. "What would the group have seen if I had clicked the mouse again?" She answered her own question by clicking the mouse button. The new slide had a few bullets on problem solving. The third slide had bullets on error detection. The fourth slide was on work flow. The fifth slide was on trials and managed change. Then a curtain slide. All essential points for any systematic improvement plan.

Nan asked, "What else have you done that you want me to know about?"

Marcy replied. "I ordered copies of that book you mentioned, *Six Sigma for Healthcare*, for all managers and supervisors. The managers will get their copies this afternoon. I figured that we'd hold the supervisors' copies until you decide how to proceed with the program. I got a quote for a bulk purchase if you want to issue copies to all the nurses. We have a few extra copies to cover Sanjar, Willy, and maybe some others. If you want to give copies to Mr. Crawford and the other executives, we can cover that. I sent a copy to the head of the nursing school, just in case it wants to add a course to the training program."

Nan nodded and said, "Let's wait and see how things develop here in the nursing service, first. This next question I ask only out of curiosity. Which budget paid for the books?"

"Carl Burke looked at the budgets and the controller's manual and decided that they should be charged to the library account. He said that the books should be treated as a permanent loan."

"Who's Carl Burke?"

"Carl Burke is the cost accountant in the accounting department who handles your accounts."

"Tell me something more about Carl Burke."

"He's married to my second cousin once removed on my father's side."

Nan smiled and turned to Sanjar. "Sanjar, what did you learn about the video system and the room lighting?"

"Mrs. Mills, I find that the brighter décor has improved the video images quite remarkably. Digital cameras have a limited dynamic range, so for videoconference setups they commonly provide only a dark image. Or else the room is overlit to compensate and you get a washed out image. This room is pretty good now.

"The whole meeting was recorded, so you can look at it yourself when you find it convenient. Since you have people working on various shifts, I thought you might wish to make the video copy available to those on other shifts, perhaps not for this meeting today but for future meetings. A little time spent at the video-editing station makes the copy quite functional, in my experience."

"Do you do the video editing?"

"Yes, ma'am, I can do the editing. Let me add that the basics are quite readily acquired, and there are several others who can provide the editing function. Willy, for example, has a certain flair in video editing."

Nan turned to Marcy. "That's our same Willy?"

Marcy replied, "Yes, ma'am."

"You are the most remarkable twosome I have ever worked with. I love you both. What do I have booked for the rest of the day?"

"You have time to freshen up and look at the mail log before your late lunch with the chief financial officer and chief personnel officer. Here's the CFO's bio and a snapshot of the flowers he sent when your appointment was announced. Here's his article in a recent hospital newsletter so you'll know what his hot buttons are. Otherwise, he's a nice enough guy for a bean counter, from what people say.

"Here's the bio, recent articles, and flowers snapshot for the CPO. Everybody seems to like her, although of course, she has to take the company line on every issue that comes up whether or not it makes any sense. She'll probably want to talk about parking."

"Okay, I'll look at that information before they get here.

"Now, what's a mail log?"

"It's a disposition report that details each mail item and phone call that I took care of for you. All routine today. But people might ask you about something they sent you or called about, and it's better to be aware of what it was and what was done to it."

"Indeed. What's the parking issue?"

"The construction going on in the old wing takes up some of the employee parking slots. When the construction is over, there will be more slots than before, but right now there are quite a few slots taken up by construction machines and piles of material. The hospital has rented a lot two blocks away for the employees to use during the construction period. Some people gripe about that."

"Well, it seems to me that people always gripe about parking and the cafeteria. If it is nothing more than that, then I won't worry about it. Marcy, where did the cake come from?"

"The cafeteria offered to make one, but you know it makes everything so bland, which takes all the fun out of having a cake. So, I whipped one up at home."

"Thank you. That was above and beyond the call of duty. Anything else?"

Sanjar looked up. "If I may, Mrs. Mills, I took the opportunity to take a few snapshots during the staff meeting with your digital camera. I will put these in your online scrapbook as mementos of the day. That's in your private files, of course, not for public access."

ENDNOTE

1. More information about the commendable achievement by the anesthesiology profession, as summarized by Dr. Suzy Wong for Nan's staff, can be found in the work of Dr. Atul Gawande in the book *The Best American Science Writing of 2000*, ed. James Gleick and Jess Cohen (New York: HarperCollins, 2000). Dr. Wong's remarks are largely drawn from this source.

5

Monday Lunch with the CFO and CPO

Nan had a leisurely lunch with the chief financial officer and the chief personnel officer. Nan had known both of them before. There was the usual chitchat about her management course and how good they felt that she was in the office now. They talked about difficulties with getting enough money from the insurance companies and the government, how the new wing construction was making a mess out of the employee parking situation, which was causing a lot of grumbling, and the general state of affairs. Big-picture stuff, nothing very surprising or substantial.

Both the CFO and the CPO expressed concern over the death of Baby Thompson, and Nan said that she hadn't read the record yet and didn't know any more about it than hallway gossip. Both expressed surprise at the untimely death of Mr. Bill, given that he was right there in the VIP suites. Nan gave the same response about not reading the record yet.

The personnel VP said how hard it was to recruit and retain nurses these days, and asked whether Nan had any ideas. Nan demurred. The personnel VP then mentioned that the nursing school was part of the personnel department, as Nan surely knew, and that close cooperation was going to be provided by the school for anything Nan wanted to take up. So, it was a pleasant enough lunch.

On the way out, both guests remarked that Nan's conference room was certainly cheerier than theirs, and it wasn't that standard color of bilious green. Nan said it had something to do with the video cameras but she couldn't say just what it was.

6

Verbal Orders

"**M**rs. Mills, Sanjar left this videotape. He says it's cued up to the scene of interest and he would be pleased if you would watch five minutes of it or so," said Marcy. "What videotape is it?"

"It's a John Wayne movie from the '50s. Looks like a submarine war movie."

"Well, let's give it a look and then get him in here to explain himself."

"The VCR in the conference room is set up. Sanjar will be here in 15 minutes."

Nan and Marcy went into the conference room. Marcy loaded the tape in the VCR and fired it up. Marcy started to leave, but Nan asked her to stay and watch the tape with her. The tape started. John Wayne shouted "Up periscope." The actor standing next to him, so close they could touch elbows, repeated "Up periscope." A third actor another few inches away pushed some levers, the periscope went up, and he said, "Periscope up." The intermediary repeated, "Periscope up." John Wayne said, "Very well." Wayne peered into the periscope, found the enemy ship, and the act was repeated.

"Mark range and distance."

"Mark range and distance."

"Range and distance marked."

"Range and distance marked."

"Fire one."

"Fire one."

"One fired."

"One fired."

"Torpedo one in the water and running true."

"Torpedo one in the water and running true."

Nan stopped the tape. She turned to Marcy, thought for a moment and said, "With one husband and two sons, I don't know how many John Wayne movies I've seen in my lifetime, but I'd guess about two million. And I've seen at least that many submarine movies. They all look like this. So what do you think Sanjar wanted us to see?"

As if on cue, Sanjar came in, bowed, wished everyone a good afternoon, and asked if he could take a chair. He could.

"Sanjar, what's the message here?"

"Well, Mrs. Mills, I always wondered why submariners, in that tiny space, shouted and repeated orders that way. As a computer person, that always seemed to be redundant and inefficient, considering everyone involved could hear every word anybody spoke.

"In the computer world, redundancy is used for a particular purpose, namely to make sure the integrity of a message is preserved. But these submarine movies are from an era before computers were very common, so I don't know if there is a direct link. Perhaps this second videotape can inform us on the matter."

Sanjar produced a second videotape. Marcy ejected the first submarine movie, inserted the second one, and hit the *play* button. The scene opened with the Union Jack unfurled on a sailing ship, a man-o'-war. Blue jackets and cockade hats, glorious color. It was one of the many Horatio Hornblower adventure movies. The captain was shouting orders.

"Raise the main sail."

"Raise the main sail, aye," echoed a lieutenant about two feet away from the captain. The order was repeated three or four times more by others farther away.

"Make course due East," shouted the captain.

"Make course due East, aye," echoed the lieutenant, and that order was repeated two or three times more.

Nan stopped the machine and turned to her friends. "Okay, this is a history lesson, isn't it? John Wayne shouts his orders at somebody two feet away because that's the way Horatio Hornblower did it. Is that the point?"

"Yes, ma'am. Navies are big on tradition, and they stay with what works. So do hospitals for that matter. Perhaps all professions have this tendency. "

"Okay, but why was Horatio Hornblower shouting and why was his lieutenant, two feet away, shouting back the same thing to Hornblower?"

Sanjar looked pensive for a moment, and then he replied. "There are surely experts on naval history who can give definitive answers. I will offer a hypothesis only, a conjecture. Perhaps it is correct, perhaps not.

"Hornblower was on a sailing ship, a fighting ship. To fight against the French, in Hornblower's case, he had to maneuver his ship into fighting positions. He could only do that with the wind. Furthermore, he had to take the wind as he found it, and if he found a strong wind in the middle of a storm, then he had to make the best of it. A high wind was likely to be accompanied by a lot of wind noise, plus the creaking of the wooden ship, plus the noise of cannon fire on his ship and on the French ship. So, he had to communicate in a noisy environment.

"You might also think that the navy was a government operation and probably had too many people employed, so they might as well repeat orders instead of just standing there.

"It might also be useful to consider that things didn't happen instantaneously on a sailing ship. If the captain ordered a new course, it might be 10 minutes or more before anything happened at all. So, the captain could not rely upon his own senses to know if the order had been delivered completely and correctly.

"For example, if you are the surgeon and Marcy is the assisting nurse, and you say "scalpel," and Marcy hands you something, you will know quickly enough whether Marcy understood your order. You get a scalpel in your hand, or you don't. If you get a forceps instead, then your sensory feedback tells you that the message failed."

Nan thought for a full minute. "Sanjar, you're telling me that the navy knows how to give verbal orders in a reliable way and that we don't, except maybe in surgery. Out on the floors, we don't know how to give verbal orders reliably. You are telling me that if anesthesiologists can learn from the airline pilots, nurses can learn from mariners."

Sanjar turned a quarter turn toward the table and clicked the mouse on the laptop controlling the projector. A simple text slide appeared on the wall. Sanjar bowed again and pointed with a laser pointer at the slide on the wall. "If I may pose the problem in simplest terms, with only two actors involved, say a doctor and a nurse, then the number of permutations is quite small. The doctor says A and the nurse hears A. Or, the doctor says A and the nurse hears B. If there is no feedback at that point, then the nurse proceeds to do B. If there is feedback, by which I mean if the nurse echoes the order and says B, then the doctor has the chance to correct the matter on the spot. In poka yoke terms, given that an error in communication has transpired, the error is made evident on the spot, and the error can be corrected on the spot. So, echoing the verbal instruction conforms to poka yoke.

"Now in this next slide, we consider what happens if the doctor thinks A but misspeaks B. With no feedback at this point, the nurse does B. However, with feedback in the form of an echo from the nurse, the doctor has the opportunity to discover that the nurse was about to do B. The doctor will probably recognize that some error has been made and correct it on the spot."

Nan sat there for two full minutes. Would this really work?

"Okay, Sanjar, I think we're on to something here, and I couldn't be more pleased. Before we launch this boat, let's pick up another of the Six Sigma tools from the toolkit and think through a potential problem analysis. That is to say, let's think about how this would work, what new difficulties might arise, and whether there is some slightly modified way of proceeding that takes care of those potential problems."

"Yes, I see what you are saying. We have a general notion in mind, but we should not force it to happen. We should think ahead, think of obstacles and difficulties, and determine whether some fine-tuning of the notion will do even better."

Nan looked at Sanjar with a little more intensity and said, "People who know this stuff say that potential problem analysis works better as a group exercise because the point is to find all the negatives and get them out on the table. If the proponents of the idea are the only people looking for the negatives, they won't see them all. But others who start from a more skeptical viewpoint will see lots more negatives. So, what group do we want to involve in this?"

"Mrs. Mills," said Sanjar, "I think it is the case that one idea tossed into the thinking may well trigger much better ideas from others. Break the ice, if I may use that metaphor. Perhaps this will happen here."

Nan turned to Marcy. "How are we going to do this?"

Marcy replied, "I figured that any idea that Sanjar came up with would be a good one, and Sanjar told me that it had to do with verbal orders, so I took the liberty of booking short one-on-one meetings for Sanjar with four of the managers of nursing units where verbal orders are common. Not all of the four could be available this afternoon, but I have three booked. Sanjar told me he could be available all afternoon. One of the meetings is with a second-shift manager, because I know the second- and third-shift people always think they're being left out. Then, all of those people are booked into a larger meeting with you at the tail end of the first shift tomorrow. It's on your calendar."

"Agreed. Sanjar, do you know what to do? Do you need any support?"

"Mrs. Mills, I am honored that you have entrusted this matter to me. I believe I am prepared, and I thank you for the opportunity. If anything comes up in the first meeting that knocks this idea down flat, I will scrub the other meetings and report back to you."

"Okay. Go to it," said Nan.

"Okay, go to it," echoed Sanjar, who was already walking backward out of the conference room and bowing at the same time. He had the videotapes in his hands.

Nan turned to Marcy. "Marcy, how in the name of God did we happen to get Sanjar assigned to our department? Did you have anything to do with this?"

Marcy answered without exactly looking at Nan. "No, he just came over to see me a few weeks ago, while you were at that school, and introduced himself. He asked if the new head nurse was married to, as he says, the famous Jack Mills. I said yes. Well, at the time I didn't know whether your husband was famous or not, but I knew his name and saw it in the newspapers a couple of times. So I figured the answer was probably yes.

"At that time, another person from Sanjar's department had been named to be our contact person. The next day, I got a memo saying that routine assignments were being rotated and that our guy would be Sanjar."

"So, it's not blind luck that we got Sanjar. Or rather, that Sanjar got us. Well, I'm not going to complain. Keep me posted."

7

Monday Evening at Home with Jack

Having finished supper, Jack and Nan were relaxing with a glass of Beaujolais, which they did only on special occasions. "Jack, I have acquired the most remarkable staff in the history of the world. Marcy does all the routine stuff before I even know it needs doing. Sanjar is a computer whiz up there in your stratosphere. And Willy the gofer refinishes furniture and edits videos. Three hearts of gold. Marcy has more relatives on the payroll than any mafioso ever thought of. Anybody she isn't related to, she has some other leverage on. And she bakes pies and cakes on the side."

"I met Sanjar this afternoon. He came over to talk about security for your home computer. He is prepared to issue you a new one, so I took him up on the offer on your behalf. We talked about broadband, firewalls, distributed computing, and error prevention in software. This was after your staff meeting. Although he didn't reveal any company secrets from that meeting, he did let it be known that he thinks you're onto something with the Six Sigma push. He's thinking of ways to apply Six Sigma to his own work. You made an impression on that young man."

"He was so anxious to meet you—the famous Jack Mills—that he was beaming this morning when Marcy called you to set up that meeting. Do you think he has the goods to be a computer geek?"

"He's a supergeek already. Quite well informed on current software issues. If he wants a job, I think I can make a few phone calls and get him placed within about seven minutes, if I talk slow."

"If you do, it's over between us," joked Nan. "Well, he probably needs to move on from his hospital job eventually to find something bigger to match his talents, but please don't push him to leave. He's precious. When he wants to go, he goes with my blessings. Until that day, I'll fight tooth and nail to keep him.

"And he doesn't even work for me! He's on somebody else's budget. If today is any example, I'm going to end up the budget year $5 million to the good, and everybody else is going to be $6 million to the bad. If Marcy weren't related to the cost accountant, I can see myself being in big trouble."

"I take it you didn't really know Marcy before, other than from those cryptic endorsements people were giving her. What else have you learned about her, other than that's she's ready to be secretary to the president of the United States?"

"Secretary, hell, Marcy could be president and director of OMB at the same time with one hand tied behind her. And pastry sous-chef for the White House in her spare time.

"The personnel chief told me that Marcy's children have grown and started their own families, so she applies her motherly instincts to her job. Maybe she goes overboard. I can see that she would drive any uptight manager right up the wall. If I have an uptight day, she'll probably drive me up the wall. Until then, I think she is just perfect. What's that British word for administrative bother? Something like *bumf*. Well, with all the bumf that comes with a big department, Marcy is the best thing that could have happened to me at work. She's the greatest debumfer the world has ever known. The more bumf she debumfs, the less likely I am to get uptight. So, we're on a virtuous cycle and I love every minute of it."

"Even with the most enthusiastic oarsmen, my love, somebody has to steer the boat. Did you meet your boss on your first day?"

"Yes, I saw him at 8:02 this morning. I knew him before, but this is the first time I'm reporting directly to him. It was a strange interlude, to quote Eugene O'Neill. Looking back on that strange interlude, I now see that he was utterly wound up like a spring. He was reacting to the tension by mouthing coaching platitudes about being on the same team and pulling together and being right there beside me—or maybe it was behind me.

"He didn't come right out and say what was torquing him. He did mention Mr. Bill and the Thompson baby, so I figure that was causing a lot of it. Looking at it from his shoes, I think he sees himself with two big public relations disasters, both of which involve the nursing service—and he has an unproven quantity running his nursing service. As long as he just worries, I guess I'll be all right. If he decides to give me a bunch of help, I can see snafus until the cows come home, with his background being in insurance rate negotiations. I think I should worry about that some. Tomorrow, though, not now. Not with you and a nice fire and maybe half a glass of wine left."

"Nan, we don't have a fireplace."

"Are you going to let that stop you? Would that stop my team? Are you going to get with the program or what? "

8

Tuesday Morning's Reading of the Records

Just a few minutes before eight on Tuesday morning, Nan walked into the hospital with a bounce in her step and a smile for everyone she met. She went directly to the office of the hospital's chief counsel, Alice Newcomb, to see what she could learn by reading the medical records for the Thompson baby and Mr. Bill.

At the stroke of eight, Nan's cell phone vibrated in her pocket. Hmm, thought Nan, that's the first inbound communication on the new pocket phone, and not many people are apt to know the number, so it must be Marcy. Sure enough, upon retrieving the phone from her pocket and opening the cover, she found a message from Marcy in the form of a text page. The message announced a meeting at 9:30 in her office with someone named D. Laurel. Well, thought Nan, Marcy doesn't set up frivolous meetings, so if Marcy thinks this is something important, I'll go along with her. Nan used the keypad on the communicator to send back a return text message that simply said, "Okay."

Alice Newcomb's outer office was open, but there was no sign of Alice. Alice's secretary greeted Nan and led her to a small conference room where the records were already set out for her. There was a typed page of instructions, addressed to her from Alice, sitting on top of the records. In fact, there were two identical pages, one on each record. The message said Nan was free to read the records in that room but that she couldn't carry away any pages or copies, she couldn't take notes, and she had to leave everything the way she found it. That kind of bureaucratic blather always set Nan looking for loopholes. Could she read the records over the phone to Marcy and have Marcy take notes? Could she dictate the whole record to a public transcription service? Could she take photos with her digital camera, which didn't really have images in it, just bits and bytes? Could she hold the pages up to the window and let somebody else photograph them?

Not today. All Nan wanted to do today was to get a little more information about the cases, something a little deeper than the hallway gossip she had gathered so far. Her interest was entirely professional. She wanted to see whether there was some obvious failure in her nursing service that she needed to address. That sort of information wasn't always available in the record, since it was easy enough for anybody to refrain from writing self-incriminating information in any record. Still, the record was the place to start.

The limitations on copying and taking notes didn't surprise Nan. Litigation was in the offing, and some lawyer will certainly ask that everybody in the hospital produce all notes, files, and correspondence. So, the simplest course of action was to avoid writing anything down that didn't need to be written down.

The two records were side by side on the small conference room table. The baby Thompson file was a typical file folder with a sticker giving the name and hospital identification number. That's what Nan had expected. What startled Nan was the size of Mr. Bill's file, which was about a foot thick! Well, she had learned something already, even if she wasn't quite sure what it was.

Starting with Baby Thompson's file, she found that the baby had been born here in this hospital 10 months earlier. The sonogram and other prenatal information were in the same file. It was probably duplicated in the mother's file, but Nan's interest was limited to the baby. The record for the last admission was exactly what Nan had expected to see. The baby was seen in the emergency room on a nonemergency basis, seen by the emergency room doctor on duty who did his diagnosis. He then called the family's pediatrician, Dr. Escobar, who came to the hospital to examine the baby. Dr. Escobar admitted the baby for further tests and treatment, at which point the baby was transferred to the pediatric ward. There were further notes from Dr. Escobar, who had gone upstairs with the baby.

The baby had been given a saline solution intravenously, a drip, in the emergency room. Nothing unusual or special about that. The baby had lost weight, according to the information recorded by the emergency room doctor, probably told to him by the mother, so adding fluids to the baby's system was appropriate.

In the pediatric unit, Dr. Escobar had continued the drip and ordered a medication to be added. The baby had been weighed in the emergency room. The baby was weighed again in the pediatric unit, which was normal because medication for infants has to be scaled to the body weight. The recorded weights were one ounce different, which seemed to be reasonable.

The medication order was written into the record by Dr. Escobar. The medication was a standard item, not subject to special narcotics or other limits. An inventory of that medication was kept in the pediatric unit, replenished from the pharmacy from time to time. Dr. Escobar had written in the dosage with notes saying that the weight of the baby had been considered in setting the dosage.

The medication-delivered note was written into the record by the charge nurse, Mary Cummins. This was not the medication ordered by Dr. Escobar, at least as far as the written record was concerned. This errant medication was also a standard item available in the pediatric stores, so no pharmacist was involved in the process.

Mary Cummins's written record was on a different sheet from Dr. Escobar's record. Therefore, it wasn't obvious to Nan whether Mary had looked at Dr. Escobar's written order at that time. From the time notations, about 20 minutes passed between the time Dr. Escobar made her entries and Mary Cummins made her notes. That seemed okay to Nan.

At the beginning of the next nursing shift, more than six hours later, the on-coming nurse had looked at Dr. Escobar's order and at Mary's record, noticed that they didn't match, checked the medication at bedside, and started making calls to the unit manager, Dr. Escobar, and the on-duty emergency room doctor. Dr. Escobar arrived within half an hour and took charge. The baby was moved to the intensive care unit, where steps were taken to get the errant medication out of the baby's system. Ten hours later, the baby was transferred by ambulance to Children's Hospital. Dr. Escobar went with the baby in the ambulance.

In her notes in the record, Dr. Escobar wrote, "Medication error, nurse did not follow written instructions." The rest of the record was in the usual abbreviated style, almost a shorthand, that would be difficult for anyone not accustomed to reading records to understand. This one sentence was written in plain English with a firm hand.

The baby Thompson record ended with the transfer to Children's Hospital. Later on, Nan thought, she should be able to find a way to read the separate record made at Children's Hospital, just in case there was something to learn from it. Although that wasn't likely since the inadvertence had happened in her own hospital, she wanted to look.

What had she learned about the Baby Thompson event? That Mary Cummins had not followed the written order, but Nan had already known that. Now it was confirmed. She now knew that the errant medication had been in the baby's system for nearly a full shift, which meant that Mary Cummins had not consulted the written order during her shift.

Nan didn't know when Dr. Escobar wrote her order, since there isn't automatic time-stamping in the manual record system being used. Common sense would say that Dr. Escobar made her entries within minutes of giving the verbal order to Mary Cummins. However, there was no way of knowing, just by looking at the written record. So, that was something to think about. Otherwise, the record just confirmed what Nan had heard from the grapevine.

Time to look at Mr. Bill's record. Nan decided to start at the beginning. After reading the first several pages, it was clear why the record was so voluminous. Mr. Bill had been discharged from the Army in 1969 with malaria, probably acquired in Vietnam. He had suffered relapses periodically since then, which was common enough. Doing date arithmetic without taking notes was a little iffy for Nan, but she estimated that had been admitted twice a year, with a couple of misses, ever since then. In the past few years, there were additional entries that one might expect for a man in his 60s, such as for extensive physical exams and minor treatments.

In the past two years, a heart condition had been treated. This might have been a consequence of the malaria, or it might have been something entirely independent. Nan couldn't tell. There were three admissions in the past year with notations of heart arrhythmia. Mr. Bill had been given defibrillator shocks during two of those admissions but not during the final one. That's the sort of thing one might expect a pacemaker to be used for, thought Nan. Then she saw a notation during the next-to-last admission, "Pacemaker prescribed. Patient refuses pacemaker." So, maybe Mr. Bill didn't like foreign objects inside his body. Maybe it was a religious belief. There was no explanation given in the record.

In the final year, the record showed elevated temperature and other signs of malarial relapse as well as the heart arrhythmia. The treatment during the admission was with antibiotics for the elevated temperature and other malarial symptoms, then close monitoring and, when required, defibrillation. He had been hooked up to a bedside EKG machine each of the last three admissions.

The record showed a general deterioration in other signs in recent years, particularly during the final year. Mr. Bill was dying, slowly, the life draining out of him. It wasn't Nan's place to guess how long he would have lived, but she guessed not more than five years, maybe less. Certainly less if he didn't get a pacemaker.

Time had flown. If she would've had another hour, she would've read Mr. Bill's record again, back to front, looking for patterns. Not having an hour and not being allowed to take notes, she closed the record and asked herself what she learned. Mr. Bill had a chronic malarial condition, deteriorating heart condition, and deteriorating general health, which might be a consequence of the malaria or age. Mr. Bill was 67 years and 8 months old at the time of his death. The death notation was heart failure, not responding to defibrillation. The autopsy report wasn't yet included and might be held separately if litigation were in the offing. The medication orders looked to be normal, and there were no differences she could find between the doctor's record and the nursing record. Mr. Bill had been admitted only to the VIP suite, and not to the regular rooms, since the hospital had had one. The record didn't say how long Mr. Bill had been on the hospital board, so she would have to ask somebody.

Nan had never worked in the VIP suite. Although she had a general notion about why it was special, she'd have to find out more about it.

Now she knew what had been written down in the official record about Baby Thompson and Mr. Bill. To be thorough, she wanted to look at other hospital records that weren't included in these files, such as the computer records in the pharmacy. In either case, these records weren't likely to be definitive, so she decided to put that off.

The hospital was slowly moving in the direction of using electronic records for everything. There was a test going on in one unit. Nan made a mental note to ask Sanjar if he knew how that test was proceeding.

The phone vibrated in Nan's pocket. Nan guessed that that would be a gentle reminder from Marcy, and that guess proved to be correct. While Nan didn't need reminding in this instance, the next time she might be happy to have such a reminder coming in, particularly if she were being held up by some gabby executive.

Nan put everything back into neat rectangular piles, thanked the secretary, and left. As she was going out, Alice Newcomb was coming in. They spoke pleasantly for half a minute, Nan thanked her for her cooperation and hot-footed it back to her office.

Halfway there, she happened to see young Willy pushing a cart down the hall, making a better speed than most maintenance people Nan had known. The cart looked to be loaded down with electronics devices of various kinds. They wished each other a good morning and went their separate ways.

9

Nan Meets
Detective Laurel

Upon arriving at her office, Nan found Marcy at her station. A man in his middle years was sitting in a visitor's chair next to Marcy's desk, holding a weather-beaten briefcase that showed a lot of miles. Nan entered her private office. Two steps behind her came Marcy, steno pad in one hand, and teapot in the other.

"Good morning, Marcy. Who is this Laurel person?"

"Good morning, Mrs. Mills. Detective Laurel is from the county detectives bureau."

"*Detective* Laurel? What have I done?"

"He didn't say. May I show him in, or do you need a few minutes first?"

"Show him in. Let's find out what's going on."

Marcy went out and came back with the visitor in tow. Marcy made introductions and left the two of them alone.

"Mrs. Mills, I'm with the county bureau of detectives. I would like to ask you a few questions, if I may." Laurel produced a leather wallet, opened to show an ID card on the left and his badge on the right. Nan had never seen a real police badge up close, so she took a moment to scrutinize this one. Then she looked at the ID card to find a picture that was probably of the visitor—one is never quite sure with ID cards—and the name Samuel D. Laurel below it, along with some telephone numbers and some official-looking notations.

"Well, Detective Laurel, tell me what you want to know. I will answer any questions, subject to confidentiality limits. Before we start, I think I should make a call to our counsel just so she knows you're here."

Laurel replied, "Yes, I understand. Take your time."

Nan went to the desk telephone and pushed the intercom key. "Marcy, please call Alice Newcomb for me."

"She's holding on line one."

Nan selected line one and found Alice Newcomb. Nan said that Detective Laurel was in her office. Alice replied that Nan should stay away from confidential matters, that detective visits were not at all uncommon, and that if things got sticky to bring him over to her office where they could all talk together. Nan thanked Alice Newcomb, hung up her phone, and turned to her visitor. "Well then, detective, with all that cleared away, what can I do for you?"

"Call me Stan. That's got nothing to do with my given name, as you have already figured out. It's just that if your family name is Laurel, everybody calls you Stan. So, call me Stan. Even my wife calls me Stan. Or, Stanley, if she is mad about something.

"I'm pleased to make your acquaintance, Mrs. Mills. I think we might get to know each other. You might not know it, but people who are mad at hospitals make complaints. Most of them are nonsense, but once the complaint is filed, we have to go through some motions. If old Aunt Sadie dies in the hospital, it must be the hospital's fault. Sometimes grieving parties file a civil suit; sometimes they file a criminal complaint. Most of them just dry up after the complainants get over their grief. Still, if a complaint gets filed, I have to check it out.

"We have a complaint lodged by Mr. and Mrs. Leroy Thompson alleging criminal negligence in the death of their infant son. The complaint names the doctor, the nurse, this hospital, Children's Hospital, the ambulance company, and probably some players to be named later. Now I know you're not going to tell me anything about the particulars of this case, and I'm not asking for anything like that. What I would like to ask are routine questions about organizational and administrative matters. I don't think these questions will cause you any heartburn.

"You are the head of the nursing services here, is that right?"

"Yes, that's right."

"And your name is Mrs. Mary Claire Mills, called Nan, is that right?"

"Yes, that's right."

"Were you in this same position last week when the Thompson baby died?"

"Yes, that's right."

"Were you in town on the days in question?"

"No, I was taking a course at the university, so I wasn't present here at the hospital or even in town at the time."

"Was somebody acting for you in your absence?"

"No, I fulfilled my duties remotely."

"How did that work?"

"The individual units all have experienced managers running them. They take care of patient care. My role as department head is to provide overall direction and administrative support. I am, of course, responsible for everything that happens in the nursing services. It's my department."

"How long have you been in this position?"

"Six weeks or so."

"Well, congratulations on your appointment. Let me ask very generally about cases such as the Thompson baby case. The baby didn't die here in this hospital. He died at Children's Hospital down the road. Do you transfer a lot of sick kids there over the course of a year?"

"Yes. They have specialized facilities and specialized staff that we don't have for pediatric cases. That's normal. I don't know how many kids we transfer in the course of a year, but I could find out for you. It's perfectly normal. We transfer other kinds of patients to other specialized institutions. For example, we don't do open heart surgery here, so we transfer those patients to a specialized institution. We do have a very advanced burn center here, so some of those same hospitals transfer patients here, too. It saves duplication of very expensive equipment and facilities."

"You have a maternity ward and a pediatric ward?"

"Yes. The Thompson baby was born here. We have a pretty good sized pediatric unit, although nothing on the scale of Children's Hospital. Some of our physicians work both here and at Children's Hospital. Dr. Escobar does."

"Now, Mrs. Mills, as I understand the case so far, the doctor ordered one drug and the nurse gave the baby a different drug. Is that your understanding?"

"I have nothing to say about that. I can answer your general questions, but let's stay away from the specifics of the Thompson case."

"Fair enough. I'm just trying to understand the normal flow of things. The doctor looks at the kid and decides what drug to prescribe. The doctor writes down an order for the drug and hands it to the nurse. Is that right?"

"No. It might happen that way, but if the nurse is standing beside the doctor, the doctor gives a verbal order and writes it down. The nurse doesn't wait to read the written order. The nurse acts on the verbal order."

"What if the doctor orders a drug that sounds really goofy to the nurse? Does the nurse follow the order anyway?"

"No. The nurse questions the doctor on any unusual drug order or any unusual dosage order."

"What if there is a dispute over the drug order?"

"The responsibility rests with the doctor at the end of the day. If there is a dispute, then the unit manager is called in or maybe the supervising physician. But that's very rare. If the nurse challenges the order, it's most likely over the dosage because it's easy to misstate a quantity, perhaps saying 10 milligrams when 10 micrograms was meant."

"How about if the doctor orders the wrong drug? How would the nurse know?"

"Nurses would question an unusual drug. However, if the doctor orders one of the 10 or 20 drugs that are commonly used in that unit and in normal dosages, the nurse would not have any basis for questioning the drug order. It might be the wrong drug for the particular patient, even if it is an ordinary drug, but the nurse wouldn't know that. The nurse is a nurse, not a doctor."

"Do you have children's dosages for drugs?"

"Yes. For infants, the doctor and the nurse will take into account the weight of the baby, since many drugs for kids are figured on dosage per kilogram of body weight. The doctor and the nurse both do the calculation and compare answers."

"Now, where does the pharmacist figure into this?"

"If the order goes to the pharmacist, the pharmacist checks the drug order against others drugs the patient is known to be taking to make sure there are no interactions. The pharmacist would note any unusual dosage. The pharmacist doesn't offer an opinion on the suitability of a particular drug for particular condition—that's not his or her business."

"Where did the pharmacist figure into the Thompson matter?"

"I have nothing to say about the Thompson matter. I will say in general that the pediatric unit has an inventory of ordinary drugs that aren't under special regulations. The nurses draw from this local inventory, and the pharmacy manages the inventory level."

"Is the pharmacy open all night?"

"Yes. At our hospital, a pharmacist is either on duty or on call, always."

"Well, Mrs. Mills, you have been very helpful and very generous with your time. I really appreciate that. Lots of people try to get me out the door, as I guess you can imagine. If I have other questions, may I call you?"

"Yes, I'll try to be as helpful as I can. Marcy Rosen can always find me, and Marcy will give you my cell phone and home numbers for your file."

"Mrs. Mills, you've been great. I hope this Thompson case goes away by itself. I don't make the final decision—that's up to the district attorney—but I don't see any sign of malice. There may have been a blunder between the doctor and the nurse, and maybe that will get sorted out eventually. But a blunder doesn't constitute criminality. Civil responsibility isn't my bag, and you might have a problem there. But unless something else turns up, well, we'll see what turns up. Thanks again." Stan closed his notebook, stuffed it into his weathered briefcase, gave Nan a business card for her file, smiled politely, and left Nan's office.

Nan waited a few minutes and called Marcy in. "So what's with this guy, Stan?" Nan asked.

"Stan Laurel is the detective who shows up every month or so to check out some complaint against the hospital. He just asks questions. Seems like a nice enough guy. I did think he tried to trip you up a couple of times."

"Marcy, how do you know what questions he asked me?"

"You left the intercom open."

Nan thought that unlikely, but it might not hurt to have a witness later on, if not in this instance, perhaps in some other. "If he has been doing investigations at this hospital for some time, then he already knew the answers to all those questions, didn't he?"

"Yes, I think so. He was just sizing you up, probably figuring that this was a good chance to do his sizing, since this Baby Thompson case is not apt to be criminal."

"Did he talk to you, too?"

"Yes, he came 20 minutes early, probably figuring he could worm some good information out of me before you got here. He asked some open-ended gee-whiz questions, but I said to him that I don't know anything. I just type letters all day long, and the letters are all Greek to me. Then I typed away for a while."

"Okay, then. Let's forget about Stan Laurel until the next time he shows up. What's next?"

10

Tuesday's Get-Acquainted Lunch

Nan hosted a small luncheon in her conference room for two of the other vice presidents as part of her get-acquainted campaign. Marcy had handed her a briefing book half an hour before the luncheon with a sheet or two on each of the invitees. During the course of the luncheon, Nan deduced that Marcy had also fed each of the invitees the same sort of briefing sheet on Nan. All public information, and it was probably better to get her version of the facts in front of them than to rely on the grapevine.

The topics of discussion were the usual executive fare, the capital campaign, the difficulty of living within what Medicare and the insurance companies were willing to pay, the high turnover in skilled personnel, and the merits of the new defined-contribution pension plan, which replaced an older defined-benefit pension plan. Soon enough, the discussion got around to the Thompson baby and Mr. Bill. The VPs asked the usual questions: How was she going to handle these cases? Did she see them as signs that nursing care had to be reorganized or computerized? How was she handling the nurses involved?

Nan answered most of these questions by saying that it was too soon to know what had happened, and the autopsy of Mr. Bill had not yet been reported. Nan was concerned that people seemed to be jumping to the conclusion that if mistakes were made, it was a nurse and not others who had made them. She needed to figure out what to do about that. She also needed to face the fact that she had not yet done anything about the nurses involved. They must be feeling awful—like they were marooned on a desert island. What should she do? She didn't want to upset the chain of command, and it wasn't her place to be talking to individual nurses or other workers in the department. But she had felt enough pressure in the meeting with her boss Monday morning, and she was an emotionally secure, well-paid, highly qualified, easy-to-find-a-job nurse with a high-income husband. How would she have handled that meeting with her boss if she were lacking in any of those supports? She'd better do something.

The other topic of conversation was Nan's decorator. Nan figured that she had better say that the redecoration had something to do with getting the cameras to work right during the videoconferences she held regularly. She could plead ignorance as to the details. She also figured she had better make sure that Marcy and Sanjar were telling the same story.

After lunch, she sat down with Marcy to review the mail log and to tell Marcy, and through her, Sanjar, the answer to give if anybody asks about the redecoration of the conference room. She asked Marcy to set up a meeting with the managers who were above the nurses involved in the Thompson baby and Mr. Bill cases, saying the topic would be "support for nurses involved in exceptional events." At this point, at least, Nan wanted to be supportive, even though it was certainly possible that both nurses had made errors that had cost lives. Possible, but a long ways from certain.

Marcy nodded. Her pencil then flew over her steno pad.

11

Nan Visits a Clinic

Nan left the hospital to meet with the manager who was in charge of the four neighborhood clinics around the city, mostly in the toughest neighborhoods. These clinics were something of an experiment in "retail medicine," serving as public health clinics in neighborhoods where payment for service was iffy. The clinics were not emergency rooms and were not set up to deal with trauma or serious matters. They were set up to handle routine pediatric, prenatal, and geriatric cases that are normal in any community. The physicians were employees of the hospital and tended to be younger doctors just getting started in their careers.

Nan found the address, although she had never been in this part of town before. It didn't seem to be dangerous or hostile, just decrepit. She might feel differently if it were a Saturday night, but on a bright Tuesday afternoon, she felt comfortable being there. She did take care to lock her car and set the alarm system, though.

The manager was Margaret Kelly, better known as Maggie. Maggie was an experienced nurse who had the potential to move on to bigger and better things. Managing the four clinics was good experience because it forced her to get jobs done through others. She couldn't do everything herself because she couldn't be in four places at once.

Nan bypassed the employees' entrance and went to the clinic's front door. The waiting room was bright enough, and there were lots of people waiting, about 20 adults and six children under age 10. A couple of new mothers had babies in strollers.

There was no receptionist. Nan found a clipboard hanging below a printed note telling people to sign the clipboard, mark the time, and wait their turn. Just to see what would happen, Nan signed her name, marked the time, and sat down to wait. She also started the lap timer on her wrist watch, just to see how long it would take.

A few minutes later, a sliding glass window, opaque like the glass in a bathroom window, opened to reveal a young woman in a hospital smock. She grabbed the clipboard and read out the first name on the waiting list, then scanned the rest of the names, finding Nan's at the bottom. Startled, she scanned the room and picked Nan out of the throng. Recognizing Nan wasn't very difficult, given that her photo had been circulated to the employees in the announcement of her new position, and she was the only woman in the waiting room dressed as a professional person. The rest were a good deal more casual.

Nan was treated to a toothy smile and invited to come forward. She did, smiling in return.

"Mrs. Mills, please come in. I wish you had knocked on the glass so we would have known you were here. Are you alone? What I mean to say is, did you bring anyone with you from the hospital? No? Well, come right in. You'll find Maggie's office is just down the hallway on the last door on the left."

Nan thanked the young woman for her welcome and walked down the hall to Maggie's office. From what Nan could see in those few seconds, the consultation rooms were clean and suitably appointed. The employees looked to be busy doing the usual sorts of tasks, and patients were coming and going in the usual way. It certainly looked like this clinic was getting enough traffic, although she would have to look up the operational reports when she got back. Lots to learn.

"Nan, I'm so happy to see you. That was a great staff meeting yesterday—and how many times can you say that about a staff meeting? It's also not often that the brass comes across town to visit with us plebeians, so this makes the week doubly special."

Nan found Maggie, whom she had known slightly and who hadn't had much to say in Monday's staff meeting, to be an interesting person, one she would have to get to know better. Maggie had a slightly frazzled but eager and intense look, a combination that projected competence and authority. Sort of a marine sergeant. No, a marine sergeant would be better turned out. Well, something of that sort. Nan had checked Maggie's employee record and knew that

Maggie was close to getting her master's degree and had an excellent scholastic and performance record. So, she wondered, is what I am seeing her normal personality, or has Maggie taken to playing a role in her first management position? We all do some role playing, Nan thought, and I wonder if I'm playing mine the right way.

"Maggie, thanks for your hospitality. This is my first field trip. Next time, let's meet at one of your other clinics."

"I'll be reasonable. I'll do it your way," was Maggie's response.

Nan presumed that Maggie's reply was meant as a little joke to break the ice and took it in good part. "Well, let's say do it my way when I'm right, but tell me when I'm wrong."

A few seconds of silence followed, both women smiling and sizing each other up.

It occurred to Nan that while she had written evaluations of many nurses and nursing supervisors in her previous jobs, she never had to evaluate managers before. Here before her was a manager who was thought to be capable of higher duties, and therefore it was all the more important that Nan get the evaluation of Maggie Kelly right. Others would be reading her evaluation very carefully, weighing every word. One more thing to learn.

As she often did, she turned the question around in her mind. How did she, Nan, want to be evaluated herself? No one above her in the organization chart was a nurse by profession; they are all business types. How is this going to work? Can she get control of the evaluation of herself by others? She'd better. Yet another thing to figure out.

Wow! Lots of things to do.

"Maggie, tell me about these clinics you run."

"Well," Maggie started out, temporizing, while furrowing her brow and looking off to the side a bit. "The clinics are three years old. I've been in charge of the nursing services and clinic administration since the launch. The nursing staff has the usual amount of turnover, which is a lot. That's a problem, but maybe less of a problem here where we do pretty ordinary care. We cover a wide range every day, from prenatal care to geriatric care. We do have emergencies once in a while, but we move those off to the hospital as quickly as we can. We stabilize the patient and grab the phone.

"The physicians are pretty good. Most of them are right out of school, so there is certain amount of fumbling and bumbling while they remember which end of the stethoscope goes in the ear. But it's good training for them, and they treat every new case as if it were the most important case they ever saw, and maybe it is.

"This year I worked with the medical association to locate a few retired physicians, general practitioners, who volunteer half a day a week at our clinics. They don't see patients but rather sit with the physicians and act as a sounding board. So, they are my coaching staff. The young docs are used to that from their schooling, and they don't mind having somebody at their elbow just in case something comes up they haven't seen before. The young docs like it, and the oldsters like getting off the shuffleboard court a few hours a week.

"I think the patients like it, too. We get a lot of immigrants here. This neighborhood is all they can afford, at least at first. Other cultures often put a lot of stock in age, figuring wisdom comes with age. So when they see an older doc sitting there, they like it. Of course, Americans generally put the premium on youth, figuring everybody over 30 is over the hill." Maggie gave this a wry smile, looking directly at Nan, now. "I'm not going to see 30 again very soon, and I'm not so sure about wisdom coming naturally, but maybe there is something in both points of view."

Nan asked, "Do you do anything special for the immigrants?"

"The biggest issue is the language problem. I've learned to say 'Show me where it hurts' in every language from Tagalog to Swahili, and there are still people who stump me every day. If there are 20 people out there, there are at least 16 languages represented. Now, they all try to learn English as quickly as they can, but most of them won't admit it when I say something they don't understand. That's even worse. If I can't understand them, as least I know I can't. If they don't understand me and won't admit it, then there has been a failure to communicate and I don't even know it."

"What do you do when you are utterly stumped, Maggie?"

"We have a telephone-based service that we use. I call the service and we use two phones here on the same line. I say, or the patient says, what language we want to translate to and from, and the service puts somebody on the line who can speak that language plus English. It's expensive, so we use it only when we're stuck. I don't know if it would work in a complicated field where there's a lot of specialized lingo, but here, at this kind of retail healthcare, we ask common questions more often than not. Where's it hurt? When was the last bowel movement? Basic stuff."

"What about the business side?"

"Well, I don't know whether the clinics make any money, or whether they lose any more money than the emergency room does. I don't get to see all the financials. I do know that the heat is on, all the time, to get costs down, down, down.

"Most of our patients are covered by one government insurance program or another, since they're poor. My guess is those programs don't pay the full cost, but I'm not the one to talk to about that. What I do know, because I see it everyday, is that the patients who are supposed to make a token co-payment, like two dollars per visit, just say they haven't got the money, and we let it go. Two dollars probably wouldn't make much difference to the financial types, but it's a shaky policy to say that patients have to pay a token co-payment when we don't really mean it.

"Token co-payments are supposed to discourage frivolous use of the clinics, but I don't see a lot of frivolity out there."

Nan said, "I know from reading the newspapers that this is a tough neighborhood. Do the gangs cause you any grief?"

"No. The gangs figure we're helping the community that they think they run, so they usually don't hassle us or the patients. They figure if they hassle us, we'll just shut the place down, and then the community and they themselves would be a little worse off. So, they don't hassle us.

"They probably give us a little business now and then by beating up on deadbeat borrowers from their loan shark business. But if they break legs, those cases go to the hospital directly and we don't see them.

"We have about one attempted burglary a year—probably junkies who figure there must be narcotics in the pill box here. So far, nobody has actually gotten into the narcotics safe. There have been no arson attempts or shootings on the premises."

"After dark, are the nurses safe walking to their cars?"

"They are safe here. They might get carjacked before they get home or they might get conked on the head when they get home, but at this end they're safe. I don't mean to say that they feel safe, but they are safe. We have had zero muggings of nurses or staff in three years. I'd say it is in fact safer to work here than at the hospital, both on the job and in getting out to the parking lot in one piece. Doctors are at a higher risk, because junkies might think a doctor has some tasty pills in his black bag. They don't figure nurses to be carrying narcotics, and I'm not going to change their thinking on that matter."

"Who runs the clinics you are not at, at any given moment?"

"I have a lead nurse at each location who assigns work and takes care of first-order management issues. Anything sticky they bump to me. We are open a nominal 14 hours a day, plus however long it takes to clear out the waiting room at the end of the day, so I have a pretty large contingent of lead nurses. I pick them myself, and I give them a little coaching, but mostly they just do what comes natural. If I pick a loser, I ease that nurse out of the position. Since it's an informal position, it doesn't show in the personnel jacket of the flunked lead nurse. For those who do work out, they get a few extra nice words in the evaluation. Not that I pick losers on purpose, you understand. It's just that you never know how people are going to work out until they give it a go. They don't even know themselves until they try. I didn't know if I could do this job until I had it."

Boy, if that's not the truth, Nan thought. I've got this new job, and I don't know myself if I can do it. I don't even know what questions to ask myself yet so I can rank the answers.

"Maggie, this is a special job, different from the other management positions in the nursing service. How do you decide if you are doing a good job or not? How do you evaluate yourself?"

"Nan, you ask tough questions. I have never had a superior ask any questions like that, and you put me on the spot. I know they are tough questions because I ask myself the same questions all the time. Here's a little of what I have learned on that subject. I don't know if I will sound coherent, but since you asked, I will give you the best answer I can.

"First of all, if I do a bad job, I know about it right away because everybody tells me. The doctors tell me, the nurses tell me, the patients tell me. There are no wallflowers around here. Everybody figures God gave them a mouth to straighten me out. Some of them are nicer about it than others, but everybody gets on me in a big hurry. So that's one stabilizer of performance.

"Second, I learned the hard way not to second-guess myself at the end of the day. I'm Irish, as you can probably tell, and we Irish tend to be maudlin to start with. Any pouting about minor fumbles during the day means an evening is lost for good. So, I don't second-guess myself any more.

"I think hard about what objectives the clinics ought to meet. On the one hand, setting the clinic's goals is easy because the clinics are free-standing little enterprises. On the other hand, setting the clinics' goals is hard because there is no obvious benchmark to follow, no big sister to blaze a trail for us. Early on, I tried to set objectives as a group, getting some of the nurses involved. I finally gave that up, because while these are bright nurses, they're nurses and not managers. They don't have the same issues or viewpoints. Now, if there were four or five people in positions like mine, then we could set goals as a group, but that doesn't apply right now.

"I've read a lot of books, but most of these books were for supervisors or CEOs. There aren't many books for group managers or middle managers. If you know of some, I'd appreciate hearing about them.

"To cut to the chase, I finally figured out that nobody was going to know the difference if I do a medium job or a great job—nobody but me, that is. So each year I pick out a few goals that I can measure in an objective way. These are goals for me. They're measures of me as a group manager, so they're measures of group performance.

"I'm not talking about boilerplate objectives that people include in the regular management-by-objectives forms that the hospital uses for us. In that form, I put down a few objectives that I can't possibly fail to meet, just like everybody else. I'm talking about a few other goals that I keep close to the vest. Maybe I'll tell you what they are, and maybe I'll have trouble remembering them if you ask. If I reach these goals, I feel good. If I fail to reach them, I won't get punished. However, I do keep score."

The two sat there for a few moments, looking each other in the eye. Nan tried to look beatific, while thinking to herself that she has another gem here. Maggie is certainly capable of greater things, and it looks like it's been a long time since anybody has patted her on the back.

"Maggie," Nan said, "I have a twin sister."

"Yes, I know that. It was in the bio sheet that went around when you were named to your position. I understand you are even named for her, in a left-handed way."

"You're right, I'm named Not-Ann, complementing my sister Ann in more ways than one. And I'm indeed the left-handed twin. Since I have a twin sister, I'm used to being next to someone who thinks the same way I do, even to an eerie extent. Therefore, I know whereof I speak when I tell you that there is some commonality of thinking at this table. I've asked myself those same questions and looked for those same non-existent middle management how-to books. I know about setting private objectives just because I think they're important. That's not rejecting or downplaying the official organization's objectives, just adding on a couple aggressive goals for myself or my group.

"I haven't tried setting aggressive goals for the whole nursing service yet. Maybe I can't do that. And I won't ask you to show me your private scorecard at the end of the year. That would only discourage you from trying to reach aggressive goals next year.

"Here's what I think. I think these clinics are something special. I think they need to be better known throughout the hospital because they do something useful for the community, which at the end of the day is why we are all here. However, I don't want to do the usual rah-rah sort of publicity blitz because those blitzes usually wind up making everybody mad. So what I would like to do is to pick one special aspect of your clinics. Identify it. Quantify it. Report it up the chain of command, and let the credit flow down to you and your nurses here in these clinics. That's what I want to do, but I can't do it by myself. I don't know if you want to do it. It would require you to trust me more than you rationally would, having only seen me in this position for two days. So, I'm not asking for anything today. A couple of months from now, you can bring it up if you feel ready and have one to propose. If not, no hard feelings."

Another extended pause. Maggie finally broke the silence. "Nan, that's a lot to chew on. Let me think about it. I appreciate the offer, maybe more than you know."

"Maggie, while it is said in song and verse that everybody talkin' 'bout heaven ain't a-goin' there, I'm confident that this whole nursing service is going to succeed, all of us together, or it ain't a-gonna succeed at all. So, I am looking for steps that lead to success."

Another pause. When Nan was with her twin Ann, there were a lot of pauses because they didn't need to talk to each other to communicate. The pause was part of the conversation. Nan realized that the tension between herself and Maggie had melted away, and she hadn't even been aware of the tension until it did go away. Nan felt this deeply, to the point of needing to suppress a giggle. How would giggling in the manager's office at an official clinic look?

"Maggie, do you keep in touch with people in similar positions at other hospitals in the region?"

"Not very much. I tell myself I should go visit a couple of them to see what there is to see, but such visits aren't high enough on my action list to do them. One hospital with clinics like these that gets a lot of good ink is a couple hundred miles away. The nearer clinics don't seem to have the same standing. Visiting the notable clinics would take me away from the office for the better part of a week. I don't know if I could get invited in. I'm sure I could get the glitzy VIP tour, but I'm only interested in getting in on the ground floor and finding out what really makes a difference."

Nan said, "Yes, if I call that hospital's head of patient services, you'll get invited and you'll get the VIP tour and a big lunch and probably dinner. How about if you find out who your counterpart at those clinics is and invite that person here? If you show that person our operations without any fanfare, maybe you'll get invited there to see the same thing. It would be taking a risk, though. What do you think?"

"I'll make a few phone calls. If they don't have a travel budget, can we swing it here?"

"Yes, I'll take care of it."

Maggie looked relieved. Nan sensed that that last question had nothing to do with the hospital's money and everything to do with Maggie putting Nan to a bit of a test. Nan figured she had passed the test. It was all part of the trust-building process, Nan was beginning to understand. She had learned a lot in only two days.

"Maggie, I want you to do something else for me."

"Shoot."

"I don't know enough about the finances of the nursing service because they're all wound up in the finances of the hospital as a whole. Now these clinics are a little bit like individual enterprises, so maybe the clinics' financial books would be more comprehensible. If I got our assigned bean counter, Carl Burke, to spend some time with you, maybe together you can generate financial statements for the clinics. Would you mind spending some time figuring out the clinics' finances?"

Maggie bit her upper lip and looked off to the side again. "That's funny, Nan. I went to high school with Carl Burke. I wouldn't say he's a close friend, but we are certainly on a first-name basis. He would be a good choice because I don't think he'll spend a lot of time trying to snow me with accounting wizardry. If you're game and Carl's game, I'm game. I'd like to know more about that myself. I even gave it a whack a year ago and never got anywhere. I should have thought of Carl then. Yes, I'll do it. You want me to call Carl, or do you need to grease some skids first?"

"Give me 24 hours, then call Carl. Work out your own schedule. If you and Carl need any computer help, call Sanjar Subramaniam. Or, you can call my secretary Marcy Rosen and she'll find Sanjar for you."

"I know Sanjar. You're the first Anglo I have ever heard try to say his family name. I wouldn't try it in public myself."

"Maggie, there is one other thing I noticed on the way in. I suppose you have a lot of repeat customers, but I was surprised that there is only a clipboard out there in the waiting room and no receptionist."

"We get a lot of repeats. We even have some weekly regulars. But we get a lot of newbies too. We used to have receptionists, but an early round of cost cutting did them in. We couldn't show that they were generating revenue or sewing up wounds. I even thought about trying to get some high school girls in a future nurses club to do it, but they can't work here because of privacy and liability issues. So, we make do with the clipboard. It's not by choice."

"Do you do anything with that future nurses club?"

"I give show-and-tells and pep talks at their club meetings. We also give tours here."

"Maggie, I value the time you have spared for me, and you have given me a lot to think about. We need to do this more often. I hope we do. You're doing something very important here, and I know it. And I think you're doing it well.

"Oh, I have one more question that I can ask on the way out, if you don't mind walking with me to the waiting room door. The question is this: Suppose you find that one of your nurses has made a mistake. Not killed somebody, just failed to do something or did something minor in the wrong way. How do you handle it?"

"In the old days, I just yelled at them. Then they'd cry, even the male nurses. Then there would be hard feelings. So I learned not to do that. Then I decided to follow the army rule of praising in public and chastising in private. That's a little better, not as much crying, but there are still hard feelings. So I do it anyway for the good of the fleet, but I don't think I have figured that one out yet. When you find somebody with the key to that lock, call me first."

They shook hands at the door. Nan thought that there was still something a little odd about two women shaking hands, but rubbing noses didn't seem to be the right thing to do. And girlish waves and secret handshakes were out. So they just resorted to old fashioned masculine handshaking. Although it was a formality, Nan thought it was also a hand taken in friendship on both sides.

At the door, Maggie said, "You mentioned that you're a twin. I'm a twin, too. An Irish twin. I was born in December, and my older sister was born in January of the same year. She's Mary Margaret, and I'm Margaret Mary. So, she's Jiggs and I'm Maggie. We're close, but no telepathy. The Irish stuff ends with this generation. My married name is Szyvczyk."

That merited a smile, and the two parted on friendly terms.

12

Nan Gets the Word on Mr. Bill's Demise

As Nan was clicking her radio control device to unlock her car door, her cell phone started to vibrate. This time is was a voice communication from Marcy. "Mrs. Mills. Dr. Anderson's investigation of Mr. Bill's death has resulted in his conclusion that Mr. Bill was dead at least 10 minutes before the nurse reached his bed and tried to resuscitate him with the defibrillator system."

"Who else knows this, Marcy?"

"Dr. Anderson's office staff, one of whom is my cousin and I won't say which one. Dr. Anderson has just gone upstairs to meet with Mr. Crawford. You don't have to guess what the topic of that unplanned meeting is."

"Okay. Let's figure that Crawford will be calling my office shortly. Tell him I'm at the clinics doing an inspection and that it's too far back to the hospital for me to get there by quitting time. Tell him that I can meet him this evening if he'd like, and let's hope he has some other engagement. Book a meeting with him tomorrow after I meet with the managers we talked about before—the manager over the Baby Thompson case and the manager over the Mr. Bill case. Juggle appointments around if you have to."

"Yes ma'am."

"Marcy, there is another thing I'd like you to do. Invite Carl Burke to educate one of our managers, namely Maggie Kelly, on the finances of the clinics, both revenue and cost. Put Sanjar on standby just in case they need some extra financial reports."

"Yes ma'am. That's a good choice. Maggie and Carl Burke went to high school together."

"All right. Keep the Mr. Bill news under your hat. Call me if you need me. Otherwise, I'll see you in the morning."

"Mum's the word. Goodbye."

Nan got in the car, keyed the ignition, backed out, and headed toward the crosstown highway. Thinking about what Marcy had told her, maybe even worrying about what Marcy had told her, she pulled the cell phone out, hit the first speed-dial button, and waited for Marcy to answer. She did so promptly, saying "Good afternoon, Mrs. Mills's office, Rachel Rosen speaking."

"Marcy, it's Nan. What's with the Rachel?"

"My given name is Rachel. My mother had a crush on an Italian film star of yesteryear named Marcello Mastroianni. She didn't go to cowboy shows, so at least she didn't call me Trigger."

"Smiley Burnett's horse's name was Ring Eye. Dale Evans's horse was Buttermilk. One can see possibilities here. But back to business. I need to know more about the Mr. Bill family and the Mr. Bill business. What can you do for me?"

"Sanjar is checking the publicly available information on the Internet. I have a friend in the Nags Nags group who works in the office at Mr. Bill's car emporium. I was just speaking to her, and I'll make a few notes for you and send them to your home e-mail account. Sanjar said he would have what he can get from the Internet by noon tomorrow."

"Nags Nags?"

"It's a woman's group. We take a bus to the track once a year and mob the two dollar window. We pick the horses by the colors their jockeys wear."

"Okay, now that I have an answer to my question, I withdraw the question. Tell Sanjar to stay on the straight and narrow until I say otherwise."

"As long as I have you on the phone, Sanjar told me he will look at some standard sorts of financial reports for the clinics based on the hospital's financial databases. He has access to those databases, and I didn't ask any questions. That will get Maggie and Carl started, and Sanjar said he can generate any special report they might dream up, if they can tell him what they want.

"Sanjar asked me to remind you to plug your cell phone into the cradle by the cigar lighter when you're in the car. It charges the battery and connects the phone through the radio speakers. The phone works by voice control, so you don't need to hold the phone up to your head while you're driving."

"Oh, yes, I see the cradle for the cell phone. That's very clever. But wait a minute. It wasn't five minutes ago that I asked you to talk to Sanjar about financial reports for Carl and Maggie. Did you read my mind again?

"No. When you hung up, I paged him with a text message that said, 'financial reports on clinics.' He paged me back with the text message, 'Can do. Will do. Starting now.' You know what they say about those computer people, the good ones are a thousand times as productive as the average ones. If he's average, I'd like to see one of those hotshots."

"I'm married to one, Marcy. I think Sanjar is one, too. So does Jack. Well, thanks again, see you in the morning. Rachel."

"Please call me Marcy. When I hear Rachel I think I'm back in third grade. Goodbye."

Nan paid a little less attention to traffic than she should have on the way across town to her home. Lots to think about. As she got to her side of town, she pulled into the parking lot for the Wal-Mart store, parked, and went into the store. At the entrance, a golden-ager in a blue vest with huge buttons on it smiled and pushed a shopping cart out for her. Nan expressed her thanks and went in to do her shopping. She noticed that a couple of the items she bought regularly were a penny or two cheaper this week. But she was not there to do her regular list. She had some special items in mind.

When she got home, she found that Jack had already put something on the stove. Jack was far from being a chef and showed only minimal interest in waxing culinary, but he didn't mind doing simple things to get supper going when he was home and she was behind schedule. So, Nan changed into at-home togs and joined Jack in the kitchen. She dug out an apron, which she almost never did, pulled her purchases out of the plastic shopping bags, and put them on the table.

"Jack," she said, "I hope you don't mind talking with me in the kitchen after supper. I'm going to bake a cherry pie. This is a practice round, just in case I need to do it for real one of these days. My grandmother used to bake cherry pies, so I'm sure it's in my blood. I might need a little encouragement, though, and a lot of moral support."

"To hear is to obey," Jack said, figuring he would hear the rest of the story soon enough. He could guess a lot of it already. "While we're eating and while you're baking, let it be known that I booked a flight to Houston for tomorrow. The calls I made to clients yesterday and today made it clear that there are plenty of jobs they want me to do for them and for which they want to pay me the new rate. The rate had to go up after taking that business course, after all. Besides, if the rate doesn't go up, you don't get any respect. I still want to hit NASA to close out that old contract and sniff around for what's new, and I want to see Jick just because he's Jick. And don't tell me to look in the mirror."

"Well, say hello to Jick for me. Tell him it's his turn to visit here and to bring the whole family. Tell him how handsome I know he is, because I look at you with loving eyes every morning and night."

"I'll say hello anyway. The rest I'll save for the right moment."

As the evening progressed, Nan told Jack what her second day on the job had brought her. Very few dull moments. She didn't talk about Mr. Bill, since what she knew was gotten through informal channels, and that case showed signs of getting sticky sooner rather than later. She talked a lot about her visit to Maggie's clinics and all the management issues that had raised for her. How to evaluate managers? How to motivate managers? Maggie didn't act like she needed a lot of motivational speeches, but Nan knew that burnout was never far away for the brightly burning candle. Nan told Jack about the receptionists being replaced by clipboards as an economy move.

Jack mostly listened, loving to hear Nan talk to him and seeing that Nan was awakening to all the management issues that come with reaching her level in a large organization. Jack also knew that Nan was telling him not only to get his feedback but also to hear herself retell the stories so she could understand them better herself, thinking them through.

"Jack, when I stopped to get the makings for the cherry pie at Wal-Mart, I was greeted by a greeter. You've been there, Wal-Mart always has an oldster there to grin and hand you a shopping cart. That person is not checking out customers at the register and not stocking shelves. Now Wal-Mart is as economy-minded as any organization, while we at the hospital spend money like it came from a fire hose, and yet we have clipboards for sick people to sign themselves in, even if they don't speak the language. What kind of vibration does that give you?"

"The difference between bean counting and loving your customers has been written up a lot in management magazines. Wal-Mart loves its customers enough to drive down prices, and Wal-Mart loves its customers enough to make shopping a pleasant experience. Lots of retailers figured out the first of that duo, but it took a genius like Sam Walton to figure out the second."

"Well, famous Mr. Jack Mills, what are we going to do about it?"

"One short week ago, back when we were students, we would have asked ourselves whether poka yoke applies. In other words, is there an operational issue here as well as a marketing issue?"

Nan thought for a minute. "Hmm. There are only three rules, so we should be able to ask them out loud, shouldn't we? I think the clipboard fails on all three. The clipboard isn't particularly helpful to a newbie, because it isn't obvious what is right and what is wrong. Furthermore, the clipboard can't answer questions such as, "Did I park in the right parking lot?' Such questions can worry people who are already sick or who have a sick kid or grandparent in tow. So, no score on rule one. As for rule two, the clipboard doesn't make it obvious when the person puts down the wrong information. For rule three, maybe the person could correct an error if it were known, and maybe not. So give that one half a point. The score is one-half point on the three-point scale."

"Yes, I agree with that scoring. But I think the psychology underlying poka yoke is to reduce the stress on the worker because high stress means more goofs. The clipboard isn't being used by a worker; it's being used by the patient."

"You got me on that one, but in the healthcare game, a lot of effort goes into getting the stress out of the patient because stress complicates issues and prolongs recovery. So getting stress out of the patient who is just coming into the waiting room would go in the right direction. Don't you think?"

"Works for me. If the hospital were a private company, management would ask you to justify any incremental expense by reducing some other expense or by increasing sales. Which is it going to be?"

"I don't know. Can't we do something just because it's the right thing to do?"

"Yes, and in any organization, there are enough degrees of freedom that people can do the right thing and not get punished for it, if they know how the organization works. Top managers do that on purpose, because they can't very well tell everybody to ignore costs, can they?

"Nan, It seems to me that you have gotten things done in two days that would have taken a year if you had gone through the regular channels, and you would have had budget fights at every stage. So some members of your gang know how the system works and where the loose joints are. Turn them loose."

"Jack, I wouldn't dare turn them loose. No, I need some kind of a rein on their activities, although I do admit I love the way they get things done. And being a brand-new executive in my hospital organization, I sympathize with the top management who can't just turn the asylum over to the inmates, even if I am an inmate. This middle management stuff has its mysteries, Jack my love.

"Riddle me another riddle, Jack. You've been in big organizations, and you had big management responsibilities at a very early age, a lot younger than I am now. What's the right way to correct an employee who has made an inadvertent mistake?"

"Nan, light of my life, you have struck upon the problem of the ages. I'll tell you what I know and what I have seen myself, here and elsewhere. I'll tell you some negatives first. If the boss dumps on the employees for every little thing that goes wrong, the employees quickly learn to do as little as possible so they can avoid the scalding. Let's call that the European model because that's what I have seen in the projects I've done in Europe. Then there is the American model, in which I have to distinguish between male and female employees. I know you're a feminist deep in your heart, so you don't want to hear that there are differences between the sexes other than those differences the birds and the bees know so well. But I will tell you because I know that you won't fire me since you love me."

"You're right—I won't fire you because I love you. I will grit my teeth and hear this blasphemy."

"The American model is to give praise in public and criticism in private. So far, the same works for both male and female employees. Here's where the difference comes in. A male employee will hear the criticism, not like it at all, think of all the reasons why it is misplaced, and then be mad at the boss for telling him. Then they have a beer together after work, and it's all forgotten. No grudge, no hard feelings. The criticism sticks, but it doesn't stick in the craw.

"Now we take a female employee, of which you have many. The female employee never lets go. There are always hard feelings. My guess is that female employees just never learned to take criticism in a positive light when they were growing up. Perhaps they didn't play cops and robbers or do whatever it was that male kids did to get the message. Maybe you know; I assure you that I do not.

"Then, we have one more model: the Japanese model. In the old days in Japan, if you were criticized by your boss, your 'face' was gone. You had to go home, get out the robe, the rug, and the great big knife, and gut yourself. Then the boss was short an employee, and the employee's family had a mess to clean up in the small front room.

"What with employees being expensive to replace, the Japanese eventually found a new way. They don't criticize employees at all.

Never. No such thought ever takes shape in the mind of Japanese managers. They are completely logical. If a mistake is made, it can't possibly be the fault of the employee, so it must be the fault of the machine or the system. If there is a machine involved, the managers examine the machine. If they find that the machine is okay, the man–machine system must be at fault. I say man–machine and not person–machine because the Japanese are utterly sexist. Part of that man–machine system is training the worker to run the machine or do the task. If it isn't the man and it isn't the machine, then it must be the training. Solution: retraining.

"Now they build on this. In a factory, you see that all employees have tracking charts in plain sight above their workstations. They are tracking number of rejects or something else. The employees don't mind because the employees know the tracking charts aren't an evaluation of themselves but of the system. See how this works? If the system yield goes down below X, then the employees go to the retraining station and get a little drill on the task.

"While employees are off the line being retrained, other workers step in and start their own tracking charts. The poor performers spend their time at the retraining station. The good performers stay on the line, and productivity goes up. It is your good old-fashioned win–win sort of a deal."

"Jack, are you going to tell me of some other culture, too?"

"No, my love, I have now told you all I know about it."

"I think you told me that the European model won't work in the hospital because it lowers productivity. The American model won't work in the hospital because we have so many female employees. Therefore, we have to figure out how to do the Japanese model even though we have an American and not a Japanese culture. Is that what you are telling me?"

"Mother of my children, it is."

"Why are you so poetic this ordinary Tuesday evening, oh golden tongued one?"

"Mayhap it be the fair sight of you in an apron, toiling over a hot recipe card file. Aprons were invented by men for carnal purposes, you know."

"Aprons? My grandmother knew this and didn't tell me?"

"She probably told Ann, twice."

"My mother would do that, but not my grandmother. She would tell one of us once, and it was up to the other one to get the word by telepathy. She was closer to the old ways, you know. Okay, now Jack, aprons and carnality aside, tell me how we make this

Japanese model work in a hospital, where we don't do the same task 20 times a minute and we don't have charts over each nurse counting errors. If we did have such charts, the lawyers would have apoplexy. What are we going to do?

"Beats me. At least you have your own nursing school. If you want to train people, you have professional teachers right there who know their stuff. You probably have training stations for EKG, intravenous procedures, and all those things I don't know anything about. So it wouldn't be impossible to do. Looks to me that the issue will be unearthing the error in the first place. Once you have an identified goof, you can execute the retraining.

"Look, suppose the nurse's record for a patient at the end of a shift shows that the patient was getting his medicine two hours late. The supervisor says to the nurse, 'The patient got his medicine two hours late, and therefore, we have a system problem. To cure the system problem, retraining on medicinal timeliness is in order. Please report to training station two at three PM.' No accusation and no evaluation of the employee in a personal way or any way at all is given. Just a retraining directive. The nurse can hardly argue that the medicine wasn't on time, and a short retraining drill is not hard duty. Now to make this work, you would have to tell all employees that retraining isn't punishment and no black mark goes in their personnel files. If you don't say that and mean it, the employees will find a way to sabotage the whole caper."

"Jack, father of my children who, I'm happy to say, look a lot like you, this sounds more complicated than I first thought. Retraining isn't punishment. Needing retraining isn't a negative. Being retrained is a productivity booster. Use the training resources we already have. Start with objective defects, not subjective or suspected defects. Never criticize the employee. That sounds pretty hard to do."

"It's easier in Japan, because managers would never criticize the employee in the first place. Nor would they ever say anything to an employee or anybody else that might cause offense. They think through what they're going to say before they say it. They engage a sensitivity filter before their mouths.

"Nan, let's start with something worth bothering about that has an objective measure."

Nan thought for a minute, then said, "Needle sticks. You're stuck or you aren't stuck. Nobody ever does it on purpose, so it must be inadvertent. It's important because, in extreme cases, it might kill somebody. Not likely, but it might happen. If the stickee is the patient or a passerby, then litigation ensues. Needle sticks."

"Okay, I think I understand that one. How do nurses stick themselves with a needle?"

"Sometimes it's just sloppy work, waving a sharp instrument around. Sometimes the patient flinches or lurches and throws the nurse's aim off."

"Are there standard ways to teach a trainee not to stick herself or himself? Also, are there standard ways to secure the patient so that flinching or lurching doesn't happen or at least doesn't throw the nurse's aim off?"

"Yes. There are training videotapes. There are exercises and drills done by all student nurses. There are mannequins to practice on. There are pediatric and geriatric drills. There are drills, drills, and more drills."

"All those drills and still needle sticks are a management issue?"

"They are enough of an issue that there is a whole industry out there inventing needles with snoods on them so that the pointy part isn't exposed until the last moment. Those needles are bulkier and harder to handle, and they cost more. I don't care about the cost in comparison to the problem, but I do care that they are harder to handle. And as a member of the executive team, since I was told by my boss yesterday to care about extra costs."

"Is there any needle-stick data on new nurses versus old nurses?"

"New nurses do it in training but not much in their early practice. Of course, a few nurses are klutzes and shouldn't be sticking anyone with sharp objects. We need to weed those nurses out or put them on permanent retraining status, as the Japanese would. The nonklutzy new nurses remember their drills and take extra care. Then there are mature nurses who do everything instinctively and extra-mature nurses who have more bad luck with sticks. It's not that any group is immune, but I think that's the distribution in a gross way. Suzy Wong was talking about the bathtub curve yesterday. Do you know about bathtub curves, Jack?"

"Yes, electronics are particularly prone to following a bathtub curve, so I get the image immediately. Almost telepathically."

"Maybe needle sticks follow the bathtub curve when plotted against nurse maturity."

"What professional groups was Suzy Wong talking about?"

"Airline pilots, and I guess military pilots, and anesthesiologists."

"And what do they do to counter the bathtub curve?"

"They retrain everybody whether they need it or not, to keep them in the low-bottom portion of the bathtub curve!"

"Do they sentence pilots who make a mistake to take the retraining over again?"

"Yes, I think so, although I guess I would have to ask Suzy again or maybe a pilot."

"Do you have a group that does a lot of needle work that would be up for a little field trial?"

"Jack, you know very well I do. Now for showing off your arcana and sitting there like a lump while I did all the hot stove work, you're going to have to eat the first piece of this pie while it is still hot and the ice cream is melting all over it."

13

Wednesday Morning's Breakfast

Jack was reading the morning paper and eating his customary cereal and sipping a glass of orange juice. Nan was having toast and yogurt. Nan tried to tempt Jack with another piece of the cherry pie to add to his breakfast, but without success.

"Nan, I love you day and night, and I love your cherry pie for supper, but not for breakfast, thank you very much."

"My first cherry pie since I was in home-ec class, and it's going to go to waste. Unless you want to take it to Houston with you on the plane."

"I don't think it would get past the security screeners, particularly if they happen to be hungry. Besides, you said you were doing that one just for practice, and it came out just right."

"The crust is undercooked and you know it. But I love you for saying it. Let's talk a little shop. I have two nurses who were involved in fatal events last week. I don't know if either one of them did anything wrong, and I may never know for sure. As a distant executive, I can weigh the evidence and stroke my chin and be dispassionate. As the leader of what I want to be a team, I want to project that I'm on their side. I bet they are crushed by all this and they probably think that the organization is going to put them out on the end of the plank. I don't know whether you've ever had any life-and-death events in your business experience, but tell me how you think I should handle this. I mean, what do I say to the nurses involved and to their supervisors and, through the grapevine, everybody else in the department?"

"I don't know. I've never had quite that experience. Life and death aren't completely foreign notions for engineers. People get killed in practically every big construction project. People get killed by software systems that go completely kaflooey. I've known people who died at their desks because they literally worked themselves to death. But those cases are still quite different from what you're faced with.

"I will tell you how *not* to handle it. This goes back several years to when I was working as a lower-level manager. There was litigation over whether or not the paint used for a product conformed to a contract specification. It's hard to believe that this was worth litigating, but as I recall, the customer was mad about something else and used this as an opportunity to beat up on the company. Well, the company could defend itself with its own lawyers, and there was always some kind of litigation going on. In this case, there was an engineering specification for the paint, and the specification bore the signature of a young engineer. Since his name was there, the other party named him as a defendant. Now, the litigators weren't serious about suing this engineer since they were claiming millions of dollars in damages. They knew they couldn't get a seven-figure amount from him."

"I know how that happens, Jack. In malpractice suits against surgeons, they always start by naming the surgeons, the hospital, and everybody in the room. Then they drop off the small-pocket defendants later on. So I understand what you're saying about naming this engineer."

"Well, the interesting thing happened next. The company's chief counsel sent a letter to this engineer with copies to everybody in management. The letter said that the company considered the engineer to have been its agent, who was doing the company's work under the company's direction. Therefore, the company would provide counsel for the engineer and pay any judgments entered against him. So far, so good. Then in the next paragraph, the company's lawyer said, 'If however you are found to have been personally culpable in the matter or to have deviated from company policy, then you are on your own.' You can imagine how that made the engineer feel, since he had no way of knowing what some jury of nonengineers might decide about the chemistry of a paint specification. He was just as far out on the plank as the nurses you are talking about. So, don't write any letters saying the nurses are on their own.

"Nan, I know you want to be protective of these nurses and all the other nurses. How did you handle it when the boys got into some kind of mischief at school?"

"When they were little, I don't think I handled it very well. By the time they were in junior high school, I had figured out the best thing to do was to start by hugging them. They were always in everything together, so it was always both of them. I'd tell them that I loved them and that they had to face the consequences of their actions like the men they were becoming. Then I told them I would love them no matter what, and so would you. Does that apply here? I don't know whether or not these nurses are guilty of anything. They might not even know themselves. Nobody may ever know."

"I think it is closer to being the answer than giving them the cold shoulder or having a lawyer write a letter to them."

"Well, at least it's a place to start. I also need to keep the chain of command in place. If I jump in and bypass the management layers, I'll alienate management, which I certainly don't need the first week on the job. Now, do I get a smooch before you fly away to Texas, or not?"

Nan got to the hospital a few minutes before eight AM and started up the steps thinking that the week was going by in a flash and that she had the same iron butterflies in her stomach that she had had the first day. So many things going on, all of them so important. Life and death, even.

Marcy was at her desk. Nan wished her a good morning and went directly into her own office. Marcy was two steps behind with the teapot and the steno pad. "Mrs. Mills, you are on call for a meeting with Mr. Crawford around 8:30. Mr. Crawford elected not to seek you out yesterday evening because he had to attend a big meeting with the city fathers for the capital campaign. My guess is he will be a few minutes later than 8:30, but that's beyond our control.

"You asked to see the managers who are responsible for the nurses involved in the Baby Thompson and Mr. Bill cases. That's Vivian Smith and Claudia Benedict. They will be here at 8:15, and right now they are having breakfast together in the cafeteria.

"I recommend we skip the mail log this morning. There's nothing very interesting or out of the ordinary. It's on your computer if you want to check it later. Right now, there is a videoconference to follow up on the videotapes of John Wayne and Horatio Hornblower from yesterday. Is that okay?" Nan nodded in the affirmative. "This videoconference is on the computer network. Sanjar will show you how to join in, if you haven't used the new computer setup."

Sanjar appeared, walking frontward since he was coming into the room, and extending his usual bow. Nan confirmed that he can bow while walking both frontward and backward, something she should practice herself in case she needed to be dramatic sometime.

Morning greetings were exchanged. Sanjar pointed to an icon on the computer desktop, which Nan selected with her mouse. Click. The screen filled with five new windows about the size of the bubblegum picture cards the twins used to collect. One of them was of herself. By looking at herself in the little window, she realized that lights around her computer screen had brightened like lights around a vanity mirror so that her face was well lit from a flattering angle. The room lights had gone down, so that the background was out of focus. She noticed that the faces in the other windows were not so well treated, meaning that her station had the benefit of Sanjar's development project and the others did not yet. As the participants spoke to each other, she noticed that the frame around the little windows changed from gray to a bright blue for the person who was speaking at the moment. That's handy.

There were four participants in addition to Nan herself. Two were managers and two were nurses that she knew by sight but not more than that.

"Good morning everybody," Nan said, to get the videoconference going.

Jennifer Dawson, manager of the maternity department, responded with a smile. "Nan, good morning. We are calling to follow up on the verbal instruction issue and the videotapes some of us saw yesterday. We have a proposition to make to you, which we will get to immediately, since I'm sure you have a lot on your plate today."

Nan could hardly disagree with that, but she wondered what the grapevine version of events might be these days.

"Jenny, I'm happy to be with you. Sanjar is here with me, checking on the video setup. It seems to be working at this end, anyway. You all look radiant this morning."

Jennifer took over again. "Okay, let's go. Nan, you know Martha Krug, your third-floor manager. You will want to know the two other nurses with us on this hookup, Maria Navarro and June Bergstrom. Martha and I brought these two young women into the loop yesterday, and they have something to say. Over to you, Maria."

Maria Navarro responded, and the frame on her window turned bright blue. "Good morning, Mrs. Mills. I'm happy to meet you."

Nan replied, noting the change in window frames again. "Good morning to you Maria. Please call me Nan."

"Yes ma'am, if you will call me Mopsy as everybody else does."

"Did you say Mopsy?"

"Yes. My baptismal name is Maria Pilar. I'm named for my grandmother, who was named for Santa Maria de Pilar, a popular saint in Spain. The Spanish nickname is Mapi, so I was called Mapi as a child. When we moved to this country, I was in grade school. My schoolmates couldn't quite get Mapi to work, so they called me Mopsy, and I have been Mopsy ever since. I will let June explain to you later why her name is Junebug."

Nan maintained a pleasant smile, since she knew she was on camera, but she wondered what had happened to picking names out of the Bible. Maybe those were all nicknames, too. How could anybody know? "Okay, Mopsy. Tell us what you've got."

"Right. June and I saw the videotapes yesterday and got the idea like a bolt from the blue. My husband is a resident over at the university hospital, and I called him to get his reaction. He heard John Wayne in the submarine, and he got the idea. He was working second shift yesterday with two male nurses. He told them they were going to play submarine, and he was going to be John Wayne. They made up name tags. My husband's name tag said The Skipper. One of the nurses was Ward Bond, and the other was Chill Wills. They did physician's verbal orders and echo responses all evening and never missed a beat. They didn't feel self-conscious about it, and none of the patients or other staff complained. They all probably thought they were goofy, but no complaints and no mistakes all evening.

"My husband says that verbal orders are a worry there because they have not only a lot of foreign doctors in training but also a lot of foreign nurses. I know from my own experience as a child that I never wanted to admit it when I couldn't understand what was being said in English. So I bluffed my way through. My guess is that these foreign doctors and foreign nurses do the same, because that's human nature. So, repeating verbal orders can't hurt and it might help. So, please consider this an endorsement from those of us who have been brought into the discussion. We all know this is a serious matter in medical care."

Nan asked, "Okay, this works for three guys. How is it going to work for three women or some combination thereof?"

Mopsy replied, "I don't know about an all female group or a female doctor and male nurses, but the most common combination is certainly the male doctor and female nurses. I don't have any field data on that combination, but I did check it out with my sister-in-law, who is a psychologist, or as she says, a shrink. She says that male–female communication is flirtation as far as the man is concerned and that every man loves to hear his words said back to him. So, according to the family shrink, it's a lead-pipe cinch. We need to check it out in a prudent manner, just as we would check out any new procedure.

"Now, Junebug has something to contribute, something important."

"Mrs. Mills, good morning. Please call me Junebug. I would like to tell you why I'm called Junebug, but I have been sworn to secrecy. Wild horses couldn't pull it out of me. In any case, that's not the subject of this call, so let me get to the point.

"All of us have sat through staff meetings where somebody drones on about an important new program, and our minds go blank after three minutes. So, I propose that we get the message out a little more dramatically. I'm a member of a little theater group in town, and I have access to their costumes and creative people.

"Last night, I put something together, and I have gone over it with Mopsy, who thinks this will work. I'd like your permission to try it out on a group of about 50 of your staff, plus a few of the physicians. This will take maybe half an hour. We've booked a video session for noon today. We have also booked a video session for noon tomorrow if you want to review and edit the videotape before we go public."

Nan considered the potential problems if she told them to launch and if she told them she wanted to edit the videotape first. On the one hand, this was the first of Nan's Six Sigma initiatives to involve the real workers in the department. If this initiative fizzled, it would be all that much harder to launch the next one. On the other hand, two of her managers appeared to be ready to go along with it, and these two young women had the bit in their teeth. They had even done a beta test, to use Jack's and Sanjar's lingo, already. Which to do?

"Junebug and Mopsy. Let's go for noon today. I'll tap into the video session if I can free my schedule. If not, I'll check the videotape later on today or this evening. I can do that, can't I, Sanjar?"

"Yes, ma'am," Sanjar said quietly.

"Jenny, please inform Gretchen van der Schoot in the nursing school of what's going on. She may have something to say from the nursing education perspective."

"Yes, I will do that, Nan. At a matter of fact, I talked to Skoots about this last evening for that very reason. She will be on the video link today, maybe with a couple of her faculty."

"Very well, Ladies. You have gotten my day off to a bright start. Let's get all the feedback we can from this first trial group. By the way, how did you pick a trial group?"

Jenny responded. "We posted a note on the electronic mail system. We said that there would be free popcorn, without giving the subject, and said that attendance would be limited to 50 nurses. That always works. We had 50 nurses signed up in half an hour."

"Okay. Who is going to report back on this and when?"

Martha Krug, the third-floor manager, spoke for the first time. "That's my task, Nan. I'll have an edited videotape and my own analysis of the questionnaire we're going to hand out, electronically, for you by the close of business today. Willy is doing the video editing. Have you met Willy?"

"Yes, Martha. I've met Willy." Nan waited for a moment and then said, "Okay. Anything else? No? Then let's give it a go. I look forward to all this. A happy day to all."

Nan clicked the mouse, the video windows closed, and the room lighting returned to normal intensity. She turned to Sanjar and Marcy. "Okay. Are there any technical issues in doing these video sessions, Sanjar?"

"No, ma'am. It's standard video stuff, predominantly a broadcast from the principal room, with capability to get audio and video back from the other rooms over the dedicated videoconferencing links and over the computer video links such as you were just using. I am guardedly optimistic that it will work, technically. As for the content, that is far from my area of specific knowledge."

"Okay. Anything to add, Marcy?"

"Not on that subject. As for your schedule, your managers are here for your next short meeting. Detective Stan Laurel will be here at nine AM, and I have cleared time around noon for you to watch the video session that you just authorized. The rest of your day is as planned before."

"I'm not sure I will be back from Mr. Crawford's office by nine o'clock. Can you keep Stan warm for me?"

"Yes, ma'am. Stan likes chocolate chip cookies."

"Very well, show in my next guests, if you please."

Marcy turned and left the room. Sanjar did his bow-and-walk-backward number out the door. Vivian Smith and Claudia Benedict came in. Marcy came back in, two steps behind them, with a new pot of tea on a tray with three cups and saucers. Her guests eyed the room décor and the saucers with equal envy.

Nan started. "Vivian and Claudia, thank you for coming. Here's what's on my mind, and I seek your advice on how to proceed. We have two nurses who are caught up in life-and-death cases. One of them is Mary Cummins in the baby Thompson case. The other one,

I'm startled to find myself saying, I don't have a name for. Names apart, for the moment, here's the issue I see from my perspective as department head. We have two employees who probably feel like hell right now, not knowing if they did something wrong and not knowing how the department and the big bosses are going to treat them now, while things are still up in the air, and later on. Are they going to be sued? Fired? Shunned? Vilified?

"At one extreme end, maybe one of them willfully harmed a patient. That is so remote a possibility that I'm going to set it aside and never talk about it again until somebody puts concrete proof on my desk. I just don't think that's the situation.

"That leaves the rest of the range of possibilities: that the nurses did everything right or that they made inadvertent errors. We all make inadvertent errors, and we all work to root them out. So, I'm not going to shun or blame any nurse for making an inadvertent error. Plus, the largest probability is that they each did exactly the right thing according to professional standards. So let's play the odds and start there.

"Now, what I would like to do is to go to them, hug them, and tell them that I'm on their side now and forever. If I do that, then I have to follow through, and the whole department has to follow through. I can't speak for the other departments or for the suits, but I can fight for them tooth and nail if it comes to that. Okay. I've done all the talking. Over to you."

The two managers had not only been quiet while Nan spoke, they had been still. They were clearly worried about this, and they probably figured they were going to get caught in the crossfire no matter how it went. After half a minute of silence, Claudia Benedict spoke, quietly, looking alternately at Nan and Vivian.

"The nurse who was caring for Mr. Bill is named Angela Copperwaite. She goes by Angel and she might be one. She has been in nursing about five years, and the last two years she has worked in the VIP section. We pick the nurses with the best skills and bedside manner. The nurses like the VIP section because we staff it a lot more heavily than the other floors, and the nurses have more time to spend with each patient. The patients all love her. She has good skills and has all the certifications anybody would want for that job. She is an agreeable employee. Always there, always on time, always cheerful. We could use more like her any day.

"I heard her story, in person. I know that you want to talk about how to deal with the affected employee and not about the case, so I'll save that for another time."

Nan turned to Vivian. "Vivian, I know Mary Cummins, and I have always thought her to be a first-class nurse. Tell me how she is taking this."

Vivian replied, "Mary is taking it hard. She is really depressed and blaming herself. Mary has been here a long time, which is different from Angel's status. Mary certainly knows about cases in which the hospital blamed the nurse before getting any facts. She has also seen the suits run for the tall grass and leave the nursing staff holding the bag. The lawyers don't know anything about nursing, but they're always quick to blame the nurse. So, based on the institutional track record, I think if I were in Mary's shoes, I'd be doing some worrying, too. Hell, I *am* doing some worrying, both for her and for myself."

They sipped the tea for a moment of reflection. Then Nan spoke, quietly, looking to each of them in turns. "They don't know me personally. If I run up to them and give them a hug, they'll think that I'm crazy or that I'm Judas, giving them the kiss of death. So what can we do?"

More stirring and sipping. Marcy appeared with a new pot of tea.

"Well, we could get your decorator in. He certainly knows how to brighten a room," contributed Vivian. That moment of levity lifted the pall of uneasiness that hovered over the room and gave Nan some hope that they could find a solution.

Claudia spoke. "When I talked to Angel, I tried some temporizing words, but I don't think she left the room with much confidence that management is on her side. So, I need to talk to her again. This time, I can tell her that management is on her side. I'd like some help with the phraseology, but I'm certain that it's my job to work with her through this. You can help, and maybe you want to meet with us, but it's my job."

Nan said, "Fair enough. Let's figure out what to say. Vivian, what would you like to say to Mary Cummins?"

"Based on what we just said here in this room, I'd like to say there is more brightness in this room than just the new paint job. What I'd like to say to Mary is, 'Mary, you're a wonderful nurse and the hospital knows it. We are on your side, and you can count on me to be right there by your side through thick and thin. I personally don't think you did anything wrong. If an inadvertent mistake was made, we don't punish people for making inadvertent mistakes. Then I will tell the same thing to my supervisors and let the word get out in the usual way."

Nan turned to Claudia. "How does that work for you?"

Claudia reflected for a moment. "Yes, that's pretty good. I can say, and mean, 'Angel, I'm on your side in this and so is the department management. I think you did everything right, and if an inadvertent mistake was made, we don't punish people for inadvertent mistakes. I can make sure everybody gets the word. And believe me, everybody is waiting to hear the word.

"Nan, I know you're speaking sincerely here today. I also know that you're not the final authority—that's up there with the suits. Nobody expects you to work miracles, but everybody will be looking with a beady eye for the first little crack in your position. So if we go down this path, which I'm more than happy to do, you're inviting lightning to strike you from a lot of different directions.

"If you can make this stick, it will be a red-letter day for sure. If you can't make it stick, then we are back in the same old funk."

More stirring and sipping. Nan spoke. "Okay. You two speak to the nurses involved. I'll make an announcement of some sort to all the troops, not mentioning these cases but also not leaving any doubt what I'm talking about. Then after a week or so, I would like to meet with both of you and Mary and Angel to reinforce the message. Meanwhile, if you hear of anything happening inside or outside the department, let me know. Marcy can always find me.

"Anything else this morning? Very well, thanks for giving me your time and your thoughts on this difficult matter. We are setting off on a long cruise together, and the better job we do steering the ship as we launch, the better it's all going to be."

Vivian and Claudia went out. Marcy came in to say that Mr. Crawford was parking his car and would be in his office within five minutes, so Nan just had time to freshen up before going upstairs. That seemed like good advice, so Nan followed it, contemplating the two major topics she had already dealt with that morning—and it wasn't even nine o'clock yet.

On her way past Marcy's desk, Nan paused to say, "Marcy, see if you can put me with Gretchen van der Schoot today and then try a videophone connection with Maggie Kelly, in that order. The topic with Skoots is retraining, and the topic with Maggie is needle sticks. If Skoots isn't available, then postpone Maggie, too. I'll be pleased to see Stan Laurel when I get back. Notice that I did not say, 'if I get back.'" With a small, conspiratorial smile, Nan picked up the pace and headed upstairs to see her boss, the hospital's chief operating officer.

14

Wednesday's Meeting with the COO

Nan was ushered immediately into Crawford's office. Crawford's secretary was just a little more formal and distant than was her normal practice. Nan found that easy to read and easy to interpret. She was going to get the wire brush. So, her organizational antennae were improving rapidly, and a week before she would have said that such phenomena don't exist. They say people should learn something every day. In Nan's case, it had been unavoidable this week.

Mr. Crawford was ready for her and extended his hand in formal greeting. Crawford gave Nan a smile that brought the image of an undertaker to mind. Nan suppressed her urge to grin and managed a professional, cool smile instead.

They were not alone. Already seated at the small executive conference table, which would double nicely as a poker table, was Alice Newcomb, chief counsel. So, not only was Nan to be outmuscled but she was also outnumbered. Nan had not had great expectations for this meeting, but now she saw that the downside was truly down. Would she be offered up as the sacrificial lamb? Made to run the executive gauntlet in her shift? Fired? Well, Jack made a good income, so she didn't need the job anyway. There was a shortage of nurses all over town, and Nan had kept up her licenses. It would have been fun, though, to carry out the Six Sigma projects just now starting. She had been looking forward to the lunchtime show to be staged by Mopsy and Junebug. Maybe they'll let her stay through lunch, Nan thought.

Maybe she needed her own lawyer. Marcy probably has one on a string someplace, somebody's cousin. What could she win in court? Free parking for life? An organ transplant voucher? What could she lose in court. Life? Liberty? Happiness? The last would be the first to go, surely. But, thought Nan, Jack loves me, Jake and Bake love me, and my sister Ann loves me—that's all that matters. So, be cool and let them show their cards. Then I'll decide what to do.

"Good morning, Mr. Crawford. Good morning Alice—I'm pleased that you could be with us. Since you are here, I'm doubly convinced that this is an important meeting on an important matter. Mr. Crawford, I believe you called the meeting. So let's drop the ladies-first policy and go right to what you have on your mind."

Crawford maintained that same funeral smile. The skin on his face seemed to be drawn so tightly that she thought it might be painful for him. Such compassion she found in herself at this moment!

Alice had a detached professional air about her this morning. To preclude any doubt as to who might be the lawyer present, she had a yellow legal-sized tablet in front of her. Nan had known Alice rather better than the other suits before all this, and she now saw that Alice had chosen sides, naturally enough, and that the gulf between them would never be lessened. No enmity, just distance. All the world's a stage, and all the men and women merely players. This was definitely her day for Shakespeare.

No points for either side, so far.

"Nan," Crawford enunciated, "You are correct in saying that Alice is here because these are delicate times. We need to stay out of the deep water."

Crawford needs a better speech writer, Nan thought. He was better off with the locker room clichés of Monday. Those could be mixed and matched without restraint.

Crawford continued. "Alice, why don't you bring us up to date on matters, from the big picture perspective?"

Alice looked down at her tablet, which appeared to be blank after the date written on the top line. "Nan and Phil, here's where we stand. There are two key cases. One is the Baby Thompson matter. There are two developments. One is that the family members have withdrawn the criminal complaint, which never had much of a basis anyway. They have continued with their civil damages suit, so there is no change on that front. The second news item is that Dr. Maria Escobar, the pediatrician in this matter, has retained defense counsel and has entered an affidavit to the effect that she wrote the correct medicine order on her physician's order record and that she spoke out the same correct medicine order verbally at the time. She was as surprised and as concerned as anybody when she learned that her order had been disobeyed. When awakened by a call from the nurse on the next shift, she had rushed to the hospital, analyzed the situation, and taken immediate steps to move the baby to Children's Hospital. What happened after that does not concern us, other than that the baby died there as a result of errors made by the hospital's nursing staff. If this runs to its likely conclusion, the hospital will pay damages on behalf of itself and on behalf of its agent, Nurse Cummins. I do not state that as an offer to settle. I am merely projecting the present state of affairs.

"Please understand that our conversation here is protected as communication between you two as senior hospital management and me as your legal counsel. Nothing said in this room today is subject to subpoena or any other order under law. It is absolutely confidential. Please treat it that way."

Alice then kept her face down but lifted her eyes up to engage first Nan and then Crawford, asking "Are there any questions on the baby Thompson matter? Then we will move along to the case of Mr. Bill's untimely demise. Dr. Anderson, our chief medical officer, has finished his personal investigation. You may well know that he does personal investigations once or twice a year at most. This was an exceptional matter in his eyes, and he took immediate charge of getting the medical facts on the table. I applaud him for doing so.

"In my view of the applicable law and regulations, Dr. Anderson could have ordered an autopsy on his own initiative. However, he got the family to agree to an autopsy, so there will be no dispute about that later on. Dr. Anderson interviewed all the people involved, and there were quite a few, including the cardiac rescue team that was called to the VIP suite to attempt to resuscitate Mr. Bill. Dr. Anderson has integrated all the information from the limited amount of computerized information together with the contemporaneous recollections of the people involved. He has established to his own satisfaction a time line for the events in question.

"Dr. Anderson has concluded on the basis of his own medical experience, and he expects any panel of experts that might come along to agree with him, that Mr. Bill went into severe arrhythmia and ineffective blood circulation at least 10 minutes before the nurse attempted defibrillation. Those 10 minutes of delay turned a severe condition into a lethal condition.

"An inspection of the EKG monitor at the bedside and the alarm connection between that EKG machine and the nurse's station has shown that the machine and the alarm are in good working condition. As it happens, the service record for that particular EKG machine shows that the machine was given a complete checkup less than a month ago as part of the overall hospital electronics maintenance program. A number of other EKG machines were checked at the same time. I understand that all four of the EKG bedside machines now assigned to the VIP suites were validated at that time. In addition, there were checks made this week, after the unhappy event, and the particular machine was shown to be in good working order.

"Therefore, Dr. Anderson, whose analysis I believe you will respect, has concluded that the only credible reading of the events is the following: Mr. Bill went into severe arrhythmia and ineffective circulation. The EKG machine recognized the irregular heart voltage pattern and triggered the alarm at the nurses' station. The alarm sounded the audible warning and the flashing warning on the alarm panel. Ten or more minutes transpired before the nurse, Angela Copperwaite, responded to the alarm, recognized the condition, and applied the defibrillator to attempt to resuscitate Mr. Bill.

"Dr. Anderson found that there were three registered nurses on duty in the VIP suites that shift. One was occupied with another patient. One had left the floor to pick up an order at the pharmacy after verifying that Nurse Copperwaite was available to handle calls during the brief time it would take her to go to and from the pharmacy, in accordance with standing procedures. Dr. Anderson therefore concludes that Nurse Copperwaite was derelict in responding to the alarm from Mr. Bill's EKG monitor for reasons not yet known.

"Dr. Anderson interviewed Nurse Copperwaite. I was present at that interview at the invitation of Dr. Anderson. Nurse Copperwaite was cautioned that she could engage counsel on her behalf at that point, at hospital expense. She declined. I repeated the offer to pay counsel for her, and she declined again."

My God, thought Nan. Angel Copperwaite must have been sweating bullets at that time, seeing the whole executive suite lined up against her. At least they might have given her the chance to invite her manager, or even me, to sit in by her side. I would have walked out, if I had been her. Well, here and now I can say to myself that's what I would do in Angel's place. But if I were Angel's age and if I thought myself to be completely and utterly innocent, what would I have done? Asking for counsel would have been the right thing to do, again easy for me to say, even though it would project guilt. A tough call for Angel.

Alice Newcomb continued. "If Nurse Copperwaite was derelict, then since she was acting as an agent for the hospital, the hospital is financially responsible for her actions. Any legal actions against her by the state or by an accrediting agency to remove her license to practice nursing is beyond my interest since that would not involve the hospital one way or the other. I do not say any such action will come to pass. I am only declaring that the hospital would have no interest in the matter.

"Disciplining the nursing staff is your affair, not that of the hospital's executive officers, because you are the senior nursing executive with responsibility for your department, within hospital guidelines. Dr. Anderson's report is available to you to read in my office, under the same restrictions that applied yesterday when you reviewed the files on the two cases we have spoken of this morning. I will be pleased to make Dr. Anderson's report available to you immediately after this meeting if you so wish.

"Dr. Anderson acted within his responsibility, in my opinion, when he contacted the family and summarized his findings in lay terms. Indeed, he would have had no right to withhold his report from the family. Dr. Anderson had made them aware of his inquest when he asked them to permit the autopsy, so they were already alert to the matter.

"The family was accompanied by counsel. On the advice of counsel, the family gave notice to Dr. Anderson, then later to Mr. Crawford, and again to me personally that the family will consider all its options for recovery of damages from the hospital and any culpable parties—meaning Nurse Copperwaite, her supervisor, and perhaps even you as the responsible executive—by civil action. In addition, the family gave notice that it would enter a criminal complaint for criminal negligence and perhaps other breaches of the law against the hospital and against the persons involved.

"In my opinion and based on a career of dealing with such matters, although this is as egregious an affair as I have ever seen, the criminal complaint will die of its own weight in due course, and the hospital as the party holding fiscal responsibility for Nurse Copperwaite and any management involved will settle the matter as quietly as possible. This will certainly get into the news because the criminal complaint is a public document. So there will be some adverse publicity. Particularly so, given that Mr. Bill was the chairman of our board of directors and given that the Baby Thompson matter is in the public news and happened the same week.

"Just to clear away one matter, please be advised that if you are called or named in a complaint, then the hospital will provide you with competent counsel. The same holds true for Nurse Copperwaite and any other employee. However, if you or Nurse Copperwaite are found criminally responsible, then you are on your own. Do you want to have that in writing?"

Mentally comparing what Alice had just said with Jack's story at the breakfast table, Nan surmised that a standard letter must be given to all young lawyers as part of their office start-up kit to put employees on notice that the employer will support them up to the point that they really need support, then the rip cord will pull itself. The employers don't even shout "Happy landings" to the employees as the ground accelerates up to meet their falling bodies.

"Nothing in writing at this point, if you please. I speak for Nurse Copperwaite on this matter as well. If either of us has a change of mind, you will be notified."

Nan's mind was going a mile a minute. For the first time, she realized that she and Jack held everything jointly, and that if she were to lose a judgment in court, he could lose his livelihood as she was losing hers. Better get that fixed right away. Usually men hide their assets in their wives' names. Here, she was the one with the greater exposure to catastrophic loss. Better speak to Jack about that this evening so he can get it going. They had a lawyer, but they had only used him to handle the house purchase and to settle some property on the twins as a sort of insurance plan. Nuts—that's going to be expensive for no good reason. Stronger terms were coming to mind, so she mentally changed the subject.

What's the most and the least she could get out of this present meeting? She needed to project strength, not fear or weakness, yet not too much independence from the team. First, she had to push Alice out of the conversation and assert her right to speak directly to Crawford.

"Alice, you have made an excellent summary of complicated matters. You have a gift for summarizing matters. Other lawyers I know get caught up in the sound of their own voices. You cut to the chase and speak in terms even I can follow. You have offered to let me see Dr. Anderson's report. I accept that offer, right after we break up here. We don't need to take Mr. Crawford's time with that, since I'm sure you have already read it in detail."

With this last phrase, Nan turned her attention from Alice to Crawford and smiled a little more warmly than she wanted. She paused. Before Nan could continue, Crawford spoke. "Now, Nan, you know I want you to call me Phil. We're all on the same team here, and we don't want to be any stuffier than we have to be. Duress should bring us together, so we can share our strengths, not push us apart."

"Thank you, Phil. I will take that as an expression of support. And I thank you for it."

"Abso-damned-lutely you have my personal support. Abso-damned-lutely. Alice's too. We can't stop people from bringing suits and complaints against us. Happens all the time. Sometimes we deserve it, and most of the time we don't. We can't stop them, but we can learn our lessons and stop the bleeding by getting the right management team onto the field with the right playbook.

"Here's what I want from you, Alice." Crawford turned to Alice. Nan guessed he was temporizing while he thought of what to say to her. That's a skill Nan needed to cultivate, too. "Alice, you have the baton on all legal matters. You say what page in what hymnal and who sings what parts. Got that? We're counting on you. You know we don't keep a big stable of lawyers here. We count on you to cover that base. You know that you have my full confidence and that of the CEO and the board, and can take that to the bank."

Crawford showed a little more tooth, but he was still as tightly wound as he had been at the start of the meeting. Nan thought again that Crawford had been showing executive skill by having Alice deliver the bad news so that he could hold himself above the fray and judge the players, the moves, and the countermoves. He's good, thought Nan. A little nutty in the phraseology department when under stress, but he's not slobbering yet. Is that me, 20 years hence? Nan asked herself. Heaven forfend. I pray that Jack rescues me from myself before I get to that stage. Still, how people act under pressure isn't readily known, even to themselves. That was one of the more interesting topics in the human relations segment of that business course. When Philip L. Crawford is under pressure, he reverts to locker-room clichés and puts somebody else out front to catch the arrows.

With his gaze on Nan now, Crawford continued. "Nan, we need a recovery plan for the nursing service. I mean something we can talk about in public. We won't link it directly to these events, but we're not going to fool anybody who is paying attention. We cannot ignore these events and pretend they didn't happen. I am not saying anybody did anything wrong, but I am saying that somebody didn't stop something bad from happening when they might have. I don't want any scapegoats or sacrificial lambs. You'll need to go through your own disciplinary processes in regard to these two nurses and these two cases, but that will never be public information if I can help it. The nurses are entitled to due process, however that applies to internal processes, and they are entitled to the benefit of the doubt. If something went wrong because somebody made an inadvertent error, well, we don't punish people for inadvertent errors. Maybe they need a good talking-to or reassignment, but that's all up to you and your departmental procedures. But that's all going to be on the q.t., so we need something else we can talk about with outsiders and other interested parties. We don't want a smoke screen; we're not out to bamboozle the public here. We want to restore the public's confidence, and we are going to do that by shooting straight pool.

"We need to move on this. It's getting close to noon on Wednesday, so let's have something for the press on Monday. That gives us four and a half days to get it right. I don't think this should go out as a press release. That will look phony. How about some newsletter or something that goes to the employees, something that we wouldn't mind if it got into the hands of the press? Hide this leaf in the forest, as somebody said. Is there a hospital bulletin or something that would look sort of normal if it comes out on Monday, Alice?" He turned to his chief counsel.

"Yes, Phil. I checked the pattern with the personnel department, since they are in charge of employee publications, even for the individual departments. The nursing department newsletter is due next Wednesday. We could move that up a couple of days without attracting any suspicion, I think. That would work, don't you think, Nan?" Alice had turned to Nan, and her smile was a little less distant. The team dynamic was taking hold.

"Monday it is," Nan said, adding a few watts to her own smile. "I will be pleased if you would review any text, Alice, just to make sure. Since this will be for all the employees of the department, it will not be soaked in medical jargon, just plain English. May I ask you to do that?" Nan knew very well that anything in ink on these subjects was going to get vetted by Alice and probably by additional lawyers brought in to watch Alice, so Nan was stealing a march and making a virtue of necessity.

Crawford was beaming. "Ladies, I knew we had the right team here. I knew we could pull together. We are going through dangerous shoals right now, so we have to keep the oars close to the boat and follow the claxon." Nan thought he probably meant to say coxswain, but she kept quiet. "Now, do we have our marching orders clear in our minds? Alice, you have the baton. Nan, you have the quill pen to write a recovery plan but, of course, don't call it that. Alice vets everything, and Nan you take care of any disciplinary action. I don't want to hear about the plan or meddle in any way. If you decide to terminate anybody or apply any severe discipline, just do it with human resources so it doesn't snap back and bite us where it hurts. Okay, ladies?"

Crawford put an even more severe look on his face as he continued. "Don't let this leave the room, but I was suffering flip-flops in the old tum-tum last evening at that capital fund-raising campaign meeting. We pulled it off, though, because we have a good track record of serving the community. Besides, the word hadn't gotten out yet about how Mr. Bill went. The next event is going to be a lot tougher if we don't get our socks pulled up. We can weather this if we pull together.

"I'm counting on you. The whole institution is counting on you. We are not important as individuals; the institution is what counts. But we have to act as individuals for the good of the team. For the good of the fleet, as my father used to say after he mustered out of the navy after the Big One. We won that one, and we can win this one. Okay Alice? Okay Nan?"

Hands were shaken in all directions. The tension in the room was little lighter than before, but it was still tense. My very first high-pressure meeting, and I'm wringing wet, Nan thought to herself. I hope it doesn't show. I'll need a change of outfits before I catch pneumonia from the air conditioning.

Even so, Nan thought she had held her own. She got no action items that she hadn't given herself beforehand. She had stood her ground and moved up a peg or two in the estimation of Alice Newcomb, Nan figured. Philip L. Crawford had tried to pull her in rather than push her away, so it was a satisfactory meeting, all in all. What more could she have asked for?

Well, it would have been nice if Phil or Alice had said that they didn't think for a moment that any nursing error had been made, no matter what Dr. Anderson thought he had found. That would have been nice, but it would have required Crawford to go against the findings of his own chief medical officer. That will be a while, I think, that will be a while, Nan thought to herself. But it won't take forever.

Nan and Alice walked together to Alice's office, which was nearby. Nan noted that Alice had not thought of some last thing to say to Crawford on the way out, a little something to project status. Good. That's a plus for me, Nan thought. Alice doesn't think she outranks me, right this minute. I'll have to cultivate that thought in her little mind, horrid though it is of me to think that way, even under duress.

"Alice, I'm used to reading these medical reports, so I'll just be a minute or two with Dr. Anderson's document. Then I need to move along to get that action plan going that Phil wants. I'm anxious to have you review it soon because you might have some ideas to include. I'm not at all selfish when it comes to getting the best ideas I can find or borrow. Maybe we can set a time for early Friday? I'll have Marcy call to check your availability. Will that be all right? If I have started in the wrong direction entirely, I'll have the weekend to set it right."

"Nan, I think Phil is handling these cases exactly right. He doesn't insist on doing all the thinking and all the work. He has the board's perspective, which he needs to have. He has the pulse of the community. He's a great COO. We are lucky to have him here during this crisis."

Nan wondered whether Alice was wearing a wire, with that speech. She didn't expect Alice to be catty about their boss, but this was the far opposite of cattiness. Another thing to wonder about. This executive stuff had its own mysteries, for sure.

"Alice, I'm new to all this, and I'm so happy that you have extended a hand of help and friendship to me. All this, all of a sudden. Well, we can do it together, and I will value your help beyond measure."

Big smile. You can't lay it on too thick, Nan thought. That was something she learned in the marketing segment of that business course. Can't lay it on too thick, even with a trowel. Now, if I could only bow and walk backward at the same time . . . No, I have to read Dr. Anderson's report first. Nan went to the little conference room in Alice's office complex and found Dr. Anderson's report laid out for her. It was only about 10 pages long and quickly absorbed. The time line was not hard to find, even though it was based on anecdotal information and not computer time stamps. The condition of the body as observed by the cardiac rescue team plus what could be learned from the autopsy had persuaded Dr. Anderson that Mr. Bill had been in arrhythmia for at least 10 minutes, maybe 15, and that was enough to kill him. Action within two or three minutes would very likely have saved him. Maybe not, but the probabilities were that way. There was no sign of stroke or any other exogenous event that would have taken him with or without timely action by the nurse.

Dr. Anderson had asked Angel, or Nurse Copperwaite as he called her, about the time lapse between hearing the alarm and getting to the bedside. Angel had told him that when she heard the alarm, she had started the lap timer on her wrist watch, as she always did so she could have the times for the record. The elapsed time when she gave Mr. Bill the paddle treatment was one minute and 45 seconds. She knew that because she had stopped the lap timer then. She had that one datum of information, and she rested her defense on it. She had refused to be drawn into any argument about whether she had been paying attention to the alarms or not. She simply said she was at the nurses' station, she heard the alarm, she started her lap timer, and she went to take care of Mr. Bill. End of story. She appeared to be confident of herself, but she seemed nervous at the same time. Nervous! Nervous! I'll show you nervous! thought Nan. What an inquisition. I wonder where they keep the dunking stool around here. Or the truth serum—that would be more up to date.

Nan thanked Alice and Alice's secretary for their hospitality and returned to her own office. Stan Laurel was waiting, contentedly by the look of him, and nibbling on a chocolate chip cookie. The road to a man's heart is through his stomach, her grandmother had been fond of saying.

Nan gave Stan a smile and asked if he could give her just a minute to freshen up. Nan went into her office, where, to her surprise, she found her own traveling suit bag. She opened the zipper a few inches and found two of her business suits inside, with accessories to match. Marcy came in, two steps behind her, with a pitcher of iced tea.

"I took the liberty of thinking you might want a change after that meeting. I called Mr. Mills and caught him at the airport. He authorized me to take care of it. He said something about cherry pie, but we had sort of a noisy cell phone connection at his end, so I didn't quite make it out. You can change here, but I think Stan will wait if you want to go to the executive ladies' room upstairs to change. The other things you asked for have been taken care of. Is there anything else?"

"Marcy," Nan felt a twinkle forming in her eye, "I need to tell you that my husband is falling in love with you, sight unseen. I give you fair warning that he's mine and I fight for what's mine."

"Yes, ma'am." Marcy looked a little uncertain for the first time since Nan had met her. That was a whole three days ago!

Nan took her suit bag up to the executive suite and took her time changing. She felt refreshed when she returned to her office, thinking that maybe the hospital should have an executive swimming pool for such occasions.

"Stan. What can I do for you today?"

"Mrs. Mills, I have two things to tell you. One, the complaint has been dropped in the matter of the Thompson baby. I figured that that would happen, as I told you the other day. Yesterday, in fact. The other thing is that a complaint has been entered in the matter of the untimely death of Mr. Bill. I'd like to talk to you about that, if I may."

Nan smiled, turned to her desk to push the intercom button, and picked up the handset. "Marcy, get Alice Newcomb for me, if you please."

"Alice is holding on line one, Mrs. Mills."

Nan pushed the button for line one. "Alice, Detective Laurel is here with the matter of Mr. Bill on his mind. Please tell me what to do."

"Nan, just put Stan on the phone, and I will give him the standard VD lecture. No surprises."

"Stan, Alice Newcomb would like to speak to you for a moment." Nan smiled at Stan and handed him the receiver.

Stan said hello, listened to words he had certainly heard a million times before, said thank you, and hung up. He returned to his seat at the table. He said he knew she would not answer any specific questions, but he would like to get an idea of what was supposed to be happening in the VIP suite for Mr. Bill. Stan said he had already glanced at Mr. Bill's medical record, with the permission of the family and Dr. Anderson, and he had read Dr. Anderson's report, which had been given to his office when the complaint was filed. So he knew what a layman could know after reading such reports. Nan thought maybe he knew just a little bit more than he was letting on, but she accepted that this was his way. And it wasn't her place to change him.

"Well," Nan said, "How can I help, without discussing Mr. Bill's case in particular?"

"Why didn't Mr. Bill get a pacemaker a year ago?"

"I can't help with that one. I will say that people refuse to have pacemakers every day of the year, and that's their call. They have their own reasons."

"Why did Mr. Bill get a pacemaker this time, if he didn't want one six or 12 months ago?"

"I can't help with that one. Maybe his family or his surgeon can tell you. I truly don't know."

"Why didn't the surgeon stick the pacemaker in right away, as soon as Mr. Bill gave him the nod?"

"Without speaking of Mr. Bill's case in particular, I will say that a surgeon will try to clear up infections or other stress on the body before doing surgery of any kind, simply to reduce the risk to the patient. Pacemakers are pretty common these days, but cutting open the body and inserting electrodes into the heart muscle isn't to be taken lightly in any case. Pacemakers are for sick people, people who have a lot of strain on their systems. So, surgeons must balance the risk of waiting a few days for the antibiotics to work with the risk of an arrhythmia crisis. That's their profession, and it's pretty hard to second-guess them."

"How do you account for the 10-minute delay?"

"I have nothing to say about that."

"Do you believe the nurse's story?"

"I have nothing to say about the nurse's story in particular. I will tell you that I believe what nurses tell me until I have reason to change my mind. Nurses deal with life-and-death issues everyday, and they take their responsibilities seriously. It's part of our profession. And by profession, I mean the oath they take when they put on the nursing hat and pin. Or perhaps I should just say pin, seeing that nurses hardly every wear the pointy hats anymore. I'm not wearing my cap, although I'm pleased that I still have it. Here's my pin, right on my lapel. I don't wear it every day anymore, but this seemed like a good day to wear it. "

"Did you have enough nurses assigned to the VIP suites at the time in question?"

"I have nothing to say about that."

"Do you believe the nurse's story?"

"I have nothing to say about that, and Stanley, you had already asked that question."

"Is there any way to reconcile the nurse's story with the other facts as we know them?"

"I have nothing to say about that."

Stan closed his notebook, which he had never looked at or scribbled in the whole time they were talking. He clearly used it as stage prop, the way men used to fiddle with their pipes to stall for time. Nan was getting to like Stan Laurel, although they were not exactly on the same team here.

"Do you mind if I talk with the nursing manager of that section and other nurses in that section?"

"That's not for me to say. Check with Alice Newcomb. Please take into consideration that they have patients to attend to, and we're running a full census these days. I know you will, you understand. I just say that sort of thing for the record. Also, if Alice decides to sit in on any interview you make with any member of my service, I want you to know that Alice is on my side, not on your side."

"I never doubted that for a moment. Thank you for your time. I hope you won't mind if I find a need to talk with you again in this matter. At least we got the Thompson baby matter to go away. That was too sad a case to drag into a criminal proceeding. At least Mr. Bill had had a full life. I'm not condoning foul play, you understand, just pointing out the obvious difference between the two cases."

Stan offered his hand, which Nan took but didn't shake, figuring that a shake would be too formal for the circumstances. Polite smiles in both directions. Stan left, finding some reason to stop and talk with Marcy, who produced a box of chocolate chip cookies, from which Stan selected the biggest one. Then he left.

Nan thought about calling Jack to ask about EKG machines, but Jack would be in transit. Wait until evening, when they can talk at leisure. Nan really liked to talk with Jack. One might call it love. She did.

Nan glanced at the mail log on her computer desktop. Truly ordinary stuff, as Marcy had said. The telephone log was integrated into the same file, and the word ordinary leapt to mind.

Marcy came in carrying a bud vase with two beautiful pink rose buds. Marcy handed Nan the card. It was from Jake and Bake, as were the roses, with best wishes on finding work. That was a direct way of putting it, and she smiled and treasured her boys. She also wondered just for a moment if Marcy had put them up to it, but she decided she didn't want to know. Another phone call to put off until evening. She could make phone calls and bake cherry pies at the same time, now that she was getting the hang of it.

15

Skoots Pays a Visit

"Okay, Marcy, who's next?" Nan took a deep breath to get a little extra oxygen into her cranium and found that she was very pleased with the day so far. This executive stuff wasn't so bad. Not tough at all. Duck soup. She'd have to have Marcy find a Xerox copy of Philip L. Crawford's book of clichés, now that she was in the big leagues.

Marcy replied that Gretchen van der Schoot, whom she had called, was on her way and expected within five minutes.

Nan took advantage of the lull to place text-page messages to Jack, asking him to call her at home at around 8:30 that evening, and to Jake and Bake, to ask them to call her around 8:00. They were usually punctual, so that should work out. The twins called home by calling the 800 number associated with their residence telephone line, so the charge appears on the home telephone bill at the end of the month. That was cheaper and more convenient than other systems they had tried when Jack had traveled a lot when he was getting his consulting business going. Besides, she didn't want the twins to have any reason at all, ever, not to call home. She missed them, and while she could console herself by reflecting that they were growing up and had to live their own lives, she didn't want to let go any sooner than she had to. Not with such delightful kids.

Gretchen van der Schoot came in the office, followed two steps behind by Marcy, who had a new pot of tea. Skoots had been running the nursing school for eons and was considered one of the fixtures of the institution. "Good morning, Nan. Congratulations on your appointment to your position, and I admire your redecorating work here."

"Thanks for coming over, Skoots. We'll make it your place next time. The paint job has something to do with the video cameras. I guess you do a lot of video link work these days, too."

"Yes, we do more and more of that. They tell me that the links will eventually be over the Internet, but for the next few years, videoconferencing and remote education will be over dial-up video links. If your paint job helps the cameras, that's something we want to learn from you. Never too old to learn, I keep telling our faculty members. Some of them are actually older than I am!" Skoots added with an overly loud chuckle, revealing a nervousness that Nan hadn't expected or had ever seen before in Skoots, whom she had known on a casual basis for several years. Skoots wasn't young, but she was not that close to retirement either.

"Skoots, I'm interested in increasing the amount of retraining we do for my nurses. I know we do periodic recertification for some procedures like CPR, but I'm curious to know if we can do retraining on routine tasks such as titrations, dosage calculations, injections, and so on. This is in line with what some of the medical professions are doing and follows the airline model of putting pilots through simulations every year. The idea is that people get sloppy doing tasks, even the tasks they do every day, and it does no harm and probably some good to put them through the paces once in a while.

"Now the retraining might be periodic, like the pilots do it, or it might be event driven. Say a nurse does a titration wrong. Rather than yell at her or him, we just say, 'Please take the titration retraining module.' The retraining isn't meant as a punishment, just as an acceptance of the fact that the titration was improperly done. That would better than pretending the event didn't happen. And it might communicate that management wants titrations done the right way and might communicate that we're not blaming the nurse but rather just fixing the system.

"So far this is just in the thinking stage. Some industries have gone this way, and it strikes me as something we can look at. Naturally, I would want to do it with your faculty and facilities rather than duplicating what you already have or going to an outside trainer."

Skoots smiled brightly and said, "Nan, I believe in training. That's where I have invested my professional life. So we certainly agree at the top line. As for the practicalities of adding any significant amount of training, there are some things to consider. First of all, we are in different departments. The nursing school is an autonomous unit in the sense that nobody bothers to second-guess what I do, and it has a free-standing budget, meaning I have separate and distinct budgets and accounts for which I'm responsible and accountable. I report to the vice president of personnel, who isn't a nurse and doesn't have too much of a clue about what the nursing school does but does know how to read a budget report.

"We hold the charter for training within the hospital enterprise, so if you decided to set up your own training programs, there would be a big turf battle. Since you just said that you don't want to do that, I'm only telling you that for background.

"We have a cost transfer system, rather than a cash system, for training your nurses and other employees. We plan a level of that activity for a budget year. Then as three nurses, say, come over to take a short course, we run the cost for the training service through our books and over to your books. It's all Monopoly money at the hospital level, since it goes out of one pocket and into another, but it's noticeable at my level. Now you might think that if you sent five extra nurses over to me for a training course, that increase would be a plus for me because I would get credit on my budget. That's true in small increments, but if it took an extra instructor or overtime pay for one of my regular instructors, then I get whacked on the cost line or the head-count line. Right now, the school is running full, and I'm short one instructor. While I can do anything you want in the long term, say the next budget year, I can only do a little bit this budget year.

"Our operations are limited not only by money, as in budgets, but also by other administrative limits. We have a head-count limit that is separate from, but just as rigid as, the money limits. We have limited physical space and a limited number of each kind of equipment, like titration units, so we can handle only certain class sizes. That's money, too, but it's capital money, which is a separate negotiation every year.

"So, we have very limited flexibility in the short term. In the long term, starting with the next budget cycle, if you endorse an expansion, I'm sure that senior management will go along with increases anywhere you think them necessary. You can look at us as an internal service organization. You are our customer, and we want to provide the training services you want. We can only do that if you give us a plan, a forecast, that we can use to size capacity."

Gretchen gave Nan a very pleasant and perhaps motherly smile, exhibiting confidence in her position. Indeed, it was the ultimate bureaucrat's position that everything is possible except for all the reasons why nothing is possible.

This was yet another learning experience for Nan. She needed more help with the ways of the bureaucracy, and she thought she knew where to get it in this instance. But that was for later. What could she do right now that would make this a winning meeting for Skoots so that she'll want to cooperate in the future? Well, cooperation might be too strong a word, but what could she do right now?

"Skoots, do you have self-paced training units, maybe computer based, that deal with topics that don't really require supervision, such as getting to work on time?"

"Yes and no. We've looked at some commercially available units, but we never bought any because they didn't fit a planned need. I could get one or two units on a trial basis, maybe, from one of the publishers if you like. We could keep the training unit on a laptop computer. When you authorize a nurse to take the retraining, a school faculty member could open a training account for that nurse. The nurse could then take the course on whatever schedule proves to be convenient. If the unit is not completed within a specified time, the faculty could follow up and see why. The nurse would answer test questions at the end of the unit, and the computer would issue a grade.

"This system isn't very secure, as you can see. The nurse might have a coworker take the exam, and we would never know. But for a range of training topics, it's a good enough system."

"So, Skoots, if I had one of my managers work with you to try some retraining that didn't require any serious manpower on your side, but maybe a small amount of money, then we could get something going this budget year. And, working with you, there could be a joint plan put together for next year and the following years, for which you could add budget and staff. Is that right?"

"Nan, you know I would be pleased to work with you in exactly that way. Now the way that would work is that you would assign a lead manager and I will assign my faculty person who is in charge of curriculum development, and the two of them could work together. Then you and I could review progress and resolve any issues, in the unlikely event that there are issues to resolve. I'd love to do that."

"Okay, I think I understand this. Do you know Maggie Kelly?"

"Yes, I do. A fine young woman. If she is your pick, that will be fine. Not that I would object to any of your managers, of course, but

Maggie will be fine. Or, you could start with Maggie and put some-body else in later, or maybe rotate the duty. That's all up to you."

Nan wondered why Skoots wants to project such a maternal, or matriarchal, image of herself. Another curiosity. Being curious, Nan asked, "Skoots, I have run across many odd nicknames the past few days. I'm sensitive to that because my own nickname is pretty odd. How long have you called yourself 'Skoots'?"

"Oh, Nan, Skoots comes naturally from my name. But the family name itself has deep and odd historical roots. Dutch people didn't use family names until the time of Napoleon. When he took over, he said everybody had to have a family name by such and such a date. The Dutch couldn't force him out, so they did what Dutch people do: they made a joke out of it. They picked silly family names, like from-the-field, from-the-sea, or from-the-mill. Some were a little more anatomical, such as from-the-tube. My own family name means from-the-womb. Napoleon didn't know any Dutch, so it was our own little joke. Maybe in the long run, the joke was on us, because Napoleon left but the names stayed. Well, even if the joke is on us, we still enjoy a good joke. Dutch people are the least apt to be grumpy of all the people in the world, I think."

That was a good joke, Nan thought, a joke for the ages. She wondered if it would be worth the time required to explain to Skoots that her own married name, Mills, was the anglicized version of the Dutch name, van der Molen, meaning from-the-mills. Nan wondered if Jack had ever heard the Napoleon story. She'd ask, sometime. Sometime less filled with urgency.

"Skoots, it will be great to cooperate with you on this. I think any sign of cooperation between departments will look good up-stairs, and I think that this retraining project, if we can figure it out, will improve patient care. That's why we are all here. Thanks for coming over."

"Nan, I want you to know that I will support you every way I can. If we were one department, the budget and head-count limits, which we both know are entirely artificial, would be less of a bother. But we are organized the way we are, and I certainly can't change it myself. Maybe we should put that on the five-year plan as a strate-gic objective." Skoots extended her hand, smiled a motherly smile, and left, stopping by Marcy's desk to say hello and gain a chocolate chip cookie.

Nan thought for a moment and then hit the intercom button. Marcy answered promptly. "Marcy, go ahead with the Maggie Kelly item, the meeting with Skoots was sufficiently positive for that. Then ask Carl Burke to come over and give me a budget tutorial. Tell him I have done budgets at the unit level for years and know about lines, targets, and allocations, but tell him that I have never had to think about budgets at my new level before. Will you do that, please?"

"Yes, ma'am. As a matter of fact, Carl came over to see me a month ago and said he would be pleased to brief you on the budgetary process when that cycle starts. I'll just tell him you are responding to his kind offer and you want to get started with an overview this week. He'll be thrilled."

"Okay, tell him I want the big, big picture and not a 200-slide show. I mostly want to talk and ask questions."

"Yes, ma'am. He understands that executives have short attention spans. He briefs executives all the time. That's what he does."

"Short attention span. I think I'm developing one of those. It must be an occupational hazard. Okay, go ahead with that, then cue up the next topic for the day. I'm going to finish my cup of tea and empty my consciousness for about two minutes."

"Yes, ma'am. I will have your next group in the conference room in five minutes."

"Five minutes are even better than two. Fine." Nan tilted her chair back into a semireclined position. This is a great chair, she thought. She held her teacup in both hands, and thought about what she had learned from Skoots, beyond the Napoleon story. Skoots had proven to be a surprise. Most of her surprises this week, regarding personnel anyway, had been on the positive side. So many energetic and talented people, for whom management seemed largely to be keeping out of their way or maybe keeping the gates open in front of them. She then began to think about all the different types of people she was working with. There's Maggie, who loves what she is doing but doesn't think the organization gives a damn about her work or her. Vivian and Claudia, who both have life-and-death cases under review, are worried that the organization is looking for a way to make them hold the bag. The two nurses, Mary and Angel, have those same worries in spades. And then there's her boss, who is wound up like a top and speaks like the coach of a midget football team, and the company lawyer, who spends most of her time reading organizational tea leaves when she isn't harassing Nan's nurses.

To top matters off, she had to write a Shakespeare-quality piece announcing the nursing service recovery plan before Friday. Maybe she could have Skoots cowrite it, so that nobody who read it would have any idea what it meant, other than we can't do anything, and it's the budget's fault. Is that me in another five years? Nan wondered. Save me, Jack!

Well, she hadn't done a very good job of emptying her consiousness, but she was a little more ready for the next adventure. As Edmund Burke once said, these are the times that try men's souls.

16

The Lowdown
on Mr. Bill

Nan walked through the connecting door to her conference room and found Sanjar and Marcy waiting politely for her. I could get used to this politeness, Nan thought. Saucers for her tea cups, good paint jobs, good chair, reserved parking, and polite people. This executive stuff is okay.

"Good morning. Where do we start?"

Marcy began. "Mrs. Mills, Sanjar has looked into the public information about Mr. Bill, his business, and his family's business because, as it turns out, those are two different businesses. I looked into the newspaper items using the online database from the local paper. The newspaper charges a small fee, which Carl said he would take care of. So, I handled the social side, and Sanjar handled the business side. I also chatted for just a moment with a friend who works over there, as I think I mentioned to you the other day.

"We'll start with the social side, since that is pretty simple, really. After Mr. Bill left the army, he got married. His wife was named Agnes. He started a used car lot, built it up to a chain of used car lots, then bought distributorships for new cars. At the time of his death, he was the biggest car seller in the region. Early on, he created a marketing image of himself as Mr. Bill, which caught on so well that almost nobody knew his real name.

"Part of that promotion was to dress his wife Agnes up like she had just gotten off a Conestoga wagon in her Mother Hubbard dress and sunbonnet. She was called Aunt Agnes on the billboards, and she was made up as if she were 70 years old. In fact, she was about 10 years younger than Mr. Bill. Mr. Bill and Agnes had two sons, both of whom are in their 30s now. Both live in town and are in business, as Sanjar will tell you in just a moment.

"Sad to say, Agnes died 15 months ago, quite suddenly. She had a stroke, according to the newspapers, and she died almost immediately. The news reports hinted at a brain tumor, but the subject didn't get much discussion, since whatever it was took her so quickly. She was at home alone, in the middle of the day, when she died.

"Mr. Bill was pretty hard hit by the loss of Agnes. He withdrew from several civic organizations, although he maintained his position on the hospital board, perhaps because it was Agnes who was so interested in the hospitals. She had been president of the hospital auxiliary and head of the fund drive about every other year.

"Agnes was big into philanthropy. She gave money to everything, including the hospital, the symphony, and the zoo. No particular mention of political giving, but that wouldn't show up so much on the society pages I was checking. When Agnes died, there were very large bequests to her favorite charities, running to millions of dollars. The new wing on the hospital was started with her big bequest to the hospital, and that wing will have her name on the front door.

"Recently, like the past eight to 10 weeks, there had been mentions in the society column of Mr. Bill squiring a woman around town. She is herself a widow, maybe five years younger than Mr. Bill. Her name is Genevieve Richards, who goes by Jenny. Her late husband had been a lawyer with one of the big firms downtown, and it appears that she was left with enough money to live on comfortably. So nobody figured her for a gold digger. They were just two people who found comfort in each other's company.

"No engagement had been officially announced in the society pages, but it looks like the society column writers thought they were engaged. There were no rumors of the sons being bent out of shape about it or anything. In fact, the rumor inside Mr. Bill's company is that the sons were happy with his choice and thought that having a friend might cheer him up a little bit. The office help said he looked a little livelier after he took up with Jenny Richards.

"That's all I have to report. Sanjar has some business information for you."

"Yes, Mrs. Mills, I do have some limited information. Much is available about businesses on the Web these days, particularly about public companies that have to file reports at the state and federal level. These reports were always said to be public reports, but until the Web came along, it was almost impossible to find them. Now it is a matter of a couple of keystrokes, and even federal agencies like the Securities and Exchange Commission have Web sites with tons of information. Today the issue is more often what to do with the flood of information once you have it.

"Mr. Bill did not publish his own financial statements about his private wealth, but his companies had done so.

"Let us start with the car distributorships. They are owned by a corporation named MB&AA. You can guess the names behind the acronym. Although this company was founded by Mr. and Mrs. Bill, it is now a publicly held corporation with about 200 shareholders. Mr. Bill was the largest shareholder, but he owned only a small percentage of stocks. Mr. Bill was chief executive officer and chairman of this company, and he drew a salary of about $300,000 a year, so he was able to maintain his lifestyle without any financial strain. He sold off his stock in this company partly to fund another investment, which we will get to in a minute, and partly to fund the charitable giving that his wife favored. Mr. and Mrs. Bill had held their stock jointly, and her interest in the stock passed to him upon her death.

"Mr. and Mrs. Bill appeared to own their home near the country club free and clear. They did not own any other property in this county in their own names. If they owned stocks and bonds or other real property elsewhere, that would be hard for me to find.

"Let us now talk about the other family businesses. There are two. One was founded by the older son, an electrical engineer who does general consulting, mostly in computer designs for industrial purposes. He does not manufacture any products; he just does engineering designs for others. In the past, he has done a wide range of engineering consulting, and I gather that he got into the industrial computer design field just because that's a good field to work in. I don't find any patents registered or assigned to this company. This company is just called Gordon Schneider Engineering. Gordon holds a bachelor's degree in electrical engineering from the state university, and he is registered as a professional engineer with the state licensing agency. That is all very normal. This company is not publicly held so I cannot give you very much in the way of particulars. From the size of the office it has on Second Avenue, I'd say he has about fifteen to twenty employees. That is not unusual for that kind of a specialty company."

Nan knew that engineering consulting companies could be quite small. Jack employed only himself, although he had a network of consultants he respected and with whom he pooled interests once in a while.

Sanjar continued. "I have one other small item regarding Gordon Schneider. You may know that the hospital is having its electrical and computer circuits studied because some of the engineering drawings are so old and so poorly maintained that there are questions about the reliability of the networks in case of, say, a fire that would damage one wing. That work is being done by electricians, since it is mostly a matter of walking around with some meters and taking measurements of continuity. It is done quite cleverly, but it does not take engineers to do the work. It does, however, take an engineer to supervise the work and to evaluate the findings. Gordon Schneider is the engineer who has the contract to do the supervision and evaluation. The contract pays him one dollar. So, this is, in fact, a charitable contribution of his time and professional effort, quite consistent with the family's generosity to the hospital over the years. I suppose he comes to the hospital from time to time to supervise this work, but I do not know him by sight. We could perhaps query the visitor's log, but since he is a VIP as well as a contractor, the hospital might have issued him a pass.

"Just in case you are wondering, if he charges a dollar for his own time but charges a big fee to provide electricians so that he can make a profit on that, I may inform you that the electricians are hired directly by the hospital maintenance department, so there is no profit to Mr. Gordon Schneider anywhere that I can find. It is simply a charitable contribution of his time. Since Gordon is a registered engineer, his report has standing, and the hospital saves $50,000 to $100,000 in money that it would have had to pay someone else to do the same work.

"Now, for the final company. I do not wish to say that the engineering company is low technology, for it certainly is not. I will, however, say that the other company is high technology, the highest technology, a leading technology for the new century. This is something special.

"The younger son, Edgar, holds a doctorate in medicine and a doctorate in microbiology. For several years, he has been developing what are called protein markers, which are chemical entities that permit a drug company, say, to measure whether a particular protein is present in a sample. This technology is thought to be very important in developing new medical drugs, new military defenses against chemical weapons, and perhaps other very important things. There are a number of patents with Edgar listed as the inventor, all of which appear to be assigned to this company.

"The company is named Schneider Protein Markers. It has some products in the marketplace. The products are of two kinds. One is the chemical material that does the sensing; the other is a computer device that interprets the reaction and presents a measured value. These products appear to be consistent with the products of other companies that offer similar technologies.

"The company has done so well, after many hard years of R&D, that it was poised to issue stock in what is called an initial public offering, or IPO, when the high-tech market collapsed in 2001. The company did not need investor money just to exist as it was, so Edgar withdrew the IPO and continued to run the business in its previous mode of operation. Since the company had enough cash to carry on, it stayed in business in a period when lots of start-up companies were folding. I am sure you have seen newspaper stories about such companies on the front page as well as on the financial page over the past couple of years. The biotech field did not get hit as hard as the telecommunications field, but investors got scared out of the venture market all at once.

"An IPO is a public document, since it is an offering to sell stock to the public. Schneider Protein Markers issued public information about itself the first time around, and updated the same information as recently as two months ago. In this public document is every minute detail about the financial structure and the key men and women in the company. Naturally, investors want to know the company's financial structure. Any investment in a start-up company is an investment in the key personnel, first and foremost. So, we—and anybody else who wants to bother to look—may know all there is to know about the financial structure and condition of this company.

"The strategy put forward by most lawyers who write these documents is to include everything, absolutely everything, so that they cannot be accused later of withholding information. They prefer to hide precious information in a mountain of data so that the precious information is simply buried. Well, we are not interested in precious information at this point, just the general structure, and that is certainly evident in the public reports. Glorious information, if I may be poetic.

"This company has offices and laboratories on Second Avenue, next door to the engineering company. From the financial statements and from the size of the parking lot, the company has something like 50 employees. That's a nice size for a high-tech start-up company.

"The second son, Edgar, founded the company more than 10 years ago. He started it with his own money. He had his brother Gordon do the industrial computer design and paid him in stock. His father purchased stock over the years to a total of about $15 million. These purchases were before the IPO. They were simply private investments. The price of the stock was different each year. The upshot is that, at the time of his death, Mr. Bill owned about 75 percent of the company, brother Gordon owned about six percent, and Edgar owned the balance. Edgar has been drawing a small salary to support his family, which consists of a wife and two kids, in middle-class style. So this fits a classic family business profile."

Marcy spoke up. "The story at the car company is that Mr. Bill was tickled pink about the prospects of the biotech company, and he loved to brag about how smart his two boys were to be up with the leaders in a brand new industry. If there were any recriminations about the money he put in, he hid it well. Actually, everybody thinks he loved being the biggest shareholder in a brand new company. No family tensions at all."

Sanjar took up his tale. "Mr. and Mrs. Bill owned the stock jointly. When Mrs. Bill died, all her residual estate, after her enumerated bequests, passed to Mr. Bill. There is no inheritance tax on a bequest from a wife to a husband, so there was no particular impact on the company or on the family finances.

"You might be wondering what the impact would have been if Mr. Bill had married again. The updated IPO documents do not mention any future wife by name, but they do say that if Mr. Bill were to marry again and precede his new wife in death, then the widow would have only a life interest in the stock, and the stock would pass to the two sons upon her death, to be divided three to one in favor of Edgar.

"Investors want to know these sort of details, because if a big block of stock winds up in the hands of inheritors, then control of the company might change in unanticipated ways. So a life interest for a new wife is a good means of protecting the other investors. This also means that the new wife, should she become a widow, cannot sell the stock during her lifetime, which also pleases investors.

"From what Marcy reported, the new fiancée was not in need of money to live on, so she had no particular reason to object to the life-interest terms." Sanjar looked up from his notes. "That is the end of the factual information. If I may now distinguish those facts from the next few words, which are speculation, I wish to offer the following interpretation of the facts as I see them. May I do so?"

Nan nodded in the affirmative, amazed that anyone, even Sanjar, could mine such information out of those IPO reports. Jack had considered going public at one time and had prepared some of those documents. She thought she understood what Jack did for a living until she read those reports, at which point she didn't think she understood anything at all. They were the most obscure and opaque documents she had ever seen—all gobbledygook. With some biochemistry thrown in, the IPO reports for Gordon Schneider Engineering must have been real stinkers to read. "Yes, Sanjar, I will be very pleased to hear your interpretation of these facts."

"Thank you, ma'am. I hope to be worthy of your trust.

"I see the following. Mr. Bill prospered in his car business to the point of being quite wealthy. He and his family moved to the best neighborhood and joined the gentry of our city. Mrs. Bill took up philanthropy. The sons grew up and started businesses. The engineering business did not take any serious capital investment, but the protein marker business did. It needed a lot of money for laboratory equipment, plus a lot of money to pay for R&D labor over several years. Mr. Bill sold off his stock in his car company, little by little, to fund his investment in the protein marker company. I would guess he paid for Agnes's charities out of his annual surplus.

"Then, quite unexpectedly, Agnes died. She was not elderly. She was 10 years younger than Mr. Bill, so it was extremely unlikely that she would precede him in death, particularly when he was known to be in poor health, with a recurring need to be hospitalized for treatment once or twice a year. My speculation is that they had done their estate planning on the expectation that he would go first and leave his estate to her, including the stock in the protein marker company. He might have included a few token charitable bequests, but the bulk of the estate would pass to her, which would escape any tax bite. Then, several years later, she would die and make generous bequests to her charities, and she would leave the residue of her wealth to the two sons.

"It is very difficult to find a way to get wealth to pass from generation to generation and not give up a lot of it to the government in estate taxes, which run more than 50 percent after a threshold level. The success of most trusts and other legal tricks depend on people dying in the right order. If they die in the wrong order, as was the case here, or perhaps I should say in the unlikely order, then the tax man comes to call.

"In this case, it wasn't the tax man who came to call, it was the list of charities who wanted their money from Agnes's bequests. Mr. Bill liquidated millions of dollars of his car company stock to provide the cash for those bequests. He chose to hang on to the protein marker stock, which makes sense. The car company is mature, and the stock price will not go up or down much in future years. The start-up company stock value will be much higher, 10 or 100 times higher, in just a few years, with any luck. So, he did what I would have done in the same circumstances.

"That is not to say that Mr. Bill was in tough straits. Not at all. He had his salary income from the car company, he had his real estate, and he had his protein marker stock. He remained a wealthy man. If he were to marry a rich widow that would not diminish his wealth in any way.

"The protein marker company has not needed his cash investment for the past two years. It has some revenue from product sales, and it has gotten a couple of research grants. The company is at or near breakeven cash flow. It needs new capital to fund expansion and growth, but it expects to get that from the public investor market rather than from Mr. Bill's wallet."

Sanjar paused. Nan reflected on what she had heard from the two of them. She added, mentally, what she had found in the medical record, which she was not at liberty to discuss even with her immediate staff. The medical record had showed that Mr. Bill's health deteriorated after Agnes died, and he had even refused a pacemaker that was medically indicated. That showed he was not interested in living. Many widows and widowers die within a year of having lost a spouse, so that did not clash with her understanding of how survivors behave. Then, in the past few weeks, Mr. Bill had found a new life interest and a potential fiancée, Genevieve Richards, so he decided that he wanted the pacemaker. That also fits. People want to live if they are enjoying life.

"Sanjar, do you know who the executor for Agnes and for Mr. Bill might be?" Nan asked.

"Yes, that is listed in the IPO document because the executor has control of the property, and that's important to investors. That is to say, the investor might want to know the executor for Mr. Bill's property, and the document adds the information that the same person had been executor for Agnes. The executor is the family lawyer, one Randall Pinkston, who is with the city's largest law firm, Pinkston-Graves. I think the name on the door was his father's."

Nan had seen that name in the report done by Dr. Anderson. While it was being said that the family had given permission for the autopsy of Mr. Bill, the report indicated that the permission was given by Randall Pinkston. If he was executor, that seemed to be okay. If the family had wanted to squawk about it, Dr. Anderson would at least have written that in the report.

So, thinking about the financials, Nan tried to think things through. Sanjar had been clear enough. Mr. Bill had largely liquidated his holdings in the car company, and he had liquidated a block of that stock to make good on Agnes's bequests to charities. He had a good annual income, but he had not had millions of dollars sitting around in a cookie jar or a passbook account. He had still held his real estate and maybe some other investments, and he held stock in the protein company that was likely to be worth a big pile of money in the near future and for which he had paid, over the years, several million dollars.

The sons would inherit that protein marker stock. They would have to pay the inheritance tax, which would mean coming up with a few million dollars to pay the tax man. They might have to sell off some of the company stock to pay the tax man, or maybe they can get most of what they need by selling the real estate or borrowing against future prospects. It's pretty clear that Mr. Bill did his sons no favor by dying when he did. His death was going to cost them millions in cash. Maybe he had a big life insurance policy.

"Sanjar, do you know if Mr. Bill had a big life insurance policy?"

"It is stated that he is insured by the protein marker company as a 'key man' but only to the extent of $3 million. Key man insurance is purchased by companies so they can buy the key man's stock upon death. It is quite ordinary. It is also, simply put, life insurance, and the premium depends on the risk the insurance company takes of having to pay off. Given Mr. Bill's chronic health conditions, as evidenced by his recurring hospitalizations, the premiums were so high that the company carried only that amount of insurance on him. That will not be enough to provide sufficient cash to pay the inheritance tax, although it will go in that direction."

Nan tried to guess the amounts involved. She guessed that the sons would still be a couple of million short to pay the taxes due. So, her previous conclusion that the sons would have to scramble to pay the tax man still stood.

If Mr. Bill had waited a few years to die, the federal inheritance tax rate would have gone down enough that the $3 million would have covered the tax. Not a timely death. So, Mr. Bill's sons get hit in the wallet by his death, and Genevieve Richards suffers emotionally if not financially from the death. The only one to make out is the lawyer, who gets to charge an executor's fee, but that didn't seem like a sufficient reason for any untoward action. Not that she knew of any untoward action that would have done Mr. Bill in, lying there in bed, 20 feet from the nurse and strapped to electronic heart monitors and alarms.

No motive, no means. Nada. This looks like a dry hole. She had already paged Jack to call her that evening, so she might as well ask him how EKGs work. Even if it didn't matter now, she liked to talk with Jack, just to listen to his voice, the way he talked to her. I don't know how he talks to clients, Nan thought, but he certainly charms me.

"Sanjar, you said Gordon Schneider did industrial computers. Are they different from office computers?"

"Well, industrial computers are quite a large and varied group of digital machines. First of all, they are ruggedized because they tend to be in less benign locations than on office desks. Second, many, but not all, do not use an architecture in which you put in a program CD-ROM and the computer runs any program you put in. They tend to have an architecture in which they perform exactly one set of programs, and those programs are in nonvolatile memory. There are various degrees of nonvolatility, but there are many cases in which the only way to update the program is to take out the memory chips and put new chips in. Sometimes the memory chip and the processor chip are the same chip. These are commonly slower and less exotic chips than those in office computers, and they are not changed very often, so this is an affordable solution. Loading the program in is called burning the chip, although, of course, there is no fire involved. It is done with ultraviolet rays and that sort of thing. "I am sure Mr. Mills can give you a more elegant explanation."

"Sanjar, you have told me quite enough about them. I just wanted to get the distinction. I don't want to build any in my basement. Come to think of it, Jack might have been doing that in the basement without telling me.

"Well, okay. There is no evidence of foul play, and there is no sign of a motive for foul play, at least as far as the family is concerned. I'm happy we looked, even if we didn't find anything. Thank you both for your painstaking efforts. Let's table this for the time being. If you have any notes on what you have been doing here, just put them in your pocket. No point in stirring up curiosity among others about what we are doing.

"Well done." Nan gave each a big smile, a sincere smile, to reinforce her words. Quite a remarkable little action team she found herself with. "Before we break up, Sanjar, may I ask you what other hospital projects you are working on? You have been so quick to respond to these unscheduled efforts for me, I'm getting concerned that I will be getting you in trouble elsewhere."

"Mrs. Mills, my work is quite elastic, and I try to be efficient in my assigned tasks so that I can be available for interesting opportunities, such as those you pose. There is one other potentially interesting project that, in fact, touches upon your nursing service. That is a bar code project. We have bar coding for pharmacy and for supplies, but we do not bar code patients and employees, nor do we use bar code at the point of service. Some hospitals are doing that already and we don't want to get too far behind. So there is a small pilot project getting started, but it is not far enough along to take up much of my time nor to show whether it will be beneficial if implemented full scale. Still, that is likely to be the future, so I wish to keep abreast of it."

"That does sound like the distant future. We must be the last industry to embrace bar coding to the maximum. My sister Ann is in retailing, which was one of the first industries to fully embrace bar coding. That's sounds like a good excuse to call her just to talk about everything and maybe bar coding, too."

Sanjar left, bowing and backpedaling in that peculiar way.

Nan turned to Marcy. "May I ask you something, Marcy?"

Marcy turned to face her and said, "Yes, of course. I will tell you though that we need to vacate the conference room because people want to set up for the lunchtime theater."

"Okay, we can talk while we walk. We have known each other for three whole days—well, two and a half days. When the job you now have first came open a few weeks ago, there was another applicant who had more seniority than you. She interviewed for this job and for the one in purchasing. She chose purchasing. Do you know why?"

"I don't know the answer. I do know that word was going around that you would be hard to work for, very demanding and autocratic."

"Me? Me? Who would say such things about me?"

"I did."

Nan found herself standing alone in her office, wondering what to make of that. The only thing she was sure of is that she believed Marcy when she said it. What a wondrous world she found herself in. She wondered if she would tell Jack that story, and if he would believe it. Nan wasn't quite sure she believed it herself, but she thought she probably should, true or not. Wondrous.

17

Bean Counter Session

Marcy came back with Carl Burke in tow. No teapot this time, since it was getting close to lunch time.

"Carl, thanks for coming over on short notice. I know about budgets from the bottom up because I used to do unit budgets and identify needs—down to the number of pencils—a year in advance. I now need to understand how budgets work from my level up and from my level down. Can you help me?"

"Mrs. Mills, I'll try."

"Call me Nan, Carl."

"Yes, ma'am."

Nan thought to herself that she was winning a cultural war, bringing manners back into American civilization. "Carl, what triggered my call to you was a meeting I just had with Gretchen van der Schoot. Just last week, I was in this management program in which the finance professor was saying that finance provides money to the productive parts of the organization, any organization, so that they can do their job. That sounded great. Now, in the first week on this job, I'm told by Skoots that I can't do what I want to do because her budget won't let me. So there is something missing here, and I need to understand what."

"Nan, I can tell you that both your finance professor and Skoots are right and both are wrong. I can best show you both sides with a couple of graphics." Carl extracted a CD from his pocket, removed it from its case, and popped it into the computer on her desk. Two keystrokes later, a pie chart appeared.

"Here's a pie chart of your budget, with each pie wedge being one of the categories of expense that you are responsible for. When you were doing unit budgets, you wrote down numbers for each of these categories plus some numbers that are lumped into the miscellaneous wedge."

Nan recognized the categories and saw that while one wedge was the biggest, there were half a dozen of significant size.

Carl clicked the mouse and a new pie chart appeared. He continued. "This is the same information, but this time you see only two pie wedges, one being the costs that are associated with employee head count and the other being everything else."

The head count wedge was about 90 percent of the whole pie. Well, okay, Nan thought, salary, statutory benefits, pension charges, vacation, and training are all tied to the number of employees. For a large department like nursing, 90 percent is probably right. Costs related to employment overwhelm all other costs for her kind of an operation.

Carl clicked the mouse again. A line chart appeared. In this chart, a line tracked the authorized budget for her department over the past 18 months and another line tracked the actual expense. The "actual" line ran a little below the authorized budget line. Carl watched her as she watched the chart, then he clicked again. A new line chart appeared that was similar in shape to the preceding one. The new line chart showed the authorized head count and the actual head count for the past 18 months. Based on these line charts, Nan concluded that the way the department stayed on the good side of the authorized budget is, or has been, to stay a little below the authorized head count.

"Carl, is this as obvious as it seems? Are you saying that paying attention to head count is the way to have a happy budget outcome? But don't we have to figure in the difference in cost between a senior nurse and a clerk?"

"Yes, but that's second-order. The mix you have of professionals and support personnel is more or less fixed by the nature of the work. If you have to choose between hiring two clerks or one nurse, you will make that decision on which choice supports your mission, not on the basis of dollars."

"Carl, those tracking charts show that this department is always a few kilodollars under budget because the head count is always a few heads short. Has that been a conscious decision, or in other words, did the previous administration play a game by claiming a need for more personnel than they actually needed?"

"I wouldn't say it was a game. First of all, it is hard to keep the head count up to the administrative limit because you have people who quit or retire, you have people you hire to replace the leavers but who are not on board yet. That dynamic alone almost guarantees that the actual head count will be a little lower than the limit, even if you hire people in anticipation of turnover. So this is the natural run of things.

"As for playing games, sure, there are a lot of games played. One is to ask for more than you need so that if you get ratcheted down in budget negotiations, you can get by with the reduced number. True bureaucrats do that for an additional reason: anything that doesn't get done in the next year can be blamed on the failure of higher management to approve the original budget. So that goes on. It's not the best organizational dynamic, but it does go on.

"Then there is the budget transfer game. Marcy got your office and conference room painted in a way that is much better than the standard-issue bilious green. Now she could have, with your permission, done the same thing and charged it to your budget. The cost to the hospital is the same either way. I went along with her on the budget transfer gambit because Marcy was taking a little bit of a risk that the new paint job would turn out poorly, that the video cameras wouldn't work with the new paint, or someone would raise Cain because of the nonstandard paint job. So, I didn't want it to be too easy for anyone to figure out what the extra paint job had cost. As it happens, it seems to be a very nice décor. Marcy and Sanjar showed me that the video cameras work much better, so now all the other executive offices will get this kind of a decor in the next cycle. In other words, a little bit of a game is okay, in my opinion, to support or reward some initiative. We can't have too much, though, or we would spend all the hospital's income on, say, competitive office designs. I can't say that I know where to draw the line, but I know there is a line out there someplace.

"To get back to your issue with Skoots. If the roles were reversed and you had her job and somebody came in with a new idea to try that might lead to better healthcare for our patients, then you are the kind of person who would have gotten right to work on it, leaving any budget wrinkles for me to sort out. I'm the kind of person who would have gotten out the steam iron and smoothed out the wrinkles. You are confident that if you do a good job, no one is going to get on your case for a few temporary wrinkles in the budget. Not everybody has your self-confidence.

"You have an instinctive view of the hospital's mission and the big picture. You quoted your finance professor as saying the purpose of the finance department is to get resources into the hands of the productive managers. I heard the same thing from my finance professor, and I hear the same thing from the finance managers here in this organization, and I'll bet you are surprised to hear that. I don't mean that we have unlimited resources or that money should be thrown at every nutty project that comes in over the transom. I just mean that your big picture and the finance managers' big picture are the same big picture.

"I'll add, at the risk that you think I'm tossing a little flattery your way, that not every vice president figures that out as quickly as you have. Either your instincts are those of a natural born executive, or you had one heck of a finance professor."

"Carl, there are other accountants in your department who have jobs similar to yours. Are all of them wrinkle removers, or do you have some who think they are there to protect the purity of the budgetary process?"

"Honestly, it's about half and half. I'm matched up with your department because you have the largest budget and the largest productive role in the whole organization. I didn't have to break any arms to get this assignment, but it's pretty well known that I slash tires when I don't get my way."

"You slash tires!"

"Well, I meant that as a joke. No, I don't slash tires. I don't even put salt in the sugar bowl."

"Carl, I have heard so many unbelievable things this week that, for a moment, I didn't know how to take your remark. I think I knew it was a joke, at least I hope I knew it was a joke. In any case, please don't slash any tires or put any salt in the sugar bowl. "Well, I have two matters you can help me with, both are sort of connected."

"I know about the first one, Nan, the financial analysis and training project for Maggie Kelly. Maggie and I talked briefly on the phone. We go back all the way to high school. I used to date her sister, Jiggs, at one time. They were great kids. Intense, but fun. Maggie was dating somebody else at the time. Jiggs and Maggie were in the same grade even though they weren't twins, just close together in time. I was in the same grade. Jiggs was a laugh a minute in those days."

"Carl, the personal training program for Maggie, if it works out, will be the template for all unit managers, or maybe for those unit managers who are interested, so that they will have the bigger picture. I have been a unit manager, and the picture I could see was pretty small. We need to prepare the unit managers for bigger roles, and maybe this will help. I don't want people optimizing their own little turf. I want them optimizing for the good of the whole organization. I can't be doing all the thinking for the whole enormous department.

"The other matter now has two parts, but it might eventually have more. The first item is to work with Maggie to figure out how she can hire receptionists for her clinics. She told me she used to have them, but she got beat down on head count to meet budgetary constraints. I can see from those few slides you showed me that there is no departmental reason why Maggie can't have her receptionists. Now if she can do it with volunteers or something to keep costs down, that's fine. But we need to provide what we need to provide."

"Nan, finish your list, then I can say something about how dumb decisions like that get made even in good organizations."

"Okay, I think I want to hear that, and it can wait. The other item that involves Maggie and budgets is Skoots. Skoots won't lift a finger until somebody solves her own little budget problem, and she will defend her position to the death. What do we do about that?"

"Tell me how much money you need, and if it is less than a zillion dollars, I'll take care of it. How much do you need?"

"Well, Carl, I don't know yet. What I have in mind is to do a lot more retraining of nursing service personnel. You know how airline pilots go back to the simulator every so often? Nurses participate in retraining classes for some procedures to keep up their certifications, but I'd like to provide retraining sessions for routine procedures— procedures that get botched because people get sloppy or didn't set the task up properly. Inadvertent error. It works for pilots, it might work for us.

"I see this as a personalized retraining program. If a nurse forgets to write down the blood pressure on the chart, she gets a 15-minute retraining session on why it is important, how it is to be done, and how the record gets used later on. Now every nurse knows this, but if the choice is between yelling at the nurse who forgets to do it or sending her to a nonjudgmental retraining program, then I want the option to do the retraining. Some of this retraining might just take a videotape. Some of it might take supervised work with an instructor. I don't know yet. I don't know what's available. I don't know if it will be accepted by nurses or if it will cause a revolt or mass exodus. There are probably more things I don't know. But I would like to try. Other industries do it this way with pretty good success. We need performance improvement, if you believe what you see in the papers, and if this is a good mechanism, we ought to try it. After all, we have this perfectly good training school right here under the same roof. If we can't try this kind of retraining, we are really stuck in the mud."

"So, you're saying you want to institute nonjudgmental retraining when somebody makes a goof rather than the wire brush. That would be a revolution if it were applied in the bean counter world, I'll tell you that right now.

"Nan, I told you I just spoke briefly to Maggie, just a few words to set up a more substantial meeting. We didn't talk about any particulars. I just told you I have known her since high school, so I'll tell you that she seemed to be cautiously optimistic that you mean what you say. I will just say to you, and later to Maggie when I meet with her, that I'm on your team. As John Wayne used to say, 'Just tell me which hat to wear and which window to come in.'"

Carl continued. "Since you don't have a dollar figure in mind yet for working with Skoots, I'll set up an account with $50,000, taking it from your year-to-date underrun, just to take care of things incrementally. If Maggie gets to a firm number, then she and I will get back to you so that you know what's going on. I know and understand Skoots, and I'll take care of her budgetary worries. We might want to plan a little more in for next year's cycle, and the best way to get that done is to have a few success stories to tell at budget hearing time. Incremental is always the way to go. If it's a dud, we'll bury it. If it's a winner, we'll spiff it up and tell the suits how smart they were to authorize it last year, whether or not they authorized it.

"Nan, that gets me back to the budgetary battles and how even good things can get screwed up sometimes. You know that nobody else in the executive ranks here is a professional nurse. Dr. Anderson is a physician, so he knows more than the others, but the others don't have a clue. They are good people, but they are not nursing professionals. So, they have to rely on you on all matters related to the nursing service. The only other input they have is the level of complaints from others, particularly patients and physicians. They don't know how to evaluate complaints, but they can hear them and count them. Did you ever do any horseback riding, Nan?"

"A couple of times on vacation. Nothing serious. Why do you ask that?"

"Did you saddle your own horse?"

"No, somebody else always did that for me."

"You saddle a horse by throwing the blanket on the horse's back and then the saddle. Then you reach under and grab the cinch belt, put it through the harness ring on your side, and snug it up. If you stop there, when you step up into the stirrup to mount the horse, you're going to fall on your can because while you were pulling the cinch tight, the horse was puffing out his chest and stomach to keep the cinch loose. I'd do the same if I were in the horse's place. So, once you get the cinch snugged up the first time, you put your knee in the horse's midriff to cause the horse to exhale. Then you snug it up for real."

"You're telling me that a knee to the belly is necessary to get rid of the bloat."

"You got it."

"So this Kabuki dance only works if both players know the script. Any horse that doesn't puff out his chest still gets the knee in the belly but doesn't have any air to exhale."

"Right again."

"And if the horse develops a resistance to knees in the belly, the rider winds up falling on his can."

"Indeed."

"So this is a game that straight arrows like me can't win."

"Nan, as they say at the track, winners find a way. You're a winner. You're going to have a lot of help from a good stable crew, and so far as I can speak for my finance department, you're not going to run out of hay. A full nosebag, that's my motto."

"That's an image I'll put on my refrigerator to discourage midnight snacks. Now, Carl, the particular training topic that has come to mind that would involve both Maggie and Skoots is needle sticks. That is, accidental punctures of the skin of the nurse, the patient, or even a passerby with a syringe. Nobody will dispute that needle sticks are always inadvertent, so it is a good prototype. They are not trivial, not with all the blood-borne diseases these days.

"I have not yet proposed this topic to Maggie. When I do, I may hear that she has a different topic to try first. I will accede to her choice. So, when you talk to her, you may hear needle sticks and you may not. Either way, please don't tell her that I want her to do needle sticks because she will think I'm pressuring her through you."

"Got it. I'll wait for her to name the topic. In fact, I don't need to know the topic. I just need to know what numbers to tweak in the budgets."

"Carl, this has been very informative. I appreciate your help, and I'm counting on you to get us through this. I understand that you went out of your way to get assigned to my department, which I deeply appreciate."

"Nan, I look at it this way. A guy who gets a job as an assistant football coach does so because he wants to be the head coach. Now, he can latch onto a poor head coach and hope that head coach gets fired so he can move up, or he can latch on to a good head coach so others will want to recruit him, figuring he learned some magic formula from that good head coach. I prefer that second approach because I can maybe learn something from a good head coach. I don't want to be head nurse, but I'd sort of like to be chief financial officer here or at some other hospital one of these days."

"Let me know if you need a letter of recommendation. Carl, I keep finding people here with rather odd nicknames, including Maggie and her sister Jiggs. Since I have an odd nickname myself, or at least a nickname for an odd reason, I'm curious about nicknames. In your case, I'm curious for the opposite reason. You have a straightforward given name. Did you miss out on the trend?"

"My baptismal name is George. I used to be called Curly because I had a mop of curly hair. Then my forehead started growing faster than my hair, and Curly sounded pejorative for a guy going bald, so it got rounded off to Carl. Longtime friends still call me Curly. I don't mind. It brings back memories of getting hair in my eyes."

Nan laughed and extended her hand in friendship. Carl took her hand in the same spirit, closed out his computer files, turned, and left the office.

Marcy came in to say that she had taken care of the prior assignments and she would confirm with Maggie Kelly for later on in the afternoon if that was still the plan. Nan said yes. Marcy said it was time to freshen up for the lunch theater. Nan was free to attend at any of the conference rooms being used or she could watch it on her computer screen over the data network. The biggest group looked to be forming in the auditorium, and she could go there if she wanted to. Nan decided that she didn't want to overpower the people who were doing all the work on their own initiative. Yet, she didn't want to be perceived as hiding in her office, so she said she would go to her own conference room and maybe stand against the wall. Marcy made notes on her steno pad, smiled, and left.

Nan found herself with a few minutes to stretch her arms and relax. She had never before had such control over her schedule that she could in fact refresh herself mentally and physically between meetings. She realized that this was largely due to Marcy's ability, and perhaps instinct, to space meetings out a little. Nan's organizational clout also prompted people to schedule meetings around Nan's schedule rather than their own. Still, her schedule was consistent with what her operations professor at the management course had said to the class. He said you need to have a little buffer inventory in your production line or the line would be so high-strung that management would always be in a panic. Nan knew plenty of managers who were always in a panic. But that wasn't her style. Cool and in control, with due allowances for minor upsets—that's the executive Nan, she thought. This is also the executive Nan who has two patient deaths in recent days that haven't been sorted out yet. I need to keep the heat up on both of those cases. I need to know what happened so I can take remedial action, Nan thought. I even owe the suits a written remedial plan with a draft due in 48 hours. How can I remedy what I can't identify? Maybe I need a little panic in this operation just to get things moving. Yipes!

Nan hit the intercom. "Marcy, did I ask you yet to set up a meeting with Mary Cummins, Angel Copperwaite, and their two nurse managers?" Marcy said it was booked for 3:30 that same afternoon. That gave Nan three hours to figure out what to say. Then she asked Marcy to keep an eye out for Stan Laurel and asked that the detective be sent her way if that would be convenient for him. Time to keep track of the players. She thought for a moment and then said to Marcy, "Marcy, I want you to track Willy, too." Marcy responded in the affirmative.

Nan thought about the sports analogies that Carl had used. She was used to them, since that's the way Jack and Jake and Bake talked to each other and sometimes to her as well. She had watched high school head coaches while the twins were growing up. The twins were good enough to make some teams but not good enough to be starters, let alone stars. They liked being on the teams, so she liked it along with them. The coaching dynamic she saw, though, was the opposite end of what Carl had been talking about. What she had seen was that the head coach who had good assistant coaches wound up with winning teams. After all, it was the assistants who did the work while the head coach was giving speeches to the boosters club and the town civic associations. What she saw for herself, so far, is that she had attracted some absolutely wonderful assistant coaches. Two days before, she had been thinking about the need to develop a replacement for herself as part of her responsibilities. Now she saw that she had to find higher positions in the hospital or elsewhere for these wonderful people so that she could make room for the next crop of assistant coaches. She could already see that every loss would be painful, but it was just as necessary to get them going in their careers as it was for her to nudge her twins along in the same way. That might be the smartest strategic move she could make. Maybe I need to talk about this with Jack, Nan said to herself. He's a smart guy, and besides, I like to talk with Jack.

18

Lunchtime Theater

Nan heard voices from her conference room, the usual titter one hears through a connecting door. Nan opened the connecting door to find half a dozen happy faces at the conference room table, and she found Willy bringing in a huge bag of popcorn. Willy looked to be making delivery rounds to all the announced conference rooms participating in the lunchtime theater. That reminded Nan of something, so she stepped back out, went to the other door, and asked Marcy to see if she could figure out how to keep track of Willy's whereabouts is for the afternoon and the next couple of days. Marcy nodded in the affirmative and made notes on her steno pad. Nan then remembered that she had already asked Marcy to do that. Hmmm.

Nan went back to the conference room, where she could see the video screen was up, showing live coverage from the auditorium. The auditorium stage lights went up and the house lights went down. Junebug stepped to stage center. At least Nan guessed that it was Junebug. That was confirmed when she started to speak.

Junebug was dressed in an oversized beret, monocle, military-cut white shirt with open collar, jodhpurs, and high riding boots. No whip or two-foot cigarette holder, so she had not gone entirely Hollywood. Close, though. She did have a megaphone in hand, which she put to immediate use.

"Ladies and gentlemen, I call your attention to our lunchtime theater, the best being offered today anywhere in our fine organization. This will be participative theater, and you will each have a part to play. Knowing your eagerness to play your parts, I call now for *curtain going up!"*

The curtain went up. There was no stage setting, no actors. Junebug spoke again.

"We set the scene. The year is 211 before the common era. Rome has decided to conquer Spain, which the Romans called Iberia. The place is the Senate of Rome. The audience will play the part of the Senate. Soon a Roman general will enter, stage left. At that time, we need to have marching drums to give the cadence. You folks on the right side of the aisle are the drums. You say dum, dum, dum on your cue.

"To herald the general, we need trumpets. You on the left side of the aisle are the trumpet section. You say ta-da, ta-daa with a good brassy sound on your cue.

"When the general comes in, he will say, 'Hail Senate of Rome.' You all respond, 'Hail Publius Cornelius Scipio.'

"Okay, everybody know your lines? All right. Camera. Action. Cue the drums. Cue the trumpets. Cue the general. Cue the tribune!" Junebug walked backward to exit, stage right.

The drum section dum-dum-dummed at a brisk marching pace. The trumpets were awful but enthusiastic. The general entered, stage left. The tribune entered, stage right. The general was dressed as might be expected. Brass helmet with red brush on top. Chest plate with elaborate decoration. Short skirt of the Roman Legion design. Shin protectors, long red cape, and small round shield. No sword in evidence, but it might have been covered by the red cape.

This might have been an imposing presence on stage, except that the actor playing the general was Mildred Paulson, known as Empie, who was all of four foot nine and weighed not an ounce more than 80 pounds—the tiniest adult woman Nan had ever known. Empie had worked for Nan two years before, and Nan knew her to be the perfect extrovert for this comic role. Not only was everything so big on her that it dragged on the floor, the helmet must have been stuffed with two boxes of Kleenex to keep it up high enough on her head so that she could see out. She looked like a pro football player's kid wearing daddy's helmet.

The tribune turned out to be Mopsy, who was costumed in a white robe that looked like what a senator or tribune might wear. She was made up to emphasize her dark eyes and Latin look, which made a striking effect. She was a very pretty young woman.

"Hail, Senate of Rome!" shouted Empie in a very big voice.

Junebug had come back on stage, staying on the right. She gave a big chopping motion with her right hand in the direction of the audience to cue their response.

"Hail, Publius Cornelius Scipio!"

The tribune then said, "General, we charge you to be the one who brings Iberia the blessings of our empire. Do you accept this responsibility?"

The general responded, "I hear, and I obey. I will return with my shield or on it. I go. Farewell, Senate of Rome!"

Two young women dressed in fishnet stockings and abbreviated costumes appeared, stage-right, carrying a large board with the next line for the senate to say. Junebug gave the audience its cue, and the senate shouted, "Hail and farewell, Publius Cornelius Scipio!"

The general and the tribune left the stage. After not more than three seconds of empty stage, the marquee girls were back, marching across the stage carrying a board that said, "Six years have passed."

Junebug was back. "Cue the drums. Cue the trumpets. Cue the general. Cue the tribune!"

The drums drummed and the trumpets trumpeted. The general and the tribune entered from opposite stage sides. The tribune was dressed as before. The general wore her same uniform plus a huge raccoon coat, most of which was dragging on the floor behind her. The general saluted and said, "Hail Senate of Rome. I went, I saw, I conquered."

Reading from the board that appeared, stage right, in the grasp of the two girls, the Senate replied, "Hail general of our legions!" The tribune joined in that salute.

The tribune then said, "General, why are you wearing that fur coat?"

The general responded, "Hey dude, it gets cold in *Siberia.*"

Junebug shouted through her megaphone, "Curtain!" and the curtain rang down.

The audiences in the auditorium and in the conference rooms were laughing over the play and groaning over the wordplay, and a fair amount of the popcorn was getting onto the floor. In short, people were in stitches.

The marquee girls were back with a new sign board that said, "Act Two." Junebug was back, too, saying, "The scene is the coast of France in 1805. This stage represents the deck of the HMS Victory, man-o'-war of the British fleet. The other locations, the conference rooms, are ships of the French fleet. The British commander is Admiral Nelson.

"This is an action scene, in high winds and a heavy sea. You on the right in the audience are the wind. You need to make wind noises for a heavy gale. You on the left are the heavy sea, lapping against the wooden ships. Let's hear a good lapping sound from you right now to check the audio." The audience members on the left dutifully made loud lapping noises, or what passed for lapping noises. Junebug then said, "Audio test for the wind," cueing the right. Wind noises of sorts ensued. "All right. Keep it just that way. You in the center are the ship itself, groaning against the sea and the wind. Remember, you are held together with wooden pegs, so groan a lot. Let's hear your groan." That part of the audience did its best groan. "Okay. Wait for your cue.

"Curtain! Cue the wind, cue the sea, cue the ship. Cue the admiral!"

The wind howled, the sea lapped, and the ship groaned. The curtain rose to reveal six actors, one dressed as a British admiral with cockade hat. The others were dressed in what might have been British navy costumes of that era.

The admiral said, "Signal the fleet to attack immediately."

The officer standing next to the admiral said, "Signal the fleet to attack immediately."

The rating standing next to the officer said, "Signal the fleet to attack immediately."

The Admiral said, "Make all sail."

The officer said, "Make all sail."

The rating said, "Make all sail."

The admiral said, "Make your course west by southwest."

The officer said, "Make your course west by southwest."

At this point, the admiral stepped forward and put his hand up beside his mouth as if to speak in confidence to the audience, and said, "Goodness, did I say west by southwest? I meant to say west by *northwest*. Why we would have missed the entire French fleet and I would have been just terribly embarrassed when that story got around." This was followed by a mincing step and moue, then the admiral returned to his previous position.

The admiral said, "I say, make your course west by northwest!"

The officer said, "Make your course west by northwest."

The rating said, "Make your course west by northwest."

Junebug stepped forward with her megaphone and shouted "Freeze!" The actors on stage made a dramatic display of freezing themselves into fixed positions. Junebug continued, this time addressing the video cameras. "Each of the remote conference rooms constitutes a French man-o'-war. You now go into action. You have two lines to speak, which will be on the cue cards as you now see." The marquee girls were back with new cards. "First you recognize that the English are attacking, so you shout, 'The perfidious English.' That's like saying 'Damn Yankee.' Except it's in French, so you have to make it sound like, 'Lays ahn glay pair feed!' Try that, now." Junebug gave her arm stroke to cue the remote audiences. Nan chimed in with her approximation of the desired phrase, as did the others. It sounded pretty bad, but the enthusiasm level was high. Junebug continued. "Now, you fight back with your cannons. You have fighting ships with at least 100 cannons. Fifty of them are pointing the wrong way, of course, but that's true for the British, too. You can't fire all your cannons at once, or your ship would turn over, so you have to fire them one at a time. You'll have to figure that out for yourselves, but you can handle that. All right, cue the French ships! Action on stage!"

Nan and her bunch, not exactly shouting but putting plenty of energy into it, did "Les anglais perfides" as best they could, then took spontaneous turns doing boom, boom, boom. The British actors continued as before, shouting and repeating orders, although Nan could no longer hear what they were saying. She wondered if they could hear themselves, which, she knew, was exactly the point.

After a good minute of boom, boom, boom, and howling winds, lapping seas, and groaning ships, Junebug shouted through her megaphone, "Cut. Curtain!" The curtain rang down.

The marquee girls were back with a new sign, which attenuated the laughter. The sign said, "Act Three."

Junebug shouted, "Cue the geisha."

A young woman in an elaborate geisha gown entered stage right, taking tiny, shuffling steps in her sandals. The young woman was a nurse Nan knew well. The nurse was cast against type, since she was a first-generation Congolese American, and a good sport. Very clever move, thought Nan, getting everybody involved but not conforming them to stereotypes. Marie-Jeanne Mkumbo was her name.

The geisha bowed, opened her fan, and spoke to the audience. As she did, the marquee girls were back, this time holding several boards. The boards had Marie-Jeanne's text, although the boards were facing the audience and cameras, not Marie-Jeanne.

"Wise man say, prevent the error resulting from inadvertent action.

"Design each task so that it is easier to do it right than to do it wrong.

"Make any error obvious, immediately.

"Allow any error to be corrected, immediately.

"This is called poka yoke. Honorable audience will now please say with me, 'poka yoke.'" After the audiences chimed in with "poka yoke," the geisha bowed and shuffled off stage.

Junebug hollered, "Curtain," and the curtain rang down. Junebug then strode to center stage, took off her beret, and put down the megaphone. She spoke in a pleasant but serious tone to the audience. "Ladies and gentlemen, doctors, nurses, and friends. We do a lot in our line of work on the basis of verbal orders. Usually that works, but sometimes it doesn't. Navies have been giving orders in noisy and stressful conditions for hundreds of years, and they figured out that the safest way to give orders is to say back the order as it was heard. That confirms the order is correctly received, and it makes any misunderstanding immediately obvious so that it can be corrected. Whether the error was a misstatement or a misunderstanding, the error gets noticed and corrected. We are humble enough to learn from the navies of the world or from anybody else who can give us the wisdom of their experience.

"Some of us have been considering this issue, as you can see from our little dramatic vignettes today. We ask you to consider this practice. If you and other responsible parties are game, we would like to try it out in a limited way to see if it works better than our traditional practice. Thank you for the gift of your attention."

At this point, Junebug produced from behind her back, where it must have been placed in her hand through the gap between the curtains, an enormous plumed hat straight out of Cyrano de Bergerac. She did an exaggerated deep bow, sweeping the air with her hat, and exited back through the curtain. The house lights came up. The marquee girls were still on stage, in front of the curtain, holding the board that said, poka yoke. The video link was then closed.

Nan found herself laughing to the point of tears, and she saw that everybody else in her conference room was in the same state. Popcorn was all over the place. Nan didn't know everybody in the room, so she took a few minutes to walk around and introduce herself. Then it was time for people to get back to their floors, so the group disbanded. Nan walked through the connecting door into her office. She closed the connecting door and went to her desk. A moment later, she could hear a vacuum running in the conference room. Marcy, she guessed, but then she guessed Willy. It didn't matter, other than the fact that somebody had thought the matter through and figured that popcorn was going wind up on the floor and a little sweeping up would not be amiss. Nan hoped that others had thought that far ahead, too. Potential problem analysis.

Nan had skipped the popcorn and had skipped lunch. Then she noticed a cafeteria salad on her desk, along with a linen napkin and nonplastic flatware. Linen napkins? I love this job, admitted Nan to herself. Nan sat down and worked slowly through the salad. It was pretty crisp for a cafeteria salad, and she had worked up an appetite during the morning. She had lots to think about. The session with Carl Burke was informative. She had learned the magic of macroeconomic budgeting, and she understood the saddle–horse analogy completely. Something to keep in mind for the next budget planning cycle.

The theater piece was entertaining, but that's a long way from being effective. The employees who showed up for the show were probably the most free-spirited people in the department, so they might be up for something new a long time before the rest of the department might be. She hoped that Skoots had at least watched and maybe had some popcorn. Junebug said she had invited some physicians, but that might just have been Mopsy's husband and his friends, who would not exactly be making free choices in the matter. How should she nudge this along? Junebug's final speech to the audience had been just right. So far, it's just an idea based on the experience of others, thought Nan. We can't be sure it will work for us, or be accepted by us, until we do a trial run. Maybe I should put a program in place. Maybe I should ask what Mopsy and Junebug have in mind. It may be that their skills are theatrical and not programmatic. Something to think about.

After finishing her lunch and practicing a little relaxation therapy for a couple of minutes, she went to the door and asked Marcy to come in for a planning session. Marcy followed Nan back into her office, steno pad in hand.

"Marcy, did you watch the lunchtime theater?"

"Yes, I watched it on the video link with a couple of the other secretaries down the hall. Everybody got a big kick out of it. I think we all got the message about inadvertent error and those three rules. I didn't understand the Japanese word at the end."

"That's poka yoke, the name for this method for getting rid of errors. It's a Japanese word but the word is the same in all languages, like aspirin and shampoo are the same in all languages.

"Marcy, what should we do to express our appreciation to the people who did all this theater work? They must have worked all night on it on their own time."

"You sent bouquets and letters of appreciation to Mopsy and Junebug. You sent a single flower and a note of thanks to each of the other actresses. Copies of the notes went to all line managers of the people involved. You sent a notice to all your managers asking them to view the videotape, which Willy will edit, if they didn't see the live performance. You have a draft of a letter to go to Mr. Crawford and the vice presidents on your computer desktop. The letter explains that you were taking advantage of your staff's skills to get some interest in a new management method that might help avoid inadvertent errors in the future and that you expect to test in a trial run in the coming weeks. The letter also lets them know that the videotape is available if they have a few spare moments and wish to see it. I figured they would hear about the show through the grapevine, so you might want to get your version out there first. "

Nan opened the document file and reviewed it. It looked to be about the right tone, matter-of-fact and informal, so she told Marcy to send it at her convenience. Nan was not surprised, but nonetheless relieved, that Marcy knew instinctively to let her review documents that were going to the suits. Politics, politics.

"What about follow-through? How do we get the new procedure from theater to reality?"

"Mopsy came by to show me the questionnaire that she and Junebug are sending to everybody who showed up in the audience plus a number of physicians they work with here. They want to get some feedback. They asked in the questionnaire if verbal orders are a matter of concern, if other solutions were known, and that sort of thing. The questionnaire looked pretty basic. It's a decent place to start because it might smoke out those who are going to oppose any change just because they can't stand change.

"Mopsy said that they would have the questionnaires back by tomorrow evening. They want to summarize the results and go over them with their managers. At that point, they will look to the managers, and I suppose to you, for direction. If you want them to start a pilot program, they will. If you want to assign the pilot program to a manager or project specialist, that's fine, too."

At this moment, Willy knocked on the door, which was opened, and stepped in carrying a mixed bouquet of flowers. Willy handed the card to Marcy, who opened it and handed it to Nan. The card said that the bouquet was from all her admirers in the nursing service theatrical group. So, the group would have beaten her to the punch, if Marcy hadn't been on the ball. I love this job, thought Nan.

19

Who Owns
the Machines?

Nan went to the door to speak to Marcy. "Marcy, ask Carl Burke if I have bedside EKG machines on my budget, and if so, if there is any reason why I can't move them around to suit myself. If he says I have EKG machines, send a note in my name to Claudia Benedict in the VIP suites to tell her to red-tag the three remaining EKG machines so they won't be used. Tell her to draw three or four from the storeroom or from other floors, preferably other makes. Leave the impression that I think there might be something wrong with the machines, but make it seem like routine checking, not suspicion. Do you get the idea?"

"Yes, I will call Carl first, then I will send Claudia a short note in your name. She will then call me to ask what it's all about, and I'll say I think you just want to set them aside until they can be rechecked again because there might be a defect or something. That's not too unusual around here, and we might find she has red-tagged them herself."

"You're right. You're on to a better line of thought there. Check Carl, then call Claudia and just ask if she is red-tagging the three EKG machines and if she needs any help getting replacement units. .The right outcome will have those three machines red-tagged but held in the VIP suites under her nose. If they go to the electronics shop or an outside testing service, we won't be able to see what's going on. Got it?"

"Yes, ma'am. Now, Mrs. Mills, you have the United Way kickoff meeting in 15 minutes. That will take most of an hour. You're not expected to be a speaker, you just need to show up and smile for the group photographs. Mr. Crawford invited all the vice presidents, and he is apt to count noses. After that, I'll have your other meetings lined up here."

"I understand that showing up for United Way kickoff meetings is part of the duty, so I don't mind, and I value what that organization does. It will give me time to cogitate. Does my suit look all right for a United Way kickoff meeting? Not too casual, not too stuffy?"

"You might want to change to those black shoes with the higher heel, but the suit is fine."

Nan changed her shoes, touched up her makeup, and headed up to 'suit land' for the United Way kickoff meeting.

20

United Way Meeting

Marcy proved to have been right about the shoes. This was the high-heel set. The assemblage Nan found in the chairman's conference room included the mayor, a couple of city councilmen, a couple of clergymen, some civic activists who were often featured on the local news, and a few children who, Nan supposed, represented the community served. The little boy on crutches was cute. A little girl in a Serbian, Croatian, or some such costume who must represent a dance group supported by the United Way. An Eagle Scout was there, although Nan thought that organization was on the outs with the United Way because of its exclusionary rules. That's one to stay away from, Nan figured.

Nan introduced herself and exchanged pleasantries with as many people as she could get to. Crawford and the other suits were doing the same. Nan found herself pleased to be seeing that Crawford appeared to be entirely in his element here. Alice Newcomb was there, but she was mostly talking to one woman Nan didn't know, not mixing with the invitees. Maybe she was afraid she would get sucked into talking about the recent unhappy events, which were front-page affairs in the local papers.

Crawford eventually called everybody to attention and urged people into the chairs so the program could commence. The local news channel had camera crews, and there were a few people who looked like reporters, notebooks at the ready. Crawford gave enthusiastic introductions to all the people from outside the hospital, and then he just said that his senior staff was there to support the program without making individual introductions. That was fine with Nan.

Half a dozen short speeches followed, all as predictable as the tides. Earnest people, important messages, but a shopworn presentation. Zero spontaneity. Maybe the hospital suits had tested this format and selected it as the best possible way to get money out of wallets. Or maybe they had been doing it for so many years that it just seemed sort of flat.

Mentally, Nan compared this polished, professional set of presentations to the lunchtime theater her gang had put on. Spontaneous, everybody involved, outrageous costumes and casting, a continuing flow of laughs, and a message. Now, which got the message home better, these set-piece speeches or her comedy? If a week from now she were to ask 10 people the message of each presentation, which message would have gotten the better score? Which message would have gotten a better distribution through the grapevine?

As the meeting continued, Nan thought about the Thompson baby, poor little tyke. Would the maritime practice of repeating verbal orders have saved the baby's life? Were there any better ideas out there?

Nan thought about Mr. Bill. No witnesses, no one with a motive, no benefit to anyone, including himself since he had a new love in his life, for Mr. Bill to kick the bucket. It seemed to be down to Angel's word against the EKG machine. Angel's word against a computer box. Are people going to believe the EKG machine over Angel? People might feel the machine has no malice, never gets tired, never watches television when it should be working, never does anything wrong. If this case goes to a jury in a civil or criminal trial, which will the jury believe? Which would I believe if I were in a jury on such a case?

As Crawford was wrapping up and thanking everybody for attending, Nan tuned back in to the proceedings. She didn't appear to have missed anything, she hadn't fallen off her chair, and she was still smiling the standard smile, so things seemed to be all right for the moment. People rose, and the photographers set up to take some shots of the dignitaries and some groups. Nan waited, and eventually the photographer wanted a shot of everybody present, so Nan moved along with the group and added her formal smile to those of all the others. Nan noticed that the politicians seemed to be the best at doing that toothy smile that looked just right on the television screen. It must be a practiced skill, she thought.

The group broke up, the hospital executives moved in the direction of their offices, and Nan heard "Mr. Bill" mentioned by more than one voice. Alice Newcomb came up alongside Nan as they were walking and said, "I hear you were doing amateur hour at lunch today. Are you going Hollywood?" Alice seemed to be smiling in a friendly way, but then you never know with lawyers.

"We were communicating among ourselves to expose an idea to the group, to get some feedback before actually trying it in a pilot test. Some of the nurses belong to the city's little theater group, so they did it with a dramatic flair. That little theater group is one of the beneficiaries of the United Way, as I understand it, so the timing was good."

"Lawyers all think of themselves as thespians," Alice responded. "Did you tape that for later viewing by your other shifts? If so, do you mind if I give it a look?"

Nan was now looking into Alice's eyes to see if a friend or foe was making this request. She couldn't tell. Alice had probably practiced that pose before a mirror in law school. In any case, Nan wasn't in a position to say no, so she smiled and said that a tape had been made, and if it was any good, it would be edited and given to later shifts for viewing. If Alice wanted to see the edited version, that would be fine with her since the whole idea was to get some new ideas into the nursing service. If Alice had any to contribute, she would be pleased and appreciative.

Nan wasn't quite sure what she had just said, but it had a good ring to it. Maybe she was part thespian herself. In any event, she bought some time so that she could view the tape before offering it to the executive staff.

Nan had not had any opportunity to speak to Crawford, beyond a wave of the hand from him across the room. He had registered her attendance, and she had gotten her mug in the group photo, so Nan had evidence to show if anybody questioned whether she had shown up. She had, and she could prove it.

On her way back to her office, she passed Willy, who was pushing his cart full of equipment. A carnation was pinned to his coveralls, and he was smiling grandly.

21

Stan Pays a Visit

When Nan got back to her office, she found Stan Laurel sitting in Marcy's visitor's chair, nibbling a chocolate chip cookie. Nan smiled and went into her office. Marcy followed, two steps behind, steno pad in hand.

"Stan Laurel was in the building so I asked him to come by at this time. He got here early, just in case there were any cookies left. I talked to Carl Burke about the EKG machines, and he says all the bedside equipment used by the nursing service is yours, as far as the bean counters are concerned. They are charged to your budget, and they are in your care, custody, and control. You may do with them what you will.

"I sent that note to Claudia, who called me immediately to find out what was going on, as we guessed she would. I told her, and she said that she had thought about red-tagging them, but she had only been able to scare up one spare from other floors, so she was only part-way there. She can rent them from a durable medical equipment vendor if you want to do that."

"Yes, tell her to rent enough machines so that it is extremely unlikely she will have to use those three. Tell her to red-tag them and keep them under her nose until I can get a test lined up by an independent testing lab. Did she happen to say what happened to the one that Mr. Bill was using?"

"She did. She said that she had tagged it that day, then Detective Laurel came around a couple of days later and left with it. She hasn't seen it since. She wrote down the serial number and capital tag number just in case we have to write it off. Carl Burke knows how to do that."

"Okay, Marcy, give me a minute to change my shoes, then send in Detective Laurel." A minute later, Stan Laurel came in and sat down, a pleasant and neutral smile on his face.

"Hello, Stan."

"Hello, Nan. That sounds like a vaudeville exchange, doesn't it? Speaking of which, I watched your lunchtime theater today on somebody's computer screen. I will bet you had a much bigger audience than you planned on. I thought it was pretty funny, very cleverly done. I didn't follow what it was all about, but it was entertaining. I even got some popcorn."

Nan wondered if Sanjar could figure out which computer stations had tuned in. Something to ask about. In particular, she wondered how many computers in the executive suite had been tuned in.

"Stan, I'm told that you took away the EKG machine that was attached to Mr. Bill. If you're going to keep it, I'll need to write it off and buy a replacement. It's not a big deal. I just don't know your intentions."

"We took it downtown and had an outside technical company run it through its paces and write a report. The report said it was working the way the manufacturer said it was supposed to work. The consultant also looked inside the box to see whether there were any foreign elements or bombs or anything. He said it looked the way it was supposed to look.

"Right now, the machine is in our evidence locker with a numbered tag on it. It will stay there until the district attorney releases it, which would be after any trial. So, you might as well write it off. If it's like most computer stuff, it will be completely out of date by the time you get it back."

"Okay. Is there any other movement in the Mr. Bill case?"

"None to talk about. I don't know that the case constitutes criminal negligence, but that's up to the district attorney. He's figuring on running for higher office next year, so that might mean he will want a high-profile case so he can be on the tube every evening, or it might mean that he will sink the case so he doesn't make enemies. He doesn't consult with me on such matters."

"Stan, are you running down any other cases that involve the hospital?"

"There's usually something going on. There's one case, but it has nothing to do with the Thompson baby or Mr. Bill. I can tell you about the complaint that was filed, since that's a public record. I can't go beyond that.

"The case is a drug complaint. The complainant alleges that a pharmacist, a pharmacist technician, and a nurse are involved in stealing drugs out of the drug inventories here, smuggling them out of the building, and selling them. The quantities are not large—your inventory controls are too tight for any significant heist—but they're more than what's called recreational quantities. So, if this is true, it's more than just some folks putting a pill in their pocket and taking it home to brighten, or is it to dim, a weekend. The complaint only names everybody as John Doe or Jane Doe.

"If it is going on, we will catch them. We always catch the amateurs. We catch a lot of the professionals, but not all of them, I'm sorry to say."

Nan felt a cold chill at the thought of one or her nurses, or anybody for that matter, stealing medicine, although she knew that it happened in many hospitals. She had known two nurses over her career who were drug addicts. So, she couldn't say it can't happen here. It could. She had read of doctors and pharmacists who were addicts. They had access. They had temptation. They had very little to stop them in a society that can't make up its mind whether drug addiction is a medical illness or a criminal matter.

"Stan, it troubles me to hear that this might be going on in my hospital and my service. If there is a nurse involved, we need to get him or her out of here before he or she harms a patient. I want to help that nurse, but I want to provide that help after the nurse is out of here. So, if you want any help from me or my management team, you have but to ask."

"Thanks, Nan. I don't know of any help we need right now."

"Are you around town the rest of this week, Stan?"

"Yes, so far as I know. Do you have something you want me for?"

"No, not at this moment. I just have a feeling that something is going to happen on the Mr. Bill case. I don't know what, and maybe I shouldn't even have mentioned it until there is something concrete to talk about."

"I deal in nonconcrete all day long. I'm pretty sure I'm around all week, and my pager number is on my card. Just send me a text page saying 'chocolate chip cookies,' and I'll use the siren."

Stan left on pleasant terms, and Nan saw him stop to cadge another chocolate chip cookie from Marcy.

Nan asked herself if she really thought anything was going to break in the Mr. Bill case. If so, what? She really didn't know. Feeling stumped on the Mr. Bill front, Nan asked Marcy what came next.

Marcy said that Dr. Escobar had asked if she could stop by. Dr. Escobar had indicated that she happened to be available right now if that suited Nan. Nan said that would be fine.

When Dr. Maria Escobar arrived, she went to Nan, shook her hand, and extended her congratulations to Nan on Nan's being named to her important position. They had been acquaintances for a long time, and Nan was struck by the haggard look on Dr. Escobar's face. After the usual pleasantries, Nan waited for her visitor to begin.

Dr. Escobar took a very deep breath and sighed a very heavy sigh. She sat with her hands in her lap. Finally, she began. "Nan, I've had pediatric patients die on me before. This Thompson baby, though, pulls at me from the grave. I don't know when I have been so struck right down to the soul. People tell me I look like hell, and if I do, it's a correct reading of how I feel.

"I don't know what happened. Mary Cummins is a wonderful nurse. If I needed a nurse for my family, she would be at the top of the list. I've worked with her for years and years. But something happened. I'm pretty sure I called out the right drug by name, and I know I wrote down the right drug by name. If Mary heard something else, I have to guess she misunderstood me. I feel that if I had misspoken, I would have caught myself at the time."

"I read Dr. Anderson's report, and he says that you have written and signed a statement that you gave the right order."

"I wrote that with my malpractice lawyer holding me by the wrist and moving my hand up and down. Her advice was to say what I believe to be correct. To say that there is one chance in a thousand or a million that I misspoke doesn't do any good. Of course, my lawyer said that if I knew I had misspoken, then I should say the truth. She just wouldn't let me say that I honestly think I did it right, that I have done it right a million times over my career, but this one time I might have done it wrong. I can see her point of view, and that's what I pay her for, but it doesn't help me sleep any better.

"I don't think I did it wrong. I don't think Mary Cummins did it wrong. But that baby is dead, and somehow between the two of us well-meaning and experienced professionals, we did it. I won't say it that way in court, but that's the way I feel today and how I have felt since it happened last week. I don't know if I'm going to get over it or not. I may need to close my practice and go sit in a cave for six months."

"Maria, I hope you don't do that. Talk to a therapist, but don't leave your patients behind. They need you, and they aren't blaming you for what happened. Don't you see that?"

"The patients I have seen have not talked about the case, but I get the feeling that you're correct. They may be worrying about me and what I might do to *their* kid, but they aren't blaming me."

"Maria, since it wasn't your fault and it wasn't Mary Cummins' fault, it must be the system's fault. So, we have to learn how to make the system work better. That's my job, so far as the nursing service is involved."

"I saw your lunchtime theater production. That was as close to a smile as I have come in a week. Lots of energy. I know many of those nurses, and it looked to me like they were having a great time. It also looked like they thought they have something to say about handling verbal orders. Maybe so. I've seen lots of submarine shows on television with my husband, who is a big John Wayne fan, of course. I always wondered why grown men, inches apart from each other, shout out those orders then repeat them six times. Maybe it is a throwback to sailing ships and iron men in wooden ships.

"I thought Empie was a scream in that raccoon coat, 10 sizes too big for her. She's a dear. She has so much to teach the younger nurses. I'm pleased to see her join in with them in this production. What are you going to do next?"

"Lots of ideas look red hot until they are put into practice. So, we are starting with a survey of opinions from interested parties. Then we will try to decide if a pilot program might work. What do you think?"

"I had first thought we should jump ahead with computerized physician's orders, but if I'm standing right next to the nurse, and we both have our hands on the patient, how are we going to get a computer into the mix? So I don't know. Maybe we ought to do a pilot program of one of those computer systems, too. What do you think?"

"I'm coming to understand, Maria, that as big as we are, we are too small to invent everything ourselves. We need to tap into the wisdom and experience of others every chance we get. As for computers, my husband is the biggest computer geek there is, and if he likes computers, I like computers. If we can get the John Wayne technique to work, we can do that immediately and without spending any capital money. We can then look at those computer systems over a little longer time period. They keep getting cheaper, which is in our favor."

"Nan, I want you to sign me up for every pilot program you run. If you want me to twist some arms in the physicians' lounge, just give me names. If you want me to get the professional societies lined up, say the word. I never want to see another baby die that way,

Nan. Not ever. And I want to be able to work side by side with Mary Cummins without causing her to worry about my screwing something up. Well, Nan, I've taken up a lot of your time. Thanks for talking this out with me. Count on me for whatever comes next."

They shook hands, and Dr. Maria Escobar left, looking a tiny bit less depressed. Nan hoped that she stopped for a chocolate chip cookie.

22

Gordo Appears

Marcy came in to say that Mr. Gordon Schneider had asked for an appointment, and if now would be convenient, he could be here in five minutes. Nan was surprised by this development, and she found herself pleased to have the chance to meet the elder son of Mr. Bill. Nan told Marcy she would be pleased to receive Mr. Schneider at his earliest convenience.

Well, thought Nan, whatever he has on his mind, it can't be as much of a drain as that session with Maria Escobar. That was a real downer. I don't know how shrinks listen to people's problems all day long and not need a shrink themselves. Maybe it did Maria some good, though, and maybe the next time we meet she will be her old self. I devoutly hope so.

Marcy returned to usher in a young man with an athletic look about him. He had blondish hair combed back on the sides, with one lock of hair down over his forehead—a boyish look that was quite striking. A handsome and attractive man. Bright eyes. Open look to his face. He wore a standard business suit and a fashionable tie, not at all overdone but looking well turned out. A good first impression.

Marcy announced him as Mr. Gordon Schneider. Nan rose from her chair, accepted Gordon Schneider's extended hand, and invited him to be seated. He did so.

"Mrs. Mills, I'm Gordon Schneider, son of the late Mr. Bill. I'm in the building today because I have been doing some contractor work for the hospital. I've been getting the documentation straight on the electrical and communications networks in the older parts of the complex. That's been going on for several weeks. I don't work at the hospital every day, and this is the first day this week that I've come here, so it's the first chance I've had to come by and express my congratulations to you on your being given this important position. As an engineer, I always look to see who is in charge of getting the work out the door in any organization. Here, that's you. The physicians and surgeons have something to do with it, but it's mostly up to you, or so it seems to me."

"Thank you for your kind wishes, Mr. Schneider."

"Please call me Gordo, everybody does. It's a corruption of my given name, and it's Spanish for 'fatso.' I used to be on the chubby side when I was a kid, and my father called me that. It stuck. He was a Marine, and everybody had to have a nickname. You've probably seen that if you ever watch the old war movies on television."

"Gordo, I understand you are doing this work for the hospital pro bono. That is commendable. Not many contractors do that for the hospital."

"Well, it's not exactly pro bono, I'm being paid one dollar. That sounds silly, but it is better to have a commercial relationship for liability reasons. If I do something stupid here and, say, cause a fire, my company's liability insurance will pay off if there is a commercial relationship but not if I'm here as a volunteer. I don't plan on starting any fires, but that's the reason for it. My lawyer made me do it that way.

"I understand that you're married to the famous Jack Mills."

Nan was beginning to wonder if Jack had hired a public relations firm to get the message out that he is no longer Jack Mills but rather 'the famous Jack Mills.' Either that, or maybe he actually is famous in his profession. Should I love him more or less if he really is famous? Should she just call him *Famous* for short? Famous Jack didn't have the same literary value as Famous Amos, though. Not as much of a ring to it. That's something for his PR firm to work on.

"Yes, I have that honor."

"Mrs. Mills, you say that with a twinkle in your eye, so I suppose you think it's funny that strangers come up to you and practically ask for your autograph because you're married to Jack Mills. He actually is very well known and highly respected in professional circles. Jack has made a name in software architecture for industrial computer systems. So, perhaps we will meet one day, and I will ask him directly for his autograph."

Gordon Schneider produced a boyish, closed-mouth grin that twisted up on one side and down on the other. Her twins used to do that, Nan remembered.

"Mr. Schneider, I want you to know that I'm extremely sorry for your loss of your father just a few days ago, right here in the hospital. I meant to say that first thing when you came in. I can't say that I knew him, but I certainly knew of him because of his work as chairman of the hospital's board of directors. It must have been a shock to lose him so suddenly."

"Thank you, Mrs. Mills. And please do call me Gordo. Everybody does. To me, 'Mr. Schneider' is my father, not me. And even that sounds strange to me, because everybody called him Mr. Bill. Kids in school thought that Bill was our family name.

"My father was on the hospital board, but it was really my mother's pet charity. She was big on the hospital auxiliary and on all the fund-raising committees and beautification committees. She was into some other charities, too, as well as the fine arts, such as the symphony. But the hospital was where she put most of her energy and my father's money. Not that he cared about the money. He had plenty, and he liked to indulge my mother's enthusiasms. That's why he volunteered me to do this networking study, and it's why I agreed to do it. Helping out the hospital is our family tradition.

"My brother Edgar is carrying on the tradition in his own way. He has a biotech company here in town that is going to make a splash in the medical field one of these days. His company produces protein markers. I suppose you know how that works and why people want them."

"I know the general idea—that marking proteins with a dye makes it possible to determine whether particular proteins are present or not present in a sample. Do I understand correctly in that they don't use dyes anymore and that it's all computerized?"

"Well, no, there are computers involved, but the real magic is in finding chemicals that attach to particular proteins and are thus detectable, so it is still the dye concept. I don't know if Gar calls them dyes or if there is some new buzzword. Gar is short for Edgar, of course."

"You lost your mother just a year ago. You have had your share of losses recently. You have my sympathy."

"Thank you. It was a shock to lose our mother. She was always the picture of health and vitality. She got her exercise, saw her doctor, and kept her weight down. Then suddenly she had a stroke and died, in the middle of the day at home.

"While we never talked about it, my family always expected our father to go first. He was 10 years older than our mother, and women live longer in general. Plus, he had never fully recovered from his war years. He got some kind of malaria that he, in good Marine lingo, called 'the crud.' He also took a round through the intestines and just about died in a rice paddy. The field medic stuffed him full of gauze to keep everything inside, but it was half a day before they could get him on a chopper and back to a field hospital. They sewed him up, got him over the infection, and he went back to his outfit, outside the wire, as he used to say. He was not the kind of Marine who wanted to fly a desk. He wanted to be with his squad."

The boyish look was still there, but talking about his mother and father was bringing tears to the eyes of Gordon Schneider.

"From his picture up in the conference room, I would say that you look a lot like him."

"Yes, I guess I do. My brother favors our mother more. My father grew up here in a middle-class family. He was pretty good at sports in high school. He went to a small college so he could be on the college teams. He wasn't big enough or exceptional enough to have made the teams in the Big Ten or the other big colleges. He was in the ROTC program, and after college, he qualified for an officer's commission in the Marines. It figures that he chose the Marines, doesn't it?

"Off he went to Vietnam. He lived to tell the tale, although he didn't talk all that much within the family about his war years. He came home with a chest full of medals and the crud, plus those scars on his belly.

"You probably only heard the protestors' version of Vietnam. That wasn't my father's version. He was proud to have been there. He loved every man in his unit, and I bet they loved him. Some of them died over there, and he came pretty close. He belonged to the American Legion and about six other veterans' groups. On Memorial Day, he was in the parade carrying the flag or a carbine. He figured that his generation had that war to fight, and they fought it. He didn't regret a minute of it, although he would have been happier if Ho Chi Minh had gotten the crud instead of himself.

"After he came back from Vietnam, he started a used-car lot. He had some name recognition in town, and selling used cars is mostly a matter of working really long hours and making sure you give the customer a good enough deal that he will recommend you to his neighbors. Then he married our mother, who was only 18 at the time, and the business started to take off. It was Mom's flair for publicity that started the Mr. Bill and Aunt Agnes promotion on billboards. Those billboards caught everybody's fancy. I don't know why, but they certainly did. So they opened more used-car lots around town, and they invested in a new-car dealership. When the Japanese brands were expanding, they invested in a couple of those dealerships. Over the years, they kept the Mr. Bill and Aunt Agnes promotion going. They treated people right, so they sold a lot of cars.

"Mom liked to play the socialite, but part of that was marketing, too. Getting your name in the society page for free beats buying an ad, and it sells just as many cars.

"Dad figured that selling cars was fine for his generation, but he had the notion that his sons ought to be in science, one way or another, because that was the real future. So he pushed us to take the college prep courses in high school and enroll in colleges with strong science and engineering programs. Maybe he was right. In any case, I went for engineering and Gar went for microbiology. He even got an MD and a PhD, which impresses the heck out of me and pleased Mom and Dad to no end.

"I have my own small engineering company. It's right next door, over on Second Avenue, to Gar's biotech company. Gar's company is growing like mad and is getting to have a good reputation in that field. It took a long time to get there—more than 10 years.

"Dad bankrolled Gar's company. He bankrolled my company, too, when I was getting started, although that was a smaller deal. Dad put millions into Gar's company. He sold off most of his car dealership holding-company stock to do so, and he did it with a smile. He figured that Gar's success was a lot more important than selling cars.

"You're probably thinking that there was a big sibling rivalry between Gar and me because Dad gave him more money. We fought a lot as kids, because that's what brothers do, particularly in a Marine family. But we are also each other's best friends. If Gar does well, I do well, too, because I own a good percentage of Gar's company.

"When Gar was getting started, he needed a computer system designed for protein marking. I created that system for him, and he paid me in stock. We took out a patent on the computer design, and he gave me a block of stock for that. I've updated the computer system every year or so, and he gives me more stock. I don't need cash from Gar, since my own business produces enough cash for my family, and the stock has a glimmer of a hope that it will be worth a lot more at some distant future date. Taxwise, taking the stock from an unknown company is a lot better than taking cash.

"About 10 years ago, Dad started thinking about his estate planning. He realized that he was going to die a wealthy man, and therefore the government was going to take a big bite out of what he died with. So he started giving Gar back some of his stock every year as a gift, as much as he could without paying those gift taxes. Gar had given Dad stock every time Dad had given him money for the company, which was not only fair, it avoided gift taxes at that time. Then, being more than fair to me, Dad gave me stock when he gave Gar stock, up to the gift limit again. I would have inherited it eventually anyway, so Dad was just being extra cautious in not doing anything that would cause enmity between Gar and me. I don't think anything would have, but you never know. By removing any source of enmity, Dad just made sure that we were more apt to do the right thing than the wrong thing. He explained all this to us at the time, and he had his estate lawyer tell us all over again.

"Nobody figured on Mom going first. We all figured that Dad would be the first to go, since his health wasn't so hot and he was quite a bit older than Mom. So his estate was set up to leave almost everything to her, and her will was set up to make some large bequests to her favorite charities, including the hospital. When she died first, Dad had to find the cash to honor her bequests, so he was faced with selling his car stock or his stock in Gar's company. He decided to sell his car stock, or a lot of it anyway, and hang on to the protein marker stock. Family pride, I suppose. In any case, that's the way it worked out.

"Dad was active in his car company right up to the end, and that paid him plenty. Gar and I have successful companies, and I guess it would have come to the same thing in the end."

Nan waited a minute, then asked, "Did Gar maintain his company under family ownership? I ask because my husband thinks about taking his consulting business public sometimes. He hasn't done it yet, but he might the next time he gets the urge."

"Gar's company is still held just by the immediate family. He looked at taking it public at the peak of the dot-com bubble, but by the time he got the paperwork done, the bubble had burst and you couldn't give IPO stock away with hockey tickets. Then Mom died, and he had to do all the paperwork over because that constituted a material change in ownership, since she owned Dad's stock in common with him. Now Dad is gone, and he is going to have to do it all over again.

"Gar's company doesn't need new investment to do R&D or cover marketing costs. He's in the black on his own. He can let the company grow at a steady pace just on internally generated cash flow. But, he has some employees he wants to hang on to, so he pays them stock bonuses. That stock isn't worth much to them until the company goes public. By going public, there will be a market for that stock, and the employees' stock will be worth a bundle. That's pretty common among successful startup companies. When Microsoft went public, it had billions of dollars of cash in the bank. Bill Gates didn't need a capital infusion, but he needed to make a market for the stock he had given to key employees. It's the same with Gar.

"If your husband wants to talk about that some time, I'd be happy to go through it with him, and so would Gar. That brings me back to where I started when I came in the door. I came in to ask if you would mind introducing me to your husband sometime so he and I can talk about computers, architectures, net-based computing, and all those things we've been doing all our adult lives. There are not many people like Jack Mills around."

"I've been hearing that a lot lately. He always told me the same thing, and I always believed him. However, if Jack told me the moon is made of green cheese, I'd believe that, too. Tell me something about your father's illness, if that isn't too painful a subject."

"It's not painful. He had the crud for as long as I have been alive, so I never knew him when he didn't have it. I guess it was some form of malaria because he would have nightmares and hot sweats followed by cold sweats. He took pills of some kind. The past several years he was hospitalized for maybe a week at a time about once a year.

"It might have been more than just malaria, though, because he had something with his feet. Every couple of years, his feet would develop a really awful smell, and he wouldn't be able to walk for several days. Then it would go away. He went to doctors, but I think it just went away on its own. So maybe that was part of the malaria, or maybe it was some other tropical disease. It was pretty awful, whatever it was.

"He developed a heart condition that eventually killed him. I don't know if that was from getting old or a part of the crud. It seems to me that a lot of athletes get heart conditions, although I don't know that as a scientific fact. He was a good athlete up through college, and he played a pretty decent game of golf later on.

"Dad's health went to pot after Mom died. Maybe that was just the last straw; you'd probably know more about that than I. I've read that a lot of surviving spouses just lose interest in being alive and they in turn die within the year. Is that really so?"

"Yes, it's true, mostly among the elderly. I don't consider your father to have been elderly, and he had his sons right here in town to maintain an interest in being alive."

"Well, he was in his late 60s. But with the crud, his body was probably a lot more elderly than his birth certificate says. Gar and I were close to him, but he and Mom had something special."

By this time, Gordon Schneider was very close to tears. Nan figured she should change the subject. "Gordo, will you tell me about your consulting project here? I know it has something to do with the new wing, but I haven't heard what it's all about."

"Sure. The new wing is my mother's doing. She gave a bequest to tear down that old wing and rebuild it with the latest in medical technology. Maybe she should have given the money five years earlier so it might have done her or Dad some good.

"The old wing was pretty old. It was properly built for its time, but that was before air conditioning, huge MRI machines, and electric gizmos all over the place. So, the wiring in the wing had been upgraded two or three times. When other wings were added on, the wiring was patched and so on.

Over the years, the diesel generators have increased in size and rating, and a better understanding has been developed about the reliability of electric supply. And, of course, electricity is much more important to life support systems than it was back then.

"You might think telephone wiring has remained pretty stable over the years because it carries only a tiny current and runs at a low voltage. But, in fact, telephone wiring done 40 years ago looks pretty quaint now. When the hospital added a computer network, sometimes new wiring was used and other times the old telephone wiring was patched. And now the new wing has fiber-optic cables everywhere.

"The other thing we always find when documenting old electrical and communications networks is that the old drawings and blueprints, which were drawn by hand, have all kinds of small errors in them. You surely know that they are all drawn by computers these days. You may think that's to save labor cost, but in fact a good drafter with a pencil can create a drawing as fast as a computer drafter can do it. The old-time drafters had a lot more going for them than a pencil. They had all kinds of tools, tapes with patterns, and specialized photocopying equipment. What the old-time drafters could not do was get all the little details right. The dimensions didn't add up, or there was an error in a list. These are errors that computers never make.

"Over the years as renovations were being made to the hospital, the engineering drawings and blueprints were revised again and again, sometimes with more care than other times. When the work started for the new wing, the electrical contractor found that circuits were not connected to their assigned primary sources the way they were supposed to be. They were just connected to the handiest source. That makes a difference when you try to make sure that you have two or three supply circuits for each major unit of the hospital, so that if one circuit gets shorted out, it doesn't short out all the others. So, the board decided to put up a little money for an engineering check of the power and communications circuits throughout the complex so that there will be a solid baseline for future developments. The general contractor hired some additional electricians and technicians to do the field work, and they hired me for a buck to study the results, calculate the reliability of the power and communications circuitry, and recommend a long-term plan to bring everything up to snuff."

"I notice, Gordo, that you said 'field work.' Does that mean something other than working here in the hospital?"

"'Field work' is anything that's not done in the office. In this case, work is being done not only at the hospital but also at other outside locations. For instance, on the electric supply side, the hospital buys electricity from the local power company. The hospital is a big electrical load. It would be good if the electric company fed the hospital from two different circuits rather than one. So part of the field work is to get in a power company truck and drive along the pole lines to see what the story is. Two feeder circuits to the hospital might look good at this end, but they might go back to the same transformer yard a mile away. So a transformer fire, which isn't uncommon, at that yard would wipe out both supply circuits. That's what we found. It doesn't require a panic reconstruction program, but it is something to get done over the next few years as the power company does other work in this district. As a matter of fact, I think the power company will use the new hospital wing as an excuse to reconnect its distribution circuits all the way back to their high voltage distribution grid. So, that will be a small, positive increment to the reliability of the electric power supply to the hospital.

"The issues with the communications networks are similar but more convoluted. You have telephones, cell phones, radios to public safety service centers, radios to ambulances and helicopters, and Internet networks. You also have entertainment cable television coming into your patient rooms, and one of your Internet connections is through the cable company.

"If you look at the hospital drawings, these communication lines are separate from one another. But if you go look with your eyeballs, you'll find that every telephone pole down the street has some wires for electric power, some wires for telephone, and a bundle for the television cable service. If a driver knocks down one pole, then you might lose all those lines in one swoop.

"I had another customer who had gone to great expense to get data networking from two different companies, so that he would have redundant capacity in case something went wrong. Something did go wrong. There was a fire in a manhole in a street a block from his building. He found that both his suppliers had their circuits running in the same underground conduit, and one fire wiped them both out.

"You'd think that cell telephone service would be separate from wireline telephone service, and it is, as far as the cell tower. Then the cell tower connects by wire or fiber-optic cable to the terrestrial circuits, pretty often at the nearest telephone company office. Fires in telephone company offices happen once in a while, and a fire can knock out the cell phone service, too.

"Since these services are supplied by different vendors, they don't think about commonality and single points of failure. They also swap services with each other, so just buying from two suppliers doesn't guarantee physical separation. Somebody has to get in the truck and go look. That's part of what is being done.

"I'm not spending much time in trucks myself, but I have done enough of that in the past on other projects. This time, I just got the vendors into one room, told them what we were about, and told them that they would never get on the liver transplant waiting list if they didn't cooperate. They cooperated, and I think they learned something themselves because we agreed to report back to them all that we learned. They have other customers with the same interests, so we're doing something for the community as well."

Nan said, "Someone told me that you're testing our electronics equipment, too."

"Yes, to get a planning database. The nameplate ratings on electronics equipment are fine for sizing peak capacity and for fire ratings, but in a big operation like this one where you have hundreds of electronic machines running, you need to have some information on the average current flow as well as the peak current flow. A lot of devices draw high current for a few seconds while they are warming up, then they draw a low current. Not all machines are started up the same second, so at any one time, most of the machines are drawing only a low current. Having both values allows for a better job of planning not only electric supplies but also the air conditioning system because all that current winds up as heat to be carried away by the air conditioning system.

"When Dad died, I had a terrible moment when I realized that the EKG machine he was hooked up to was one of the machines we had taken down to the test room and run for an hour to get the peak and steady-state currents. We took four EKG machines from the VIP suites, so we would have a decent statistical sample. Then we took them back. They were only off that floor for half a day. I had done those measurements myself that particular day. When Dad died, I thought that I might have screwed the EKG machine up somehow. Then I heard that the police had taken that particular machine and had some EKG specialists check it out. They found it to be in perfect working order. That was a relief, I'll tell you."

"So when you tested it, you found it to be okay?"

"Yes, but I was just doing current measurements, not functional tests. I didn't have any leads hooked up to anybody's heart, so I wouldn't have known if I had messed up the internal workings. When handling equipment, you always run the risk of creating a hidden defect. The right thing to do is to put the equipment through a complete functional test before returning it to service. I made sure this week that functional testing is part of the procedure we follow when handling all electronics.

"With an EKG machine, you'd think that would be a minimal problem because the nurse hooking it up would either see a reasonable trace on the screen or not. Still, the right procedure to follow is to perform a functional test, and that's the way it's going to be for all the rest of the equipment we test."

"I can see that that would have been a frightening moment, Gordo. What do you do with the bigger machines that you can't get on a cart?"

"The big machines have built-in current meters. We just read the dials. It would be possible to measure their current with different kinds of indirect meters, but we didn't have to since they have the built-in meters."

"Has the young man named Willy been moving these machines around for you?"

"Yes, he's a bright young man. I tried to get him interested in engineering, but he is deep into furniture refinishing, of all things. He told me he refinished your furniture while you were away at a management course." Gordon Schneider took a moment to run his hand along the edge of the small conference table and looked closely at the rest of the furniture in the room. "I would have thought this was all new furniture. He must have a pretty good touch."

"Some is new, some is old, but I can't tell the difference. He does have the touch."

"That's like my mom. She was the artistic one in our bunch. Willy told me this morning that he was going to edit the videotape of the lunchtime theater today, so I watched the theater from one of the computer stations. That was a lot more fun than any college lecture I can remember.

"I understand from those skits that you want to see if the navy system for saying back every verbal order will reduce the incidence of verbal communication errors. That seems reasonable to me. Certainly worth a try, although I guess you can't tell the doctors what to do. They might go along, and they might not. And there might be times, like in the middle of an eyeball operation, where you don't want any noise at all for fear the surgeon might twitch."

Nan nodded and said, "We have some expression of interest and support from a few doctors. We haven't gone far enough to know anything definitive yet. We are taking a survey this afternoon as a starting point. The male doctors all seem to visualize themselves as John Wayne in a submarine when the subject comes up."

"I had the same thought. 'Up periscope!'" Gordon Schneider continued, after reflecting for a moment. "That comic theater pulled me in several directions. I was hoping to see a solution to the error, whatever it was, that killed my father. I was hoping that everybody in the building was as blue as I am over the loss of my father. That's maudlin, I know. But I see that you have done what I myself have tried to do, which is to get busy with work and not dwell on unhappy events. I know you deal with life and death every day, and I know that comic relief is necessary, or more necessary, for you as it is for us civilians. And it was funny! I know it got me laughing, and that's a pretty good trick these days."

"Thank you. It came out pretty well, maybe a little longer on enthusiasm than talent, and maybe a little longer on theatrics than on content."

"No, I don't agree with that evaluation. My mom did that Aunt Agnes shtick over and over again, and people liked it. It was comedy, and it got people to think about buying a car. If you look at one of her billboards, you look at her, not at the car. So that was 99 percent entertainment, and yet it got the message across. I think your theater did the same thing. It entertained, and it got the message across. My guess is the message will stick a lot longer than if you had read an announcement over the loudspeaker system.

"Are you thinking about EKG machine errors, too?"

Nan answered, "I'm thinking about them, but I don't know what to think. The machine has been tested by experts, and they say it was working. We have never had any such difficulty with an EKG machine, and the obvious conclusion is that the machine is just fine. So something other than the machine is at fault. Human error, maybe. Maybe something we haven't thought of, yet."

A moment of silence. Gordon Schneider was sinking into deep reflection again. Nan thought she would try one more change of subject.

"Tell me, Gordo, do you have numerical goals in mind for infrastructure reliability?"

He brightened up again and replied, "Yes, eight nines—that's, 99.999999 percent uptime. In everyday terms, that's less than one second of nonperformance during a year. That's better than any one system such as the electrical supply can do. So, the hospital has the power company supply, plus its own diesel generators, plus battery backup on vital equipment. Then the circuitry has to be checked to be sure that items that are supposed to be isolated from one another are in fact isolated. Finally, you have to be sure that nobody is cross-connecting loads to separate circuits. Only then can you reach that kind of reliability. The same holds true for the communications links.

"The trick is to avoid common modes of failure and single points of failure. In other words, you need to avoid the situation in which one catastrophe can knock out two of the systems or machines at once. Like maybe one room getting flooded and that room is where all the circuits pass through."

"That sounds like something my husband talks about when I overhear him talking with his clients."

"Yes, I'm sure it is. All engineers think in those terms, although it's a lot easier to talk about than it is to achieve it."

"Did I understand from one of the newspaper reports that your father was engaged to be married?"

"Just about. He had certainly taken an interest in Genevieve Richards the past few weeks. They had known each other for years, but this spark was something new. Gar and I were happy that he was maybe getting over his depression. We had been worrying that he might just give up, or he might marry some teenager and fly off to the Caribbean. Mrs. Richards is a substantial person with her own wealth, so she isn't at all a gold digger. At least he was sufficiently interested in her that he was interested in trying a pacemaker. He had refused a pacemaker when his cardiologist recommended one last year. So, that's one more disappointment in all this—that he didn't get the pacemaker and didn't marry Mrs. Richards and have some years of comfort.

"Well, I have prevailed upon your hospitality too long, Mrs. Mills. I'll make my exit now, and I will not be tempted into a chocolate chip cookie. I'm more a macaroon fancier, myself."

Gordon Schneider stood up, smiled that boyish smile, and offered Nan his hand. She took it, thanked him for stopping by, and promised to introduce him to Jack at the first opportunity.

What should I make of that? Nan asked herself. He seemed to be sincerely troubled by the loss of both his father and mother. He seems to be settled into a comfortable life. He seems to be working here on that circuits project in part to keep himself busy. The remark he made about being frightened that he might have damaged the EKG machine seemed to be authentic to her. It was certainly human nature. Nan had fits of that sort herself with other patients who had taken a bad turn after she had done something to them or for them. He had cultivated that boyish charm, and he probably sold a lot of cars off the lot working summers during his college years.

Did he tell her anything she didn't already know? She already knew about the protein marker company. She already knew the father had sold off his car company stock to fund that company and to honor his wife's bequests after her death. She learned something about Mr. Bill's recurring malarial symptoms, or whatever tropical disease he had. It sounded like malaria plus something else with the feet. General deterioration coincident with depression was not a surprise. A recovery when the new life interest came along was no surprise either. There are strong connections between body and soul.

Did this nice young man have any reason to murder his father? No known motive, Nan thought. He had more access than his brother or his father's fiancée, since he comes into the hospital regularly. He might have gone up to the VIP wing without being noticed, given that his project takes him around the building and people are used to seeing him. Most female nurses would very likely notice him if he went by, but even they would get used to seeing him around and not think anything of it.

Did Mr. Bill have some enemy I don't know about? Some car dealer rivalry? she asked herself. So here I sit, with no motive and no known means of carrying out a murder. Anyway, Mr. Bill died of natural causes, heart failure. If any human is culpable, it looks like it's Angel Copperwaite. I truly, truly want to believe it was not Angel.

23

Sequestering the Evidence

"Marcy," said Nan into the intercom, "Please see if it is possible to have the security people post a guard next to the red-tagged EKG machines in the VIP suites. I think I would like to preserve those EKG machines just the way they are for a few days. If there is a budget issue, Carl Burke will take care of it, as you certainly know yourself."

"Yes, ma'am."

"Marcy, you are usually two steps ahead of me. Did you already do this, too?"

"No, ma'am, I didn't think of that. I understand that the machine that was attached to Mr. Bill isn't there anyway. It is downtown in the police evidence locker, from what I hear."

"Yes, that's what Stan Laurel told me, too. So that one is safe. I don't have any reason to worry about these other machines, but Marcy, I just have a feeling about this, and I want to be doing something."

"Yes ma'am. What do you want me to do?"

"Marcy, chase Willy down and see if you can find out when he took the four EKG machines from the VIP suites down to the test room, when he took them back, if he took them anyplace else, and anything else of that sort. Let's see if we can construct a time line on these machines. Then cross-check the time line with the people on duty in the VIP suites, and see if they have anything to add.

"You see, this Mr. Bill case boils down to Angel versus the EKG machine, since there are no witnesses and no other tangible evidence. So let's see if we can keep other people's hands off these machines for the time being, and let's see what we can find out about where they have been. I don't know what I'm looking for, so let's keep this low key."

"A rent-a-cop in the VIP suites is not low key."

"Put out the story that it's a bodyguard for one of the VIPs. That won't work with the staff, but it will dazzle the visitors. They'll probably want one for themselves, and maybe we can create a new revenue stream. Make sure the security department takes this seriously, so they provide backup coverage when the assigned guard takes a comfort break. You'll think of something, won't you?"

"The day shift lieutenant is somebody I can get to."

Nan thought that sounded like something out of *The Untouchables*, but she preferred to think that Marcy had something benign in mind. "Okay, you take care of it, and I will feel better."

"Yes, ma'am."

"What's next?"

"I blocked out 45 minutes for you to work on your recovery plan, which is due Friday at noon. But, I just got a call from Alice Newcomb's office. Mr. Crawford and she would be pleased if you could find time to counsel with them at 3:30 PM. That's about 10 minutes from now. She said the topic is professional decorum."

Professional decorum? I'm in favor of it, Nan thought. So far as she knew, Alice and Crawford were in favor of it. I wonder what this is all about? "Marcy, did Alice send an agenda or any background material for this meeting? Is this a topic I should be up on? Did this come up last month? Am I on a professional decorum committee without knowing it?"

"I checked the correspondence and notice files. Nothing comes up. I don't know of any such committee or team. Even if it is a select committee organized by Mr. Crawford or the board, somebody up there would have called me. So, I don't think so."

Well, Nan thought, I'll have to play this one by ear. Nan thought back over the few, but meaningful, contacts she had had with Crawford and Alice this week. The one was a blast in her direction because of the two unexplained deaths. Not enjoyable, but understandable. Then the next meeting was sort of neutral, with Crawford saying he didn't want to punish innocent mistakes when the hospital was financially liable anyway. Then the United Fund meeting, which was neutral. Now this, whatever it might be.

With Alice, Nan had first been miffed that she was playing the big-shot executive lawyer and no longer a friend. Then that seemed to warm up a little. So, Nan felt no particular reason to be concerned about Alice for the moment. Well, I have 10 minutes to spare, and how many managers can say that?

24

Dressing-Down

Nan walked briskly to the executive suite, nodding at the people she happened to meet in the hall. She knew some of them and was, apparently, known to all of them. Most exchanges were friendly, a little beyond just being polite, so that was a good omen.

Nan found Crawford waiting for her at the door of his conference room. He looked uptight and grim. So, Nan thought, I must have stepped in something. He invited her in, mostly with a nod, and stepped aside to allow her passage. Nan found Alice Newcomb seated at the small round table, with the same look on her face that Crawford had on his. Well, she knows her master, thought Nan. She knew that dogs tended to look like their masters, so maybe that applies to lawyers, too.

Crawford and Nan sat down. Crawford looked to be getting up the courage to say something distasteful, so just to be devilish, Nan spoke first. "Mr. Crawford, thank you for including me in that United Fund meeting. That's a good program, and the hospital gets some of the benefit of those collections they take in. I had never had any occasion to be in the same room as the mayor and the other dignitaries, and I envy the way you and Alice move in those circles." Nan topped that off with a pleasant smile and waited to see if she had upset Crawford's footwork. Alice appeared to be unmoved. Lawyers!

"Nan," began Crawford after inhaling a breath so deep as to have caused apoplexy, "Nan, we've got a problem. I know you're new to your position, but we have to put a cork in this bottle right now before it gets out of hand."

Nan waited to hear what is was that she had done. She kept a neutral, pleasant face. She wondered if Marcy had another change of outfits for her, just in case this got a little warm.

"Nan, we have an institution wherein the people of our community are born, where they are sustained throughout their lives, where they are comforted in their final hours, and where many of them die. They come to us at many of the most important milestones of their lives. They come on their own behalf, on behalf of their families and loved ones, and on behalf of their neighbors. We are the locus of this community."

Nan thought that to be a very nice expression of the role of a community hospital.

"It's not that these events happen in sequence. Rather, all of these events are happening every day—babies being born, illnesses being treated, surgery being performed, and people living out their last hours. It is therefore incumbent upon us to be sensitive to the fact that while some of the community are here in celebration of new life, others are here in sorrow. We express our sensitivity to their sorrow by the way we comport ourselves. That's what we call professional decorum."

Uh oh, thought Nan, now I see what's coming. She kept her face unchanged, paying polite attention to each word Crawford said. I should have Sanjar fix me up with a wire so I can record these meetings for posterity, Nan thought. I'd better be quick about it because I don't think I'm coming very close to Crawford's expectations for a head nurse.

"Nan, this comic theater business at noon today fell far below our expectations in professional decorum. Skits at some nursing convention off site might be okay. Comedy skits here, broadcast to every computer station and every video network node, making fun of the fact that verbal orders which go awry can leave people dead here, as you know they did last week—well, that was extremely poor taste.

"I'm severely and utterly dismayed by this turn of events. Just a matter of hours ago, we were talking about you putting together a recovery plan for the nursing service to get us beyond the issue of those two untimely deaths that your service was involved in last week. Then this happens. Nan, I don't know if you're with the program here or not.

"I want you to be with the program. I want the hospital to have the benefit of your skills, training, and leadership. The board and I thought you were ready for this big step up the management ladder.

Now I'm shaken by this series of events, none of which have gone in the right direction.

"Nan, I want you to ask yourself a few questions. Don't answer them now, just think about them and we can meet again on Friday afternoon. I'd suggest tomorrow, but I'm committed to be at the state capitol for meetings, and that shoots the whole day. Maybe it would be best if you have a couple of full days to consider the questions anyway."

There was a very slight pause, and Nan jumped in. "Mr. Crawford, when I was offered this position, I did something that was intended to be dramatic. I wrote a letter of resignation and left the date blank." Nan dug into her handbag to produce an envelope addressed to Mr. Philip L. Crawford, COO, followed by the hospital's formal postal address. She handed it over. "This is something I have seen in movies, and I thought it had a certain flair. I know I serve at the pleasure of the board, so I wrote an undated letter of resignation."

Crawford opened the letter and read it quickly. It was only a few lines long. Nan continued. "You may fill in the date any time you like, including right now."

Crawford said, "Now, Nan, let's not talk about resignation in the heat of the moment." Crawford put the letter back in its envelope. He did not give it back to Nan, he passed it along to Alice Newcomb. "Let me give you these questions. You can reflect on them, and we can talk Friday afternoon. Here are the questions: One, what are your goals for yourself and for the nursing service? Two, what standards of performance do you put forward as measures of your progress toward those goals? Three, what range of novelty or innovation are you willing to consider, and where do you draw the line? Here I am considering means as distinct from ends. Four, are you, today, the person for this important position in the hospital organization?"

Crawford continued. "This is a somber moment for me, Nan. I found you to be the best possible candidate for this position. I don't want to find myself to be wrong, but I'm sorely vexed at this moment."

Nan looked at Crawford for a full half-minute, then she looked briefly at Alice Newcomb, who had found something on her blank tablet to stare at. "Mr. Crawford, those are basic questions that I have asked myself. I believe it would be better to put off answering them for 48 hours, and it is good of you to give me that reprieve. Since this seems to have been triggered by the lunchtime theater event, may I ask you if you saw it yourself?"

"No, I was at a luncheon downtown. I heard about it from a number of people the moment I was back in the building. I don't know if Alice saw it."

Alice did not respond, since Crawford had not turned to her. Nan could not decide if that meant Alice had or had not watched the program. Nan could ask her, but would she believe the answer? Lawyers!

Nan spoke. "It was intended for the 50 people in my department who signed up, but we did not take any steps to limit others from viewing it. It didn't occur to me that anyone else might be interested in a nursing procedure. As for the style, I approved it beforehand, so if anyone has punishment coming, it is I and no one else. I will be ready Friday afternoon. Until then . . . Alice, Mr. Crawford, good day."

Nan stood, offered her standard nursing smile to each of them in turn, and left the conference room. She walked at a steady pace until she was out of Crawford's office complex. Then she slowed down to a funereal pace. She wanted to think. She wanted to talk with Jack, badly. Was that love, or was that an indication that she wasn't really ready to handle this job on her own? No, she knew she was ready. Three days into the job, she knew she could handle it. She could make a difference to nursing that would stand up for the ages. She liked this job, and she was going to fight to keep it. But she wasn't going to rescind that undated letter of·resignation because she did indeed serve at the pleasure of the board, which meant at the pleasure of COO Philip L. Crawford. She had to live with that. If she couldn't live with Crawford, if she couldn't win him over, she might as well go home and teach herself to knit.

Charm wasn't going to work, because she couldn't charm Alice. Alice had a lot more access to Crawford that Nan was ever going to have. If not charm, then it had to be performance. Unimpeachable performance by Friday.

25

The Four Nurses

When Nan got back to her office, she was surprised to find that Marcy was not at her desk. Nan knew that Marcy had things to do besides parking at her desk, and she appreciated the fact that she did them. Even so, it was the first time that Marcy had not been there.

Just as Nan was entering her office, she saw Marcy coming toward her from the direction of the cafeteria, pushing a cart with an oversized pitcher of iced tea, a second pitcher of ice cubes, several glasses, a small dish of lemon wedges, those small envelopes of sugar, and napkins. Only paper napkins today.

Marcy spoke as she approached. "I didn't think you would want to change with only one meeting left on the calendar today, so maybe a glass of iced tea will do. The last meeting is with Angel Copperwaite, Mary Cummings, Claudia Benedict, and Vivian Smith. I have their text page set up, and I'll just hit the mouse button here to send the page. They are on notice, and I told them you had been called up to the executive suite on short notice. I moved some other things over to tomorrow morning. Nothing urgent, from what I could tell."

Nan said, "Marcy, the iced tea is heaven-sent. I may guzzle it all down before our guests get here."

"There's more where that came from."

"While I am guzzling, would you do one other thing for me? I'd like to keep track of sightings of Gordo Schneider. Anywhere around the hospital, but in particular anywhere near the VIP suites. And if you can get estimated sightings of Gordo for the past few days, all the better. Capisce?"

"Capisco, and that's all the Italian I know. Yiddish, I can do, but not so good the Italian."

"You knew two words of Italian, I only know one. I don't know why I am thinking like an Italian today, or worse, maybe I do."

"I thought of another Italian word. Vendetta."

Nan laughed. "Okay, enough with the Italian. Where are we with the rent-a-cop for the VIP suites?"

"He's in place, he has backup and relief replacements, he has orders, and he has a modest supply of chocolate chip cookies. Coverage will continue, 24 hours a day until you say otherwise. The cover story is the buzz of that entire floor. Bodyguards have never been in the VIP suite before, so everyone is atwitter. I think Claudia figured it out, but she won't breathe a word."

Nan saw the first of her visitors coming down the hall, so she waved a greeting and added one more instruction to Marcy. "Marcy, I am expected in Mr. Crawford's office at this time on Friday. Friday is shaping up to be a red-letter day. So keep Friday afternoon open, and try to keep tomorrow, that's Thursday I think, and Friday morning open as best you can. I know you carried over items from today to tomorrow, and that's fine. Pass the word to the home team to stay on call tomorrow and Friday so that we can move quickly on some things. This would not be the week to take vacation days. If things don't develop as I think they might, I can spend the free time to write the plan to give to Alice Friday noon, and I have a little homework from Mr. Crawford to take care of by Friday afternoon, too.

"When is Willy doing the edit of the lunchtime theater?"

"He said he would have a rough cut first thing tomorrow morning. It will be on the computer network but under password control. You have access using your biometric fingerprint. Willy said he would add a musical background to the sound track over the weekend."

By this time, all four of the invitees were standing there, not wishing to interrupt and not certain whether to proceed into Nan's office or into her conference room. Nan shepherded them into her office, which was big enough for the group.

When they were seated and partaking in the iced tea, Nan began. "Mary, I've known you for eons. Angel, I have known you by sight but I don't recall that we ever talked to one another before. Claudia and Vivian, we have been talking to each other all week." Pleasant smiles all around, although all the invitees appeared to be nervous. The managers were accustomed to talking to their vice president, but the nurses were not. Although that contributed to the state of nervousness, the underlying reason was surely the deaths of Baby Thompson and Mr. Bill. This was the first senior management contact they had, if Nan put Alice Newcomb's inquisition out of her mind. So, she had to do this right, get the right message across, and get the right outcome. Whatever happened in the next few minutes, the whole nursing staff and most of the rest of the hospital would know about it by dawn.

"I want to talk about the deaths of Baby Thompson and Mr. Bill. Those deaths are on all our minds, and I want to tell you how I'm approaching this, so you'll know.

"Alice Newcomb told me that she had talked to you, Angel. Did she talk to you, too, Mary?" Mary nodded in the affirmative. "Alice probably gave you one of those you're-on-your-own statements or maybe even a letter. Let me tell you here and now that you're not on your own. Whatever happens from this hour forward, you have my full support, the support of the hospital, the support of the nursing association, and the support of anybody else we need to line up. Alice can . . . a Navy expression comes to mind, which we can perhaps leave unexpressed in the interest of professional decorum.

"As near as I can reconstruct these two cases, neither one of you did anything wrong. Mary, Maria Escobar came to see me on her own initiative to say that she doesn't understand what happened, she doesn't think you did anything wrong, and she doesn't think she herself did anything wrong. She did an affidavit saying that she gave the same verbal order as the written order because her malpractice lawyer browbeat her into doing it. I repeat, Dr. Escobar does not think you did anything wrong. Neither do I.

"Mary, I'm sure you're taking this pretty hard. If you want to transfer to a different unit, you can do that immediately with a free choice of units. Every one will be glad to have you. And Vivian will not be glad to lose you."

Nan checked body language with Vivian and Claudia, both of whom were nodding in the affirmative, emphatically.

"If you wish to stay in the pediatric unit, then what I want you to do is to be sure you work with Dr. Escobar. Vivian, I will leave it up to you to arrange that. Mary, you and Maria Escobar have shared a horrible experience, and you have a better chance of getting things going again by being mutually supportive. I know that Maria is heartbroken because she told me so. If you have seen her around, she looks a wreck. Our hospital needs her, the same as it needs you. So, Mary and Vivian, you have some action items here. Mary, if you want to see a post-trauma therapist, you're covered.

"Now, before you two respond, I want to talk to you, Angel. As near as I can understand what happened to Mr. Bill, no one has any evidence or a witness to say that anything was done wrong, certainly not by you. What we have is an unexplained death by natural causes. Any accusation against you is based on conjecture. As far as I'm concerned, you did nothing wrong at all. If somebody makes a complaint against you, then you have my support, the hospital's support, and the nursing association's support, just as Mary does, or anybody else in this department. We stand together.

"I'm willing to believe that there are nurses who do willful, malicious, even criminal acts. In those exceptional events, we get them out of here. We get them out of nursing if we can. But those cases are extremely rare, and if we never see them in our professional lives, other than on television, that's fine with me. That simply doesn't apply to these cases at hand, and that doesn't apply to the run of cases that we see year in and year out.

"We have mistakes in nursing, because we have human nurses. Those mistakes are inadvertent, and we need to learn how to reduce and even eliminate inadvertent errors. I spent the past six weeks in a management course, and that is one lesson I took to heart. It is possible to reduce inadvertent errors.

"Did any of you see the lunchtime theater today?" All four nodded. "Consider that the kickoff of my pet project for the rest of this year or however long it takes. We're going to redesign our manual tasks so that they are more apt to be done right than wrong, so that any error is immediately evident, and so that any error can be corrected on the spot.

"The theater was about verbal orders, a message that I hope came through the comedy. I don't know if the navy's way of repeating orders will work for us, but it's a candidate for a pilot program anyway. If it works, fine. If not, let's all look to see what other industry has already solved this problem and find a way to apply it to nursing services.

"Mopsy and Junebug are taking a survey this afternoon to get some instant reaction about the lunchtime theater, so we'll have some information to deal with shortly, maybe even this week.

"Reducing inadvertent errors in verbal orders is only one part of my pet project. Working in various ways with electronic equipment is another. And Maggie Kelly is looking at ways to get receptionists back into her clinics to take a little of the stress out of the patients who go there for their health needs.

"We can't do everything on our own. We have to get a lot of cooperation from physicians and maybe other departments and specialists. We can put forth our interests and our recommendations, we can fight the bureaucracy, and we can plead with others. We have to do our homework and make our case. I think we will win our share of cases and then some. Now, I have been doing all the talking. It's your turn."

Silence.

Nan spoke again. "One thing I meant to say at the beginning of the meeting but didn't is that Philip L. Crawford, our COO, emphasized to me this week that the hospital administration doesn't punish people for making inadvertent mistakes. If they happen, they happen. He's not interested in anything other than our learning to do things better, improving our system, and taking care of our patients."

Angel spoke up, with a pained voice. "Then why did he send that lawyer woman to scare the hell out of me?"

Nan looked at her evenly and replied, "That won't happen again. That is part of our system that needs some attention, and I have the ball on that one. What she said to you is not hospital policy, and I quoted Crawford to you just 10 seconds ago. Lawyers must practice in front of a mirror to learn to say things in the most hurtful way possible. I'll take care of that. You'll get a letter from her correcting her statement to you, or the hospital will get a new lawyer. Mark my word."

Mary Cummins said, "Can I have one of those letters, too?"

Nan smiled, maybe for the first time in this meeting. "Yes, Mary, and now everyone is going to want one."

Nervous laughter all around.

Vivian Smith looked at Nan, then at Mary Cummins. She put her hand lightly on Mary's forearm and said to her, "Mary, I hope that what Nan just said sounds a lot like what I told you the other day after talking to Nan myself. I want you to stay in pediatrics, but if you want a transfer, it's with my blessing as well as Nan's. I've known Maria Escobar for years, and I think she is a wonderful pediatrician. I don't want the hospital to lose her, and yet I haven't known what to say to her the past few days. Now I think I know what to say, and I'll go say it. I'm going to say that she and you and maybe me should sit down quietly real soon and work on a plan to get us back on track again. I think she wants that, and I hope you want that, too.

"I'm also going to tell her that it doesn't matter whether she misspoke or you misunderstood. What matters is that we have to change our system so that neither kind of mistake can get by us next time. We need to fix the system, not punish the people."

Mary blinked back a tear and said, "Vivian and Nan, I have loved being a pediatric nurse all my career, which seems like all my life. The past few days, I've been wondering if I can ever face a mother or a doctor or a child again. I was seriously thinking of hanging it up. Now I think that would be a mistake because it wouldn't get rid of the hurt. Now I want to get back in there, bandage up some knees, and listen to some tall tales of how those knees got skinned. I want to stand next to Dr. Escobar the next time she pokes and probes some little kid, and I want her to know that I'm paying attention when she gives orders. If we can fix the system so that verbal orders don't go awry, no matter what, then I'm all for that, too. So, Vivian, if you can set something up yet this afternoon with Maria Escobar, I'm ready to give her a big hug, have a good cry, and figure out what to do next."

Angel spoke up. "That still leaves me out on the end of the plank with a criminal complaint hanging over my head."

Nan replied, "You're not on the end of the plank. You're in the middle of a huddle, surrounded by your defenders and supporters. There was a criminal complaint against Mary, too, which was withdrawn by the Thompson family after they cooled down a little. What I know about the complaint against you is that it was filed, not by the family, but by the lawyer who is the executor for Mr. Bill's estate. He filed it to preserve his rights, which is the same as saying he filed first and will think about it later. I want to get that lifted, and I think I can do it. Even if I can't, there is no basis for any criminal action against you. There might be civil litigation because there is already a lawyer involved, but the hospital is financially responsible for you and for all of us, so don't worry about that."

"Nan," said Angel, "You tell me not to worry, and I don't want to worry, but I am worried. This case could ruin my career, and I did everything by the book. This is just awful. While I appreciate the fact that you're expressing support, and I appreciate every kind word that Claudia has said to me, I still feel awful."

Claudia figured this was the time for her to speak up, so she said, "Angel, it's okay to feel awful, just don't feel alone. All for one, that's our motto, and Nan for all. You do a fine job in our VIP unit, and I hope you'll stay with us. I know you can get a job anywhere with a phone call, but I don't want you to go, at least not until this is all put behind us." Claudia put her hand on Angel's forearm.

Nan said to herself, these are nurses with the healing touch. Let's hope it cures some wounded hearts and souls here.

After a moment, Nan said, "You all said that you saw the lunchtime theater. Did you sign up to attend? They had to scrounge to get 50 people to sign up, the way I heard it."

They all spoke at once, saying that none of them had signed up but they had all watched it on the computer network. Then Vivian said, "I didn't pay much attention to the notice because it looked like one more how-to lecture, and I've seen my share of those over the years. Then I heard through the grapevine that Junebug was going to be the director. Since it was at lunchtime anyway, I tuned it in on the computer.

"It was a scream. Empie in that raccoon coat. Marie-Jeanne in that kimono. If 10 percent of our training classes were like that, maybe some of the stuff would sink in. I got to thinking about John Wayne in a submarine. My husband takes possession of the television anytime there's a John Wayne movie on."

Claudia asked, "Are you going to do all your training programs like that? If so, we need to get a bigger auditorium."

Nan replied, "This was spontaneous. Junebug and Mopsy seized the idea and wanted to do it their way. I just tried to get out of the way. Tell me, do you think we were too jocular in those skits for a hospital setting?"

Vivian said, "Now that's fuddy-duddy thinking if I ever heard any. Laughter is the best medicine, and besides, who taught more generations how to express themselves than Will Shakespeare? He did comedies. We were not in the cancer ward, we were on closed video circuits and computer circuits. Nobody saw or heard anything who wasn't going to some effort to do so. Humbug. It was great, and I think we ought to do it a whole lot more. Get some of those bean counters and those other uptight suits up on stage in a fright wig and maybe somebody would think they're human."

All agreed. The lunchtime theater had already passed into the departmental folklore, and nothing Nan could do would blot out a single line. Not that she wanted to, she thought it was pretty great herself.

The meeting broke up, Nan shaking hands all around. Nan had given herself an action item: to get Alice Newcomb to write a new letter to Angel and Mary. I wonder how I'm going to get that done, she thought to herself.

26

Wednesday Evening
on the Phone

Nan stopped at Wal-Mart and picked up ingredients for more cherry pies. This time, she got the ingredients for the crust so that she could make the crust from scratch. If her grandmother could do it, she could do it.

At home, she made a feast of leftovers, then put on the apron, got our her recipe books, and started making the crust from scratch. How hard can this be? She made three crusts so that she could try different baking times and get some statistical data, figuring that her master's degree ought to be a big help in this undertaking. If she started with nine, she could test baking temperature, too, and have a lot of data. Well, we start with three, and then we'll see, she said to herself.

She had the crusts out of the oven and the kitchen cleaned up well before 8 o'clock, at which time the phone rang. She answered, finding Jake and Bake together on the line. That saved her the bother of figuring out which one she was talking to, because they could fool her if they wanted to.

"So, Ma, how's the new gig going?" asked one of them, Nan didn't know which.

"That's a tough question."

"No, Ma, it's never a tough question. It's the answer that's tough."

"Okay, I'll tough it out and give you an answer. It's going. On the upside, I have some delightful and effective people trying to make me look good. On the downside, we have two inexplicable patient deaths, and my nursing service may be blamed for both of them. In the short run, my boss stopped one micro-inch away from accepting my resignation this afternoon, and the chief lawyer for the hospital seems to have the soul of a spider. That's not too bad for three days on the job, is it?"

"What's the long run, if there is one?"

"In the long run, there is a thirst for better ways to do our work, to eliminate errors, and to be the best nursing unit in captivity. But the difficulty with long runs is that they are made up of short runs, and if I get fired Friday, there won't be any long run."

"We'll love you anyway, so don't take any guff from the old goat." The twins actually said that in unison, which brought Nan back memories of her childhood days with her own twin, Ann. They had done that all the time, and it wasn't until much later that they realized that not everybody said things that way.

"I love you, too, both of you," said Nan, meaning every word. "Have you found any time to go to class yet?" she asked, with only a little trepidation.

"We take turns, and nobody notices. We can tell Dad, though, that that computer stuff is out, nanotechnology is in. Biotechnology is big, too."

"I'll be sure to tell him. He's in Houston with Jick, and I expect him to call shortly. Boys, I wanted you to call so I could thank you for the flowers and your card. It was a very kind thought."

"Ma, you're welcome. We're happy for you. Besides, it was really easy to do because Marcy called us and asked what we wanted to say on the card and what kind of flowers we wanted. She claimed she could tell us apart, too, but we don't think so."

"Boys, Marcy does have powers, but I think they are not quite mystical. Thank you for calling. I love you."

"Bye Mom. We love you too. And thanks for the chocolate chip cookies."

27

Jack Calls Home

Still shaking her head after her talk with her sons, Nan fixed herself a cup of tea. At 8:30 on the dot, the phone rang. Nan picked up the handset and said, sweetly, "I love you."

"Hey, if you answer the phone like that, you'll have the happiest telemarketers in the world calling you. They won't care if you buy their vacation packages and aluminum siding or not."

"Jack, you know I can see your cell phone number right here in the caller ID display on the phone, and I'm not going to tell you how I answer the phone when it isn't you."

"Well, you're going to be putting 'hello' into the dust bin of history in a big hurry. Besides, I love you whether you answer the phone or not. So, what's up?" Jack asked.

"Where do I start? I handed in my letter of resignation today."

"Wow! You really know how to get a new job off to a rocketing start. So, are you going to join my business or are you going to learn to knit, or what?"

"It wasn't accepted. It wasn't handed back, either, and that's where I stand with the suits. The letter is without a date, so the boss can pencil in a date any time he wants to. I'm being called on the carpet Friday afternoon. I have to show just cause for why I should be kept on the job and show that I have the proper team attitude."

"Is this the mild mannered Nan Mills, whom everybody loves, who was always the model employee? Or do I have the wrong number?"

"I may be the wrong number for this job, Jack. After three days, I love it and I hate it. I think I left the mild-mannered bit behind someplace. Besides, you're the mild-mannered one."

"Being mild-mannered is easy if you're in control. I run a one-man company, so I'm in control and ever so mild when it comes to manners. Being mild-mannered in a big organization with lots of bureaucracy takes a gift. You've got that gift, Nan, you just don't have things under control yet. Hey, you haven't even been there a week. So, you're learning on the job. We all have to do that. There's no amount of schooling that tells you how to ride that bucking bronco before you get up in the saddle and the gate opens. Your gate just opened. Let it buck a little, and you'll get the hang of it. If you get thrown off, you'll have lots of people there to dust you off and get you another bronco. That job is just a job. It's not your life. So, play it for laughs, learn a lot, and if it works out, fine. If it doesn't work out, there's another bronco born every minute."

"Jack, I think you're mixing your metaphors more than usual tonight. Anyway, I want to know about EKG machines. I know what they do. I want to know how they work. I'll even tell you why. The Mr. Bill case boils down to this. Mr. Bill had a heart condition, so he was strapped to an EKG machine, which had an alarm that sounded at the nursing station if Mr. Bill's heart stopped or started to have an erratic beat. The alarm went off. The nurse went to the bed and hit him with the paddles to get the heart going again. He did not respond. The cardiac rescue team was called and did what it could, which turned out to be not enough to recover Mr. Bill. A medical investigation said his heart had gone out at least 10 minutes before he got paddled.

"Some people, including the lawyer for Mr. Bill's family and estate, think the nurse was dawdling and got to the bed 10 minutes after the alarm. There is no time stamp on anything, so it's impossible to know from that kind of independent data. So, it boils down to our nurse, whose name is Angel, against the EKG machine.

"Angel is a good nurse, and even a mediocre nurse or a poor nurse would respond to that kind of an alarm. It's like the bell in a firehouse, the bell goes off and everybody lines up to slide down the pole to get on the fire truck. No thought required. So that leaves the EKG machine. Tell me how it works."

"I know about oscilloscopes, which is the engineering version of an EKG machine. Here's how they work. There are electrical leads that connect, in your case, to the patient's body so that differences in voltage can be measured between any two connection points. I think the heart voltages are in millivolts, and that's plenty strong to be picked up, provided the leads make good connection to the body. I think you use a conductive paste to fix the lead connections to the skin.

"Inside the box, the voltages are detected by a little circuit and converted to digital values. The processor stores the values temporarily in its memory, and it generates the waveform on the display. The display is just about the same as a television or computer display, except that instead of scanning line-for-line down the screen, it draws the curve on the screen by moving the beam from left to right and up and down—the same way you would draw the trace with a pencil. But that's a detail, not an important feature. Then there are some knobs to set the size of the trace on the display screen and to set the time base for the trace. You say there was a remote alarm, so there was some logic programmed in to recognize nonnormal conditions, which I will guess amounts to loss of signal or missing high pulse, but it might be a more sophisticated analysis than that. There's probably a socket to connect the machine to a computer network for remote display, and there's probably a driver to connect the machine to a printer or a strip-chart recorder."

"You say there's a memory, like a computer memory?"

"Yes, it would have at least a small memory because I think an EKG machine can freeze the display, can't it? In that case, it would have had to store the most recent trace so it can repeat it for as long as the freeze is on."

"So there is a computer inside the box, a computer with a memory?"

"A computer, but not quite the same as the one on your desk, which is a general-purpose computer that runs any program you load into it. It's a special-purpose computer that is programmed once, at the factory, and it only runs that one program. Since the work being done by the EKG computer is trivial compared to what computers can do these days, a very cheap computer chip is used. If there is a revision to the software, you just yank out the old chip and pop in a new one."

"So if a hacker wanted to mess with the software, the hacker would have to get inside the box, pry out the old chip, make up a new one, and push in the new one. I suppose he could pry the old one out with a screwdriver, but how would he program the new one? Doesn't that take some big machine to do? And how would he figure out how to change the program?"

"Your thinking is correct, but you wouldn't use a screwdriver to lift out the old chip. There are special tools that look like a staple puller that you use to extract the old chip. As for making a new chip, that's called burning the chip, and you use a chip burner. There are chip burners for every chip maker's product. Although they aren't as common as laser printers, there are, I'd guess, thousands of them in the country for every major chip line. They are a PC attachment, and they come with software that controls the burner. That's the small-lot version. The EKG factory probably has a bigger version that burns a hundred or a thousand chips in an assembly line sort of process. These chip burners are used for a lot more products than just EKG machines. They're used to make anything from cell phones to pencil sharpeners.

"That leaves one task for your hypothetical hacker. He has to figure out what the old program was so he can mess with it. That takes some less-common software, called a disassembler, that reads the bits from the old chip and works backward to figure out what the program was. Disassemblers are a lot less common because the original programmer doesn't need one. That person knows the code since he or she wrote it. But they exist, and if you want one, I can probably find one, if you can tell me what chip is in the EKG machine. While you're at it, tell me more about what's going on. Why do you think there is a hacker, and who is your suspect? Do you think somebody croaked Mr. Bill, and if so, why?"

"I don't know what chip is in the EKG machine. Until this minute, I didn't even know there was one in there. Can somebody just look inside and read off a part number or something? Is it stamped on the outside of the box?"

"It might be in the manufacturer's literature, and in any case, you'd want to have somebody look in the box. The part number is stenciled onto the chip, and the chip will be in plain sight because it is designed to be replaced in the field."

"Okay, I'll think about how to do that. Can I do it myself?"

"Have Sanjar call me—that is, if he is included in your circle of confidants in this caper."

"He is. I'll send him a text page this evening and have him call you tonight or in the morning."

"Tonight is fine. Sanjar might never have worked with this kind of programmable controller, but he'll understand immediately what's required. Now if you want to get serious about this, we're going to need some equipment and access to the particular EKG machine."

"The particular EKG machine is locked up in the evidence locker at the police station. I'll have to think about how to handle that part. Can you find that disassembler software there in Houston?"

"Here, or on the Internet. They're commercial products. Tell me more about what's going on. Why do you think there is a hacker in the woodpile?"

"I don't have any positive evidence or clues. All the evidence is negative. First of all, I want to believe Angel, and the only factor other than Angel is that EKG machine. So, that's by process of elimination.

"That elimination works against me when it comes to finding somebody to put the black hat on. The family members inherit Mr. Bill's estate, but they don't get anything they don't already have, and they will have a big tax bill to pay. So that doesn't make any sense. There is a fiancée, but she is already rich and would have only a life-interest in the property, so that doesn't make any sense. There's the family lawyer who will get a big fee out of handling the estate, but he was probably already collecting big fees every year from Mr. Bill, so that doesn't make any sense. If there is a business rival or another enemy, I haven't found out about that person yet.

"Marcy and Sanjar did a search of the public documents, and Mr. Bill's son, Gordo, told me a lot of things that confirmed what Marcy and Sanjar had found, so I think they did a good job. I can send that to you by e-mail, if you like."

"Post it on my Web server there, and I'll pick it up in the morning. That's slightly more private than e-mail. Do you remember how to do that?"

"Yes, I've done that often enough in the past. I can do it. If I can't, I'll call you or the twins."

"Okay. Let's table that until I can gather some information from those reports and whatever Sanjar can find out in the morning.

"What happened on the baby case?"

"The baby is still dead. Everybody is still saddened by it. Nobody can find out exactly what went wrong, and the doctor and the nurse are each worried sick that they were the one who made the blunder. So we are all cogitating on how to prevent it from happening again. That's what got me fired today, or almost fired.

"We thought about verbal orders and how to make them immune to inadvertent error. We thought about John Wayne in the submarine. A couple of nurses grabbed onto the idea, checked with kith and kin, and organized some comic skits that they ran at lunchtime. They were in the auditorium, and we had video links to some conference rooms where a total of 50 people had signed up to participate. The video links are public, in the sense that anybody who is on the network can tune in. Some people tuned in and got bent out of shape because we were doing comic skits in the hospital during the lunch hour when some people in the hospital were dying of cancer or sclerosis or a brain hemorrhage. So they moaned to the COO, who had not seen the show, and he called me on the carpet with his lawyer there to be a witness."

"How many people tuned in?"

"It must have been everybody in the whole building, and maybe all the ships at sea. The video runs over the data network, so I guess it might have been seen in Timbuktu if somebody knew how to link in."

"Is there a videotape of it?"

"Yes, our man of many talents, Willy, is editing the raw footage down to a final version. Word is that he wants to add musical highlights to it over the weekend. Maybe he writes music, too."

"What else is going on, Nan? Not that that doesn't sound like enough."

"Back to the baby Thompson case. I think the nurse and the doctor are going to be able to pull themselves together again and get back into their professions. I see positive signs. I hope and pray for the best. I've bumped into some bureaucratic walls I hadn't imagined existed, and I have to learn how to navigate the bureaucracy a lot better. I have found some guides, but this is driver's training in braille.

"Jack, do you remember telling me the other day about the company you worked for writing letters to employees telling them the company was right behind them until there is any trouble and then they're on their own?"

"Yes, that's a fond memory that always gives me a warm corporate feeling."

"Well, our chief counsel didn't write that in a letter, but she told it to Angel and I think to Mary Cummins, the nurse in the Baby Thompson case. I told them both I would get the lawyer to write them a new letter by the end of this week. I don't know how I'm going to do it, but I have to try. And I had better succeed."

"Nan, lawyers don't have any position on anything. Corporate lawyers flow with the power. If they think you have the mojo, they'll do what you want. If they think somebody else has the mojo, then you're out of luck. So, get some mojo and show it off. That's all it takes."

"Thanks, I think. Jack, I have been with the lawyer three times this week already, and she has been two or three different people. You're right, she goes with the mojo. She would never cross the boss, but the way she pays attention to me depends entirely on how she reads the mojo of the moment. You have a keen insight. Maybe that's why I love you."

"Nan, I don't know why you love me or why I love you. I'm just happy it happens to be so.

"Let me tell you the short version of what I've been doing here with Jick. It's poka yoke applied to software architecture, something

I was talking to Sanjar about on Monday. The world is moving rapidly to distributed computing on lots of different computers linked by networks. Most of these will be somebody else's computer running somebody else's software, and the networks belong to somebody else, too. There are computer operating systems, network operating systems, browsers, and the applications themselves. The poka yoke connection is how to make errors obvious in this kind of system. A programmer can debug his application to start with, but he has no control over all those other elements out there.

"You've seen that even our checkbook software updates itself without asking permission, using the Internet to get the updates from the vendor's Web site. Imagine a whole slew of software doing that at any time. There is no stable, known, certified condition. It's all uncertain.

"Now, each vendor makes sure that its updates don't inadvertently introduce errors into its own software. However, the vendor doesn't stop to ask the users how they're using its software or whether its updates are screwing up other applications that the users are running. To be fair, there might be 10,000 or a million users, so the vendor couldn't possibly check with all of them.

"So here's what Jick and I are thinking, and I want to talk this over with Sanjar soon, plus a couple of other guys in the business whose opinions I respect. I think we should build in some testing that runs right along with the actual application. Periodically— maybe on every cycle—the error-checking code can run known cases to see if the right answer comes back. If not, the code can raise a red flag. And I think we will want to save up some known answers and compare each result to the known answers to see if the result seems reasonable.

"A lot of software does that internally already. For example, suppose you're filling out an online form to buy a book from a bookstore on the Internet. You're supposed to enter your telephone number in a little box. If you put in something that doesn't look like a telephone number, the software will let you know about your error. I want to apply that kind of reasonableness checking to each calculated value or database value in every networked application."

"Won't that slow everything down a lot?"

"I don't think so, but maybe. I don't think so because computers are so blistering fast that they are idle most of the time. Because the computer is so much faster than the fastest network, that idle time is going to increase in this new scheme. On the human scale, everything is very fast in a computer. On the chip scale, there is a lot of white space that can be used for other purposes, and maybe poka yoke ought to get some of that white space.

"It won't be enough to stand up at some conference and read a paper on this. I'll need to think it through in detail and figure out what might go wrong, how some bad guy might exploit it, and how to institutionalize it, if it's a good idea. But I like it. Jick likes it, but that's not an independent check, if you know what I mean."

"Yes, Jack, I know. I thought you engineering types used three or four computers side by side so that if one failed, the other computers did the work."

"Yes, that's done in airplanes, military applications, power plants, and chemical plants—situations in which the consequences of a computer failure outweigh the cost of adding a redundant computer system. That kind of an architecture is great for dealing with hardware failures, but it might surprise you to hear that it is only mediocre when it comes to software errors. Even if you have four separate teams writing programs for completely differently chip sets, if one team makes a design error, it's pretty likely that the other teams will make the same goof. It's called common mode failure. Still, if hardware failure is a critical issue, then having redundant computer systems is the right thing to do. What I'm talking about would not replace that: it would deal with a different set of issues. I'm just talking about detecting upsets in the networked computer system. What you're talking about goes further and fixes any upset on the fly by using duplicate computer setups."

"I think I see that. In any case, Jack, if you think it's a good idea, I think it's a good idea. What were you doing this evening before I so rudely interrupted?"

"I'm at Jick's house, where we just finished a family dinner with lively nieces and nephews. Everybody's fine here. I spent most of the day setting my traps so I can maybe catch some consulting business. Tomorrow, Jick is getting us a private tour of the mission control room, that room you see when there's a big shuttle launch. NASA engineers have been doing research for 30 years on man–machine interfaces, and they must know more about it in a practical way than anybody else on earth. You nursing types have a lot of computer displays these days, don't you? Maybe it has some relevance to your department."

"I'd never thought about it quite that way, but my new mode of learning is to steal ideas from everybody, even John Wayne. Give my love to Jick and family." Nan paused for a moment, and then said, "Jack, can you be back here by noon on Friday? I think things are coming to a head. No, I should tell it straight. I'm bringing things to a head. I think it has to be Friday or my mojo is going to go up in smoke, and I might as well buy a rocker and learn to knit."

There was an interlude of half a minute. Jack seemed to be figuring out how to juggle his commitments there. Then Jack said, "Nan, you are a lot more important to me than any business meetings here. My little company has too much business already, so if I miss something here, to heck with it. I'll catch a red-eye or an early-bird flight and be there by noon on Friday. I guess you want the chip business on the same schedule, and I think that can work. You want me at the hospital door by noon on Friday, is that right?"

"I love you, Jack. See you at noon at the hospital on Friday."

"To hear is to obey. I love you, too. Till Friday noon, at the hospital. You see how we're playing John Wayne in the submarine here? Maybe we can make that into an adult party game."

"Forget the adult party game. Goodbye, Jack."

"Goodbye, my love."

I love to talk with Jack, thought Nan. I love Jack. I love my job, too, I think, so I better figure out how to get the 47 balls I have up in the air to come down in a neat pyramid. And I need to find out where I can get a king-sized bottle of mojo.

Nan went to her computer station and checked kitchen supplies on the web. She needed more pie pans and a six-hole pie carrier or two three-hole pie carriers. She could probably find them in town and maybe save a buck, but who had any time? She found what she wanted on a Web site, requested overnight delivery, and gave her credit card particulars. The parcel delivery services in town had standing orders to leave any packages on the doorstep, so Nan would not have to be home to sign for delivery in the morning.

Okay, Nan said to herself, not everything is going badly, at least not yet. Some things are actually going well, and the lunchtime theater that may have gotten a vice president fired will live in hospital folklore for many years to come. I don't even hate anybody, and I admire Crawford even if he is on my case. There are a couple of people who don't do their job in a way that pleases me, so I'm going to have to get them to bend or live with a stone in my shoe. Lots of stuff to learn in this new job.

28

Laying the Snare on Thursday Morning

Nan strode into her office a few minutes before eight AM, thinking that she had adjusted to executive parking and a very nice office without any difficulties at all. She went into her office, and two steps behind her came Marcy with a pot of tea and her steno pad. I love this woman, thought Nan, even if she does send cookies to my kids at college. She's probably ironing Jack's shirts and starching his collars, too. Who was it who told me that Marcy was not the secretary for an insecure boss? They got that right. Maybe that will be my continuing test of security. She makes a good pot of tea, too.

"Marcy, good morning to you, on this our fourth day together. Doesn't it seem like a million years?"

"Good morning, Mrs. Mills, and yes, I think you have gotten off to a good start. You certainly have the best people in the department all stirred up. And people in other departments, too. It's like they had been waiting for a spark."

"Well, if our spark starts a forest fire, we'll have plenty to write in our diaries and plenty of time for diary-writing."

"I can get a job downtown any time I want. I know some people. I like working here because there's plenty going on."

Nan elected not to pursue that line of inquiry. "Okay, Marcy, what do we have on the griddle today?"

"Yes, ma'am. Maggie Kelly is first, in a few minutes, to talk about receptionists. She will be back later on with Carl Burke to talk about finances, but I don't have any details on that. There is a senior management meeting to outline the capital program planning cycle leading up to next year's capital acquisitions, and there is a vendor presentation on computerized patient records. The hospital has been looking at that computerized system for years but hasn't had the money to buy it, from what I hear. There have been some little pilot programs but not a major commitment. You don't have to attend either of those meetings, but they seemed to me to be important enough that you might want to consider them."

"I need to go to the capital planning meeting so I can learn how the system works. The other one, I don't know if I have enough depth on the technology side. I know the idea, of course, and I've been reading about them for years. Do we have a poop sheet or something on what's going to be said?"

"Yes ma'am, it came in by e-mail."

"Please send it along to Sanjar and ask him if he can attend. If he knows this stuff already, then he shouldn't waste his time. Speaking of Sanjar, I'd like to talk with him on the telephone before I meet with Maggie, if that's possible."

"Yes, he's out here raiding the cookie jar. He says they don't do cookies like that in India, and he is trying to adapt to our local culture. I'll send him in."

Sanjar came in with a cookie in one hand, showing his respect with a bow and his best wishes for the new day.

"Sanjar, I think we need to do something in the Mr. Bill case that will involve some computer work. I talked at some length about it last night to my husband, Jack. He's in Houston. He is thinking about the EKG machines, and he may need you to do some legwork here."

"I will be honored to render any assistance. Any mention of the famous Jack Mills on my résumé will be worth its weight in gold. But, if I may express my ignorance, I thought Mr. Bill's EKG machine had been impounded by the police?"

"The real one is impounded by the police, but the other three that were in the VIP suites that night have been impounded by me. I have a guard watching them. They are red-tagged to keep them out of service. If we pull one of those for examination, then that will get a lot of attention. What we need to know today is what kind of chip is inside, from what Jack told me. Do we have other machines of the same make on another floor? We have EKG machines all over the place, but I don't know how many of them match Mr. Bill's machine."

"I should be able to figure that out from the inventory records. We usually buy them in substantial quantities at a time, because it is something of a bother to have to service too many different makes. I will take care of that."

"Okay, I think you have Jack's cell phone number, so please contact him soon and follow his directions. He may want you to buy some computer equipment, a chip burner I think it is called, and if you do, get overnight delivery here to the hospital so we can use it tomorrow from noon on. Get my credit card numbers from Marcy to pay for everything."

Nan had not given Marcy her credit card numbers, but she knew that Marcy would have them filed away for some eventual emergency. And a spare set of her car keys and a house key and her shoe size. Nan was coming to realize that's just the way she wanted it.

Nan thanked Sanjar and wished him on his way. It occurred to Nan that she ought to ask about sightings of Gordo Schneider. She stepped to the door, but Marcy wasn't there. Okay, I'll check on that later, she said to herself.

As she returned to her desk, Nan found a flashing icon on her computer screen indicating an incoming video telephone call. She clicked her mouse key, the room lights went down, and the halo of lights around the computer screen came up. That's what they call a key light in the movies, I think, Nan thought to herself. Every actor and actress has a key light so that shadows won't fall on their faces. I have my own key light.

Maggie's face appeared in one of the windows on the screen. Nan's own face showed in another window.

"Good morning, Nan. I don't know how you manage to be such a glowing image on this video phone, when I look like the bride of Frankenstein."

Maggie's image was a bit off, the camera was too close to her and pointing from above, so her forehead was magnified out of proportion to the rest of her face. There were shadows on her face from the ceiling lighting, and the background was too brightly lit, giving poor contrast for her face.

Nan said, "Maggie, you look like a dream. Where are we with the receptionist caper?"

"Carl Burke and his wife Wags came over to our place last evening. Carl is an old high school buddy of my husband Cash. We were all in the same high school gang, and I don't mean like today's gangs. We were just kids together, like the old Dead End Kids or the Happy Days kids. Carl was Curly in those days. He had a mop of curls that would put Bobby Vinton to shame. He was the envy of every girl in school. Cash's name is Casmir, but he likes Cash better. I'm not sure what Wags's real name is, something on the order of Wilhelmina. So we talked about old times, and we talked about how to do the receptionist caper, as you rightly call it, so that we get the job done and don't spend all your money.

"To boil it down, what we are thinking about is hiring some of the women from the neighborhoods around the clinics. Some of them speak four or five languages, and they know the drill. A lot of them don't have work papers, and some of them are hiding from abusive husbands or boyfriends, so just putting them on the payroll doesn't do it.

"There is an agency that would hire the women to our specifications and contract them to us. I don't mean pimps, I mean a legitimate business that was set up with some help from the state employment agency. We would interview the candidates, give them the same physical exam we give volunteers, and screen out the TB cases, the addicts, and the carriers. They would serve at our pleasure. The agency would pay their FICA taxes and even a little money into an IRA pension savings account. The agency also gets them a bank account so hubby doesn't spend all the money they earn on booze. We can pay them as much as they are earning off the books in some sweatshop, maybe more. This agency says we can audit its books. Carl says he will do that himself because he doesn't want us to be involved in any shady deals.

"I know that at least one of these women was a nurse in her home country. She doesn't have papers, but maybe we can work her in as an aide and get her paperwork straightened out over time so that she can get her state license."

"Maggie, you know we need every nurse we can scrounge up, and if we get one of them in, maybe she'll know some others."

"Nan, one of them was an oculist in her home country. All kinds of interesting people out here."

"I can believe that. Okay, Maggie, are we set then on this topic? Does Carl have everything in hand?"

"He tells me he can handle it, and I haven't pressed him for details. I believe the three of us are meeting later this morning, so you can ask him in person."

"Okay, over and out."

Maggie said something of the same, and Nan closed the video link. Nan went to her door to see if Marcy was back. She was. Nan asked her to step into her office, to get away from the traffic in the hallway.

"Marcy, Maggie is in the process of having an agency hire women from local neighborhoods to be receptionists for the clinics. Carl Burke is taking care of the finances. It's departmental money but not our head count, since they are employed by the agency. Carl will audit the agency to keep it clean. I'm sure word will get around, probably distorted out of shape, so I want you to know what I know. This might not work out, but it's worth a shot."

"Having a receptionist there is a good idea. I hate it when I go to a doctor and find a clipboard instead of a human being."

"Marcy, have there been any sightings of Gordo Schneider?"

"Yes. I was just over getting the report from the security lieutenant, because I didn't want to do that on the phone. Lou, as everybody calls him, says that he posted a guard on all shifts like you said. Around supper time last evening, Gordo showed up and was surprised to see a guard there, like everybody else. Gordo talked to the nurse at the desk about nothing at all for a couple of minutes, then left.

"Around three o'clock this morning, there was a telephone call to that nursing station asking for the guard. The guard took the call, and it turned out to be some kind of wrong number or wrong person.

"The first thing this morning, Willy appeared at the VIP nursing station with his cart, with orders to take the EKG machines down to the test area. The guard politely told him no. Willy said okay and left. On his way back downstairs, Willy stopped by for a cookie and told me that he had been sent for those machines so they could be checked and that the guard had said no because of orders from you. So, he stopped by here to see what he was supposed to do."

"Who had told him to go get those machines?"

"I asked him. He said there was a note on his phone when he got in this morning. It wasn't signed, but he didn't have any reason to think anything about it. A lot of people leave him written, voice mail, and e-mail notes, since he is the lowest ranking gofer in the whole establishment.

"I told him that those machines were being held for the time being and that we would tell him when they are released. In the meantime, he should not hold his breath. He took a cookie and left, heading back downstairs to get his next batch of orders."

"So, do Willy's story and the guard's story jibe?"

"Yes, they do."

"Okay. Let's keep up the Gordo watch and see what happens. Marcy, get us a large conference room for tomorrow, starting at noon. We'll need a table that we can do some computer work on and some chairs set up in classroom style. Maybe two dozen chairs. Anybody else can stand. Get Stan Laurel here, and have Willy and the guard move those three EKG machines to that room at noon or a little later, maybe half-past. Put out the word to the people who are involved in the Mr. Bill matter that they may want to join in. It's optional, of course. Then tell the department managers that I'm having a meeting on the Mr. Bill matter and any of them who are interested are welcome if they have some free time. If anybody else asks, tell them it is for senior management only, but all senior managers are welcome, since there are no secrets in our department. Sanjar will be involved with the computer equipment. He may need to buy some equipment, and I told him to check with you to get my credit card numbers for the purchases. Deliveries will be made here to the hospital, but we don't want them marooned on the receiving dock, so that may take some attention.

"We'll also need Lou, the lieutenant, and our new friend Gordo Schneider. One other thing. I want open admissions to this meeting, but I don't want anybody watching over the video links or computer networks. Can you arrange to kill the video links?"

"If I can't, Sanjar can. Executive meetings are set up that way, so we should be able to do the same thing."

"Please make all this happen, Marcy."

"Yes ma'am. I'll check the large conference rooms and boot somebody out of our training room if I have to. The conference room upstairs is usually open, because most people are afraid to ask to use that one. There is a way to handle express shipments at the receiving dock, and I'll take care of that. Sanjar doesn't mind when I help him, not like some men who can't stand to have anybody help them. Some women, too, I suppose.

"Mrs. Mills, forgive me, but I believe you have a position paper due to be delivered to Alice Newcomb by noon tomorrow. You have about half an hour before that capital budget meeting if you would like to work on that now."

Nan thought that learning to bug the boss must be the most delicate task a secretary or an administrative assistant ever has to learn how to do. Marcy did it pretty well and earned a smile from Nan.

"Yes, in fact I now have three things to write before tomorrow noon, one for Mr. Crawford, one for Alice, and the one you mention, which is to be reviewed by Alice before going into the departmental newsletter. None of them is very long, but I need to get each word right. Make each word tell, as my college prof used to say. I'm going to make each word tell."

Nan went back in her office and picked up a pencil with a nice point on it and a tablet of yellow paper. To work! She knew what she wanted to say in all three cases, and she needed to think through the sequence of events for what she had planned for tomorrow.

29

The Capital Budget Meeting

All the suits turned out for the first meeting of the capital planning cycle. Nan took a seat close enough to the front to let people know she thought this was an important topic but not so close that she was apt to be called on to comment on the odd thing here and there. She looked around for Carl Burke, just out of curiosity, without finding him. She saw two or three people who worked in the same group as did Carl, so that department was amply covered.

There was the now-standard PowerPoint slide show giving the past five years and the next five years. Millions of dollars. The hospital was a big operation, and it had perpetual needs to grow and to upgrade. Every year, some part of the building needed to be remodeled and modernized, and that would go on forever. The new Aunt Agnes wing took a lot of dollars for steel and concrete, and it took more dollars for furniture, electronics, beds, computers, and such. Big bucks.

Some of the equipment would be purchased on Nan's say-so, and she supposed she was free to kibitz on everything else. But she was attending this meeting just to get a feel for the whole process. How did the suits decide what to spend capital money on? They could hardly decide for themselves, and they therefore had to put a lot of trust in their professional service people, the chief medical officer, and herself. They could go see what other hospitals are doing, and they probably will, just to get a free lunch. But at the end of the day, they were managing something they couldn't possibly understand in any detail.

Nan thought, then, that the same applied to her. She had been an expert on the nursing done in her unit when she was a unit manager. Now, while all her department was involved in nursing, there were too many specialties, and Nan had to trust her unit managers on the details, even details that entailed million-dollar decisions. Nan felt comfortable with that, at the moment. But, 10 years from now, when technology will have changed every detail of how the work gets done and new specialties will have sprung up, how will she handle that? Nan could see that she had better learn how these suits cope with these mysteries, so she can do it herself sooner or later.

The speaker was showing a time line for the next several months. The time line showed the due dates for submissions and drafts, review periods, outside review periods, milestones, and board review dates. So it looked to Nan that the method is to draft, review, critique, redraft, re-review, recomment, and eventually converge on one version. How much time would we save by just writing down the final answer? Yet, she answered herself, that's the whole point, no single person knows the final answer, so they need to get a lot of input and review. They were probably also figuring on putting a knee in the gut, to use Carl's apt analogy of saddling a horse, to get the bloat out at the end of the process.

Adding up all the requests would surely give a completely useless and wildly expensive total. So, they would need to get the bloat out, and even then they might have to put off some expenditures for later years. She would need to be sensitive to that, because the items most tempting to put off were probably the capital equipment she will need to keep the nursing service up to date.

Very interesting stuff, Nan thought. There's something to learn here. This iterative process seems likely to grind everything down to a common denominator, making it a bland product with nothing very clever in it. She'd better make sure she has a little capital money in a cigar box to sponsor a few innovative projects each year. Carl Burke can probably tell her how to do that.

Nan made a mental note to ask Carl Burke if there was somebody in the bean counter corps who was charged with looking out for her interests in the capital planning process. If not, she had better create one. Otherwise, she knew whose gut was going to get the knee.

30

Thursday Morning Meeting with Maggie and Carl

The planning meeting broke up, and the presenters were thanked effusively for their efforts, which did indeed seem substantial to Nan. The people all spoke earnestly to each other about the importance of the capital planning process, and then they disbanded.

Nan returned to her office, smiling and nodding to people she happened to meet along the way. No one appeared to be scurrying to stay out of her path. Yet.

Nan found Maggie Kelly and Carl Burke waiting for her on Marcy's visitors chairs. Nan smiled in their direction, went into her office, counted to two while waiting for Marcy to follow her in, and turned to see what Marcy might have to report.

"Mrs. Mills, I understand that Sanjar has been in contact with your husband on the computer matter and will be ordering some equipment for overnight delivery. He is also organizing some computers here, but I don't know what exactly he is doing with them. I had Sanjar check out our training room. He says it will do quite well for Mr. Mills's purposes because it is set up with ceiling cameras over the frog table and a big projection screen so that the audience can see what's being done on that table.* The room has chairs for 50 people. We can take some out if you want."

"No, 50 will be more than we need, but don't bother taking them out."

---

*So-called in memory of the days when frogs were dissected thereon.

"Okay. There's an audio system and plenty of computer network and power connections right there at the frog table. The training room isn't set up like the auditorium, with stage lights separate from house lights, so every part of the room has about the same light intensity."

Nan thought for a minute and responded, "That's probably good. Anything else?"

"Other things are going along. No sightings of Mr. Schneider yet this morning, but his office accepted my call. His secretary said that she was sure he would attend your meeting tomorrow and invite his brother, Edgar. She will confirm that with me this afternoon. Also, Sanjar tells me that he saw the technical version of that vendor presentation on the electronic patients records. He says he prays you hold him excused from attending that meeting. He'll go if you tell him to, but he's just excited about working with Mr. Mills."

"Okay, let Sanjar go ahead with what he's doing and send in Maggie and Carl, if you please."

Marcy went out, and Maggie and Carl came in. "Good morning, Carl. Good morning again, Maggie. Tell me where we are."

Maggie had shed the frazzled look. She had fixed her hair a little differently, and she was dressed in a skirted business suit rather than the clinic smock. But the big difference seemed to be in her whole being. She looked like she was playing the world dead even. So, maybe there's something in this young woman that marks her for better things. I'd better groom a lot of managers, thought Nan, because I won't be able to keep them all.

Maggie began. "Carl is laying out a financial program for me, drawing from the hospital's general business presentations that are done for the board. Carl will create some homework so that I can manipulate the numbers and see how things work together. Carl has a business model on a spreadsheet, so you can change one item and see the ripples. I don't know how long it's going to take for the model to soak in, but Carl says he can stand it as long as I can. I think he likes to show off how much he knows." With this, Maggie gave Carl a friendly smile and a jab with the elbow. Carl took it in good part. "Then we will start on the clinics as a pretend business unit. Carl says he can work up a model on a spreadsheet using the real numbers by the time I'm ready for that."

Nan thought that to be pretty good progress for one day. She asked, "Carl, do you think that this has prospects for being a training course for all the managers on Maggie's level, eventually?"

"Yes, I think some of it can be carried over. My experience with this kind of model training is that the first iteration of the training plan looks good until you try it, then you find out everything that's wrong with it. We do this kind of model training for new people in our department because most accounting types have never thought about how a not-for-profit company operates. But I think we can get what you want in two iterations.

"Maggie's group has some characteristics of free-standing business. Some other units really don't, so that's going to take some thought. I understand you want to have unit specificity so that managers will naturally want to dig in, rather than some general blather that doesn't hit home."

"Yes, that would be ideal. However, if we fall a little short, I don't think that will be the end of the world. But let's not give up the goal until we give it a try."

"Maggie doesn't have any particular accounting background, and I don't suppose most of the other managers do either, so I'm digging up some general-introduction self-paced training material that I found a while back. It helps get through the jargon and the basics. Accounting isn't complicated once you get past the mumbo jumbo we use to keep everybody confused."

Nan asked, "Maggie, is this going to fit with what we talked about the other day?"

"Yes, I sort of like being the pioneer woman, and if I can figure this out, so can the others. Considering how busy everybody is, I like the self-paced idea. I'm sure it will be more work for Carl, but that might do him some good. It might even make his hair grow back so we can call him Curly again."

Knowing how sensitive some men are about baldness, Nan was relieved to see that Carl thought this to be pretty funny. She guessed that they were indeed old friends who could josh around with each other without inflicting pain.

Maggie said, "Nan, I chased down Skoots to ask about retraining programs for individual nurses. She said she was eager to do anything she can do. Then she went into a song and dance about fiscal constraints and capacities and priorities that I couldn't follow. Maybe that's evidence I need this financial training course. Anyway, I spoke to Carl about this just now while we were waiting outside. Carl said he would check with Skoots today to see what the problem is, or if there actually is a problem."

Carl said, "Skoots can be pretty bureaucratic, so this might be a paperwork problem, or it could be real. I'll find out today and recommend some action if any is required. If it is just budget money, I have already set up the first $50,000 as we discussed yesterday. If she has some other problem, I'll have to figure out what it is before I try to fix it."

"Okay, please do," said Nan. "Maggie, there is something else I want us to discuss. Maybe I'm dreaming up too many things for you to do all at one time, but let me tell you anyway, just so I won't forget it entirely. I have been looking for problems that are worth fixing and that we can find a fix for. So far, we're trying to reduce inadvertent errors by improving verbal orders and implementing individual retraining. We're also going to hire clinic receptionists to reduce patients' stress. One other problem came to mind, and that's needle sticks. Do we suffer needle sticks the way I remember them from my days in a pointy hat?"

"We have needle sticks down to one or two a month because we use the new syringes with a cap over the needle. They are clunky to work with because it takes an extra hand to get the cap off, but we don't have as many sticks as we used to. Needle sticks are probably down by a factor of five at least. It's a good topic, though, because it's usually the nurse that gets stuck."

Nan responded, "Maybe that is well enough in hand so we should look for some other problem to solve."

"Nan, I'm not happy with one or two sticks a month," said Maggie, showing some intensity. "Maybe we look at training people to use the new syringes in a way that gets the sticks down from one a month to one a year. That wouldn't hurt anybody's feelings. And maybe the vendors will have taken some of the clunkiness out of their products by then. Syringes aren't the only clunky equipment we have, you know."

Nan thought to herself, yes, that's clearly the better idea. I admire people who have ideas, even if they trump mine. "Okay, I see your logic, and if you take that up as a project, let me know how you come along with it."

"Nan, I'm not trying to duck this responsibility, but I wonder if you would go along with this. Our biggest incidence of sticks has to do with kids because they flail around when you're trying to inject them. We see a lot of kids, but the pediatric unit sees more than we do. I wonder if you would go along with a joint project between my clinics and Vivian Smith's pediatrics department? We've never tried anything exactly like that. I can't speak for Vivian on the matter, but would you go along if it's okay with Vivian?"

Nan turned to Carl Burke. "Carl, if there is some expense here, is there any difficulty if two units are involved?"

"Nope. Inside your department, it's all the same."

"Nan," said Maggie with a little different look in her eye, "Vivian and the whole pediatrics unit need something to think about besides that terrible Baby Thompson case. Maybe Vivian would want to take the lead on this project, and I can play second fiddle. Or maybe not, I don't know yet, but I'd like your permission to talk with her about it and maybe dump it on her if she doesn't watch out."

Nan thought this to be an unusual way to do team building, but she couldn't think of any reason to oppose it. It might work, and giving Vivian something else to think about had been a worry of her own. Nan replied, "That's fine with me. Don't twist her arm more than about halfway around. Do you have enough in the way of statistical background to deal with low-incidence event tracking?"

"Yes, I've had a couple of graduate stats courses, and Vivian has a master's degree, so between the two of us, we should be able to muddle though. I know the statistics prof in the nursing department at the university, so if we need some help, I'll call her."

"Okay, then. Thanks everybody. I'll look for some feedback from you, Carl, after you talk to Skoots."

After they left, Nan checked the mail log on her computer, which looked to be ordinary, and she checked her schedule with Marcy. "You have a salad bar luncheon with a cross-section of your department. There will be about 20 people, mostly nurses. I put out the word to the managers and supervisors that they were not to monopolize the meeting and they should let the worker bees talk. The invitation just said an informal chat and a free salad. It's in the training room, so you can size the room up for your purposes tomorrow."

31

The All-Hands Luncheon

Nan went to the training room. She found that the salad bar was set up and that most of the invitees were already there, some of whom she knew and some not. She spoke to each person as she entered. Since it appeared that nobody else was willing to make the first salad, she headed to the salad bar. The others queued up promptly after her.

Nan sat at the front but went out of her way not to take anything that would appear to be a power location in the room. She chatted with those seated nearest to her for five minutes while she nibbled at her salad. Then she called for the group's attention. "Folks, the only agenda item today is to get to know each other. I'm not going to make a speech because I'm putting what amounts to a speech in next week's edition of the department's newsletter. I've only been on the premises in this position for four days, so I don't have very many positions to defend. Just tell me what's on your mind."

After not more than six seconds, one of the male nurses spoke up. Probably male aggressiveness, Nan thought.

"I know this isn't your fault, Mrs. Mills, but we don't have anybody else to complain to. I will speak for myself on this, and others can speak for themselves if they want to. What I have to say is that the present employee parking stinks. It stinks, big time. Real big time. Stinko.

"The construction for the new wing has taken up half the regular employees' parking lot. It also took up some of the visitors' lot, so they took some more of our places and gave them to the visitors so they didn't suffer any inconvenience at all. They rented a parking lot two blocks down the street so they can say that the same number of slots are available, but that's a joke. We run three shifts, which means there are always cars already in the parking lot when the next shift drives in. You see? That's about as elementary as anything about a hospital can be, but the yo-yos who run the facilities don't have a clue.

"You probably noticed that I'm a male nurse. So, if I'm on the night shift and have to walk in the dark down to that other parking lot, I'm not at much risk of getting mugged. My many associates of the female persuasion do not have that immunity. So, there are plenty of reasons to get this straightened out."

Well, Nan thought to herself, I have at least one employee who isn't intimidated by my presence. She said, "Thank you. Duly noted. What else?"

"Nan," said a nurse who had worked with Nan before, "you can't imagine what a mess they have made with this parking situation. I'm on my feet for eight hours, then I walk two blocks to my car. That's just not right."

Another nurse spoke up, "Mrs. Mills, why do the employees get the short stick here? I don't see the facilities people giving up any of their slots. The doctors' parking lot is never full. It's like the old gold mine story: they're getting the gold, and we're getting the shaft."

"There's nothing like a good walk in a cold rain to make you think about all those want ads for nurses that run in the paper every Sunday."

"You park in the executive corral, so you don't know how the common folks are being treated here."

This went on and on. This wasn't exactly what Nan had conceptualized as a group feedback meeting. She didn't want to burn the whole meeting on a topic she could do so little about, no matter how much heartburn it was causing to her troops. How was she going to get herself out of this mess?

Finally she put both hands up above her head and called a halt. "Okay, I get the message. Let's organize a committee of six people to put your parking complaints and concerns down on paper, together with any data you have. Tom, is that your name? We haven't been introduced, but I will take the liberty of appointing you scribe. If anyone wants to be one of the five other committee members, sign up with Tom. Tom, you go over what you write with your supervisor and manager, then bring it to me. You can write down anything you want to write down, but just bear in mind that this document is going to go to the hospital executives with your names on it, so a little care in your choice of words will not go amiss. Now, for the rest of this meeting, we're not going to talk about parking."

Nan put her hands down on the table and waited to see if that would quell things. It did. After about a minute of murmuring, one of the employees said to her, "Mrs. Mills, the news release that went around about you last week said that you had earned the Black Belt rank in Six Sigma. I think I know a little about that because my brother works in a factory that makes a big deal out of Six Sigma. My brother talks about process yield, machine setup time, and other things that don't seem to have much to do with a hospital. Can you tell us something about that?"

Nan liked that topic a lot better. "Yes, I can say a few words about that here, and you'll be hearing more about it in the department's newsletter and other places. We might even organize some Green Belt classes in the future, with emphasis on the kind of work we actually do, not factory work.

"Since our time together today is limited, I will just talk about eliminating error caused by inadvertent actions. That's the kind of error that arises in nursing, since none of us makes errors on purpose. They just happen inadvertently. Now you might think that all we have to do is to be advertent, if that's a word, and the problem would go away. But, it doesn't work that way. Eliminating or reducing inadvertent errors requires that work tasks be designed with three simple rules in mind. First, it should be easier to do the task right than to do it wrong. Who could argue with that? Second, if an error is made, it should be immediately obvious. Third, it should be possible to correct the error on the spot.

"Those are such simple rules that you'd think that everything we do would have been designed with those rules in mind, since they are just common sense. I'll give you all the homework assignment to think about some task you do today to see if those rules are followed.

"There is a related matter, and that's what to do with a person who makes an inadvertent error. My answer, and the hospital's official policy as uttered by our chief operating officer, Mr. Crawford, is that we don't punish people who make inadvertent errors. We retrain them, and we do that without prejudice. Airline pilots regularly go back to the simulator for training. They don't go through retraining because they suddenly don't know how to fly a plane. They go through retraining because they want to get better at what they do both in regular flying and in being prepared for emergencies. As an airplane passenger, I think that's just fine."

Nan turned to the young woman who had raised the question. "Emily, is that your name? Your name tag is at the limit of my eyesight these days. We are different from factories because we do a lot of things with our hands. Factories are all machine setups and robots. We are manual. So, we need to think about how to improve manual operations that haven't been an issue in the factory for the past several decades. We do hands-on care, and I think that's one of the best things about nursing. I hope you do, too. So, let's see if we can better ourselves in how we do manual tasks. These simple rules might help."

Emily asked a new question. "Mrs. Mills, can we decide for ourselves how to do things? It seems to me that the doctors are in charge of everything we do."

Nan answered, "Emily, we need to get cooperation from physicians and others. There are regulations and practice standards that were put in place with the right intentions. If they are off kilter, we'll get them changed. I can tell you that doctors are every bit as concerned about this issue as we are. Many of you know Dr. Suzy Wong who runs the anesthesiology service. She did a short talk to my staff managers this past Monday on what her profession has done to reduce errors, and it's pretty impressive. What's equally impressive is that they think they can do even better. That talk will be up on the department Web site shortly, if it isn't already there."

Nurse Tom said, "It's already up. I checked it out earlier today. It's worth a few minutes to eyeball that video file. Those lives they are saving are ours, among others."

Nan smiled at Tom and said, "I am informed that the other medical specialties are getting after themselves and have similar research programs under way. These things grow exponentially because we can learn from each other if we don't get our defensive shields up too high.

"You'll be hearing about a couple of initiatives we have launched already this week. One deals with verbal orders. We all deal with verbal orders. We don't make many errors, and when there is an error it's never clear whether the doctor goofed and misspoke or the nurse goofed and didn't understand what the doctor said. It doesn't matter much, because it's the patient who suffers for it, either way. So we are not hunting witches. We are looking for systematic changes that eliminate both kinds of goofs by making the error evident if it happens and by allowing for immediate correction on the spot."

Emily spoke up at that point, offering a bright smile. "Yes, we all saw that lunchtime theater yesterday. It was great. I told my boyfriend about it, and he started doing his imitation of John Wayne in a submarine. Is that Japanese methodology?"

"Yes, and if you look at the Japanese authors, you'll find they quote American writers. The name that has stuck to it is poka yoke, and it's called the same in all languages, like the word shampoo. So, if you want to say it's Japanese, that's fine. If you don't, that's fine, too."

Another voice from the back asked, "Is there more than that to Six Sigma, and what's with the belts?"

Nan responded, "Yes, Six Sigma also deals with problem solving, error detection, change management, systematic reduction in variability, and work flow. All those have some relevance to our work, and I think we will be dealing with them in due course.

"As for the belts, that's a bit of a spoof of the martial arts. People qualified to carry out Six Sigma projects are called Green Belts. Those qualified to design Six Sigma projects are called Black Belts, and there is a higher category called Master Black Belts, who train the Black Belts. That doesn't mean you can't do something if you don't have a belt. It's just an organized way of identifying who's up to what level of preparation. I have a certificate saying Six Sigma Black Belt, and so does my husband."

The hour had gotten away from them, and it was time to wrap up. Nan stood to indicate that the luncheon was at an end, thanked everybody for coming, and walked back to her office, wondering how bad the parking situation really was.

32

The Nursing School Flap

Nan walked slowly back to her office, feeling that there were still a lot of things for her to learn about her own department. She went by Marcy's desk and into her own office. Marcy followed, two steps behind.

"Are there any action items from the employee salad luncheon, Mrs. Mills?"

"I didn't get any action items, but I authorized a grassroots committee to get together a bill of complaint about the employee parking, which is fouled up by the Aunt Agnes wing construction, as you probably know and as I would have known if I parked in the employee parking lot myself."

"Yes, ma'am. Who is leading?"

"A young man named Tom, who is a nurse as I understand it. I didn't ask what unit he is in, since I didn't want him to think I was going to launch an immediate investigation of him.

"So, I don't want an investigation. I just want to find out who he is and whether he is a straight shooter or a troublemaker. He isn't the only one who was mad about the parking, but if he is a known nutcase, I can't very well take him to suit land to protest the parking. He didn't look like a nut, so I'm hopeful in that regard."

"Yes, ma'am. You had a telephone call from your husband in Houston, who said he had given Sanjar a list of things to get for your meeting tomorrow. Did I understand that Mr. Mills will be here in person?"

"Yes, he will be here by noon tomorrow."

"I'll get him a parking pass for the VIP visitors parking, which is the same as the executive corral. He'll just need a VIP number, which I can send to his text pager."

"Good. If there was ever a VIP visitor, it's Jack."

"You have that vendor presentation on electronic patients' records at 2:30 this afternoon, and Carl Burke has asked if he could see you for a few minutes on the Skoots matter. You can do that before or after the records meeting. Carl says he will arrange his afternoon to suit yours."

"I like that in a man," Nan said jokingly. "Give me about 15 minutes, then I'll see what Carl has to report. Although, I think if it were good news, he simply would have told you the message, don't you?"

"Yes, ma'am. He sounded a little miffed on the phone."

"Okay, then. I'll go back to working on my three documents for tomorrow."

The quarter of an hour passed quickly for Nan, who was thinking deeply about her three papers. She had not yet put pencil to paper. She liked to get her thoughts straight in her own mind before committing them to paper, finding that once written, her thoughts were harder to change, and she wasn't ready for that quite yet. She'd be ready by tomorrow, but she wasn't ready yet.

Carl Burke was announced. Carl came in and took a chair at the little table. He sat with his head forward, a habit that Nan had noticed before. She wondered if that habit was a relic from the days when he could shake his head and make curls fall over his eyes. One day she would have to ask Maggie if she had any high school photos of her old gang.

Carl did not look pleased. "Okay, Carl. Shoot."

"Nan, I spent time with Skoots van der Schoot to see how to handle the unplanned expense of the training program you want to experiment with. I've known her to be a bureaucratic curmudgeon, but I have never hit stone walls like this before. She must think that this is the time for her to make a power move. I couldn't figure out why she thinks that, but I'm guessing that she heard something from her vice president about who's up and who's down on the tote board upstairs in the executive suite. That kind of word gets around, especially in the staff organizations.

"Here's what she wants. She wants you to cover all expense. She wants you to transfer two heads, which is to say her authorized head count would go up by two and yours would go down by two. And then she wants a statement signed by you and by her vice-president saying that only her department will do nursing training in the hospital. I couldn't get her to budge on any of these three demands.

"After we meet those demands, she wants to do a feasibility study before doing any work. I told her that didn't make any sense if the point is to experiment with different training regimes, but she said she can't turn her operation upside down on a bag of whims. So, I'm here to report defeat. I thought I knew how to get things done in our bureaucracy, but I've met my match today."

Carl sat there, head down, elbows on knees, one balled fist being squeezed by the other hand. Muscular hands, not what Nan would have expected for a bean counter.

"Okay, Carl, let's go through her list of demands. We had already said we would cover the expense, so the first point is okay. On the head count, if we have some white space between our actual and our authorized levels, why don't we give her two? Is that a big deal?"

"Yes, that's a departmental no-no. If you transfer head count slots, the suits will think they had authorized too many for you last year, and then next year they will cut your head count arbitrarily to get rid of bloat."

"Another knee in the gut."

"You got it."

"Well, Carl, tell me how we would reduce authorized head count if we really wanted to? Could we ever admit that we were authorized too many?"

"You combine head count change with some automation project or reorganization so nobody can tell what's going on."

"Well, I can see there are tricks of this new trade that I'm going to have to learn quickly. You're a good coach when it comes to hiding peas under shells.

"Tell me about number three, which I take it is a request that a charter be written which authorizes Skoots and nobody else to do nursing training. I understand the substance. Skoots told me she already has the charter, so tell me why that would be a bad idea."

"That's a power grab. She wants to have a piece of paper that she can use against you some time in the future, for good reasons or bad. Right now, you do some training within the department, like informing your troops about a new medical procedure or a new drug. Those are usually just briefings and maybe a show-and-tell by a vendor, and you have a training room for that. If you go for her charter deal, she would be in charge of even things like that, if she wanted to get snotty."

"But she says she already has the training charter. What am I missing?"

"She has a charter that she wrote for herself and signed herself. It has no standing with the suits. She wants a real charter signed by you, which would have some standing."

"Okay, I can see that we don't want the charter. Now tell me why she wants a feasibility study on something we can hardly define at this point."

"Bureaucrats want charters and scopes, but they don't want to have to deliver anything. As long as there is a feasibility study going on, she can take credit for everything and not have to deliver anything. She can keep a feasibility study going for six months or a year without breaking a sweat."

"Carl, our paradigm here is to learn from the experience of others. I'm learning from your experience. So what are my options?"

"Okay, I have been noodling on options. One, you can do it her way. Two, you can forget about the whole idea. Three, you can make an issue out of it with her vice president and try to work out a deal. The trouble with trying to make a deal is that her boss is just as big a bureaucrat as Skoots is. The VP will back up Skoots as a matter of principle, just as you would back up one of your managers in a turf battle. Thus, this dispute would wind up being resolved by the COO. Now I can tell you, suits don't like to have to settle turf battles because one side or the other is going to wind up mad at him. So he'll wind up mad at you, even if he settles it in your favor. In fact, he will be particularly mad at you if he settles it in your favor, because then he'll think he will have to do a favor for the other guy. So, that whole scenario is a bummer."

"So, Carl, let me review this to see if I have it straight. Skoots figures I'm short on mojo right now, and she is taking advantage of that to expand her empire."

"Right. Mojo is the word. It's all organizational politics, perceptions, and pecking orders. Mojo is right."

Nan thought this through. Skoots has a bad attitude, that's what this comes down to. Skoots could do everything that Nan wants and take some credit for it if she wanted to, but that would take an attitude adjustment on Skoots's part. Nan didn't think hitting her with a two-by-four would play well in Nan's present circumstances, and she refused to ask Marcy if she knew anybody in that line of work.

What was that expression the twins used to say? Something about applying heat until the other guy saw the light.

"Marcy, will you join us when it is convenient?" Nan asked through the intercom.

"Yes, ma'am." Marcy came in, armed with her steno pad and a pencil.

"Marcy, by 10 o'clock tomorrow morning, I want Gretchen van der Schoot to be firmly convinced that she and her nurses training school are being transferred to this department on the first of next month."

"Yes, ma'am. Anything else?"

"That will do it for the moment, thank you."

Marcy's pencil flew over the steno pad, then she turned and left. Carl remained seated with his head down, but even at that angle, Nan could tell he was treating himself to a very wide grin. Nan thought she should change the subject. "Carl, I sat in the first capital budgeting meeting. You weren't there, but there were several people from the financial department present. The meeting went pretty well, I thought, and it was the first time I had paid attention to the quantity of millions of dollars of capital the hospital deploys year in and year out. I have come to appreciate how you look out for me in operating expense matters. Is there somebody like you assigned to me for capital allocations and planning?"

Carl managed to straighten his face before he looked up to respond to her. "Our department divides itself between expense and capital, and planning is separate from reporting. That's pretty standard for our kind of organization. We rotate people around so they eventually know something about all phases, which I think is a pretty good policy. I've worked in all the units myself over my career. One of our people who was in that meeting is probably assigned to you, but I don't know which one. I'll check that out and do a little snooping to make sure it's the right guy or gal. If it's a junior person, and my guess is that it will be because that's sort of the way things happen, I'll let him or her know that he or she has a new big brother, namely me. When the person hears the Skoots story, he or she will be looking for protection anyway."

"Who's going to tell that person the Skoots story?"

"Nobody—everyone is going to know through osmosis. In fact, you might want to throw a bone to Skoots next week so she doesn't feel too mortified by having had her bluff called. You do want her cooperating, not sticking sticks in the spokes of Maggie's bicycle wheels. Skoots's mojo is going to be running on empty."

Carl was trying hard not to grin or break out laughing. So was Nan. But one had to maintain professional decorum, as it was pointed out to her recently.

"Carl, there is much truth to what you say. Let's see how this plays out tomorrow. After all, we're bluffing, too."

"Nan, do you mind if I attend your noon meeting tomorrow? I don't know what's going on there, but it figures to be something special, the way wheels are turning around here."

"Carl, I consider you to be one of my personal staff, and I will be pleased if you can attend. I've invited the people who are directly involved, and I've told my managers and some others that they can attend if they want to. I guess we didn't declare a topic for the meeting, so that might keep attendance down, what with everybody being so busy."

"I don't think attendance will be down. In any case, I look forward to being there." Carl stood, smiled politely, and turned to leave. While he was turning, she thought she saw Carl's smile expand into a very big grin.

This executive stuff is all right, Nan thought. Get the right team and the right mojo, and this job is really easy.

She picked up her pencil, holding it but not writing with it, lost in thought.

33

The Electronic Patients Records Meeting

Marcy reminded Nan when it was time to go to the vendor presentation on computerized patients records. This was a vendor presentation made by one of the leading vendors in the field. The presentation was slick, with animated PowerPoint slides, video clips from happy customers, and impressive-looking charts of return on investment. None of that surprised Nan, and she had no way of guessing whether the arithmetic was correct or not. Nan knew that the hospital had been studying electronic records for years, as she supposed all hospitals were doing. Nan had learned from Sanjar that some kind of a pilot study was going on in the hospital, but she didn't yet have any information about that or about how it was going.

Nan did know that if the hospital went whole hog for electronic records, the way her nursing staff did its work was going to change, big time. So, she needed to make sure that this profound change would be managed in the best possible way. A disaster she didn't need. She didn't need any embarrassments either.

She noted that the vendor was bragging about their bar code scheme. Nan knew that bar codes were on everything these days, so that seemed reasonable. But how would that work at a patient's bedside or in the emergency room? Would bar codes be the final solution to patient-misidentification problems? Giving new mothers the wrong baby? Supplies that get lost after delivery to the floors?

In her new mode of looking to benefit from the experience of others, Nan thought of a person she knew really well, a person who had spoken to Nan about bar coding when it was first taking off in that person's industry—her twin sister Ann. She decided to call Ann that evening, while the pies were in the oven.

Nan collected the glossy brochures, made a note of the hospital person who seemed to be in charge of evaluations, thanked everybody in sight, and returned to her office.

34

Jack Calls

"**M**rs. Mills, Mr. Mills is on line one," announced Marcy. Nan thanked Marcy and went to her desk to pick up the handset. "I love you," she said into the telephone.

"Nan, you really have to stop answering the telephone that way. What will people think? Besides, I wanted to say that first, and I almost did before I realized it was Marcy who was answering your telephone calls."

"Let's not pursue that. What brings you to call, other than to say you love me, which is sufficient reason, of course."

"Jick and I have been running on all cylinders here. Jick found a guy who knows all there is to know about disassembler software, the software I was telling you about last evening. He showed me the latest version, which is a lot better than the kind I used several years ago. The new version has a built-in editor that helps sort the code. The disassembler doesn't know anything about what the purpose of the program is, so it just assigns names like A01 and A02 to the various lines of code it reads in. Then the user has to figure out each line's purpose, such as whether the line is a counter for some loop or a time function. You still have to play detective, but the editor makes quick substitutions so the whole process goes pretty fast. The editor can find the range of loops and substitute colors so you can see the pattern of the code pretty quickly. Fortunately, EKG programs are only 10 to 20 pages of code, not a thousand like you'd see in other programs, because the EKG machine is quite simple. He gave me a copy of his disassembler software to go by. Ours won't be quite the same, but it will be a leg up.

"I talked to Sanjar, and we worked out a list of software and hardware to acquire. Sanjar found an EKG machine from the same lot as the machines of interest. He opened it up so he could read the part number off the chip. It's a standard chip from a leading manufacturer, so we can find plenty of sources of supply for anything associated with it.

"Then Jick and I spent some time getting a tour of the mission control center. The room isn't as big as it seems on the tube, but it is still big. Lots of workstations. We talked to the guy who performs man–machine research. He's a great guy who knows his stuff. I'll give you the long form when we're together some time, but for now I'll boil it down to the short form.

"NASA built this room more than 30 years ago, back when computers could hardly do anything, so the individual displays were primitive and hard to figure out. NASA trained the experts to deal with those limited and complex displays. Then over the years, as computers got more powerful, NASA upgraded the software and displays. The displays are now a lot easier to understand. Although the control center staff members had not made a lot of mistakes reading the old displays, since they're really committed and drilled, they had made some. Since NASA has started using the simplified displays, the error rate has gone down. So, experts make fewer errors when the displays are simpler.

"NASA even has a rule of thumb on display complexity: When the displays get to the point that a civilian can look at the display and know what's going on, then that's simple enough. NASA works on reducing complexity until it gets to that point, after which it starts working on something else.

"NASA learned something else. Experts don't like to be helped. Very rarely did any expert ever ask that his display be simplified, which might be a macho thing or maybe they just feel that they have mastered the complexity. There is a corollary to this. NASA has a lot more turnover in those jobs than it used to have. The experts think the challenge has gone out of it, so they get bored and go look for a different assignment."

"Jack, that's interesting. We use a lot of electronics machines these days. We don't have any say-so over their display designs, we just get what the vendor offers. I suppose there are some nursing society task forces on this, but I don't know for sure. The doctors would probably have more clout. I was just in a vendor presentation on an electronics patients records system that the hospital might buy. I just sat there like a lump because I don't have the competence to ask any questions. Now you have given me one question I can ask any computer-type vendor. Let's call it the NASA test for display complexity. Don't tell NASA we're using its name."

"NASA will be thrilled, since pushing technology transfer to the civilian sector is a big deal for the organization. Maybe I can get one of the experts to write a paper on it. Do you want to be a coauthor?"

"Not me. I couldn't bluff my way through. How about you or Sanjar?"

"Maybe both. This is worth some thought. Speaking of thought, I was reading the newspaper this morning, and I saw a report that a brain surgeon had started drilling holes in a patient's head only to discover halfway through that the surgeon had the x-ray in the viewer backward, so that he was drilling on the wrong side of the poor guy's head. He caught it in time, but I'll bet his insurance rates are going up."

"Jack, I heard that on the car radio when I was driving in this morning. That was awful."

"Does that kind of thing happen all the time? I've had a few x-rays in my time, and I remember taking the twins for x-rays after some ball game episodes, and I never understood how the doctor could tell if he was looking at the front or the back of the x-ray. I suppose it doesn't matter most of the time because he can tell by what he is looking at, but an x-ray of the left foot looks like an x-ray of the right foot if the film is backward, doesn't it? That's a man–machine interface that maybe you can do something about."

"To mark the front of an x-ray film," Nan said, "we put a small white dot in the lower right-hand corner. Some places stamp a serial number on the image. But x-ray machines aren't like your 35mm camera that puts the time and date right into the picture. The stamping is done later and may or may not get put on the right way.

"When I was in training, I was the nurse standing next to a doctor who was starting a chest procedure. At the last moment he discovered that the x-ray was reversed. He about had a stroke on the spot. He recovered in time. I used to wonder if he bothered to write that up in the medical record. I'd bet maybe two doughnuts that he didn't. I would have, because I'm pure of heart."

"Nan, you are indeed pure of heart and one in a million," said Jack. "Okay, I pass that along for whatever good you can make of it, as our lawyer friends say. I'm booked on the early-bird flight in the morning. I upgraded to first class so I won't look like a derelict when I get to the hospital.

"Sanjar told me he cased the room we're using, which he says is your training room. He's getting a new PC for us to use so there won't be any other programs loaded that might interfere. That's overkill, and that's fine with me. He said you get a shipment every month, so he will just seize one of the PCs that hasn't been delivered to a user yet.

"I got that workup you did of public information about Mr. Bill's family businesses. I don't see any motive for wanting to off Mr. Bill. I guess you reached the same conclusion. Jick and I tried to figure it out, but we can't. So, Jick got hold of a financial planner who has been trying to sign Jick up as a client. The guy does financial planning, trusts, and other tax dodges. Jick gave him a short summary over the phone, and the guy said two things immediately. First of all, you can't conclude that people are wealthy just because they say they are. Second, there is a big difference between being wealthy and having any money. We sent him the file by e-mail, and we're meeting with him this evening to see what he has to say. It's all public information, so that didn't seem to be risking anything. I'll let you know what we learn when I see you in the morning. It's probably nothing. After all, you and Jick are both smart and neither of you found anything. Modesty forbids me mentioning myself in this matter."

"Okay, Jack, if the financial planner finds something, that will be great, and if not, we are no further behind."

"I love you Nan. Or as I used to say when you were rooming with your twin sister, I love you Ann or Nan as the case may be. That still goes."

"I love you, too, Jack or Jick as the case may be."

After hanging up the phone, Nan thought about NASA display complexity and x-rays. It seemed to Nan that everybody in health-care had some anecdote about a backward x-ray. Usually caught in time, thankfully. Nan walked out to Marcy's station and asked, "Marcy, how do I find the telephone number for Philomena Stewart, or Meenie Stewart if you know her by that name. I'd like to call and ask her something. She still runs the roentgenology department, doesn't she?"

"I'll get her for you."

"No, Marcy, but thanks. I can still dial a telephone."

"Yes you can dial a telephone, but no you can't make your own calls to people. They'd have a heart attack if they find themselves talking to a vice president. I have to warn them first. I'll get Meenie Stewart and set up a video call. Just click the icon on your computer when it flashes."

The limitations of the executive, Nan thought. I can play power games with other departments, but I can't make my own telephone calls. Nan went back to her desk, and when the video link icon flashed, she clicked the mouse. Her key lights came up and the room lights went down. She saw herself in one computer window and Meenie Stewart in the other.

Meenie Stewart had trained as a nurse and had then specialized in radiation therapies. She had worked herself up to being in charge, which was a big deal these days with MRI and PET-scan equipment to go with the old-fashioned x-ray machines. X-ray was not part of Nan's department, so Meenie did not report to her. Meenie and Nan had known each other for years, and Nan was hoping that the organizational distance wouldn't inhibit their friendship.

"Nan, you look great on this video link. I always look at myself and see one of the Three Stooges. Maybe all three of them. What brings you to call? I hope it's not business."

"Meenie, you look just great from here," Nan countered. That was a generous extension of the truth, because in fact, Meenie's face was poorly lit and somewhat distorted by her camera's position. Shadows did her face no favors. "My call isn't exactly business, and it isn't exactly social, although the next time I call it will be all social. We need to catch up. This call is about something I heard on the news. This brain surgeon was drilling the wrong side of the patient's head because he had the x-ray film backward in his viewer."

"Yes, I heard that on the radio this morning. That's yucky. I'm glad it wasn't my case."

"I remember assisting at a surgical procedure when I was in training that was a pale version of the same mistake. Does that happen often?"

"I don't know the incidence rate. It happens. I have had a couple of personal exposures to it, and I hear stories every once in a while. There are documented cases from other institutions of that happening and the wrong leg getting sawed off and that sort of thing. Everybody is supposed to check three times, and I suppose that catches most of them but not quite all. I asked a question like that to one of the radiologists here a year or so ago. He told me that they train themselves to make sure."

"Wouldn't it be better if any passerby could look and point out the flaw?"

"Maybe, but I don't know how much experience you've had trying to get doctors to do the most obvious things. Popcorn on granite."

"Meenie, sometime would you pull some x-ray films that would be a problem if they were viewed backward, like a foot or a hand or a kidney. I'm not looking for x-rays that took people to court. I'm just interested in seeing what the state of the art is."

"Sure, I can do that. I've got an intern trainee standing right here, and as soon as she finishes mopping the floor and polishing my shoes, I'll put her on it.

"Is there more to this story, Nan? I hear you're stirring things up over there. And let me add that I was deeply saddened when I heard about Mr. Bill and the Thompson baby. Did x-rays have anything to do with those cases?"

"No, there was no x-ray involvement that I know of in either case. And I don't know if I'm shaking the department up or it is shaking me up. The latter for sure. I haven't been fired quite yet, although there is always tomorrow.

"I'm looking for procedures we can do better in this service, and part of that is stopping practices that lead to error. Maybe x-ray films that look the same front and back, at least to a civilian, are something that could stand some attention. Who knows, maybe we should put colored frames on the back. I'm just poking around to see what I can learn before the routine tasks take up 200 percent of my time."

"I'll be over in the morning with a few samples. If you get serious about this, you know me, I want to play. If it comes to getting cooperation from the radiologists, I've got enough dirt on every one of them to get plenty of cooperation."

"Meenie, you're a dear. Let me or Marcy know when you're ready. I'll be looking forward to seeing you in the morning."

"I'll book with Marcy. Tell me, Nan, can I come to your meeting at noon tomorrow in your training room? It's so mysterious, I'd hate to miss it."

"You're welcome to come. It's an open meeting, and I didn't mean it to be mysterious."

"I hear Jack is going to be there."

"Yes, Jack is the main attraction."

"No wonder you didn't make any announcements, you'd have to get a bigger hall."

"Good-bye, Meenie."

"Good-bye, Nan."

Nan told Marcy to expect a call from Meenie and to fix it so she and Meenie could see each other in the morning. Then Nan said that that was enough for one day. She had shopping to do, so she left.

35

Thursday Evening

Nan stopped at the local Wal-Mart to get her baking supplies for the evening. Upon arriving home, she found the pie carriers that she had ordered on the Internet waiting on her porch. She lugged everything into the kitchen and planned her evening around baking times. She could cook two cherry pies at a time in her oven, so that meant three times 55 minutes to get six pies, plus some setup time. She'd get that started and make herself something to eat while the first pair of pies were in the oven.

Having practiced the two preceding evenings, Nan had cherry pie baking down to a drill. She preheated the oven and got to work on the pie shells. Soon enough, the first pair were in the oven. Nan did a simple stir-fry for her supper while she thought about everything that had to come together like clock-work the next day.

When the second pair of pies were in the oven, Nan figured that Ann would be finished with the family supper at her house, and she placed a telephone call to Ann. No video link was available, but then she knew exactly what Ann looked like.

"Ann, it's Nan."

"Yes, I knew you were calling. What's up? Has Jack decided to trade you in on a new model? Did the twins flunk out already? How's the new job? Did you go to any classes when you were at that management course? Or did you and Jack play hooky?"

"Jack is still around because he still has that crush on you. The twins don't talk to anybody but each other, so I don't know if they go to class or not. But they have just developed a taste for chocolate chip cookies. I'm not going to tell you what Jack and I did at that management class. Besides, this call is strictly business."

"What kind of business, your kind or my kind?"

"Yours, because it gets around to being mine. You bar code everything, don't you? We seem to have bar code in the future here, and I want to learn what you already know so I won't have to learn it the hard way."

"Yes, we bar code the crap out of everything. It works better in some circumstances than in others. Or maybe I should say that it worked immediately in some circumstances and not so immediately in others. It worked immediately in highly structured places, such as the warehouses. The other extreme was the checkout counters. We do general merchandise, so we have little items, big items, big counters, and big shopping carts. We also have checkers who work on their feet for eight hours, are badly paid, and marginally motivated.

"What we found at the outset was that inventory control and cash realization were worse with bar coding than before, not better, the way the vendors had promised. We had to dig in to find out why. We found that the checkers who used to eyeball a big bag of something at the bottom of the shopping cart didn't want to bother lifting and lugging that big bag around to get the bar code reader wand to read the code on the bag. So, they didn't bother to scan it at all. We found that if the bar code tag was in an awkward place on the merchandise, the checker would just throw it in the shopping bag without trying very hard to scan it.

"Then we found that although the scanner would beep when it read something, the scanner didn't know what it was reading. Sometimes it was the right thing, and sometimes it was the wrong thing. There was no display that the checkers could check as they went along because they were working with their heads down, pushing the merchandise across the scanner as fast as possible. Checkers are graded on speed, not bar code precision.

"And then if a checker found a mistake, it was a whole big hassle to make a correction. So rather than hold up a line of customers, some checkers didn't bother to make any corrections.

"That was expensive R&D for us, but we eventually learned that we had to do three things to make bar coding work at our checkout counters. We had to redesign the counters and the checkers' workstations so that it was easier for the checkers to do it right than to do it wrong. We had to make it possible for the checkers to see what the computer was ringing up as they scanned items. That way, the checkers could immediately see whether an error occurred. Finally, we had to simplify the correction process so that the checker would not hesitate to make a correction if necessary.

"Those changes all sound pretty basic to you, I'm sure, Nan, but we are just simple peasant retailer types, fumbling along here with this high-tech stuff."

"Ann, those rules make a lot of sense to me. I think our unstructured workplace is just as hard to structure as your checkout counters. Maybe worse. So this is going to take some work on our part."

"What you'll find, Nan, is that bar coding works like a champ in the supply room, pharmacy, and other places that have a lot of structure. The suits will see that and think that bar coding newborns and amputees must be just as simple. I don't think it will be."

The oven clock started its raucous call, so Nan walked quickly to the kitchen, taking her cordless telephone with her so she would not have to break off the call. "Nan, is your house on fire? What's that racket?"

"It's the oven clock. I'm baking cherry pies."

"You? Cherry pies? Don't tell me any more, I'll get guilt pangs."

"I'll tell you all about it next time we see each other, Ann.

"Good-bye. Thanks for knowing everything about bar coding."

"Good-bye, Nan, and I don't believe that cherry pie story for a minute."

At 10 o'clock, Jack called again to tell her what he and Jick had learned from the financial planner. Jack said that Jick had signed up as a client on the spot.

36

Friday Morning

Nan parked her car in the executive coral and organized the items she had to carry into the hospital. She had two three-pie carriers plus her briefcase and handbag. The latter two had shoulder straps, so it was theoretically possible to make it in one trip. As she got as far as the door, Willy spotted her and offered his cart and himself for her service. Nan accepted, and they walked together to Nan's office. Willy struck Nan, once again, as one of the most obliging young men she had ever met. She hoped her twins were half so obliging as they went off into the adult world.

Once they reached Marcy's desk, Nan asked Willy to wait a moment while she and Marcy organized the day. Nan asked Marcy to arrange for the pies to be taken care of in the cafeteria kitchen and warmed so they would be ready for cutting about one o'clock in the afternoon in the department training room. They discussed what else they would need, and they settled on ordering a range of soft drinks for 30 people, napkins, plates, and flatware. Nan had no idea how many people would show up or if anybody would be in the mood for cherry pie, so she pulled the numbers out of the air. Marcy said she would ask a friend in the auxiliary to see if the auxiliary had any flowers on hand that would make for a centerpiece, which she didn't mind doing considering how many bouquets they had gotten from Nan, which is to say from Marcy, in the past few weeks.

Nan left Willy with Marcy so that Willy could truck the pies to the cafeteria once Marcy had things organized. Nan wanted to work on her three documents, all due in just a few hours, but she was in the habit of checking her e-mail first. Marcy had already gotten rid of the junk e-mail and routine bumf, so the to-read list was short. One was from Maggie Kelly, her manager for the clinics.

Maggie reported that she was moving ahead on the receptionists front and that she had spoken to Vivian Smith about the notion of doing a joint project on needle sticks between the clinics and the pediatrics department. Vivian had made positive noises and had a bagful of anecdotes about needle sticks, so Maggie would keep moving that along.

Maggie then wrote that she was thinking about the way her clinics operated, first-come, first-served. That was eminently fair, but it wasn't very efficient, especially as viewed from the patient's perspective. Maggie had been to see her dentist the week before, and she was struck by the fact that there was only one other person in the waiting room. If a low-tech dentist's office could manage itself that well, why couldn't her high-tech clinics do the same?

Maggie at first answered herself by saying that she had to deal with unexpected events, which was certainly true. But on the other hand, most of her traffic was pretty routine and could be scheduled well ahead of time.

Still, the zillion languages her patients spoke made it difficult to do even simple tasks like set up appointments over the telephone, because it was so much more difficult to understand heavily accented language over the phone. So it was more complicated than just announcing that appointments could be scheduled.

If she got her receptionists going, then the four receptionists at the four clinics would, at any time, cover a good range of languages, so if she could shift calls back and forth, she could probably handle the language issues, using the computer network so that any receptionist could book an appointment for any of the clinics. If they got stumped, they could use the fee-for-service translation setup. So, Maggie wrote, she can see how to do the mechanics. What she could not see was how to do the scheduling with a mix of scheduled and unscheduled work. Did Maggie have any references on that?

Nan wrote back that Maggie should establish a service level for the unscheduled work, such as a service level that said an unscheduled patient would be seen within 45 minutes 99 percent of the time or some other combination of maximum wait time and confidence level. With that requirement in mind and the average number of unscheduled patients in, say, any two-hour period, they could work out the number of time slots to hold for unscheduled patients. If the number of unscheduled patients was greater in the morning than in the afternoon, or if some days of the week or the month (like the day after payday) had more unscheduled traffic, they could make the model a little more elaborate to cover those variables, so long as they could figure out the pattern. Then they would use the Poisson distribution that's built into their spreadsheets to figure the arithmetic. Nan offered to show her how. Actually, Nan figured that with this much of a hint, Maggie could figure it out for herself, given that she had had a couple of statistics courses.

Nan was pleased that Maggie was showing an interest in the operation of her clinics. That was a level of abstraction that some nurses never reached. Scheduling the appointments would reduce the inventory of people in the waiting rooms quite a bit. Given that on any day some of the kids in the waiting rooms would be loaded up with germs, reducing the body count in the waiting rooms would reduce the contagion factor, which would be for the betterment of the community. Well, Nan thought, if I can get two or three of the other managers to be as interested in improving operations as Maggie is, I can coast for the next two years.

Nan closed her e-mail application and picked up her still-pointy pencil and the yellow tablet. Nan was still thinking of how to make these documents work together. She wasn't quite there yet, mentally. Noon was still hours away.

Marcy came in to organize their day. The noon meeting was on and the invitees were invited. Gordon Schneider's office said that Gordo would not only attend but he would also bring his brother and their lawyer who is also the executor for the estate of Mr. Bill. Other curious people had called to ask what the meeting was going to be about, and Marcy had pled ignorance to all. The arrangements seemed to be in order, and she had arranged with the receiving dock to page her when the express shipments arrived for Sanjar. Sanjar himself was already in the training room, unpacking a new PC and setting the training room up for the noon meeting. The cafeteria effort was organized, and Willy was on call to hustle to the receiving dock and to go back and forth to the cafeteria as needed. The guards were still guarding the three red-tagged EKG machines in the VIP suites. There were no sightings of Gordo Schneider to report.

Nan wanted to ask Marcy if and how she had undertaken to apply organizational heat to Skoots van der Schoot so that Skoots would see the light on the training turf battle, but Nan decided she probably didn't want to know. She'd wait and see how it played out. On any other day, that event would make the highlight film, or the blooper reel, but today, there would be a lot of competition for the highlight film's top spots.

Marcy said Meenie Stewart would be along in five minutes with some exhibits. Okay, thought Nan, that might be an interesting diversion for the morning, and she needed diversions to keep the butterflies down.

37

Meenie Comes to Call

Meenie came in, after being announced by Marcy, and laid out a half dozen x-ray films on the small conference table. There was a shot of a foot, one of a hand, one of a skull, and so on.

First, Meenie laid them out frontward. Then she told Nan to turn around for a moment, during which Meenie turned some of them over. Then she asked Nan to turn around and tell her whether it was a right foot, a left hand, and so on. Nan got about half of them right.

Then Meenie said they would do it again, and that Nan should look carefully for the white dot before calling her answers. This time, Nan got them all right.

For the third drill, Meenie said they would do the same thing, but this time each would be covered with a sheet of paper. Meenie would uncover each one in turn, and Nan had one second to call each one. This time, Nan was back to batting .500.

Then they traded places, and Meenie was to call each film within one second of its being uncovered. The first time, Meenie got every one right. Nan shuffled things around, turning some over and some not, and they did it again. This time, Meenie got five out of six correct.

They stopped to figure out what that meant. After discussing it, they decided that Nan was better than a civilian would be, and Nan might as well have been flipping a coin. Meenie was an expert, and she got 11 out of 12 correct, which is better than 90 percent. That's good for a batting average, but not so hot for making a call that might put life or limb in jeopardy.

But was that a fair test? Probably not, because it wasn't very scientific. But it was interesting. Meenie said she would talk to the tamest of her radiologists to see if that person could come up with a better test that was still simple like this one but a little closer to real life.

They talked about the NASA criterion, that the display, or in this case the film, had to be so obvious in its meaning that a civilian could understand it. The white dot mark on the front side of the x-ray film sort of satisfied that requirement, but just barely. This certainly called for something better than what was being done. So, they made a pact to work on this together, with Meenie having the ball. She would call on Nan for organizational, political, and moral support. They didn't think they would need any money in the short run, but Nan said she would find some money if the need should arise.

Nan volunteered to poll her managers to ask for x-ray goof anecdotes, but Meenie said she could get a zillion of those, so they were beyond that point. Nan acquiesced. Meenie left, full of enthusiasm. Nan returned to her yellow tablet.

38

Mojo

At 10:30 AM, Carl Burke put his head in the door, displaying a big grin. "Guess who just called? Did you guess Skoots van der Schoot? Then you win the Kewpie doll."

"Carl, I want to hear it all, but first I want to know how you got past Marcy."

"She's not here. She's down in the training room doing something with Sanjar. His packages just got delivered, and Willy was sent to fetch them. I think Marcy just wanted to make sure everything connected. She's good at follow-through."

"Marcy is good at everything. Now, tell me the story."

"I was sitting at my desk, adding up the pennies column in our latest report, and my phone rang. It was Ms. Van der Schoot, who wished to say that she had been thinking about our conversation yesterday, and she thought maybe she had put her position rather badly. She wanted to try again. Her position this morning is the following:

"On the matter of expense, she could make a contribution from her budget because she had been short one body for a few months and has an underrun right now. She wants to contribute that, which wouldn't be a big deal compared to the nursing department, so it was sort of a goodwill gesture.

"On the matter of head count, she thought we ought to put that off until we see how the project grows, and if she needs some additional head count next year, then she will ask for it in the usual way and hope to get an endorsement from you at that time.

"On the matter of the charter, that seemed to be premature, too, and we ought to see how things develop.

"On the matter of the plan, what she had meant to say was that we all should take notes as we experiment so that we can write it up in the standard planning document style at the end of the trials.

"Most of all, she wanted me to say to you and to Maggie that she thought it was a splendid initiative, and everybody could count on her to do her part and more. She even had picked up a couple of items in one of her trade journals that might be worth discussing some time."

Carl flopped backward in his chair, arms and legs akimbo, and enjoyed a big laugh. "Nan, that was the fastest strategic retreat I have ever seen in this organization. She imploded like the Great South Sea Bubble. It was beautiful. I wish I had recorded that call for posterity."

Nan limited herself to a polite smile, what with professional decorum and all. "Carl, I'm burning with curiosity over how Marcy did this. I'm also pretty sure I don't want to ask her. How are we going to find out?"

"Oh, I already know. It was a classic—this one goes in the case books for all future organizational climbers to study like Caesar's Gallic Wars. Like chess moves. It was beautiful. This morning, the print shop clerk calls Skoots to check the spelling of her name and title on her new business cards, the cards that said 'nursing service' in the middle of the address. Then the painters, Eddy and Joe, wander into her office and eyeball around like they're estimating the time it will take to repaint the office. When asked what they were doing there, they just said they had a work order to paint the office by the first of the month for the new occupant. They don't know anything else. They just paint where people tell them to paint. When they left, Skoots put two and two together and got 17, just like Marcy figured she would. Now a different kind of person might have checked with her boss or asked around, but Skoots figured she had to move her bets over to the other side of the table."

"What's going to happen when the first of the month comes around and no reorganization?"

"Nothing. Reorganizations get put off all the time. And there is nobody she can ask without looking like a doofus, so she won't ask. She'll just sit there and be polite to everybody, particularly to you. The suits never admit that they're contemplating a reorganization, and they won't give her a straight answer if she asks. The standard answer is that the board is happy with the present organization but is always considering its options. What's she gonna make of an answer like that?"

It hadn't taken too much heat for Skoots to see the light, Nan thought. Now she'd have to think of some bone to throw in Skoots's direction. A bone thrown that way would probably be interpreted as a hint that the reorganization was going ahead, one day soon. A bone thrown per month could keep this going indefinitely.

"Carl," Nan said, placing her hand lightly on his forearm, "Mum's the word."

"Mum's the word. Chinese water torture won't get a word out of me. Besides, I didn't do anything except add up the pennies column on my sheet. But I'll tell you right now, Nan, this is one for the ages. The word will get around, and your mojo is going to be up, up, up. Nobody but nobody is gonna mess with you. Even if the suits find out about it, and I'm not going to be the one to tell them, they'll chalk it up as a point in your favor. They admire office politics skills, like they admire the golfing skills of Tiger Woods if they play golf—and they all do. Sheer admiration."

"Okay, I understand, but let's keep it mum as best we can."

"Can Joe and Eddy come by for a piece of that pie this afternoon in the training room?"

"How do you know about the cherry pie?"

"Everybody knows. The cafeteria gang can't keep a secret worth a hoot."

"Of course, they can come by for pie. If they miss out, I'll bake them one of their own Monday. Unless we're all fired in the meantime, that is."

"I don't mind if I get fired. I know some people downtown. I'd probably make out better someplace else, but I like this place. Lots goin' on. Bean counting can be pretty dull if you just sit around and count beans."

39

Nan Makes Notes on Bar Code

After Carl Burke left her office, Nan set about writing notes on what she had learned from Ann about getting bar coding to work in unstructured environments. She added the obvious points of connection to the bedside situation in hospitals, and she added what she thought might be a first-draft specification to give to vendors who want to sell bar code–based electronic records systems to the hospital. When she was done, she attached her notes to an e-mail message to Sanjar, asking him to give the matter some thought. No schedule, no due dates.

Nan had no information about any procurement schedule for such systems, since none had been identified in the meeting the day before. It didn't sound like there was any definitive schedule in that meeting, but Nan admitted to herself she was not yet accustomed to reading signals in such meetings. If there was a schedule, Sanjar probably knew it and would act accordingly. So, she had done what she could, and now she would have to trust others to follow through.

40

Nan Writes Her Documents

Nan opened new document files on her computer and, finally, wrote out the three documents she had in mind for this day. She wrote letters to go to Angel Copperwaite and to Mary Cummins. At the bottom of each letter was a space for Alice Newcomb's signature, if she could get Alice to sign them. She wrote Crawford's big-picture questions and her answers to them. She wrote the "recovery plan" requested by Crawford and which was to go into the departmental newsletter the following Monday, if it could get past a review by Alice Newcomb.

Nan wrote all these documents consistent with how she thought the rest of the day would go. That was more than a little brash, but the calendar did not have enough slack for her to do otherwise. Nan thought they were as good as she could make them, so she saved the files on the computer, printed a set to carry with her, and made envelopes to match. Then, Nan checked with Marcy to confirm that the noon meeting was still on and that everything else was still on track.

Nan stood by her desk, reminded herself that her job was not her life, that Jack loved her, Jake loved her, Bake loved her, and Ann loved her, and that she made a pretty decent cherry pie. With a platform like that to stand on, she might as well play to win. Somebody might be keeping score.

41

The Noon Meeting

Nan went by Alice Newcomb's office to drop off envelopes. Alice was not there, which is what Nan had expected. Nan had taken an extra set of those papers, just in case Alice turned up at the noon meeting.

Nan proceeded to the training room, arriving there at the stroke of noon. She found her husband Jack and Sanjar huddled over the frog table, looking at manuals and using electrical probes and instruments to poke around inside an opened EKG machine. They had a PC and a gaggle of computer parts and hand tools on the frog table. What they were doing was made evident to the audience by two large screens on the wall. One was the image from the frog camera mounted in the ceiling and looking down on the work being done by Jack and Sanjar. The other screen was a projection of the display screen of the PC on the frog table.

Nan went to the front of the room and took the speaker's rostrum next to the frog table. Nan looked over the audience, which she could see plainly because the room lighting was uniform. She had invited some people and had told others that the meeting was open if they wanted to attend. The only stipulation she had made was that the video links were closed, so that anybody who wanted to see what was going on had to attend in person.

Nan found all of her managers present. Maggie Kelly was sitting with Carl Burke and, surprisingly, Gretchen van der Schoot, chatting away. Dr. Suzy Wong was sitting with the chief of medicine, Dr. Anderson. Claudia Benedict and Angel Copperwaite were sitting with Vivian Smith, Mary Cummins, and Dr. Escobar. Alice Newcomb was seated beside Philip L. Crawford, on whose other side were four members of the board of directors of the hospital. There were four departmental vice presidents, seated with each other and with some assorted spear carriers from their departments. Meenie Stewart was there, with two radiologists.

Nan walked over to Alice Newcomb to hand her the envelopes and then returned to the rostrum. Near the front, Nan found Gordon Schneider seated next to a man with darker coloring but otherwise resembling Gordon, whom she took to be Gordon's brother, Edgar Schneider. Seated next to Edgar was a man with an elegant look and a thousand-dollar suit, whom Nan thought she recognized from newspaper photos as lawyer Randall Pinkston, executor of the Mr. Bill estate and, no doubt, attorney for the Schneider brothers. Nan found detective Stan Laurel seated next to Randall Pinkston and, at the other end of this grouping, the hospital security head, Lieutenant Lou. Scanning the room, Nan saw hospital security people standing at ease beside the two doors to the hallway. Additional security people were standing at the fire exits. Curious, thought Nan.

Nan put her papers on the rostrum, then she went to the frog table, smiled at Sanjar, and kissed Jack on the cheek. She asked about the state of their work.

Jack said, "We are checking out our setup. Things look okay so far. Sanjar got the right equipment delivered, and my plane was on time, so we are off to a good start. Sanjar has a wireless microphone for me here. I have not turned it on. If you want me to explain what we are doing, just give me the word." Jack gave her a confident smile.

Nan looked over to Sanjar, who seemed to be thrilled with what was going on. Nan returned to the rostrum and addressed the audience, setting her face into a pleasant but rather formal smile. "Ladies and gentlemen. Our purpose here today is to examine the EKG machines assigned to the VIP suites last week when Mr. Bill met his untimely demise. The particular machine that was in Mr. Bill's room and attached to him is no longer in the hospital. It has been impounded by the police. Therefore, we are not examining *that* machine.

"To assist us in this examination, I have engaged a software consultant, namely, my husband Jack Mills. It is customary for the hospital to pay its consultants one dollar, and I have one dollar here to pay Jack." Nan produced a small picture frame enclosing a dollar, a Confederate Dollar, they had acquired from a souvenir shop during a trip through Old Dixie several years before. Jack came to the rostrum, took the frame, shook Nan's hand, returned to the frog table, and positioned the frame so that the audience could see the joke on the wall screen. "Jack will now explain what he is doing. Let me add that Jack is being assisted by Sanjar Subramaniam and others of the hospital staff."

Jack turned on the wireless mike that he had attached to his shirt front. He looked out to the audience in a friendly, professional way, and began. "Ladies and gentlemen, my purpose is to determine, if I can, whether or not the software in the computer chip inside the EKG machine has been modified. This is like looking for a virus in your computer. A computer virus is a software program that got into your computer somehow and does something that not you, but somebody else, wants it to do. If you get a virus in your PC at home, you probably got it over the Internet or from a contaminated floppy disk. The EKG machines being used in the VIP suites do not have Internet connections, and they do not have floppy drives nor CD drives. What's more, the chip inside is different from what's in your computer at home. This is what's called an industrial computer and has its program burned into the chip for all time. It is a single-purpose computer, not a general-purpose computer. To change the code, it's necessary to take out the old chip and put in a new one with the modified program burned into the new one.

"With this in mind, the insides of the EKG machine are laid out to facilitate changing the chip. The chip is pulled with a chip puller like this one." Jack held up a hand-sized device that looked more or less like a staple puller. "The chip itself is quite inexpensive, just a few dollars even in small quantities, and they can be bought at supply houses or over the Internet." Jack turned to Sanjar and asked, "Did you buy these chips locally or over the Internet?"

Sanjar answered, "I got these from a standard supply house over the Internet. All quantities are readily available. I got the chip puller and these other items at the same time so that I would be sure that we would have compatible equipment because there are small differences from chip manufacturer to chip manufacturer."

Jack resumed. "This item here is a chip burner. It is attached to the serial port of the PC we are using here. The so-called burning is done with ultraviolet light, and it just writes the program code into the chip. Then the chip is inserted into the EKG machine's chip socket, and it is ready to use. Chip burners are quite ordinary equipment, and I'm sure there are dozens, if not more, here in the city. This one is a one-holer, as you can see, the kind that would be used by an engineer or technician doing development work. For high-volume manufacturing, there are bigger burners that can handle large volumes expeditiously.

"Let me add that the PC here on the table, and I am told this is called the frog table, is a brand new computer just taken out of its box this morning. It has no application software loaded on it other than what we have installed for our purposes. We did that just to make sure there was no extraneous activity going on that might confuse somebody, particularly us.

"This EKG machine was taken from the third floor and replaced there by a rented EKG machine so that they would have enough for their patients. We took this one because, as near as we can find out, it was never tested or handled by anybody during the recent equipment testing campaign. So this is our null example or baseline.

"We have removed the cover and pulled the chip. We have inserted the chip into the socket of the chip burner. We have used the PC to read the chip's burned-in code. Using software called a disassembly program, we have recreated that code in a form that human beings can read. That's what you see on the screen above me and what I see on the PC screen here, in smaller scale."

The screen showed many short lines of what looked like algebra. Groups of lines were in different colors. Jack continued. "Using a standard text editor, I could modify this code in some way to suit myself. I could then burn that modified code into a new blank chip and put that new chip into the EKG machine. I would have, in effect, given that machine a virus. In short, anyone who has experience with this kind of computing, access to the right EKG machine, and a few hundred dollars worth of equipment, can give that machine a virus.

"Getting rid of the virus just requires doing the same in reverse. Take out the chip with the virus and put back the original chip. The same tools would be used.

"Now, I have never seen the code for this EKG chip before. I could eventually determine what each line of code does, which would take most of the day. Fortunately, we won't have to do that. Instead, we will just compare this code from this chip in this null machine with that from an EKG machine we suspect may have the virus."

At this time, Willy came in, pushing his cart with three EKG machines stacked on it. Willy was accompanied by a uniformed guard from the hospital security service.

"Willy, I'm Jack Mills. Thank you for your help this morning. Do I understand that you have brought these machines from the VIP suites, and that these are the machines that were in the VIP suites last week?" Willy responded in the affirmative.

Jack turned to the guard accompanying Willy. "And you, sir, can you tell us that these machines have been out of use, red-tagged, and under guard by your department since that was requested by Mrs. Mills?" The guard answered in the affirmative.

"Very well. Willy, if you will, put any one of those three EKG machines up on the frog table, Sanjar will remove the cover. Please arrange the EKG machine so that the frog camera can pick up what you're doing."

Willy took the top machine on the stack, put it on the floor, and selected the second machine to put up on the frog table. Sanjar used what looked to be a standard nut driver with a ratchet handle to remove several small machine screws with hex heads. He put the screws aside, lifted the cover off gently, and put the cover aside. Sanjar then used the chip puller to pull the chip. He placed the pulled chip in the socket of the chip burner, and clicked the mouse. Then, he stood aside, smiling respectfully at Jack Mills.

Jack continued. "As we look at this code that the disassembler has read from the chip from this EKG machine, we see what looks to be the same as the other one from the null machine. If we look at it line by line, we might find some differences. Let's do that, but let's let the computer do the comparison. We'll just tell it to compare the two code files and highlight any differences. There is nothing very special about this process, most text editors will compare files in this way."

Sanjar clicked through three windows on the PC screen rather quickly, and then the screen filled again with lines of code. This time, only one small group of lines was highlighted in a red color. Jack and Sanjar looked at the code for a full minute, then they conferred with each other. They nodded affirmatively, and Jack turned again to the audience.

"I suppose that most of you have never looked at computer coding at this level of detail, what's called machine code or assembly code. That's okay, because this is quite a simple code segment. It's important to see what it does, which we will get to in a minute. It is important to see where this virus is put into the original code. Let's take that second point now and then get back to what the virus does.

"Sanjar and I speculated that the virus would be attached just where the null copy of the code turns on the alarm at the nursing station, since we speculated that the purpose of the virus would be to mess with the alarm logic. By working with the board layout and a voltmeter, we were able to identify that the chip originates this alarm by changing the voltage on its pin 15. All computer chips communicate with the outside world by changing pin voltages, we just needed to figure out which one. We did that this morning.

"I will stipulate that there are other places that the virus might have been attached, but we thought this to be the most likely. Events have proved us to be correct in our speculation. If we had been wrong, it just would have taken us another hour or so to figure it out.

"If you look just below the red section you see here," Jack pointed to a part of the text using a laser pointer he had produced from his shirt pocket, "you see the word PIN015. So we know that this whole block of code deals with pin 15.

"Now, lets's determine what this virus, the part in red, does. First, we see that this is a loop that will be repeated 750 times." Jack pointed at some particulars in the red code, which looked like Greek to most people in the audience. "Here we see it checking for the clock, so that the loop will be repeated over 750 seconds. That's 12½ minutes. Here you see a reference to a section of the normal code that I will tell you sets the EKG machine into 'freeze display' mode. Sanjar and I investigated that this morning, and I can show that in detail later to anyone who wants to see it. Finally, just below this loop, the red code is setting a permanent flag.

"Let me now step away from these details and tell you what the virus does. First of all, the virus does nothing at all until the EKG tries to activate the remote alarm. Then it delays for 750 seconds, during which it causes the EKG screen to continue to show a frozen image of the most recent complete trace. Then, it sets a permanent flag so that the delay is never done again. This has the effect of delaying the alarm by 12½ minutes and providing a display that would appear to be normal at first glance for that period of time. Then it eliminates itself so that later functional testing would not reveal the virus. I understand that Mr. Bill's EKG machine was tested by the police after the fact and found to be in good order.

"That finishes our part of the program. Before handing the spotlight back to Nan, I just want to say that I have never seen these machines before and therefore I have never handled these chips before. Sanjar, let me ask you if you have ever handled these machines or these chips before, just for the record."

Sanjar responded, "Yesterday I took the cover off what we are calling the null machine so that I could identify the chip part number so that I could order the correct equipment that you see here. I took a digital photograph so that I would not have to rely on my memory. I replaced the cover. So, yes, I have seen the null machine before. I did not handle the null chip yesterday, I simply looked at it with my eyes and with the camera. As for the machine that Willy brought in, I have seen it with its red tag upstairs in the VIP suites, but I have never handled the machine and certainly not the chip."

Jack thanked Sanjar, Willy, and everybody in general, and then with a smile he handed off the meeting to Nan at the podium. Nan addressed the audience. "When I learned from Dr. Anderson that he thought there was something so unusual about Mr. Bill's death that he was doing his own investigation, and when I read Dr. Anderson's report on Mr. Bill's death, it seemed to me that either the duty nurse had been very slow in responding to the EKG alarm, or else the alarm was delayed. I wanted to know more about the machine. At that time, I did not know that there is a computer chip inside an EKG machine, but fortunately I had near to me people who did know such facts, as you have just seen.

"The EKG machine that had been at Mr. Bill's bedside had already been removed to the police station. I learned that four such machines had been located in the VIP suites, and that they were in a pool. As one was needed for a patient, it was taken from the pool. It would be impossible to predict ahead of time which of the four machines would wind up with which patient. Therefore, I concluded that if anything was amiss with any of the four machines, it was amiss with all four. What Jack called a virus. If one of the machines had a virus, all four had it.

"The other possibility was a random failure of the particular EKG machine at Mr. Bill's bedside, but I learned that the police had already tested that machine and found no such fault. Therefore, it looked like something was wrong with all four machines.

"I ordered the remaining three machines red-tagged so they would not be used on any other patient until this was sorted out. We rented some machines from a durable equipment dealer down the street so that we would have enough machines to take care of our patients.

"Jack has shown that one of those three red-tagged machines has the virus. I'll bet a Confederate dollar that the other two have the same virus, and so does Mr. Bill's machine down at the police station." Nan paused and looked around the room. Every eye was fixed on her.

"There is another question, obvious to all. That is, who would want to interfere with life-saving nursing care for Mr. Bill? If he had any mortal enemies, I didn't know of them. If his family wanted him out of the way, what motive did they have? His recently declared romantic interest seemed an unlikely suspect.

"Having access only to public documents about Mr. Bill's family, I learned that the untimely death of Mr. Bill's wife of many years, known as Aunt Agnes, had drained Mr. Bill of most of his liquid assets so that her bequests could be satisfied. That left Mr. Bill with some real estate and his controlling interest in the company founded by his son Edgar and which Mr. Bill had bankrolled to the extent of about $15 million over its early years.

"One of the public documents of interest is the offering memorandum, or perhaps it is called a prospectus, written about two years ago in anticipation of an initial public offering for Edgar's company, which does biotech work in protein markers. That is what is popularly called an IPO. That IPO did not happen because of market conditions at that time. It has recently been updated, so it appears that Edgar Schneider and his board anticipate trying the IPO market again in the near future.

"The IPO documentation covers the ownership of the stock in detail. It says that Mr. Bill had the largest block of stock and that block of stock would pass upon his death to his two sons, predominately to his son Edgar. That may seem like an odd detail to find in a stock prospectus, but since Mr. Bill was known to be in poor health, the disposition of his stock at his death would be a matter of concern to any potential investor.

"Now Mr. Bill is dead, and the stock will pass to the sons, who will pay inheritance taxes on the bequest. If the value of Mr. Bill's stock is taken at his cost, then the inheritance tax will be $4 million or $5 million. There is a $3 million key-man life insurance policy, and the sons can probably raise the balance by mortgaging real estate or taking out personal loans. At the end of the day, they will hold Mr. Bill's stock.

"Therefore, on its face, Mr. Bill's death cost the sons millions of dollars for the marginal benefit to them of holding the stock in their own names rather than in their father's. That does not constitute a motive for a felonious act.

"Just last evening, the missing piece fell into place. A professional financial planner, looking only at these public documents, explained that the difference in tax obligation depends enormously on whether Mr. Bill happened to die before or after the IPO. Before the IPO, as I just said, the sons have to find a couple million dollars plus the insurance money to satisfy the tax obligation.

"After the IPO, Mr. Bill's stock will not be evaluated for tax purposes at his cost but rather at the market price. The post-IPO price will be at least 10 times as high and quite possibly even higher than that. Taking a low figure, Mr. Bill's stock will be worth not $15 million but more than $100 million. The tax bill will be at least $50 million.

"There is no chance in the world that any insurance company would write a $50 million policy on somebody in Mr. Bill's physical condition. Therefore, the sons would have to come up with $50 million in cash by liquidating assets. The only asset in sight is Mr. Bill's block of stock. They would have to put at least half of Mr. Bill's block of stock on the market.

"Moreover, putting a big block of stock on the market would drive down the market price, which means they would have to sell an even bigger block of the stock to raise the required $50 million in cash. They might have to sell all of Mr. Bill's stock or, theoretically, even more, although at that point it would be cheaper for them to refuse the bequest. If most of Mr. Bill's stock were sold on the market, then the family would lose control of its company, the company that Edgar had spent all of his career and most of Mr. Bill's accumulated wealth to create.

"Until recently, the prospects of Mr. Bill's living long enough to see the IPO were slim because of his deteriorating health, his refusal to accept a pacemaker, and his ongoing depression brought on by the death of his wife, whom the public knew as Aunt Agnes. Then, some few weeks ago, Mr. Bill became enamored and took a renewed interest in being alive. He decided to have a pacemaker installed.

"I don't know what a pacemaker plus an interest in being alive would do for his life expectancy. I'm a nurse, not a doctor. But I would speculate that his life expectancy would be a few years, not many years. Dr. Anderson or Mr. Bill's physician may have something to say in this regard.

"If Mr. Bill were to live, say, three more years, that would carry him beyond the IPO but not far enough beyond it for the sons to find $50 million worth of liquid assets. Nor could they count on inheritance taxes going down, not with one national political party cutting inheritance tax rates and the other party having raised inheritance taxes on large estates the last time they had the power to do so. So, they were stuck.

"I believe that Gordon Schneider and perhaps his brother Edgar took steps to interfere with medical equipment that would have very likely saved their father's life here in our hospital last week. Since Mr. Bill in fact died of natural causes and since he might have died even if he had been defibrillated promptly, I'm not the one to say what law has been broken. I will say that sabotaging four machines recklessly endangered not only Mr. Bill but potentially three other patients who just had the bad luck to get one of the four machines that were sabotaged, and that sounds felonious to me.

"Gordon Schneider, you had access to these machines. You have the technical knowledge of industrial computers. You had motive. I accuse you of recklessly endangering four of my patients. I will recommend to the authorities that criminal action be taken against you. If your brother Edgar was involved, I'm sure the authorities will bring this to light."

Nan stood stock still, glaring at the Schneider brothers. The room was deathly still.

After a long pause, lawyer Randall Pinkston stood and asked Nan if he might say a few words. She nodded to him, and he approached the rostrum. Nan stood well to the side, near to Jack, to give Pinkston room. Randall Pinkston spoke, nodding respectfully to the audience, which stayed still. "Mrs. Mills, Mr. Crawford, ladies and gentlemen. I am Randall Pinkston, executor for Mr. Bill's estate and attorney for Messers. Gordon and Edgar Schneider. I will speak on my own behalf here in matters related to Mr. Bill's estate, and I am authorized by the sons to speak on their behalf to you at this time.

"The sons came to see me at my office downtown the first thing this morning. They gave me a series of letters, some of which I will read to you presently. I served Mr. Bill as his attorney for many years, and I knew Aunt Agnes very well. I have known the sons, it seems, all their lives. I have watched them grow and succeed in their careers. I have been aware not only of the charitable acts of Mr. Bill and Aunt Agnes but also of the community support given by the sons over the years. Therefore, I find this to be a very sad occasion.

"Two of these letters that I have here in my hand are letters of admission signed by each of the sons. Each admits that the EKG machines were tampered with for the purpose of interfering with life-saving efforts that might be extended to Mr. Bill during the course of his stay in the hospital VIP suites.

"The letters differ in one regard. The letter signed by Gordon Schneider asserts that he was acting on his own behalf and that his brother Edgar had no knowledge of, and took no part in, these actions. The other letter, signed by Edgar Schneider, asserts that the entire matter was his doing and that he coerced his brother to do the tampering. I don't know how to reconcile these two statements, but that is not my duty in any case.

"Each of these letters authorizes me as their attorney to surrender them to the legal authorities and to take other such actions as will expedite a resolution of the matter before these authorities and courts of jurisdiction. I have already spoken to Detective Laurel by telephone this morning, and I will put these letters in his hands while we are both here. The surrender is voluntary, and I think this can be done with a little decorum if we try to do so."

"I have other letters from the sons renouncing any bequest of stock from their father's estate.

"I have Edgar's letters of resignation from his company, for which Edgar was chairman and CEO. I have Gordon's letter of resignation. Gordon served as a member of the board of directors. The letter from Edgar recommends that the present COO be elevated to the position of CEO, and I leave that to the company's board to evaluate. The letter goes further to assert that the patents, products, and research team of the company are strong and that his leaving the company will have little or no negative impact on the value of the company and its IPO prospects. I offer no opinion on that matter.

"Now, with my executor hat on, I have something to say about Mr. Bill's last will and testament. Mr. Bill's will stipulated that the stock in question be bequeathed to his sons along with some real property and some family mementos, and that the residue of his estate be given to the hospital, which was his favorite charity and that of his wife. Since much of Mr. Bill's wealth, other than the stock in question, had been liquidated a year ago to pay for the bequests of his wife, that residue looked to be of modest size. Not to be sneezed at, and I didn't see any sign that the hospital would turn up its nose, but not millions of dollars.

"That is now changed. The hospital stands to receive Mr. Bill's stock in Edgar's company, and I have no question in my mind that stock will be worth more than $100 million by the time the estate is settled and the IPO has taken place. The hospital is not subject to estate taxes, so all that will be yours. That surely constitutes the largest charitable gift to the hospital in my memory. I hope that the hospital will put aside the troubling circumstances and see fit to accept this gift.

"Speaking still as executor, I say now that I will approach the hospital board and you, Mr. Crawford, within the next few days to discuss something that has just occurred to me this morning and may take a little thought and discussion to put into place. That is, and I speak now in general terms and subject to improvement upon discussion, I will ask the hospital board to set aside a portion of the Mr. Bill bequest to be a fund to support operational initiatives within the hospital so that projects of modest size can be undertaken on the say-so of the head nurse, the head nurse plus the chief medical officer, or some small steering committee. I don't mean the whole panoply of the senior management, because that would just duplicate the present machinery. Something under the discretion of the line management. If you have some interest in this, I will be pleased to discuss it with you and work up some language with your counsel, Ms. Newcomb, for whom I have the highest regard.

"I have still one more thing to say as attorney for the sons. Each of them has given me a letter to give to the hospital offering to replace all EKG machines in the hospital so that there will be no taint remaining. I imagine that will run to some hundreds of thousands of dollars, and I can tell you without revealing any confidences that each of them is good for it. I doubt if you want two sets of EKG machines, so we can discuss how to deal with these offers. These offers stand apart from all other topics this morning and are offers made in good faith and without condition.

"Now, I have never thought of myself as a windy sort of lawyer, but I do have one more thing to say with my executor hat on, again. When Dr. Anderson called me a few days ago to say that he was concerned about the circumstances of Mr. Bill's death and suggested an autopsy, I took his recommendation and agreed. At the same time, I sent my clerk over to the courthouse to enter a criminal complaint against the hospital and the nurse whose name had been given to me. At that time, I had no particular notions of criminality. I was doing what lawyers do by making a filing so that the right to file would not be lost by later circumstances or developments. Today, on my way back to my office, I will go the courthouse and withdraw that complaint.

"On Monday, Alice, if this can be arranged with your schedule and that of the nurse, whose name I understand to be Angela Copperwaite, I wish to meet with you to discuss a cash settlement to be paid to Ms. Copperwaite by the estate for any anguish she may have suffered because of my action. There was nothing personal in my action, but then I suspect it may have seemed otherwise to Ms. Copperwaite. If you, Alice, or Ms. Copperwaite wish to bring in outside counsel, that will be fine with me, but please let's try to do that in the early part of the week.

"Now, I am done. I will remain here to take care of matters with Detective Laurel. If there are other questions, I will try to deal with them if I can." At that, Randall Pinkston left the rostrum to resume his seat between Stan Laurel and Gordon Schneider.

The room remained eerily quiet. Stan Laurel stood and asked Nan if he could say a few words. Nan nodded in the affirmative. San took the rostrum.

"Ladies and gentlemen, I am Detective Laurel of the county detectives bureau. People call me Stan. I wish to confirm what Mr. Pinkston has said to you just now. Mr. Pinkston telephoned me this morning and said that Gordon and Edgar Schneider wished to surrender themselves to the law, and we agreed that that would be done after this meeting. I want to emphasize that the surrender was offered before this meeting and, if I had so insisted, would have taken place before this meeting. Therefore, I was not then nor am I now relying on what we have all just seen and heard here this morning.

"I say that for the record because I don't want my boss to yell at me for letting amateurs solve this case before I did. I won't tell him if you don't. The first I knew that Mr. Bill's death had any suspicious overtones was when Dr. Anderson called me to say that there was an unexplained delay of perhaps 10 minutes between the time Mr. Bill's heart action went off kilter and the time the duty nurse tried to bring him back by giving him a shock with the paddles.

"I impounded the EKG machine and had technicians from the dealership check it out at the station. They found it to be in good order, but I kept it in the evidence locker because a criminal complaint had been filed. When I stopped by to talk this over with Mrs. Mills, she refused to discuss the case, as everybody always does, and even in general terms could not account for the delay. So, the case wasn't going anywhere. There was no mechanism that I could see, and there was no motive evident. It looked like the nurse had been slow in getting to Mr. Bill's room, or else there was something we hadn't figured out.

"Then Lieutenant Lou called me to say that Mrs. Mills had ordered the three remaining EKG machines red-tagged and guarded. Something was up, and it had to do with the EKG machines. So, I called the EKG manufacturer to get them to send hardware and software engineers here next week to do a complete analysis of Mr. Bill's EKG machine. I did not know what they might find, but it looked like the right place to dig. I think they would have found what Mr. Mills found here today, although you never know. They might not have been interested in finding anything wrong with their machines. Now that they will know what Mr. Mills found with this one machine, I think they will be looking hard to find any virus in that machine. I will be asking Mr. Mills to document what he found here today or to join us next week or both."

Stan turned to Jack and made a polite bow. Jack smiled politely in return without making much of a commitment to do anything.

"There still wasn't any motive that I could see, so I contacted the financial consultants we use in white-collar cases and turned them loose on the affairs of Mr. Bill and his two sons. They have not yet reported, but I'm confident that they will find about what Mrs. Mills reported here this morning, especially since I didn't see anybody arguing with her.

"You may think that if the Schneider brothers have already offered to surrender themselves, there would be no point in following through with this. However, that's not how we work. If there are independent ways of determining the facts, we try to find them. Also, if there is a new way of committing a crime, we like to know about it and share it with other agencies.

"When I started talking, I said that I'm not relying on anything said or shown here today. I'm not. But I *am* impressed. You got to the heart of the matter and you marshaled the talent and resources to figure this mystery out in a big hurry. That may even qualify you, Nan, for having your picture taken with the county attorney." With that, and a nice smile in Nan's direction, Stan retook his seat.

Alice Newcomb came forward and asked to be allowed to speak. "Ladies and gentlemen. I am struck dumb by what I have seen here this morning and it will be some time before I will be able to speak freely. So I will be brief.

"Randall, you suggested that we meet very soon to arrange a settlement in favor of Angela Copperwaite. Angel is here with us this morning, and if we can speak together for a moment before we scatter, we can schedule a time. I will recommend to Angel that she take outside counsel so there is no taint of hospital meddling in the matter. The hospital will pay her attorney's cost. I will name some attorneys to her if she does not have her own counsel presently. It is not my place to comment on that offer of settlement with Nurse Copperwaite, but Mr. Crawford may have something to say in that regard when I am finished.

"On the matter of the Schneider sons donating money to replace the entirety of the hospital's EKG machines, I can assure that the hospital will accept your offer. We can meet to sort out the amounts of money and who gives what.

"On the matter of the large bequest in favor of the hospital, I will be pleased to work with you on any details. You mentioned setting aside some part of that bequest to endow a fund for operational projects. While accepting any such terms is up to the board, I can assure you that I will be pleased to work out the details if the board accepts in general terms."

"I have something else to say, quite apart from these topics. I wish to say it to all of you who are present. I had a conversation with Angel Copperwaite shortly after the Mr. Bill incident. I said to her that if she were named as a defendant in the event of civil or criminal proceedings, the hospital would provide her with counsel and cover costs unless she had done something wrong, in which case she was on her own. I have probably been saying things like that to hospital professionals since I have been here. I now see that was a foolish and callous thing to say.

"Mark Twain said that a bank was something that loaned you an umbrella if the sun was shining and then wanted the umbrella back if it started to rain. Well, this hospital is not a bank. We are an organization of professional people who commit their careers to helping people when they need it most, rain or shine. The hospital administration needs to do the same and, in fact, has always done so. We just need to get my mouth in synch with our practices and policy.

"I have in my hand a letter addressed to Angela Copperwaite RN, saying that if she is named in any civil or criminal litigation arising from her professional services to the hospital, then the hospital will provide her with counsel and cover her costs, with no conditions.

"I have another letter of the same substance addressed to Mary Cummins RN, which is a separate matter. I see that Mary is present this morning, and I wish to take this opportunity to tell her this.

"Nan, I thank you for allowing me to attend this meeting this morning. It has gotten me to pull my socks up on this policy matter, and it has given me plenty of work to do on these bequests, and I love you for it."

Alice left the rostrum, giving Nan a bow and a smile that was not the usual lawyer stone-face and just might have been inviting Nan to let Alice be her friend. Nan deigned to smile and nod in return. Mojo.

Dr. Anderson came forward and asked if he could speak. "Mrs. Mills, Mr. Crawford, ladies and gentlemen. I'm the old codger in this crowd, and I want to say that I have never seen anything like this meeting during my very long career. I've learned a lot. I've learned a lot all this week. Maybe I'm not too old to learn something after all.

"I am pleased, Mr. Laurel, that my call to you in the Mr. Bill matter led you to start actions that have borne fruit here today. That was what I did right in this matter.

"There are plenty of things I did wrong. When I finished my report, I had looked at all the information available, and I had concluded that the most likely cause was that the duty nurse had been slow and maybe derelict in responding to the alarm from Mr. Bill's EKG machine. Okay, that was logical problem solving, and I think most of us would have come to the same conclusion.

"I now wish to point out for all to see and to admire that Nan Mills read my report, rejected out of hand that one of her nurses had ignored an alarm for 10 minutes or more, and set out to find the real cause of the problem. It boiled down, as Nan said moments ago, to being either the nurse or the machine. It's not the nurse, so it must be the machine. Now, if I would've had that much sense, maybe I would have gotten the right answer instead of the wrong answer.

"I'm told that Nan Mills had never set eyes on this particular nurse at that time. Now a jaundiced viewer might say this was just tribal instinct on Nan's part, not a rational action. So let me tell you about another case that came up last week. Some of you know about it, and some of you don't. I will not go into details, but the issue boils down to a failure in communications between a good doctor and a good nurse that had unfortunate consequences. When I looked into that matter, I concluded that since the doctor is a good doctor whom I regard highly, it must have been a blunder by the nurse. You can call this tribal behavior on my part, which it was.

"Nan Mills could have done the same, saying that since the nurse is a good nurse, it must have been a blunder by the doctor. That would have been tribal instinct on her part. Now tribal instinct protects the tribe, maybe, but it doesn't prevent the same communications failure from happening tomorrow or next month, in this hospital or in some other hospital. Here's where Nan Mills showed me the error of my ways and made me think for just a moment that I might be getting too old for this job.

"Nan did not take the tribal action. I'm sure that instinct is just as much alive in her as it is in any tribal leader, but she did something better. She said that if a communication got botched between a good doctor and a good nurse, then we had better fix the way we do verbal communications between doctor and nurse. Now, that's pretty smart. It's also pretty obvious when you say it out loud. Obvious. Well, lots of things are obvious after they are obvious, they just aren't obvious until they are.

"Nan did something more. She took a personal hand in getting the doctor and the nurse to put their energies into finding a better way and not into remorse over what had happened. Then she turned her organization loose to find a better way. I watched the videotape of those skits your department did the other day, Nan. I had heard about them, and the whole approach was so far away from what we customarily do around here that I was ready to be scandalized. What I found instead were some short, clever skits that made the point quickly and in a memorable way. I'll take that over a boring report any day.

"I expect most of our physicians will want to work with you to try this idea out. Any of them who don't can plan on watching John Wayne submarine movies until they get their heads straight.

"As for the doctor and nurse in this case, I see they are here today. I will take this opportunity to say to them now what I should have said to them at the time. I have known you both for years, and I know you to be top professionals. I know that any error that happened involving you two was not a failure by one of you, it was a failure of our system. Please forgive me for not having had the sense to say that to you on the spot.

"Mention was made here of an endowment to pay for innovative projects in hospital operations. I think that is timely, and I think that, with our present organization, the best way to handle it is to give Nan Mills sole discretion over the fund. Nan, you can count on the medical staff to be responsive to anything you want to try.

"I see Dr. Wong, Suzy Wong to her many friends, is here today. I have known Dr. Wong since she has been here, and I have been generally aware that good things were happening in anesthesiology the past few years. What I had not bothered to think was that there was something physicians might learn from that experience. While I was asleep at that switch, Nan Mills, her first morning in the office in her new position, got Dr. Wong to tell the nursing management what lessons have been learned, so that the nursing staff could take benefit of them. If they have a sufficiently open mind, a skeptic might say. Well, Dr. Wong opened some eyes, that led to thinking about verbal orders, that led to those skits, and that led to identifying something that has worked in the navy for several hundred years that just might work at bedside. I hope it does. But my point here is that we are going to do a better job finding ways to reduce medical error if we open our minds to the possibility that our systems just might be imperfect and that somebody else may have something useful to tell us.

"Well, I'm old and slow, but I'm not out of the picture yet. After I saw the tape of Suzy Wong's remarks to the nursing staff, I got up out of my chair and went over to ask Suzy to give the same sort of talk for the medical staff at our next meeting. If she agrees, I'll ask her to invite Dr. Gaba out at Stanford or one of his researchers to talk to us about the latest and greatest findings. Then we're going to be asking a lot more questions of our own professional societies, of ourselves, and maybe of the university faculty. It's time for us doctors to get with the program.

"Nan, I have just heard a little about your plan to do one-by-one nonjudgmental retraining of your staff. I don't know enough about that yet, but I'll be calling your office to book you for one of our medical staff meetings as soon as your schedule permits. I'm sure you're planting lots of other seeds I don't know about yet. I'll be looking forward to seeing and hearing about those, too.

"Nan, I'm honored to be on the hospital staff with you. It's going to be a lot more exciting around here now, if this one week is any indication. One last thing. Mr. Mills, Jack if I may call you that. I don't know if there is such a thing as forensic software engineering, but if not, I think you just invented it." He smiled a warm smile in Jack's direction and then in Nan's and returned to his seat.

Nan discovered that Jack was holding her hand. That was a little more demonstrative than he usually was in public, but she didn't mind at all.

Crawford came forward. "Nan, ladies and gentlemen. I want to say that this has been a learning experience for me.

"Nan, you had so much confidence in your staff and in your husband that you were willing to do this forensic software before a live audience. That takes a steady hand. I don't think I've ever seen anything like it. I haven't yet seen Suzy Wong's tape, but I will catch that later today. If Suzy has ideas that will help the hospital, I'm all for them. The same for Nan and everybody else.

"I was a big admirer of Mr. Bill and of Aunt Agnes. Their generosity has been heartfelt. I'm sorry that neither of them is here with us now, and the circumstances around Mr. Bill's passing have been given enough attention here. I will only add that when the bulk of Mr. Bill's estate passes to the hospital, it will not be the hospital so much as the community that will benefit, because that's why we are here.

"I have not yet had a moment to discuss these matters with the board, although some of our members are with us here today. Perhaps we can exchange views shortly. I believe that Alice's remarks are very close to where we will come out.

"Now I want to say to you how proud I am of myself. I am proud that I recommended to the board that Nan Mills be named to her present position as head of nursing services. I told the board that we were sticking our necks out by selecting a younger candidate who might need to take a little time to figure out how an organization like ours works and that there might be some bumps along the road. I said to the board that you could be expected to add some spark. What we have had all week were Roman candles!

"Well, I don't know if I can stand many weeks like this one, but I'm game if you are. On behalf of the board and the senior executives, Nan, I want to say how thrilled I am that you are with us. You can count on our support. And I thank Mr. Mills, Sanjar, and the rest of you for your contributions to the resolution of some problems and for your contributions to our being a better hospital today and a yet-better hospital tomorrow.

"Mr. Pinkston, your proposal of settlement in favor of Nurse Copperwaite is as welcome as it is unprecedented, so far as I know. Alice will work with you on that, and you can count on my personal participation if and when that would be useful. Thank you."

Smiling broadly in Nan's direction, Crawford returned to his seat. Nan thought he looked like he might have relaxed a little. Nan gave Jack's hand a squeeze and let go. She went to the rostrum.

"Thank you all, friends, for your kind words of encouragement. There are only a few minutes before the refreshment cart is due, so I will be brief. First, let me say that this week was different from what I had expected. The strategy professor at the management course Jack and I just took said something to the effect that an executive can't really control an enterprise. All he or she can do is get an oar in the water and try to cope with the tides, winds, and turbulence. I think my oar is in the water. I think there will be turbulence ahead. With you at the helm, Mr. Crawford, and with our able crew, I think we should be able to keep our ship upright and in good trim.

"You asked me some questions about roles and strategy a few days ago, Mr. Crawford. I am prepared to answer them now, but I think both the questions and my answers have been overtaken by events. If you agree, I'll table that matter." Crawford smiled his best beatific smile and nodded in the affirmative.

"You asked me, Mr. Crawford, to draft a plan to be circulated to the troops in the earliest convenient departmental publication. I have given a draft to Alice Newcomb, since all of you know, I am sure, that anything that looks like a policy statement needs to be vetted before seeing the light of day, which is a policy I agree with entirely.

"I had thought to present that plan to the group here today, but we have run longer than I thought we would and presenting the plan would interfere with refreshments. So if you agree, I'll have

Sanjar put the draft up on one of the screens so that interested parties can give it a look while enjoying the refreshments.

"Mr. Pinkston, your idea for an innovation endowment is an interesting one. I look forward to working with you on it, to the extent that my views will be of any value to you and to Alice. I'll conclude by saying to you, Jack my husband, that I love you. All this week people have been asking me if I am married to the famous Jack Mills. Now I know why they ask. Refreshments are about to be served. Thank you for coming, and let's follow up on all the good things proposed here today."

Nan gave the audience her best professional smile. As she concluded, the rear doors opened and Willy came in pushing a cafeteria trolley covered with pies. Behind Willy came the cafeteria manager in chef's hat pushing another trolley, followed by sous-chefs and more trolleys. Did the cafeteria have sous-chefs? If not, who are all these people in chef's hats? In total, there must be 25 or 30 pies, discovered Nan. What's going on?

The trolleys were lined up and joined by other carts with liquid refreshments, plates, forks, and napkins. The pies each had little numbered flags, and they had been cut into tiny pieces for tasting. Her gag production of six cherry pies had become a pie tasting contest worthy of the county fair!

As the crowd thronged around the food, Crawford was heard saying to all, "Watch out for the mincemeat. My wife sent that in with me this morning. She told me that she had used nonalcoholic rum. But you can't take her word for something like that. She's a trickster if there ever was one." That got a big laugh from the crowd, and the mincemeat was getting lots of attention. Her cherry pies were going fast, too, but now Nan had to wonder if her staff were each taking a taste of her pies to be polite to her.

Nan saw that Sanjar had gotten her recovery plan up on the screen, but nobody was paying much attention to it. Jack had left the frog table and had joined the throng at the pie serving tables.

Marcy was helping the sous-chefs serve the bite-sized servings of pie. Willy was holding a pie plate with one hand and taking snapshots using Nan's digital camera with the other.

Suzy Wong was talking with Angel Copperwaite and Mary Cummins. Maggie Kelly was talking with Dr. Anderson. Carl Burke was talking with Maria Escobar. The others were talking and moving around and not getting too far from the pie carts. Even Eddy and Joe, the painters, had shown up and were bellying up to the pie bar.

Stan Laurel and Randall Pinkston were going out the hall door with the Schneider brothers. Nan guessed that Marcy would put aside a share of the pie for Stan.

Nan mixed with the crowd and received kind words from all. The one with the most ingratiating smile and demeanor was Skoots van der Schoot. Taking her time, Nan worked her way over to the board members who were talking with Crawford and Alice Newcomb. Alice leaned close to Nan so that she could speak without raising her voice in the now noisy room and said quietly, "That undated letter of resignation went in the shredder." Nan didn't doubt that outcome, but she wondered if the past tense was a little off. Lawyers!

Nan gave Alice a minimum smile and turned to Crawford. "Mr. Crawford . . . "

Crawford interrupted her to say, "Nan, please call me Phil."

"Phil, then. When can we talk about the situation with employee parking?"

An Afterword on
Six Sigma

Six Sigma is a management method for achieving very high goals for correct outcomes. The "sigma" stands for standard deviations; and six standard deviations means that the remaining erroneous outcomes are way out on the tail of the normal distribution. A higher sigma count means a higher expectation of favorable outcomes.

Let's start again. Six Sigma is also a management *attitude*. The Six Sigma management attitude is:

- Face it.

- Find it.

- Fix it.

Face, find, and fix *what?*[1] The sources of error at every step in the operations. High overall results can only be achieved by having very high results at every step along the way.

Facing it is a management issue, not a technical issue. Why do sources of error linger? Because management tolerates it. When management stops tolerating errors, error sources get found and get fixed. There are Six Sigma tools to help with the finding and fixing, and there are tracking tools to make sure the fix stays fixed.

Let's face a couple of examples in the healthcare field.

Doctors have been using medical x-rays for more than 100 years. Virtually every healthcare professional has a personal anecdote about something dreadful that almost happened or did happen, because the x-ray film was in the viewer backward. Surely this is a trivial problem to solve, so why hasn't it been solved? One suspects that it's because the issue hasn't been faced.

Nurses have been using syringes for almost 100 years, and nurses are still sticking themselves after all these years. This is a little trickier problem to solve because it involves manual tasks in an unstructured work environment, but it certainly isn't impossible. With the anxiety over blood-borne diseases these days, why hasn't it been solved—not improved, not managed, not tracked, not incremented, but *solved?* One suspects that it's because the issue hasn't been faced. Let's say it another way. If there is no management commitment to face, find, and fix errors, there won't be any errors fixed.

Now let's suppose that management sees the light. What does Six Sigma have to offer? The Six Sigma management method says let's set high goals, let's go after those goals systematically, let's create a work environment where everybody is going in the right direction, and let's figure out how to reduce the number of errors that get made *by the system.*

Six Sigma appears to be a quantitative method, and quantification is important. But the way to achieve high results is to start with the belief that the sources of error are *in the system.* If people are doing things in ways that don't give good outcomes, then it's not the person, it's the system. The setup is poor, the training is poor, the workload is high, the work flow is poor, or maybe the tooling is poor. Okay, so let's face this, find a solution, and fix it.

How? Suppose a Six Sigma organization finds that some outcomes are not favorable. Six Sigma includes a full toolkit for working backward to find root causes and for dealing with them in satisfactory ways. In particular for healthcare, where many key operations are manual, there are tools to improve the outcomes for manual operations. These particular tools, which are used extensively in this book, represent a new way of looking at manual operations for many people. Therefore, new solutions often pop up when these particular Six Sigma tools are applied.

When better means are identified, Six Sigma has change-management tools that make sure the benefits are achieved and retained. Many of the individual tools have been around for 50 or more years. What's different about Six Sigma? First of all, Six Sigma is not satisfied with incremental change, for the simple reason that a large number of incremental changes may still not add up to a satisfactory solution. Six Sigma starts at the other end, with a numerical goal, and works backward to insist that each stage of the operation get into conformance. Six Sigma is results-oriented work, not busy work.

Six Sigma was created by Motorola and was soon adopted by GE, IBM, and other first-class manufacturing companies, and not just for their manufacturing operations. Financial services companies, which are classic service companies in that they have few tangible products, saw the benefit and joined the Six Sigma bandwagon. Bank of America and American Express are two such companies. Following the lead of GE, some of these companies now require a candidate for any management position, even in human resources or the mail room, to have reached the Green Belt level of Six Sigma proficiency. Mimicking the martial arts, Six Sigma has three belt levels: Green Belt, Black Belt, and Master Black Belt. The belts are attained by following courses of study. Completion of projects is always part of the training program.

While the only point of Six Sigma is to improve outcomes, a Six Sigma organization finds that each subprocess must be observed, measured, and tracked because errors anywhere in the overall process are bad. Thus, a Six Sigma organization applies process control methods to each process step. It controls the outcomes by controlling the process. There are Six Sigma tools to help.

What will it take to get Six Sigma, or any other systematic improvement program, to make a dent in the healthcare error rate we see today? First, management's attitude must change. Management gets what management supports through thought, word, and deed. Management must be willing to look at time-honored work methods and toss them out in favor of something that *works better in the real healthcare workplace.* Second, healthcare organizations must be willing to create a blame-free work environment. Third, healthcare workers must be willing to learn from the experience of others.

While leading manufacturers are striving to get beyond four sigma to five sigma and six sigma, where's healthcare? Nobody has a good measure of this, but there is not much reason to believe that healthcare is any better than the general run of service industries, for which it is believed that the present attainment level is about one sigma. Surely everyone believes that there is room for improvement. Indeed, Six Sigma says that there is a reasonable possibility of improving that ratio from a few errors out of 10 to a few errors out of a million.

In the Nan series, Nan, as a department manager, starts by teaching her own nursing department about the rudiments of error reduction, including the key point of system improvement rather than blame assignment. Nan then brings in other departments and expands the corps of believers and practitioners. In the GE case, events moved faster because the CEO at the time, Jack Welch, simply announced that all future applicants for *any* management position in GE would have a Six Sigma belt, and he followed this up by bragging about GE's Six Sigma prowess in every public forum he could reach. Well, most of you, dear readers, can't start from Welch's vantage point, but you can start from your own middle and senior management positions and have a wonderful impact on your own institutions and on healthcare in general. For readers who want to learn more about Six Sigma, there are a number of useful sources on the subject.[2]

This is life, death, and a big fraction of the gross national product.

Robert Barry, PhD
Six Sigma Master Black Belt

ENDNOTES

1. Many Six Sigma textbooks put this as describe, measure, analyze, improve, and control, or DMAIC, for short. While that is sound engineering, it doesn't convey the management point.
2. Here are a few useful Six Sigma resources. You can check the ASQ Quality Press online bookstore at www.qualitypress.asq.org for more:
   - R. F. Barry, A. C. Murcko, and C. E. Brubaker, *The Six Sigma Book for Healthcare: Improving Outcomes by Reducing Error* (Milwaukee: Health Administration Press and ASQ Quality Press, 2002).
   - *Six Sigma Forum Magazine*, ASQ Quality Press, Milwaukee, WI.
   - J. N. Lowenthal, *Defining and Analyzing a Business Process: A Six Sigma Pocket Guide* (Milwaukee: ASQ Quality Press, 2003).
   - R. A. Munro, *Six Sigma for the Office: A Pocket Guide* (Milwaukee: ASQ Quality Press, 2003).

Index